# THE HUNTED GIRLS

# BOOKS BY JENNA KERNAN

*A Killer's Daughter*

# THE HUNTED GIRLS

## JENNA KERNAN

bookouture

Published by Bookouture in 2021

An imprint of Storyfire Ltd.
Carmelite House
50 Victoria Embankment
London EC4Y 0DZ

www.bookouture.com

ISBN: 978-1-80019-314-7
eBook ISBN: 978-1-80019-313-0

*For Jim, always*

———

# PROLOGUE

*He moved undetected by the authorities, the public or his prey. It was how he preferred it until now. Because his target had changed and so, too, must his methods.*

*He finished the alert and set aside his phone, wondering who would be the next to spring his trap. He was certain of his skills. A decade-long career—with each of his victims only ever listed as missing persons, the truth of their fate never established by the authorities—made his proficiency as an apex predator undeniable.*

*Before he'd known of her, he'd been content. Now he saw contentment was not enough. Neither was complacency. To lure the ultimate target into his territory, he needed to carefully bait this trap with something she would find irresistible. So he was here, in her mother's playground, and this time, instead of hiding evidence of his work, he would display it.*

*He kept his playthings only for himself. Sometimes for days, sometimes weeks, once for a month. None were ever seen again after he snatched them from their known world and carried them screaming into his.*

*This new plan meant exposing his victims and giving back his playthings, but not before he had finished his games. She had to see him, what he was and what he was capable of becoming. He needed to tempt, capture her attention and hold it. Offer something she could not resist. A series of fresh kills in the shadow of her mother's crimes.*

*She'd come. He'd be waiting.*

*There would be two bodies, to release the scent of death, grab media attention and raise the possibility of a serial killer.*

*He had been here behind his hunting blind less than a half hour when she appeared with a dog. The canine has already greeted the departing couple in the lot as if they were related, so it is no threat to him. Rather the creature is an asset, as it gives her the confidence to move blithely into the woods alone.*

*Bird-watching. She lifted her binoculars, sweeping the limbs of the live oaks draped with Spanish moss, searching for her quarry. If she heard him, she gave no sign. Her dog noticed him immediately and wagged its tail in greeting.*

*The shove from behind sent the woman crashing down, momentarily pinning her arms beneath her. He threw himself on top of her, preferring his hands to any weapon.*

*Air whooshed from her and she arched back, lifting her head. Before she drew her next breath, he captured her neck in the crook of his elbow. She couldn't scream if she wanted to. The chokehold worked in less than a minute. Her body sagged, going limp. He yanked her hands behind her and tightened the restraints tauter than necessary, enjoying the feel of the plastic tearing into flesh. He tugged once more, savoring the zipping sound of the teeth engaging, locking her tight. Droplets of blood soaked into the fabric covering her lower back.*

*Next he secured her ankles, turning her into a worm as she roused to struggle. When she woke enough to open her mouth, he stuffed a cotton rag between her teeth. She choked, but before expelling the object, he tore the section of silver tape and secured it over her parted lips.*

*She rolled to her side, her eyes wide and frantic, darting from his face and back to her surroundings as if trying to understand what was happening. He waited, holding the leash to her dog, smiling down at her.*

*Did she recognize that the fact he'd allowed her to see his face was a very bad sign?*

*Bagged and tagged, he thought. The first step to luring the ultimate catch.*

# CHAPTER ONE

## TUESDAY

At the flight attendant's announcement, that passengers could use their cell phones, Dr. Nadine Finch discovered she had two missed calls, two voice messages and two texts. She checked the texts first.

They were both from Homicide detective Clint Demko. They'd been dating for seven months now, as he kept reminding her, each time he tried to have the conversation about moving forward. This five-month separation during her training at the FBI National Academy in Virginia had been a strain.

The first text said he would be late and the second that he was waiting beyond security, likely because her late flight allowed him to arrive on time.

She turned to her voicemail as the doors opened and the line of passengers choking the center aisle began to move.

She skipped the unknown caller and frowned at seeing the second was from FBI Special Agent Sean Torrin.

Those pesky hairs on her neck lifted. Torrin had not been in touch in months. He had been assigned to assist the local Bureau out of Tampa on a case in which she was the star witness. The murders of four couples by an emerging serial killer here in Sarasota, Florida, had been Nadine's first job as a profiler.

"Nadine, it's Sean Torrin. Listen, I got a call from the Lakeland Bureau. They've got a case down there in Ocala."

She sucked in a breath. *Ocala.* Her hometown and her mother's onetime playground. Just the mention of the place where Arleen Howler had killed eight people caused her muscles to tense. It seemed being the daughter of a serial killer never got easier and was full of all kinds of hazards, her own memories being one of the most unpredictable.

"I recommended they contact you for your opinion. The lead is Jack Skogen. Don't know him, but he's got a solid solve rate. He'll be in touch. Fill you in on the details." There was a pause. "Oh, I'll be in town for the trial. Maybe we could meet for drinks?"

Nadine glanced at the second message and the unknown number. Beside her, the man who had occupied the window seat hunched, casting her an impatient look. Nadine didn't need any of her psychological training on nonverbal communication to read his annoyance at her blocking his exit.

She stepped into the aisle, collected her carry-on, made heavier by the brick tucked inside, earned by completing the FBI's grueling 6.1-mile obstacle course. The rite of passage was fondly referred to as the Yellow Brick Road. Precious cargo in tow, she made her exit. Just outside the gate, she pulled aside to retrieve the second message.

"Hi, Dr. Finch. This is FBI Special Agent Jack Skogen. I'm in Ocala working with the Orlando field office. We've been called in on two unusual homicides. I'd appreciate your opinion. Requested you be assigned and have Tampa's okay on that. Please give me a call when you get this."

Nadine resisted returning the call and instead fired off a one-word reply to Demko.

*Landed*

Then she headed out, finding him waiting just past security. She waved from the secure side of the glass exit gates.

His fine brown hair had grown back nicely over the surgical scar resulting from the blow to the head suffered last September as they closed in on their perp—another reminder of the Copycat Killer. He kept his hair overly long on the top and it was forever falling across his wide brow.

Demko grinned, his blue eyes bright. He was again strong and fit and back on the job. They were lucky to have survived, not to have lost their lives or each other. But they both had scars. Permanent reminders of the cost of hunting serial killers.

Nadine exhaled. Seeing Demko always gave her butterflies, reminding her how much she loved him. She hurried through the sliding glass doors.

Clint closed the distance as she released the handle to her roller bag and stepped into his arms. They shared a desperate hug.

There was a difference of eleven inches in their heights. Demko was tall and muscular. She looked up at his handsome, smiling face and kissed him. The soft grazing of lips escalated like a brush fire. When she pulled away, she sucked in much-needed oxygen as he panted and dragged his fingers through his hair.

"Wow, have I missed you," he said. "Twenty weeks is a lifetime."

Her FBI coursework had been exhaustive, including basic training, firearms, academics and operational skills. She enjoyed the case exercises and scenarios the best, and 110 hours of shooting practice the least. And throughout, he'd cheered her progress and missed her as much as she missed him.

Meanwhile, Demko had been busy preparing for the upcoming trial. Because of that, they had seen each other once in the five-month separation.

"Where's the brick?" he asked, referring to her unwieldy memento of the course.

When she'd left for Virginia, she could do only three push-ups. Yet somehow she'd survived slogging under barbed wire, scrambling over cargo nets and dragging herself up cliffs using a climbing rope. And she had a brick trophy to prove it. Amazing what determination and practice could accomplish.

"Carry-on," she said, tilting her head in the direction of her bag.

His smile beamed with pride and she grinned back.

"Can't wait to see it." He hugged her again. "I'm so proud of you." He kissed her forehead.

"We need to go out and celebrate! Big romantic dinner. Anywhere you want."

She made a face and he frowned.

"What?"

"I just got a phone call from FBI Special Agent Jack Skogen."

"I'm not going to like this. Am I?"

He wouldn't because, if she took this assignment, she'd be leaving again.

As they headed downstairs to the baggage claim, Nadine tried and failed not to obsess about the two homicides Skogen mentioned.

Nadine and Clint had both thought that her new assignment in the Tampa FBI field office would mean more time together. Before leaving for Quantico, she had rented a place in Bradenton, between Tampa and Sarasota. But if they shipped her off to a field office in Central Florida, that ride to see Clint would change from twenty minutes to three hours.

"Do you want to return his call?"

"Maybe. God, I'm not even unpacked."

She had thought to have a little time to settle in up in Tampa.

"How's Molly?" she asked, referring to his puppy, who was now a lanky almost one-year-old boxer.

"Misses you nearly as much as I do," he said, taking her hand and bringing her knuckles to his lips.

Nadine wondered if she'd even have a chance to give Clint a proper hello before she was saying good-bye. So why was the possibility of fleeing Clint causing her a mixture of regret and relief? They were good together. He balanced her anxiety with calm, and she grounded his obsession with his work with a routine that included meals. But that didn't mean she was ready to move in with him, as he'd suggested. Exactly what prompted her reluctance was a deep well of murky, still water.

"How's Christopher?" she asked about his son, the boy she had yet to meet, but that, too, was something he wanted. She recognized this as a big step.

His face just lit up as he described his last weekend with his boy and all that his son was doing. The pride and love oozed from him like honey from a comb.

Meanwhile, children made her uncomfortable because they were all potential and dangerous possibilities. Children were terrifying.

His boy might be a federal judge someday. Or his mother might convince him to use a shotgun on Clint, just like Clint's half brother had done to Clint's father. She hoped that his child would grow up like him and not his uncle.

Clint gushed about Christopher's first surfing lesson as they reached the luggage claim. It was clear to anyone how much he missed him when they weren't together. Two weekends a month was hardly enough, but divorce and a job across the state made more time available only on certain holidays.

"He wants to meet you," said Clint, as the luggage carousel trundled along with the first bags.

She held her rigid smile, knowing that her assignment to Ocala would prevent a visit with Christopher yet again. The relief made her feel like a traitor.

They stood waiting with the others from her flight.

Clint shared a video from the weekend. He was different with his boy, happy in a way that he wasn't otherwise, and it made her realize just how important being a dad was for him and how magnificent he was at it. A natural.

Christopher was lucky to have a great dad. Meanwhile, she'd spent her childhood fantasizing about her missing father. In his absence she'd concocted an imaginary dad from every sitcom and family movie she'd seen. She had envisioned that father, who had abandoned the family at her birth, would be normal and kind and wise. All the things Clint was to Christopher. Nadine had dreamed that her dad would return and rescue her from her terrifying home. Of course, he hadn't and her efforts to find him had failed.

She knew from her years of therapy the depth and breadth of the scar left by her father's desertion. Listening to Clint talk about his boy reminded her more deeply of what she had lost and illustrated the truth. Clint was a great father, while her ability to be a mother was in serious doubt. Not only was she missing solid role models, she feared she lacked the innate abilities necessary to raise a sweet, funny, normal kid like Christopher.

Her doubt was placing a strain on their relationship. Because every time Clint tried to have a conversation about moving them forward, she retreated.

She wondered if this new assignment was just another opportunity to hold him at arm's length.

"That's mine." She pointed at the first of her suitcases and he sprang forward to retrieve it. After collecting the second, they headed out, reaching the parking area under towering thunderhead clouds more typical of the summer than spring. Perhaps the rainy season had already arrived.

Once in his vehicle she gripped her phone, her foot tapping away on his spotless floor mat as he got them under way.

"If you call him, you might be able to stop fidgeting," he said.

Was she? Yes, she was squirming like a worm on a hot sidewalk.

"Fine." She placed the call.

"Jack Skogen." His voice held a slight drawl, like Texas perhaps. There was a pause, and he must have glanced at the number of his caller. "Dr. Finch?"

"Yes. I'm returning your call. I was in the air."

"Flying home from Quantico."

"Yes."

"You were recommended by Agent Torrin. I'm here in Orlando from DC. Local law enforcement called us in. Seems they have identified a possible serial killer."

"Two victims?"

"Yes. So far. Both females. No IDs yet."

Nadine wished she could have Juliette Hartfield go over them. She trusted her friend who was a fine medical examiner with Florida's District 12. Unfortunately, that district did not stretch as far east as Orlando.

"I've already had approval on your reassignment. I'd like you to report immediately."

She glanced at Clint and then tapped the mute button.

"They want me now."

"Great." His words ground with sarcasm.

She hit the button to unmute and then hit the speaker function.

"I can be there tomorrow."

"Tonight would be better."

She pinched her lips. "Can you tell me anything about the victims?"

"Local authorities incorrectly initially listed them as an animal attack, but the ME listed them as homicides. That's when they called us."

"Where were the bodies found?"

"In the Ocala National Forest on the St. Johns River."

Nadine's heart jumped to a wild staccato and she nearly dropped the phone.

"That's your mother's old hunting grounds. Isn't it?"

Nadine pinched her eyes shut, dizzy with how fast this conversation went from seeking her professional opinion to delving into her past.

"Yes. We lived in Ocala."

"And many of Arleen Howler's victims were recovered from the forest."

"How is this relevant to your current investigation?" The sharp bite of her voice must have struck something because she was met with silence.

If Skogen wanted her help because he was a curiosity seeker, he could go spit with the reporters and publishers who flooded her voicemail and in-box with invitations and offers.

"I requested you because of your success profiling the Copycat Killer."

She made no answer.

"Nadine." His voice went low and strangely intimate.

Clint scowled at her phone and tightened his grip on the wheel as Skogen continued, his drawl more evident now.

"You know these predators. They don't take holidays. They don't stop. They keep hunting and killing until they are caught or die."

She did know. It was why she had made the decision to dedicate her life to hunting them. But not there. Not where her childhood was tangled up with so many of her mother's victims. The murder sites, body dumps and the ruined lives. It was too much.

"We only need you to consult."

Should she? Could she go back there and keep them separate in her mind? The past and the present. Two killers running over the same ground.

"Dr. Finch?"

"How many days between them?"

"That's one of the disturbing parts. Seems only a few days."

That meant this unsub—unknown subject—might be searching for the next victim right now. The pressure to stop the killer warred with her uncertainties.

"I'd have conditions."

Now he was the one hesitating. "Such as?"

"Could you hold for a moment?"

"Dr. Finch, I have two bodies up here."

She tapped the mute and turned to Demko.

"What do you think?" she asked Clint.

"Great opportunity. But I'm not anxious for you to disappear. Honestly, the last three months have been tough."

That warmed her heart. "For me, too."

"And are you really ready to take on the hunt for another killer?"

Was she? She didn't think so. No. How could she ever be? But she knew also that she could not sit by if a predator was out there, hunting. She'd always been determined to make up for her family's trail of ruined lives in the only way she knew how. By hunting people like them.

"If there's a killer up there again. And I can help…"

He nodded. "Then go for it."

"Would you come with me?"

He blinked at her and then returned his attention to the road, gliding up the North Trail toward Bradenton, passing car dealerships and strip malls.

"I have a job."

"Leave of absence?"

"I can request it. No promises."

"Do you think Juliette would join us?"

"All you can do is ask," he said.

"Dr. Finch? Are you there?" asked Skogen.

She tapped the screen to unmute. "Yes. I'm here. I'd like to form my own team."

He made a sound in his throat. "It's my investigation. My team."

She smiled, wondering how badly he wanted her help, and waited.

"They would not be active members of my investigation and would have to be vetted. Their opinions and input would be for you alone."

"Of course."

She noticed how, before even knowing her team, he had dismissed their importance and the value of their input while establishing his control over "his" investigation.

"I can live with that." But she believed he was making a mistake. As a Homicide detective who worked for years in Miami-Dade County, Detective Clint Demko likely had worked on many more murder investigations than Skogen ever would.

"That it?"

"No. My role as consultant for this case would have to remain confidential. No press announcements, no interviews. And no media gets near me or my team."

"My team and superiors would have to be aware of your role."

"I'm fine with that."

"Then I'll look forward to meeting you in person this evening. You'll have a room waiting for you in Silver Springs. I'll send you the details."

"Thank you."

"How long until you assemble your team?"

"Let me get back to you on that."

"Fine. Text me when you arrive so we can meet, Dr. Finch."

Agent Skogen's number vanished from the screen. She took a moment to add it to her contacts so he wouldn't spring on her again.

"So, tonight? I can't get there that fast," said Clint.

"I understand."

"Nadine, you don't have to go up there tonight or at all. Not if you think it will be too hard for you."

Hard did not begin to describe the whirlwind of emotions tearing around inside her.

"He's cleared it with Tampa. I'm assigned. His request is a formality."

She was certain of only one thing—she would do all she could to help the FBI stop this unsub.

"Another serial killer hunting in my mother's territory."

"Hell of a coincidence," he said.

"Yes." Except she didn't believe in coincidences.

*

Nadine exited the highway and tried to ignore the goose bumps as she spotted the sign for Ocala and Silver Springs. Her headlights illuminated the familiar collection of gas stations, hotels and fast-food joints that clustered about each exit. These gave way to a smattering of industrial parks and car dealerships.

Seeing her childhood home again conjured thoughts of her brother, Arlo, an inmate in Lawtey Correctional Institution, eleven years into a fifteen-year sentence on a conviction for sexual assault.

Another criminal in the family.

They exchanged frequent emails, occasional phone calls and, since the purchase of her first car after college, she visited once a month. Being in Ocala would shorten her travel time considerably.

Her heart was beating so fast. She kept one hand on the wheel and pressed the other over her rib cage to still the mad pounding.

Had she really thought to escape this place? Believed that she would never have to come back and face the memories and the pain? Meanwhile, she'd carried them with her all these years.

Why was she doing this? She hated this town, this terrible place. Hated that no one had known what her mother was really like, and that she had waited so long to tell.

As she pulled into the hotel parking area, she wondered if she had really woken up in the FBI dormitory at Quantico this morning.

Before exiting her vehicle, she checked her texts, seeing one from Juliette.

*Notified my director, requested leave.*

They had spoken before she'd left town about the possibility of Juliette joining her. Nadine barely had the question out and Juliette was agreeing, jumping at the chance.

*Great! Hope to CU soon.*

Nadine threaded her keys between her fingers. Then she stepped from her Lexus and scanned the parking area. It was well lit, and her space was close to the hotel entrance.

She wheeled the amassed luggage, still containing her yellow-painted brick, the distance to the lobby. Inside, the tropical vibe prevailed with potted palms, blue pastel wallpaper and a carpet covered with a pattern of Monstera leaves. Between the baggage station and the main desk sat a square cage on wheels. Inside was a sulfur-crested cockatoo that she went over to admire. It reminded her of Juliette's beloved pet.

"Good evening," said the chipper young woman at reception. "That's Petunia. She's a permanent guest here. Left behind in one of the rooms over a decade ago."

"My friend has one."

"Oh, fun!"

Nadine sagged on the counter.

Meanwhile, the woman before her looked perky as a cheerleader at halftime. The tag said that her first name was Rosie. Well named, thought Nadine.

"Long day?" asked Rosie.

"Endless."

"Well then, let's get you checked in so you can get to your room and relax." Rosie was a blonde with a pale complexion. She wore a cloth headband and a crisp uniform of gray-and-white polyester. Her fingers shot to the keyboard. "Do you have a reservation with us?"

"Yes. I should. It's Dr. Nadine Finch."

Rosie's carefully applied eyebrows lifted. "Oh yes. Dr. Finch. I have your reservation here. It's open ended. You will be having an extended stay?"

"Yes."

"Very good. Let me just get your key ready." Rosie ducked below the counter and out of view, popping back up like a gopher from a hole. "How many keys?"

"One." She hoped that Demko would be up here shortly, if his leave of absence was approved, but preferred spending time with him at his place.

As Rosie ran a plastic key card through the data-card system, a text from Skogen appeared, asking her to reply upon arrival so he could welcome her and relay case details.

She thought the best welcome he could give her was time to take a hot shower and get a full night's sleep.

"Here you go. The key will only open the elevator at your floor and provides you access to the common areas, like the pool and exercise room. Elevators are to the right. Tiki bar on the pool deck opens at four. We serve warm cookies at reception from three to five. Breakfast is between six and nine every morning and there is coffee until midnight right in the dining area." Rosie motioned to the empty seating area, now dark. "Do you need maps? I have some coupons for Silver Springs and information on the National Forest."

"I don't need maps, thanks."

Rosie glanced toward the empty bell stand and frowned.

"I got it," said Nadine, reading Rosie as she referred to handling her own luggage.

"Well, I'm here until midnight, if you need anything. Your room is 242, second floor and a left just off the elevators." She slipped the key card into a paper envelope and slid it forward. "Have a nice evening."

She wouldn't, but she nodded, forcing a smile.

"Hello," said Petunia, with perfect enunciation.

"Good-bye," corrected Rosie.

Up in her room, Nadine took in the space. This was a business hotel, which meant she had a kitchenette consisting of a tiny sink, microwave, coffee station and minifridge. She passed a small love seat facing a desk, continuing beyond the partition, collapsing on the bed. Her eyes drifted shut for an instant before the text chimes startled her.

The first text was from Clint and was one word.

*Arrived?*

The second was from Skogen.

*Reception says you arrived. Please meet me in the lobby.*

He'd barely given her the chance to settle in or text him herself.

She groaned and texted Demko.

*Arrived. Meeting now with Skogen.*

Nadine stared at her reflection, her expression determined, her chin lowered.

"All right, Agent Skogen. Let's see what you've got for me."

When the elevator doors opened at ground level, Nadine found a well-dressed man in a tan suit and gray satin tie standing in a posture of practiced stillness. He cocked his head to one side at her appearance and lifted a brow.

"Dr. Finch?"

This could only be lead investigator Special Agent Jack Skogen, acting as if he didn't instantly recognize her. Her photo was in the FBI database and had been in every national newspaper. His pretense that he needed to verify her identity irritated.

She gave him a once-over as she nodded acknowledgement of her identity. His physicality screamed former military, with a muscular build and above average height. His light brown hair receded slightly off a broad forehead. His brows peaked in a near-perfect triangle over intent blue eyes. He had a narrow nose, strong jaw, thin lips, and ears that protruded a little more than they should to be classically handsome—although, all in all, he was a good-looking man, and clean-shaven despite the hour.

She stepped forward, making good eye contact and holding her smile but withholding her hand, keeping it fixed to the strap of her briefcase.

"You must be Special Agent Skogen."

"Guilty," he said. "Please call me Jack."

He motioned her forward out of the alcove and into the lobby, where he took a seat that commanded the best view of both the front and back entrance. She chose a chair facing reception and Rosie, who gave her a bright smile and wave.

Petunia sat upon a wooden perch, on an elaborate play stand fixed to the cage top, her foot raised as she shredded a paper towel tube.

"It must be strange for you to be back up here," said Skogen.

Of course he would have read everything he could on her background before offering her a job as consultant. This would include Nadine's connection with her mother's arrest and her recent involvement in the apprehension of the Copycat Killer.

"Yes. I passed the development where I grew up on my way in here." Although she knew the old trailers where her family had lived long ago had been removed, to prevent curiosity seekers. One of the property owners had taken the additional step of changing the trailer park's name.

Jack kept his voice low, Nadine hoped with the intention of preventing the receptionist from gleaning any details of their conversation rather than to lend intimacy to their meeting.

"You were recommended to me for this assignment by Agent Torrin."

"So you mentioned on the phone."

"He said you were so good he thought you were a suspect."

She frowned at this revelation.

"He felt that you'd bring more to the investigation than a professional profile. It was his opinion that you have a sort of intuition."

"I don't rely on intuition. My work is clinical. Data points and logic over hunches."

"And that work impressed him, along with your innate ability to glean more from the facts and details of the case than would be apparent to an investigator."

"I should hope so or I'm going to have to ask for my money back on my education." He was trying to say that he believed her personal experience and being raised by a notorious killer gave her some sort of edge. But he was dancing around the point, and she was not going to help him because Nadine did not wish to be selected for this assignment due to her notoriety. If he had done so, he was bound to be disappointed.

Still, she was relieved that he had agreed to keep her association with this case out of the press, because she did not relish becoming the center of a media storm again. Been there, done that—twice. She believed the attention needed to remain squarely focused on finding this killer.

Despite the inevitable wobbles in her confidence that came and went, she was good at her job. Profiling required education, knowledge, experience, and identification with killers. She had all that, unfortunately.

Skogen reached in his bag and withdrew a folder, pressed it to the table and pushed it in her direction. She noted he wore a class ring on his right hand, West Point. So he was army. There was no ring on his left. This did not tell her if he was or was not married. Many men in his profession chose not to reveal personal details, including wives and children.

"Until we can get you secure access to our network."

She accepted the folder.

"I'll answer any questions you may have after you are up to speed."

"Fine." She shifted, keen to go.

"The ME tells me that the two victims died within a few days of each other, so I'm anxious to get you working on this. We'll get you full access tomorrow. There is an ID badge for you to wear at the office and at any crime scene."

"Thank you."

He smiled and sat back, hands resting on his knees. His knuckles showed thin crisscrossing red lines. She assumed he'd been out in the field because those were the cuts left by sawgrass dragging across unprotected skin.

"Where are you from originally?" she asked.

"Oklahoma," he said.

"Been to Florida before?" she asked.

"Just the coast."

That was a different world than Central Florida. There, most people were transplants from up north, East Coast and Midwesterners. Here in interior Florida were the original crackers, named for the long whips used on their oxen. Here they had citrus groves, cattle ranches, phosphate mines and farming. What they didn't have was outsiders.

He'd stick out like a Yankee in Alabama.

"How are you coming with collecting your team?" he asked.

Jeepers. He'd only offered the position today.

"I'm working on that."

"I'd like their names. They'll all need to be vetted."

"Of course." That would make for interesting reading. All the people she wanted around her had mothers convicted of murder. It was an odd club and one that no one wanted to join, but somehow they made her feel almost normal.

Another oddity was that none of them had fathers. Medical examiner, Dr. Juliette Hartfield had been born to a mother already convicted of shooting and killing her three young children to remove what she saw as impediments to a relationship with a man who did not want children. Ironically, she didn't know she was already pregnant with Juliette. Unlike the rest of them, her mother's crimes occurred before she was born, and she had been adopted by a nice couple. The strange part was that her adoptive dad was the DA who had convicted her mother.

Tina Ruz, her administrative assistant, had been born to a single mother convicted of first-degree homicide, when Tina was a teen, for her part in a gruesome kidnapping and murder of an elderly neighbor in a plot to empty her bank accounts. Tina's mother was serving her sentence of forty-five years in prison.

Demko's father had been murdered by a shotgun blast delivered by his stepson, a plot hatched by their mother, to collect the payout from her second husband's life insurance policy. She had convinced her elder son, Demko's half brother, Connor, to stage a robbery of her husband's medical offices. But the podiatrist recognized his masked attacker before his death, as witnesses testified. Now both Demko's mother and his brother were in federal prison.

And Nadine's mother had butchered four couples for their infidelity after abandonment by Nadine's father. But recently, after a conversation where Arleen had admitted to killing a man around the time her father had vanished, Nadine had doubts that their father had run out on them. She'd raised the possibility to Arlo that their mother had murdered their father after discovering his intent to leave her. Nadine wished he'd rejected the notion, but he had not. Instead he seemed to believe it a real possibility.

Had her father never returned because he was another of her mother's victims?

She wondered about this often, and if he was like his sister, her aunt Donna—a successful, smart, normal woman who had adopted Nadine when she was a teenager after she'd testified against her mother—or if he was like Arleen. Nadine was near desperate to discover that at least one parent had been kind and nurturing and normal. It was the only antidote she knew to the horror of being the daughter of Arleen Howler.

While she was up here, back in Ocala, she might just see if she could dig up more about her father's disappearance. She had to admit it was a reason she had jumped to obey Jack Skogen's orders the very same day she received them.

"I wonder if you were able to obtain release time for Dr. Hartfield?"

"Yeah, that's a go."

Nadine stifled a yawn. Skogen met her gaze.

"Sorry," she said. "Long day."

"With plenty more to come," he said.

"So tell me. How were these bodies discovered?"

"Forest service. On Sunday, one of their maintenance crews was doing trail work, clearing brush near the river, and came upon them. That was three days ago."

"The two were in close proximity?"

"Yes. In the same area. Forty feet apart. Arnold spotted the first one, which he reported was uncovered. Forest service discovered the second body in the vicinity after that. That one had been there longer, maybe a week or more. Found covered with dirt, leaf debris and some branches."

Nadine drew the folder onto her lap. "I see. You mentioned the initial victim appeared to be an animal attack?"

"Yes. Predation by something. Crushing injuries. Initially the sheriff believed the deaths were the result of an alligator attack."

"What changed their minds?"

Skogen reached into his pocket and withdrew something in an evidence bag.

"Medical examiner. She agrees that there was predation while the victim was still alive. Severed the spinal cord and would have left the victim paralyzed but conscious. But alligators don't leave their kills out of the water and they don't use these," he said.

"What is it?" She glanced down at the shiny bit of pointed metal.

"It's a high-carbon steel arrowhead. One removed from each victim."

Nadine took a moment to internalize the horror of an attack by alligators in which you were alert but unable to move. Then her mind went to work profiling. *Male, comfortable in the woods, bowhunting experience, anatomical knowledge…*

"Dr. Finch?"

She flicked her attention back to Skogen, having been lost in thought.

"I'll let you get some rest. See you in the morning."

Nadine nodded and rose to shake his hand, but the moment he turned his back, her mind latched onto her profile of an emerging killer.

# CHAPTER TWO

## WEDNESDAY

The floor of the hotel breakfast bar was sticky by the orange juice machine, and the aroma of waffles pervaded the air. Nadine continued her phone conversation with Dr. Juliette Hartfield on her wireless earbuds as she filled her travel mug.

"What does that mean?" asked Nadine. She was mindful that her conversation could be overheard, and that the earbuds and her long hair combined to make it seem like she was talking to nobody.

"Just that I arrived at work this morning and before I even opened my mouth, I was given my reassignment. Who did you have call my director?"

Nadine finished filling her mug and stepped out of the crowded room and into the alcove by the elevators.

"The lead investigator. He said he'd see what he could do."

"Well, apparently what he can do is have the director of the FBI call my boss."

"What do you mean, the director?" Nadine had not meant to sound cross, but her words held a sharp note.

"I mean the director of the entire FBI. The one in Washington. You must be into some high-profile shit."

Indeed. It appeared so.

"When will you get here?" Nadine asked.

"Soon as I can finish some paperwork and pack my stuff. You know if that hotel takes pets?"

Juliette was referring to her feathered toddler, Jack-Jack, a rescue bird with a voice that could rupture eardrums. Nadine had to smile at the thought of Juliette bringing the bird along on the investigation.

"Yes. They do, and they have a parrot in the lobby."

"What kind?"

Nadine told her what she knew of Petunia.

"They should be fine with one more small bird."

One small bird the size of a football, who could throw a single grape twenty feet and who always required a sheet under his perch as he was not housebroken.

"Do you know if Demko is bringing Molly?" asked Juliette.

"Not sure. Did you read the autopsy reports?" asked Nadine.

"Got them as an attachment last night from the District 5 ME. Grim. Very grim. I'm anxious to see the remains."

"Semen recovered from one of the bodies," Nadine said, referring to what she had gleaned from the paper copies Skogen had left her regarding physical evidence.

"Yes. But not much else, apparently. Freshwater is hell on evidence."

"There's the arrowheads."

"Yeah. Saw that. Entrance wounds are visible on the crime scene photos."

"Both bodies were found in brush near the river."

"Yeah. Got that. Oh, and the second body was moved postmortem. The blood pooling shows she died on her side but was recovered on her stomach."

Both bodies were found near the place her mother had dumped a victim. Nadine had memories of this spot, a place near the River Forest Camp.

"Do you agree with the cause of death?" asked Nadine.

"I can see where they could be listed as animal attack. But the arrowheads in the spines would have rendered the victims unable to move from the point below the severed spinal cord," said Juliette. "Victim one suffered a cervical lesion. It would have rendered her paralyzed from the shoulders down. This one couldn't move anything except her face and jaw."

"Would she have been breathing?"

"No. Impossible." Juliette paused before continuing. "The second had an injury to the lumbar area. She would have been unable to move her legs."

"So the alligators left the water to attack them?"

"Unlikely. I believe they were in the water."

"If they were paralyzed, how did they get into the water and how did they get back out?"

"Likely walked in, barefoot, based on the river mud under their toenails, and so already in the water when shot. Photos show duckweed and watermeal on their bodies and in their hair. They're aquatic plants, freshwater only. You won't find them on land. Perhaps our victims were also shot there. And they were dragged out with something. Bruising on the bodies look like the links of a chain to me."

"The animal activity was prior to death. Correct?"

"Yes. But there wouldn't have been any sensation. So no pain."

Juliette was trying to soften the horror of knowing these women likely were conscious and aware that a large alligator was tearing them apart, that they were being eaten alive.

Nadine didn't need that kind of help. She needed all that horror and the accompanying images to give her fuel to catch this killer. Two women made a series. And Nadine already saw the evolution from the first, with the neck injury, to the second with the back injury.

Was he disappointed that he could not witness the first woman struggle? Had her inability to breathe shortened his pleasure at her death?

"Could the first victim speak, before she died?" What she actually wondered was could she scream, beg and plead for her life? Could she feed this monster's need to witness her desperation?

"No. You have to control your diaphragm to speak."

So… no screaming or struggle. And a limited time before that initial victim died from lack of oxygen. How disappointing for this killer.

Their unsub had to have dangled them like baitfish and then retrieved their ravaged bodies, to dump them on the shore.

Why? So they'd be discovered?

"What do you make of one being covered and the other left exposed?"

"That's the most confusing part. So odd."

"Agree."

"You look up the ME that is working on this investigation?" asked Juliette.

Nadine glanced longingly back at the breakfast area. Her English muffin and untouched bacon were both getting cold. She'd yet to take a sip of her coffee and she had a meeting in twenty minutes.

"No. Why?" she asked.

"Dr. Pauline Kline is why. District 5's ME. I read her textbooks when I was in medical school. Qualifications up the yin-yang and all the MEs up in the central districts have ten more years' experience than I do. They certainly don't need my opinion."

Skogen had mentioned Kline last night. She was a member of his task force.

"Well, *I* need your opinion. So get your butt up here."

"Yes, boss lady. See you later on."

"Lunch?"

"I'll be tied up with the dead."

"Well, find me if you get a moment," said Nadine.

"Yes. I will."

Juliette disconnected the call. Nadine hurried back through the crowded breakfast area, added sugar to the coffee and stirred. On the way to her table, she discovered that guests were waiting before the empty chairs at her place and an attendant was wiping down the surface, readying it for the new arrivals. Her muffin and uneaten bacon had vanished.

The breakfast attendant, a small, brown-skinned woman with dark hair, met her gaze. Her brows lifted in alarm.

"Oh, I am sorry, ma'am. I see you go to elevator. I think you are finished." She had a heavy Spanish accent and contrite smile. Nadine followed her gaze as it flashed to the manager who was already approaching, glowering at the woman. Meanwhile, the couple stood, holding heavy-laden plates, anxious for both of them to disappear but polite enough to wait.

"No, no," said Nadine. "I was finished. Thank you…"

The young male manager stopped, glaring at his employee. Nadine turned to him.

"Bibi, did you toss her breakfast?"

Nadine stepped before the manager.

"She's doing a terrific job. The place is spotless."

The smaller woman took the opportunity created by her interruption to hurry toward the kitchen.

Nadine capped her take-out coffee and retrieved her briefcase, which contained her small cross-body purse, and was out the door a few moments later, carrying a small yogurt and an apple.

She noted that there were two unfamiliar people manning reception and wondered if she would be here long enough to learn everyone's name.

*

Nadine sat back in her desk chair in the temporary FBI office, situated in a vacant suite in a medical building in Ocala. The closest FBI field offices were in Maitland and Lakeland, so Skogen had set up a temporary office here. Tina had arrived before her and now sat in the outer office. Nadine took a video call from Juliette and the ME reported on her morning at the ME's office and her examination of the remains of the two bodies.

Juliette's image shrank as she shared her screen and clicked through the photographs taken at the crime scene by local sheriffs and state crime techs.

"I agree with the assessment that the remains of victim two are somewhere between seven and ten days old. Victim one died between three to five days ago."

Nadine stared at the image of the discolored remains of victim one, covered with leaf debris and sticks. The next shot showed the dump site from farther back, the body nearly invisible beneath a large live oak tree.

Nadine had begun building her psychological autopsy of the two victims, but they were sparse as they had yet to identify either woman.

"I need to go out there," she said, more to herself than to Juliette.

"Might be wise."

Juliette flipped to a shot of the second victim. This woman rested on her stomach; her legs splayed, the pose sexualized and unlike the other. Nadine knew this was the victim found with additional physical evidence, semen. The slight wound from the arrow at her lower back was barely visible and her form was pale, with some evidence of decay. The bruising about her waist, left by a chain, was apparent. Predation on the lower legs was obvious and disturbing.

Beside her lay a pile of sticks and leaves. Had someone removed them after the killer had left?

"You saw the X-rays?"

Juliette nodded, flicking ahead to the image of the objects removed from the victims.

"It's arrow points. One in each spinal column. Cervical on one and lumbar on two. Here's a thing, the point didn't break off. It's a whole arrowhead, intact. It almost seems like they weren't properly fixed to the shafts."

That was odd. Was that intentional, the killer leaving a calling card?

"Just the arrowhead? No shaft?"

"High-carbon steel arrowhead. They're called broadheads."

"Why did they come off?"

"I'm not sure."

"Don't they usually come out with the shaft?"

"Unless they break."

"Was it broken?"

"No. Intact and recovered from each victim's spine."

She needed to see that point and have Demko take a look as well.

"I'd like to see those broadheads."

"We have them."

"Progress on victim identification?" She needed that to help her build a picture of these women. They were the key to finding their unknown suspect and she did not doubt for a moment that if they did not soon figure out who, where and why he was targeting them, their killer would kill again.

"No." Juliette flicked forward to the image of both women, now on tarps beside waiting body bags. "But I understand the FBI is speaking to families of all recent missing persons. If these women are from the area, we should know fairly soon."

"And nothing, no personal items found anywhere in the vicinity?" She knew this but had to ask again. It still seemed unlikely and infuriating.

Her mother had taken all clothing from her victims to remove physical evidence. Was this perp doing likewise?

"No jewelry, clothing or objects of any kind."

Many killers saved the jewelry from their victims. Keepsakes.

Nadine stared at the image of the two dead women, allowing the anger to percolate within her.

If this were a series, then their killer might already have captured his next victim. They had to figure this out. There was no time to waste.

She glanced at a report. "And there was nothing in their stomachs. How long were they held?"

"Unknown. Best guess is two to four days. It's hard to differentiate what chemical processes began before or after death. But the second victim was definitely in ketosis. Possibly the first also, but we're unable to determine this was not due to the natural processes of decay. However, I agree with the ME's assessment that the second victim, at least, and possibly the first, were both starving at the time of death."

Was that to weaken them or instituted just for the pleasure of watching them suffer?

Juliette flicked to a close-up of the denuded bone on the lower leg of one of the victims. "Massive tissue loss for victim one both before and after death. Water in lungs indicates she drowned."

Couldn't breathe. But could swallow water. Nadine felt a chill at the image she conjured.

"And victim two?"

"Victim two died of exsanguination."

"Bled out," said Nadine. "Do you agree with the ME?"

"Predatory activity. Likely an alligator. Big one. Nothing else can remove flesh like that. Bruising around the wound on victim two shows she had circulation."

"I've seen some gruesome deaths," said Juliette. "From boat propellers, heavy machinery, automobiles. But these two top the list. Simply horrifying."

The silence stretched as Nadine tried and failed to eradicate the image of an alligator feeding on the living women.

"Have a look at these." She flipped to a photo of an arm and shoulder. "Both victims also shared similar puncture marks on the extremities, not caused by an animal, and these were also inflicted before death."

"What about these smaller wounds?" Nadine asked, referring to the red crisscrossing marks that reminded her of the sort that might be caused by a switch.

"We think that's from the serrated edges of palmetto fronds. They're pervasive. Seems they were moving through them without the protection of clothing."

Nadine took a moment to internalize that before moving back to the puncture marks and dark gaping wounds. "Do you know what weapon was used?"

"Pretty sure this was also arrows."

Nadine's brows lifted.

"It looks to us as if our first victim was hung up on some kind of a backboard or large tree and someone shot arrows at her. Multiple punctures in the extremities. The wounds are consistent with a body that was left to hang; the weight of the torso further tore the wounds. Easy to confuse with knife wounds but a knife wound often leaves bruising on the skin and you see there is none. Also knife wounds frequently show directionality, and again, there is none. The wounds are uniform and, more importantly, they are narrow and deep, so deep that with a knife you would expect to see a hilt mark. Additionally, these wounds were consistent in size all the way through the tissue except for the ones where there was tearing after initial penetration. They were slightly larger there.

The ME is going to get ahold of some arrows and see if they can make a match."

Nadine was tempted to ask her why she knew so much about arrow wounds, but then thought better of it. She knew that medical examiners' training involved working backward to identify what tool or implement made each wound.

Nadine gave a grim summary. "In other words, the victims were starved, chased, used for human target practice and then had their spinal columns severed before feeding them to alligators?"

"Yes. The perpetrator delivered no fatal wounds. In fact, the injuries seemed designed to inflict pain, rather than death. Extremities only, except for the single wound to the spine. No major blood vessels damaged by the arrow wounds. Those two injuries, only, were delivered from the rear. And though the second victim died from animal attack, she was already experiencing organ failure resulting from exposure and dehydration." Juliette wrinkled her nose. "Do you think the alligator's purpose was to dispose of the bodies?"

Nadine shook her head. "No, because then there would be no reason to remove them from the water and cover them with dirt and dead leaves."

"I suppose."

"So he shot each, in the water, with an arrowhead that remained lodged in the spinal column. Then waited for the alligators to attack?"

"He would have had a line on them, either before or after shooting them." She flipped to an image of bruising around the torso. "These ligature marks are pre- and postmortem. Seems they were chained for retrieval. Looks like the sort used to chain a dog. See the mark from the twisted links."

"Then after the alligator attack and the victims had bled out, this killer dragged them to the riverbank and dug a grave?"

"Not a grave, exactly. Victim one was loosely covered with debris and left near the water. Reminded me of the sort of treatment that bears, bobcats and panthers use to cover a food cache up in New Hampshire."

"Or a human, making a hasty effort to hide a body."

"If that's what it was, he made a bad job of it. Close to a trailhead, close to the water and guaranteed to draw buzzards."

As if this killer wanted the bodies found. "He's exhibiting them. But then why cover the first and not the second?"

"There were small bits of debris found on the most recent victim."

Nadine latched onto this. "Do you think it possible she was covered and then uncovered?"

Juliette nodded. "Might have. There's a debris pile close by."

This might mean their killer had returned to visit his victims. Nadine smiled. Such a predator was easier to catch.

"And returned to uncover her?"

"Yes. And to masturbate."

Nadine would allow herself to feel all the pain and horror of the deaths later. After that, she'd permit herself to sink into the mind of a predator who enjoyed using a living person for target practice, leaving them to suffer, then returning to continue the job. A male who planned the entire hunt, carried the chain, altered his arrows and possibly returned to his kills.

She needed information, puzzle pieces from which to construct a complete picture.

"Any indication of direct sexual activity with either victim?"

"Unable to determine with victim one."

"What about the other?" asked Nadine.

"No. We don't think so. Just the sperm on the body. But we did find something interesting."

"What's that?"

"Sperm were viable."

# CHAPTER THREE

Nadine thought about this for a moment. Visualizing the predator standing over the mutilated corpse.

*Not yet. Don't go there yet. Wait for more pieces.*

"How long do sperm survive outside the body?"

Juliette nodded, possibly in appreciation of Nadine's question. "In ideal conditions, which these were not, sperm can survive for only a few hours. This body would have been somewhere between two and three days postmortem when this happened."

"We just missed him."

"It seems so." Nadine failed to repress a shudder at the killer returning to his victims and becoming so aroused.

"But he left us solid DNA, so that's the upside," said Juliette. "Skogen already delivered the sample for processing. They're using the FBI labs to expedite the results."

It didn't sound right. Was this killer so confident in his ability that he'd leave his DNA on a body? It didn't sit well with her emerging profile of an organized killer who planned each detail. Returning to the victim held enormous risks and this guy had left each of his two victims for days where no one had found them. If he wanted to visit, why leave them in such a public place? It didn't make sense.

Judging from the timeline, it appeared this killer might be hunting for the next victim right now.

"We need to make an ID," said Nadine.

"Working on it."

"I'll come by to see that arrowhead."

"Good. Anything else?"

"Not right now."

There was a momentary pause and then Juliette closed the screen share. Her image instantly enlarged, filling the screen.

Silence stretched.

"You and Demko okay?" asked Juliette.

Concern took over at the question, seemingly out of the blue. "Yes. Why?"

"He stopped in at the ME's office. Seemed sort of sad."

"Sad?"

"Yeah. Just, off."

Nadine lowered her head.

Juliette noted her withdrawal and her voice held suspicion. "What's going on?"

"He picked me up at the airport and I was in my car driving up here less than an hour later. We didn't have any time together and these last few months have been really hard."

"I can imagine. He's been working with the DA on the Copycat Killer case, and I know you didn't have much leave from your training at Quantico."

"Exactly."

"But you two will find time, now that you're working together."

Nadine made a face.

Juliette narrowed her eyes.

"Something else?"

Nadine nodded. "He keeps talking about moving the relationship forward."

"Well, that's super." Juliette studied Nadine and her smile faded. "Isn't it?"

"Why? Why do we need to move anywhere?"

"Obviously he's missing something, or he wouldn't want to move forward."

"We're good together. What more do we need? He keeps talking about taking the next step."

"Next step, huh?" Juliette rubbed her chin, thinking. "Is he talking marriage, kids or what?"

Nadine's eyes bugged.

"Okay, clearly that's not what you want. Why is that?"

"Not everyone is cut out to be a mother."

Juliette nodded. "This about *your* mother?"

"Well, neither of us was raised by a soccer mom."

Which was true. Both Juliette and Clint were the children of mothers incarcerated for first-degree murder, while Nadine's mom was on death row.

And Nadine's mother, grandfather and great-grandfather were all convicted murderers. Small wonder worries about her own psyche had led her to study psychology and ultimately forensic psychology.

"Soccer moms, huh? That's true. But it doesn't determine what kind of mother you might be."

"Doesn't it? My role model had me carry the bloody clothing of her victims to the trash in hopes of tempting me to be like her. She was a cat bringing a wounded bird to her offspring, teaching me how to hunt and kill."

"Well, it didn't work," said Juliette. "Instead you're a profiler and you caught one of the most successful killers in the country."

"Yeah, after I got shot."

Nadine's first case as a profiler. She'd even determined early on that the Copycat Killer was imitating her mother's crimes.

Now she had a bullet wound to remind her that she wasn't as good at this job as others believed.

But she'd learned something important. She wasn't one of them. She'd had the chance, free and clear, of killing. Instead she'd seen their prime suspect arrested.

Juliette shrugged. "Well, you're the psychologist. Maybe figure out why you're stalling with Clint."

She knew why. Fear.

"You should see the videos of him with his son. He's fun and supportive. A natural. He loves children."

"Ah. And you? How are you with kids?"

"They scare me to death. They're all potential energy and dubious outcomes."

"You've worked with too many juvenile offenders. That's what you did in Orlando, right? Your first job after graduate school."

"Yes. And incarcerated felons. But I'm aware not all kids become... like my mother."

"Are you, though?"

"If I could just find my dad. See him, talk to him. If he was normal, I'd be more willing to take a chance."

"By take a chance, you mean become a mother?"

"Oh." She exhaled and stared at the ceiling. "It's so scary."

"Hell yeah, it is. But not for the reasons you think. Nadine, you'd be a great mother. You worry too much."

"Maybe." She didn't believe that for a second.

"What does Clint say about all this?"

She pushed back from her desk. "Oh, my God. I haven't told him any of this. He hasn't even directly said anything about kids because I keep avoiding this exact conversation."

"What? Why?"

Nadine's head sank. When she spoke, her voice was small. "I don't want to lose him."

"If you keep stalling and refusing to share your fears, you might. Nadine, you have to let him know. Together, you two can work anything out. He wants real intimacy."

Her tone turned disgruntled. "I'm sleeping with him."

"That's great. But I'm speaking of emotional intimacy."

Nadine huffed. She'd wanted to complain to a sympathetic friend, and Juliette had switched teams.

"All my personal stuff is terrible, painful, embarrassing or all three."

"Relationships need to move forward. At least try."

"Yes. Okay. I will."

"Promise."

"Yes." Nadine wiped her hands on the fabric of her slacks. "I don't think I thanked you for dropping everything to come up here to help me."

"Catching that deviant will be thanks enough," said Juliette. "Hey, are we having dinner together tonight?"

Nadine hesitated.

"Oh, unless you're reserving all of your free time for Demko."

"I haven't seen him since yesterday."

"Then you should spend time with him."

"No. We should all eat together as a team." Was that because she was already looking to avoid the conversation that she so dreaded?

Likely, she realized.

Juliette gave her a dubious look, then changed the subject, bless her.

"Oh, did I tell you? I got an alert after I checked in. There's a nest of burrowing owls in Silver Springs. Do you want to go see them with me before dinner?"

Nadine had more interest in making a speedy ID than she did in tromping through the woods to see owlets.

"They want a preliminary offender profile ASAP, so…"

Juliette took the rejection with a smile.

"Okay. Maybe next time. Are you getting the alerts?"

She'd shut them off instantly after getting the bird-spotting app at Juliette's insistence. Her friend was outdoorsy, but Nadine preferred air-conditioning.

"Oh, guess what? They're letting me set up my spare cage for Jack-Jack next to Petunia."

"Will he be safe there?" asked Nadine.

"I have the staff at reception's assurance and I'll keep him in his cage for now." She glanced at her phone. "Six-thirty for dinner okay?"

Nadine gave her a thumbs-up.

Juliette ended the video call and she had two glorious hours to work on the profiling, interrupted only by Tina delivering coffee before heading out for lunch. Nadine ate her yogurt and apple at her desk.

Skogen found her in the break room refilling her coffee.

"There you are," he said, by way of a greeting.

He sat at the round table using the man-spread position, occupying as much room as possible. Nadine leaned against the counter facing him.

"I have some news. Good news, I think."

"Yes?"

"Our profiler, the one we expected, has been reassigned to California. I told DC that we didn't need a replacement. They've agreed to appoint you as lead profiler."

Her eyes widened. "They have?"

"Yes."

"I'm just a consultant."

"You've assembled a team. You've a proven track record. You've completed the necessary training. There's no reason why you shouldn't take the assignment. Is there?"

Other than terror and the constant feeling that she was a charlatan, there was not.

"Nadine, don't turn me down. We need you."

"This will be made public?"

"Not at all. Your involvement will remain confidential, as we agreed."

"All right then," she said.

He rubbed his hands together in satisfaction and then rose. "Great. Just great."

He held the door for her and they parted ways.

Nadine headed for her office and set to work collecting information on known offenders who had committed violent acts involving deprivation, torture or hunting behavior. Gathering commonalities among apprehended offenders of similar crimes was, in her opinion, a far superior method of giving investigations tangible information useful to the apprehension of a hitherto unknown suspect.

She used the current crimes only, to find commonalities in offenders. This prevented succumbing to hunches, unsubstantiated assumptions or gut feelings. Data led her to her last suspect. This series would be no different.

The devil was here in these details, the pieces that would lead to the killer.

She had begun formulating both the suspect-based profile and very sketchy victims' psychological autopsies. Knowing these background characteristics and understanding psychological quali-ties helped in creating a profile of the type of individual targeted by their killer.

But the connections were forming now, an affinity to this killer building. She understood the hunt and the prey. She didn't think that the capture was the part he relished. The victims were starving at the time of death. She believed that was not so much for pleasure on the killer's part, as preparation for the hunt. He weakened them, and then, before these victims died of exposure, he released them.

Did they run or attack? The images in her head reminded her of a bullfight, the weakened animal finally facing its tormentor, the odds no longer in the creature's favor. Why did this killer feel it necessary to weaken his prey? Was he incapable of hunting otherwise?

An old toothless lion, unable to bring down healthy prey?

Or was it for the pleasure of seeing the desperation, turning them back into animals? Yes, that was it.

Stripping away all veneer of humanity. Leaving what lay deep within. Turning them into wild creatures with only instinct. Fight. Flight.

Escape or die.

But there was no real chance of survival, was there?

It only added flavor to the hunt. And he relished this part. Seeing the desperate hope in their eyes. Watching them run, naked, through the tangle of undergrowth. Knowing they couldn't get away.

She had already put forth that the unsub was likely male, an outdoorsman, but she now added hunting or trapping experience.

Nadine did not yet know if he was using an unknown lure to draw likely victims into the territory where he felt most comfortable, or was patrolling a comfort territory and capturing victims who chanced into that area. The two kinds of killers were very different, the first brought victims to him and the second attacked targets that happened into his range. One more premeditated and organized, and the other opportunistic. His method of capture remained unknown.

Time frame was approximately a week between kills and his handling of both bodies involved outdoor body dumps in a public space.

They had so little on the victims. Demko was checking local missing persons. Hopefully, they'd make an identification soon because the killer and victims were interdependent. She needed to know these women intimately to catch this killer. By focusing on the type of victim likely to be chosen she might extrapolate where she might live and what activities brought her and the unsub together.

She could not save these two. But she could give their deaths meaning by letting them inform her profile and the hunt.

For now all she had was their treatment at capture, imprisonment, murder and, ultimately, handling after death.

All such killers sprang from somewhere and she knew that, although human behavior was unpredictable, it was also repetitive. This killer showed a similar technique with both known victims and already she saw commonalities, recurring behavior. She took those behaviors and broke them down into the sort of earlier crimes in which this unknown subject might have engaged. Just before two in the afternoon, she brought the list to Skogen in his office.

"So, we should look for similar crimes committed on animals."

"Yes."

"'Hunting behavior'?" he read.

"I'm looking for similar treatment by stabbing or shooting at the living animal and/or similar disposal of the remains."

"'Using living animals as bait'?"

"Yes. Or partially covering the remains. That seems an invitation to scavengers, or possibly a way to shock the one discovering the mutilated carcass."

"How would we determine the kill wasn't animal behavior?"

"Animals don't use arrows."

Skogen glanced at her list. "'Trapping animals. Abuse of animals. Pornography related to bondage and torture'?"

"Yes."

"Sick puppy," he muttered.

"The mind determines what is or is not arousing. But that doesn't change. What *will* change is the willingness to move beyond fantasy and into reality. Once the killer makes that step, he won't turn back."

"Anything else?"

"Just what it says. We have an organized, stylistic killer who displays his victims publicly. Not acting on impulse but showing preplanning."

"Working with someone else?" asked Skogen.

"Statistically unlikely. But I can't rule it out."

"I'll get my team working on this. See what we turn up."

"It would help me to have the victims identified."

"Working on that now."

Skogen's desk phone buzzed. He took the call and then straightened, retrieving a pad of paper and pen. He began scribbling as he spoke ending with, "Okay. Get me all you can. I want to be there with the sheriff."

He disconnected.

"We have a positive ID on victim one."

# CHAPTER FOUR

*He secured his victim in a hog trap. The metal bars made a strong enclosure. If a hundred-and-fifty-pound wild sow couldn't bash her way out, neither could this petite woman he'd taken around noon.*

*She spoke little English. Where was she from? Central America was his best guess. She was about to get a taste of a North American jungle. This view included deprivation, insects and exposure. He'd taken her clothing, left her stripped bare.*

*"Liberame," she shouted, fingers through the cage, rattling her enclosure. "Let me out!"*

*They all did that. Began with demands and threats. Those soon turned to begging and tears. The power of it all rushed up within him, giving him an arousal like no other.*

*But it didn't last.*

*Why would he want to have her when he was so close to having the most rare and valuable of her kind?*

*She was not worthy. Like the others. Just a bag of skin.*

*This specimen was a worm on a hook. A lure to capture her interest and the first one that she had met. Once she knew of him, he would signal that he understood her as no one else ever could. Finally, and most important of all, he had to prove himself worthy. The male alpha for her.*

*Yes, that was what he must do.*

*He took out his crossbow and notched an arrow. When he pointed the tip at her, she screamed, holding up her mud-streaked hands in defense.*

*Pathetic.*

*The arrow shot through her calf muscle, pinning her leg to the ground.*

*The scream she gave now was truly magnificent. The horror, shock and pain combining, turning her into the animal she had always been.*

*He wouldn't let her pretend to be something more than this. She was prey. Entertainment for superior beings. A creature made for the chase, and poor even at that.*

*When her screams changed to whimpers, he left her.*

*Soon, they would have their hunt.*

\*

The name of the first victim was Nikki Darnell, the thirty-one-year-old married daughter of a wealthy developer. Skogen's team had made the ID from a missing person's report filed by Darnell's husband. Dental records confirmed the match.

Agent Skogen wanted Nadine along for the notification of next of kin. Her request to allow Detective Demko to accompany her was approved and he'd agreed via text.

But first Skogen and Demko had to meet.

Since Demko did not have his ID card, she met him in the lobby, where she found him waiting, chatting with the security guard.

The weariness melted away with just the sight of him. Sweat stained his rumpled clothing and his face was sunburned. If she didn't know better, she'd suspect he'd been fishing all day.

That was possible, but she felt certain that bass and trout were not what he'd been after.

Skogen's warning that Demko's role was only to consult with her rose in her memory. Clearly, he had already been out in the field.

Demko extended a hand and she took it, allowing him to reel her in for a kiss on the cheek.

"There's my girl," he said.

She never grew tired of hearing his terms of endearment and drew back to beam up at him. The stubble on his face made him look like a pirate. She pictured him with a gold earring and her smile broadened.

He turned to the guard. "Have you met Dr. Finch?"

The man shook his head. He was not the same guard who had checked her in. This man was black with close-cropped hair touched with silver at the crown and a head as round as a bowling ball. He was massive and reminded Nadine of a professional wrestler.

Demko cast her a reproachful look. "Which means you missed lunch."

Actually, she'd missed breakfast.

"Brought it."

"Tony, this is Nadine. Nadine, Tony has twenty years on the job in Jacksonville. His grandkids live in DeLand." He turned to Tony. "Ranchers?"

"Citrus growers."

"Nice." He turned back to her. "Ready?"

Her brow knit for a minute. He made it seem as if he had been waiting for her instead of the other way around.

"Not quite. Skogen wants to meet you."

"Later, Tony."

"Stay safe out there," said the guard, giving Demko a salute.

Demko offered his arm and escorted her back the way they had come, waiting until they were inside the office to give her a proper kiss. When she came up for air, she forgot what he was doing here. Only he did that to her, the befuddlement. Demko's kisses were like a potent drug. And like any addict, she never got enough.

"I've got a king-sized bed," he whispered in her ear.

"You know how to sweet-talk a gal." She drew back as she recalled where they were and that the lead investigator was waiting.

She'd been expecting him earlier, but he was late.

"I thought you left this morning," she said.

"Miss me?" He wiggled his eyebrows.

"You have no idea."

When were they going to have some time alone together?

"What have you been up to?"

"I checked in at the Ocala Police Department. Just common courtesy."

"And found out all you could on the case?"

"Yes."

"Then I did the same at Silver Springs. That's a small outfit. And the sheriff's office."

"And the ME's office?"

He grinned.

"That all?"

"Sheriff's office took me to the body dump."

"You questioned people?"

"A few."

"Clint, you are not an investigator here. Agent Skogen told me specifically that you are only to assist me. Process the information his team provides, is what he said. He doesn't want you interfering."

Demko made a snorting noise. "Interfering. That's a laugh. You know who has spoken to the owners of the businesses in the strip mall closest to that body dump?"

She had a funny feeling that she did.

"No one?"

"Correct."

"No more of that," she said. "At least without bringing me along."

He smiled. "I can work with that."

"Ready to meet Special Agent Skogen?"

"Lead on."

On the way, she filled him in on the ID made on their first victim.

In Skogen's office, the agent in charge stood to greet them, anchored behind his desk. He buttoned his blazer as she crossed the threshold and the corners of his mouth tipped down.

Clint Demko trailed behind her. She made introductions and stepped back as the two alpha males shook hands and sized each other up.

Nadine pressed her lips together. You needed no skills on behavioral science to see that these two hated each other on sight.

"So you got your gold shield in Miami-Dade and have been on the job in Sarasota over a year."

"Yes."

"With a solid solve rate," said Skogen, showing them he had done his homework. "But I'll remind you that this is my investigation. Dr. Finch's input is essential. Yours is not. You are here at her request and only as long as I don't find your work interferes with mine. We clear?"

Demko lowered his chin and smiled. "I understand my job here."

It wasn't the verification Skogen sought, or acceptance of his position as subordinate.

Demko had worked with the Feds and she knew that he generally found agents overbearing, with more education than experience.

"You delivered notification of death before?" asked Skogen.

"Many times," said Demko.

"Then I'll let you handle it."

Notifying next of kin was a terrible job. So this was the reason Agent Skogen had been receptive to allowing the detective to accompany him. He was anxious to foist the dismal duty onto Demko.

Nadine scowled, thinking it small of him to "let" Demko have the job that no one in their right mind wanted.

"Sure."

"I appreciate you tagging along," he said.

Nadine's mood soured further. Demko wasn't tagging along. Skogen had just assigned him a job.

"I want to make it clear to both of you that Detective Demko has no jurisdiction in this county and his role is strictly advisory."

Demko's brows lifted. "So you don't want me to notify next of kin?"

Skogen turned to Nadine.

"He always this difficult?"

She glanced from her new boss to him.

"When provoked."

She and Demko shared a smile.

Skogen changed the subject, wisely, she thought. His attention shifted to the page before him.

"Nikki Darnell's husband, Roger, listed her missing on Saturday, March 13th, eighteen days ago. He is the owner of a small business and has his state contractor's license. They rent a home in DeLand. Nikki previously worked for her father, Clem Miller, but switched jobs last February and now works for a financial planning group in Orlando. Seems to be some bad blood between father and daughter."

"I know of him. He's a developer. A really successful one," said Nadine. "He builds assisted-living places all over the state."

Demko nodded, perhaps recalling the controversy over one of Miller's buildings in Sarasota that succeeded in gaining a variance against the community objections to the high-density project.

"A man like that could have raised an army to hunt for his daughter. Gotten public awareness."

"Except my agents tell me he and his daughter haven't spoken in over a year, since she announced her plans to marry Mr. Darnell."

"Does he know she's missing?" asked Nadine.

"Unknown. All my agents could verify was that Roger and Mr. Miller are not in contact."

"And he didn't think to ask her father's help when his wife vanished?"

"Whether he thought of it or not, he has not been in contact, or so he claims."

"Disappearance in the papers?" asked Demko.

"Yes. Local only."

"And her father lives in Orlando," said Nadine.

Skogen nodded.

"Your people spoke to Darnell?" asked Demko.

"Yes, and with every family who has reported a woman missing in the last month. Nikki was on the list. Her husband has been interviewed."

"But not her dad?"

"No."

"Why?"

"We spoke only to next of kin or the person filing the report. In Nikki Darnell's case her husband was both."

"What are the details of her disappearance?" asked Demko.

Skogen referred to the page again. "Missing after she failed to return home after an early-morning walk with their dog in the state forest on Saturday, March 13th. Officially listed as missing on March 14th. Her husband located her vehicle at the trailhead she had mentioned." Skogen sighed. "No sign of either Nikki or the black Lab until the recent bodies were discovered."

"Does she often walk alone in the woods?" asked Nadine.

"Always with the dog, Char. Husband said the dog is very devoted to her and protective."

Not protective enough, thought Nadine.

"Where's her dog?" asked Demko.

"Missing," said Skogen.

"You check the shelters?" asked Demko.

"Not yet."

"How'd you make the ID?" asked Demko.

"Dental records, verified by DNA match. Hair sample provided by Roger."

"Anything from the vehicle?"

"Sheriff released it to Darnell after processing. My people are handling that now."

Nadine realized that the news they were to deliver would be a shock, the worst possible outcome, but not as great a shock as homicide notification from out of the blue. Nikki had been missing for over two weeks. Searches had failed. Her husband would be hoping for the best and fearing the worst. Unless he already knew, and her job was to assess if that might be a possibility.

Skogen turned to Nadine. "Ready?"

She narrowed her eyes and stepped up beside Demko. "We'll follow you."

His mouth went tight. "Fine."

He checked with his assistant that the sheriff was waiting outside, and they followed him from the lot.

Inside his SUV, Demko said, "He's a charmer."

On the drive, Demko explained the procedure far more clearly than Skogen, who, she suspected, like her, had limited experience. Death notification generally fell on local law enforcement and to the detectives working the case.

"You have a minimum of three. Usually a detective and two uniforms. In this case, one uniform. That will be the sheriff."

"Add to that an FBI agent and one forensic psychologist," said Nadine.

"You, me, Skogen and the sheriff. Yes."

"He'll know we have bad news," she said.

"Yeah. But some part of him will likely hold out hope. First, we try to get him to allow us inside and get him seated. We do a visual sweep to make certain there are no sharp objects or weapons of any sort within easy access."

"I see. Self-harm, or do you think he might attack us?"

"Both. People are unpredictable." He paused, then took up the explanation again. "The sheriff is there to present a man in uniform. He grounds us and has our backs. His job is to observe and protect. Step in if things get hostile. I'll deliver the news and answer all his questions. Then you ask who we can call to be with him."

"Skogen?"

"I got no job for him. After Darnell's questions, we leave our cards and are out. Sheriff remains until a relative or friend arrives. Never leave him alone. Got it?"

"Yes. I've done this once before."

"Great."

She recalled the howl of a mother on notification of the sudden death of her child. She thought that cry of agony would live in her memory forever.

"Everyone experiences grief differently," she said.

"Don't I know it. Once had a guy run right through a sliding glass window after I delivered the news of his wife's death."

"Acute stress disorder cause by psychological shock."

"Yes."

At three-fifteen in the afternoon, under brilliant blue skies, they parked before a modest home with pygmy palms flanking the entrance and assembled on the sidewalk. After a brief discussion, they rang the bell.

They were expected. Skogen's people had notified Roger that they had news on his wife.

After a slight wait, the door opened and a gaunt man, with a hawkish nose, filled the gap.

Skogen took over. "Mr. Darnell, I'm FBI Agent Jack Skogen. Might we come in for a few minutes?"

"Did you find her?" He clutched the doorknob.

"May we?" Skogen motioned to the house.

Roger Darnell stepped aside to let them pass. Nadine entered between Skogen and Demko. Skogen chose the living room, taking a seat on the couch. Demko stood before the television, just beside the couple's wedding photo, and Nadine perched between them at the opposite end of the couch from Skogen. The sheriff moved to be in clear view of Darnell, who settled in the recliner, waiting.

"Did you find her?" he said again.

Skogen looked to Demko, and Darnell followed the direction of his gaze.

"Yes, Mr. Darnell. I'm Homicide detective Clint Demko. I am sorry to inform you that your wife is the victim of a homicide. We made a positive identification with both dental records and the DNA sample you provided."

Darnell's face went red and tears sprang from his eyes. He retrieved the pillow from behind him and hugged it.

"I'm very sorry for your loss," said Demko.

Darnell pressed his face into the pillow. The room went silent except for his ragged breathing. When he lifted his gaze, he seemed lost. He shook his head slowly, processing, Nadine thought.

"What happened to her?"

Demko gave a very amended version of events. "She was attacked somewhere on the trail and died from a neck wound."

And starvation. And a spine injury. And an alligator attack, thought Nadine.

"Where did you find her?"

"By the St. Johns River. Near a trail."

"Our dog?"

"Still missing."

He swallowed hard, staring straight ahead.

"Why would someone do this?"

That one Demko did not answer. He just waited.

"Do you have any suspects?"

"As you can see, the FBI is involved. We are doing everything in our power to solve your wife's homicide."

She admired how he avoided saying killer or murder. He obviously did know what he was doing.

Nadine directed her attention to Roger Darnell. He seemed to have shrunk before her eyes. His posture drooped and he pressed a hand to his forehead.

"I can't believe this," he whispered.

Demko stepped forward. "This is my card." He placed it on the coffee table. The sheriff did the same.

"Do you have someone we can call to be with you?"

He shook his head but said, "My brother." He glanced to Nadine. "We were trying to get pregnant. We were…" His words fell off and he dropped his face into his hands as the grief pushed past the shock at last.

With Darnell's assistance, Nadine retrieved the number and made the call. Then all but the sheriff made their exit. Demko paused at the door.

"Mr. Darnell, we will be in touch."

And Nadine saw something then, a widening of the eyes as if he found the prospect of another contact with authorities as a threat. Then he noted her watching and dropped his gaze.

Nadine lingered. Darnell reached for a cigarette, his hands shaking. It might be nothing, a normal reaction to having his wife's death investigated. Certainly, he'd just had his worst fears realized. Likely he was heartbroken, trying to hold it together until they left.

"What do I do about her will and stuff?" asked Darnell. "Call a lawyer?"

Nadine's eyes narrowed. That was definitely not what should be on the mind of a worried husband upon notification of death. She and Demko exchanged a knowing look.

"Perhaps start with a funeral director?" said Demko.

"Or Nikki's parents?" she suggested.

"I can't. They haven't spoken to me since we got engaged." He glanced to Nadine. "Could you tell them?"

"Of course," said Nadine.

Darnell took a long drag on the cigarette and blew the smoke toward the ceiling.

Skogen had headed back to his vehicle as Nadine and Demko reached the SUV. She settled inside and he got them under way.

"What was your take on him?" Demko asked.

"Fairly normal until you told him we'd be back. That made him apprehensive, which could be natural. Police make people nervous. But that comment about the will. That wasn't normal."

"Yeah. I agree," said Demko.

She clipped her seat belt. "I'd like to speak to Nikki Darnell's parents, the Millers. See what they have to say about their son-in-law. Before they read it in the papers."

"We can head over there now."

"Not alone."

"I'll bring a uniform with me."

"Hadn't we better tell Skogen?"

"He's already made his decision. Doing the minimum, contacting her husband as next of kin. But if it were my kid, I'd like to hear it from a father instead of reading it in the headlines."

"Let's go. If it's my idea, Skogen can't object."

They drove through a downpour, reaching the offices of C.L. Miller Developers as the rain tapered off just before five in the afternoon.

They were met in the lobby by the uniformed officer Demko had requested. At the management company suite, Demko's detective's shield got them past Mr. Miller's assistant.

Miller stood as they entered a large office filled with heavy dark furniture. Models of building projects sat on the sideboard and framed artists' renderings filled the walls. Through the floor-to-ceiling windows stood expansive views of other high-rise buildings in Orlando's business center.

Clem Miller looked like his photos, which appeared on most advertising for his company. He was tan, fit with vibrant blond hair, out of place for a man in his mid-fifties. He ushered them into his posh office.

Miller rounded his desk, hand extended. "Detective, how can I help you?"

Demko motioned to the seating area, six high-backed office chairs ringing a round table with ornately carved legs, like bandits circling a wagon train.

"Could we sit?"

They did. Demko introduced Nadine and then asked Miller when he had last been in contact with his daughter. The man went scarlet. He blustered and blew, reminding Nadine of a bull preparing to charge.

"We've severed ties," he said at last.

"Because of her decision to marry?"

"Detective, I'm not going to discuss personal affairs with you."

"I see."

Nadine knew that would be changing because, although the FBI had deemed it unnecessary to notify the Millers immediately, they would likely soon be interviewing them.

"Is your wife here? I understand she works with you."

"She's not. Detective, what is this about?"

"Sir, I'm assisting the FBI with a homicide investigation. We've made a positive identification on one of two victims."

"The bodies at the river?"

"Yes, sir. I'm very sorry to inform you that one of those victims was your daughter."

He had gone pale and his lips were suddenly bloodless and gray. "It's a mistake."

"No, Mr. Miller. We have DNA confirmation and have a positive identification on Nikki Darnell."

"Don't call her that! It's Nikki Miller!" He was on his feet now. A shove sent the chair crashing into the credenza, toppling a statue of a dancer.

"Mr. Miller, I'm very sorry for your loss."

"I knew that guy was trouble. It's him, isn't it? That low-life, moneygrubbing excuse for a man. He did this!" He turned toward the door.

The young officer looked to Demko, who held out a hand.

When Demko spoke, it was with a tone of authority Nadine had never heard.

"Sir, you need to sit right now."

Miller gave him a look of outrage but then retrieved his chair and sat.

"He's not getting a penny," he said. "I'll see he's locked up for the rest of his life."

"You have some reason to believe that Roger Darnell would harm your daughter?"

"He tried to get me to buy them a house. He hinted he needed a new truck. Even asked me to hire him on one of my building projects. As if I would ever… The man is a parasite. It's why I cut her off. Now he'll be after the insurance money," he said to himself and then pointed at Demko. "He won't get it."

"Did he have a policy on Nikki?"

"No! Hell no. He couldn't afford to get his truck fixed. *I've* got the policy. Oh, no, the trust."

"Trust?" asked Demko.

"I put her shares of my company in a trust so he couldn't get at them. But…"

He didn't need to finish. Those shares were likely now part of Nikki's estate and without a will, they would eventually pass to her husband.

Nadine broke in here. "Mr. Miller, I'm very sorry for your loss, but I wonder if you might need to contact your wife before this story breaks. I'm sure it would be better if she heard it from the detective or from you."

He was on his feet again. "This will just kill her." He reached for the phone and hit the intercom button. "Rebecca, find my wife. Get her here and tell her it's urgent." He paused, listening. "I don't care where she is. Send someone and get her here now!"

Off the phone now, he paced before them.

"Mr. Miller, I need to get a better picture of Nikki," said Nadine. "I'd like to interview you and your wife. It will help our investigation."

Miller raked a hand through his thick hair. "Yes. Ask Rebecca. She'll schedule it."

"Fine. Mr. Miller, I am truly sorry for your loss."

Miller pressed his mouth into a tight line. But tears now coursed down his face as grief overcame fury, at last.

"Do you have any questions for me?" asked Demko.

"Questions? Hell no. My God. I knew something terrible… I should have…" He lifted his gaze to the pair of them.

Demko placed his card on the table and she did the same. They stood in unison.

"Officer Gaines will stay here until your wife arrives. If you have questions, please call."

Nadine nearly reached the door when Miller spoke.

"Dr. Finch, you find who did this to my little girl."

"Yes, sir. That's what I'm here for."

In the outer office, they stopped to schedule a meeting for the following day, then left the building. Back in the SUV, they drove in silence to the highway.

"What do you think?" asked Demko.

"Being after his wife's money doesn't make him a killer."

"Doesn't eliminate him either."

"True. I've got to tell Skogen."

Nadine and Demko made it to the hotel after eight, due to the perpetual tie-ups on I-4. She'd had a brief conversation with Skogen on their visit with the Millers en route and just received a text from Juliette that she and Tina waited in the lobby.

Tina, now wearing a yellow sundress, her makeup flawless and including false eyelashes, looked younger than her twenty-one years. Juliette, by contrast, wore jeans, cowboy boots and a paisley peasant blouse. Her only makeup was mascara and a tinted lip gloss, scented with mint, Nadine knew, because it helped mask the smell of the bodies she dissected. She wore a cross-body bag large enough for a phone, wallet and her handgun.

"We waited on dinner for you," said Tina. "Reservation at a Caribbean place."

"We had appetizers at the tiki bar. But I'm starving again," admitted Juliette.

"Great. Let's go," said Nadine. But Juliette didn't move.

"We got a hit on the second victim."

# CHAPTER FIVE

"The lab has DNA to verify," said Juliette, "but we believe we know her name. It's Rita Karnowski."

"I recognize that name," said Demko. "Sheriff's office gave me a list of all known missing persons. Her boyfriend reported she disappeared during a hike. Right?"

"Yes. On March 20th. One of Skogen's team called to tell us they made a match on a tattoo. The parents at first denied she had a tattoo, but the older brother came forward this afternoon. It's a match. They were at the ME's office and made the identification."

"Why didn't you call me?" asked Nadine.

"I called Tina. She told me where you were."

"And she fits with our time of death?" asked Demko.

"Sure does," said Juliette.

"They contacted the boyfriend yet?" asked Demko.

"I'll find out." Nadine drew out her phone.

In a moment she'd sent a text to Skogen, then waited the endless seconds for the chime notification of his reply.

She read his text aloud.

*Heading to Hugo Betters residence. Meet us. We'll wait.*

He furnished the address of Betters, Rita's boyfriend.

Demko drove and they met Skogen and the sheriff at a single-family, squatty cinder-block box with a double carport larger than the building. The only vehicle present was a Camaro missing an engine.

The house was dark and the window A/C unit wasn't running.

"You sure this is the right house?" asked Demko.

The sheriff nodded and made the approach. Unsurprisingly, there was no answer.

"Did you try his phone?" asked Nadine. Death notifications were done in person when possible, but the phone was better than nothing.

"We did. No answer and no voicemail," said Skogen.

"What about his work?" asked Demko.

"He's a subcontractor. Electrician. Working several jobs. We're trying to pin down his current location."

Skogen rested his hands on his hips, glaring as the sheriff tucked his card in the gap of the screen door and frame.

"We'll keep trying the number," said the sheriff. "And call some of the contractors I know are building in the area."

Nadine didn't like leaving a death notification, but it was Skogen's call.

He nodded and told Nadine he'd see her back at their temporary office.

At Demko's vehicle she sighed.

"So… dinner?" said Demko.

Nadine hung back. "I need to add Karnowski to my profile. Begin gathering details on—"

Demko cut her off. "You need to eat."

She nodded, accepting defeat, and climbed into his vehicle.

"I sent Juliette a text. She just got back to the hotel. We'll pick her and Tina up on the way."

Nadine said nothing. She was itching to get back to work. Both victims identified. There was so much to do.

"Maybe Skogen will locate Darnell while you eat."

*

At the restaurant, they stepped into cool air-conditioning in the lively, pink-and-turquoise-decorated interior. In the corner, a lone musician worked a set of steel drums. Her stomach growled at the smell of the Caribbean and American food. With a jolt, Nadine thought of the two young women who'd never again go out for a casual meal with friends or enjoy the atmosphere of a relaxed restaurant. But the best she could do for them was to stop this killer before he tore apart the lives of another family.

At the hostess station they were greeted by a spunky young woman who seated them at a great table in the center of the busy room. Nadine was thrilled that she had never been there before, so she could enjoy her meal without the shadows of the past encroaching.

Demko told the hostess that they were in a hurry and she took their order, instead of waiting for the server. Nadine's cheeseburger and fries were a big, delicious mess and she ate the entire thing.

"How's Molly?" Tina asked Demko.

"Good! A little confused at the change of residence. But I took her to a dog sitter today. The woman has a four-year-old shepherd and a golden retriever. Molly is in heaven!"

"That's nice. My cat spent the day under my bed. But I'm sure Muffin will adjust. I'm keeping the maid out for now."

"Wise," said Juliette. "Jack-Jack is welcome in the lobby when Rosie is there. She'll watch over him and their little gal, Petunia."

"I saw some of the kids talking to Jack-Jack," said Tina.

"Yeah, he had a busier day than I did."

At last, everyone had eaten their fill.

"That was great," said Juliette, dropping her napkin beside her empty plate.

It was the first real sit-down meal Nadine had had since leaving DC. She was finally full but had yet to relax.

That would come only after they caught this unsub. She knew this sort of killer. He was just getting started and finding him would take all of them.

She glanced about at her team. She'd never led a team and felt suddenly grateful and terrified.

"I think we should swing by the body dump," said Demko, bringing the conversation back to the case.

"At night?" croaked Tina.

"That's likely when the killer was there. Might help Nadine with her profile."

They turned their attention to her.

She was itching to get back to her laptop and the new details on their victims, but this also had value.

"Yes. Anything that will help us find this killer."

"Ready?" asked Juliette.

Tina reached for her margarita, draining the remains in two swallows.

"*Now* I'm ready."

"Bathroom," said Juliette.

"Good idea."

The two headed out, leaving Demko and Nadine momentarily alone in the crowded restaurant.

Nadine received the bill from their server and calculated the tip as Demko finished his final onion ring.

His hand went to his napkin and then to her knee. The zip of attraction sparked, and she met his gaze. There was no misinterpreting that look. Nadine's pulse jumped as she returned his smile.

"Can I come up to your room tonight?"

"You're the one with the king-sized bed."

"Great. You come to my room." He grinned. "See you later then."

Juliette and Tina returned as they reached the servers' station. Tina's face had gone pale and she was sweating.

Nadine recalled that Tina's mother's victim had been found in a shallow grave. The prospect of seeing this body dump might be touching off all sorts of emotional reactions.

"You okay, Tina?" asked Nadine.

Tina pressed her mouth tight and gave a vigorous nod.

"We can swing by the hotel. Drop you off."

"No you won't! I'm going, too."

"Not necessary," said Demko.

"I'm part of this team," she said, her expression stubborn.

Demko sighed and motioned toward the door. When they reached the exit, their hostess cast them a ready smile.

"You folks have a good meal?"

"Yes, very good," said Demko.

"That's fine! Y'all come back and see us."

Their affable hostess wished them a great evening and waved them out.


Ten minutes later, they had left Ocala behind and headed, in Demko's SUV, toward the St. Johns River, leaving streetlights behind.

On the way, Juliette told them everything she could remember about Rita Karnowski.

"She enjoyed the outdoors. She and her boyfriend... oh, what's his name?"

"Hugo Betters," supplied Demko.

"Right. Kayaked on Saturday morning."

"Big Water Marina," said Demko.

"Then you tell it," said Juliette.

Clearly, he knew every missing person's case better than any of them. Nadine recalled the name, but she'd need the files to refresh her memory.

"After eating at Big River on Saturday, March 20th, they headed to a hiking trail. Hoping to see some wildlife. She's a transplant from up north."

"Michigan," said Juliette.

"Yes. Very interested in the spring migration."

"You got this all from her file?" asked Nadine.

"I've spoken by phone to her parents," said Demko.

"When?"

"This morning."

Skogen was not going to like that, she thought.

"Before the ID?"

He nodded.

"You speak to the boyfriend?" she asked.

"Not yet."

"Because…"

"Until Skogen clears him, he's likely to be a suspect."

"What about Nikki Darnell's husband?" asked Juliette. "What did you think of him?"

"There's a big range of emotional reactions when confronting the death of a loved one. But his seemed rehearsed."

Demko took up the conversation again. "And her father has indicated there is insurance money. Ask Skogen to see if her husband also has a policy on his wife. Request Darnell's computers and check what he's been searching on the internet. If he and his wife used the same one, it will be part of the investigation."

"You think these two each killed their partner," asked Tina.

"I think," said Demko, "that you look at partners until you know otherwise."

Nadine thought of his mother, who hatched a scheme to kill her second husband for insurance money, dragging her elder son into a murder plot that landed them both in federal prison.

In the darkness, the bleached asphalt glowed gray in the headlights. Deep drainage ditches flanked them. These would fill in the summer rainy season, making an easy highway for the male gators seeking new territory.

The silence in the vehicle closed in on Nadine.

"Juliette, I want to ask a favor. Would you take a blood sample and run it for a specific enzyme sequence?"

"Sure. I order lab work all the time. Whose blood?"

"Mine."

The silence now crackled.

"If it's to add your blood to the DNA database, I'd advise against that," said Demko.

"Not for that."

"Research?" Juliette asked, her words holding caution.

"Personal reasons."

"What am I looking for?" asked Juliette.

Demko broke in. "Nadine, is this about that damned study?"

"What study?" asked Tina.

"Some doctor drew blood from felons and now Nadine is fixed on it," said Demko.

"Is this the gene sequence associated with greater frequency of violence?" asked Juliette, clearly recalling a conversation Nadine and she had had months ago.

"Yes. I want to know if I have the sequences associated with aggression."

"Why?" asked Tina.

"Because the sequence shows a strong correlation to violent behaviors, like homicide."

"You are not going to become a killer because you have some gene sequence," said Juliette.

"My great-grandfather, grandfather, my mother, and my brother all committed acts of—"

Demko cut her off. "All made their own decisions and suffered the consequences."

She said nothing to that.

"What about the rest of us?" he asked. "Do you think we're all killers because of our parents' crimes?"

"No, of course not."

"One study," said Juliette. "You can't explain criminality purely as biological. There are other factors. Ones that won't appear in the blood, genetics or the small research study you've fixed on."

"I realize that."

"Do you? Violence is not that simple. Scientists have been trying to attribute man's evil deeds to brain damage, genetics, hormonal abnormalities and, in past centuries, to the lumps on a person's head. I saw one bizarre argument linking crime to fluoride in drinking water."

"Really?" asked Tina.

"It's like trying to find the cause of cancer. PS, there isn't one. There are many contributing factors, a mix of heritage and environment. So don't place too much value on one study."

"Using your analogy, it's like a cancer screening," said Nadine. "Just something to be aware of."

"You are not like them. You're a profiler," said Demko. "You *hunt* killers."

Killers like her mother.

"Nadine, you are what you do. Not what you fear you'll do. Not what your mom did," he said. "And I know you. You're all about stopping these monsters. Not becoming one."

Monsters. That's what he thought of her mom. What everyone thought. And she was. But Arleen was also her family.

Confronting the Copycat Killer had shown her that she wasn't like her. But Nadine now had other worries. Ones that replaced her old obsession of the possibility of becoming a violent offender and ending up in a jail cell beside her mother. Over the last year, she battled a new apprehension, one triggered by Clint's desire to get more serious.

*What if the killing just skipped a generation?*

"Besides, you're almost thirty, and you've never committed a violent act," he said.

"I stabbed the Copycat Killer."

"In self-defense," he countered.

"Five times."

Demko grumbled, "Should have made it six."

For a moment there was quiet. Then Tina spoke up.

"I want the test, too."

"Fine," he said. "Take my DNA, too."

Demko pulled into the dirt parking area, rolling over uneven ground and stopping before the nearest access to the trail where the bodies of Nikki Darnell and Rita Karnowski were discovered.

He cut the lights and they sat in darkness. Gradually Nadine's eyes adjusted to the moonlight casting a wide silver band across the black waters of the St. Johns River.

Demko stepped out first, heading for the trail flanking the water. Insects buzzed in the trees. Nadine saw a blue light wink on and off to his left. Every hair on her neck lifted. She reached for her mace and threw open the door.

"Stay here," she called to the women behind her. To Demko she shouted, "Get down."

Demko fell to his stomach at Nadine's shouted order.

Nadine crouched, hurrying toward Demko, pointing. "What was that?"

"What?"

Nadine explained what she saw. Her fear was that it was a targeting laser.

"Can't be. That would have landed on a target, not flashed in the woods."

Demko moved forward to investigate as Nadine swatted at mosquitoes. Her skin was freezing despite the warm, humid air. Something brushed against her leg, making her dance sideways.

Finally he returned.

"Wildlife camera."

Had they just caught a break? Could that camera hold the image of their killer dragging two bodies along the trail?

While they waited for the sheriff to arrive, Nadine took note of how empty the site was. The river access would be busy in the early morning and possibly throughout the day. But now, before midnight, it was empty of people. Even the alligators were absent. With no sunlight, they had no reason to bask on the bank and warm their cold blood. She couldn't see them. But they were there, nocturnal hunters all but submerged, hunting fish and turtle in the river or waiting for the prey to venture too close. Possum, raccoon, armadillo and possibly a pack rat or two scurried in the dry palmetto leaves. Small night creatures also needed to eat.

The sheriff arrived, lights but no siren, and Demko spoke with him as Nadine made her way back to the lot. Demko sent them home in his SUV as the sheriff contacted the FBI to see about procedures for evidence collection on an object possibly associated with their case. Juliette drove. Nadine was exhausted and her head began an incessant pounding, heralding a blooming migraine.

The three said their good nights and Nadine made it to her room after midnight, downing one of her migraine pills. She was impatient to work on her profile. But her body wasn't cooperating. In the bathroom, she tugged on her black headband, a knockoff Versace with the gold Greca border. She'd accidentally dripped bleach on it and so it was now relegated to the bathroom. She drew her hair back with the band and scrubbed the sweat from her face, determined to push through her headache and get to work, but upon reaching the bed, she spotted the flashing red light on the phone indicating a message. She lifted the handset and pressed the message button.

"Dr. Finch, this is Rosie at the front desk. We have an envelope for you from Agent Skogen of the FBI. He asked us to deliver it to you as soon as possible. Could you please come to reception when you retrieve this message?"

What was it? A list of contractors where Betters worked? Some detail on the identified victims vital to her profile?

Nadine rose wearily. Her headache was getting worse, and the blurred vision and stomachache forecast a doozy of a migraine that her medication had yet to impact. Frustration blossomed with the pain. It was only a short journey to the desk, but her head pounded, and wavy lines disrupted her vision. They were better if she closed one eye.

On the way out, she spotted her key card and grabbed it. Closing one eye obviously affected her balance, because once in the hall, she toppled into the door beside hers and swore a string of obscenities that would have made her mother blush.

The elevator was the easy part. It had handrails, but the bright halogen bulb blinded. The light sensitivity signaled that the migraine had a firm hold. She lifted one hand as a visor against the assault.

As the elevator jolted to a stop at ground level, Nadine came to the recognition that her profile would have to wait for this headache to come and go in its own sweet time.

At the front desk, she braced against the nausea, still shielding her eyes.

The receptionist was male. She glanced to the bell stand to see one covered birdcage and one empty one. Juliette had taken to keeping the travel cage in her room and leaving this larger one in the lobby beside Petunia's. It was well past both birds' bedtime. Hers as well.

She told the man behind the desk what she needed, and he passed her a manila envelope with her name scrawled in jagged strokes.

Inside, instead of some vital document related to this case, she found four policy manuals on collaborating with the FBI and a Post-it with a message that read, *For your team. This* was what brought her down here? Fuming, she retraced her path, but the damn buttons on the elevator didn't work.

It was several minutes of fumbling before she remembered to use her key card. Tapping it to the panel, the button now engaged. The doors swept closed and the car whisked her upward. She clutched the handrail and held on, squatting as the lights swam with her vision.

*You are not puking in a hotel elevator.*

But she might. The doors opened and she stood, weaving forward with one hand on the envelope and the other over one eye. The closing doors bounced off her back leg and then opened again, causing her to spin and collide with a cylindrical trash container. It shot forward and rolled from the alcove into the hall with a deafening clatter.

She collected the pieces of the can and reassembled them, with more clattering, now certain she was going to be ill.

Nadine paused, deliberating between losing her dinner here in the bin or making a run for her bathroom.

Bathroom, she decided, dashing along. In the hall outside her room, she was fumbling with the key card when the door she had earlier crashed into opened. Out stepped an older woman. Her brown hair, streaked with gray, tumbled in waves down her back, huge glasses with thick lenses made her eyes bulge and a look of fury reddened her face. She cinched her robe and glared.

"Do you know what time it is?"

Nadine shook her head, the key card poised just above the slot.

"It's after midnight! I have to be up at four and I can't sleep with you crashing around. What is wrong with you?"

Nadine felt her face heat and her stomach gave a dangerous lurch.

The door across from her opened. In the gap stood a man, dressed in khakis and a dark shirt. He held a towel around his neck, gripping it in each hand.

Nadine's stomach roiled and she pressed a hand to her mouth.

"What's going on?" he asked.

"She's drunk or something. Woken me up twice!"

"Migraine," she murmured.

"So help her with her card and go to bed," said the man.

He met Nadine's gaze, his face a perfect expressionless mask. The door swung shut.

The woman huffed as she stepped forward and snatched the key card from Nadine.

"No respect for others. Simply unacceptable," she said, her words sharp as any schoolmarm.

The door lock clicked, and she swung the door open.

"There. No more racket or I'll call the manager."

Threat delivered, she stormed away. Nadine lunged forward, making it to the toilet before losing the sour remains of her meal.

She wiped her mouth on a hand towel and retrieved her migraine medication, downing the second bitter white pill with the crushed saltines she had in her purse.

Then she lay on the bed with a wet cloth over her eyes, waiting for the medicine to work. It did, by degrees, and she slipped into unconsciousness.

*

*Bianca Santander was living a nightmare. After her shift on Wednesday, a man had approached her at the bus stop. She'd seen him coming and called her brother. Told him they were taking her into custody.*

He'd been in a uniform, said he was from Immigration. Only after she was in his truck did she see it was a forest ranger's uniform.

He had taken her into the jungle, shot her with an arrow and left her under the relentless sun, locked in an animal cage.

Now, in the darkness, her thirst grew and the insects came in clouds. Her wounded leg throbbed and sent white-hot bolts of pain through her muscle every time she moved. The blood drew the insects in swarms, biting flies and mosquitoes. They landed, dotting her leg, biting, sucking and swelling with her blood, as she slapped and cried and finally screamed to the sky.

No one heard. No one came.

By now her brother would have told them she was in custody. They'd be calling Immigration. Trying to get an attorney to handle her case and expecting her to be deported. She had no papers. Neither did her father or two brothers. If they called the police, ICE might take them all.

She slapped, moaning at the pain caused by the contact. Then she brushed at her leg, but the insects landed immediately. Should she pull out the arrow? But she had nothing to bandage the wound. He'd left her naked and caged.

What time was it? Clouds covered the moon and stars of the endless night. A downpour at dawn had lasted only long enough to soak her. Why didn't she think to try and drink what water she could?

Now she shivered as a cold sweat dampened her skin. She was going to die here, she realized, and began praying to God, her dry lips moving with the words she knew by heart.

"Padre nuestro, que estás en el cielo, santificado sea tu nombre…"

Something big rustled in the brush. Was it him?

# CHAPTER SIX

## THURSDAY

Nadine woke well before her six-fifteen alarm. Her head was fuzzy from the medication, but it no longer pulsed with each heartbeat. Her vision was clear, and the light sensitivity had disappeared.

She carried the damp washcloth to the bathroom where she took her antidepressant, then stared at her reflection that showed dark smudges beneath her eyes.

Nadine remembered the encounter with the woman, cringing. Then she recalled the envelope from Skogen. What had she done with that?

A search of her room came up empty. She retraced her steps, dressed only in her robe. She found the trash receptacle now sitting beside the foyer table that held an artificial orchid arrangement. She pulled off the lid and there was the manila envelope.

She blew out a breath in relief and reached into the bin, retrieving the package. Nadine pressed the parcel to her chest. *Phew.* Returning to her room, she discovered the alarm on her phone sounding.

She flicked it off and noticed that she'd missed a 1 a.m. text from Demko asking her if she was still up.

She glowered at the screen.

No. She had not been. And he had not called. So far their reunion had been a bust. She pushed away her frustration because she approved of his decision to pursue evidence on that trail cam. Anything to get this guy.

Nadine fired off a text to Demko asking him to meet her at breakfast. She'd deliver the damned procedural manual to him and find out what they'd gleaned from the wildlife camera.

His reply was one letter.

*K*

Nadine spent several minutes on an unsuccessful hunt for her headband before washing up. Leaving the bathroom, she heard her phone sound with a notification. She'd missed a call from Juliette and retrieved the voice message.

"Tina and I are going to see those owls. Leaving the hotel at six-fifteen. Call me if you want to join us."

"Nope," she said to the phone and then quickly grabbed some of the few remaining clean clothes from her suitcase. She paused to stare at the plastic bag and Bubble Wrap protecting her brick, considering bringing it to breakfast for Demko to admire, but left it, and quickly dressed. Somehow, she managed to reach the lobby at 7:15 a.m. to find Tina and Juliette just coming in.

Juliette's expression beamed with delight.

"I saw them!"

"Who?" asked Nadine.

"The burrowing owls. God, they are so cute. They are only the size of soda cans, and their legs! They're like stilts."

"You shouldn't be on the trails alone."

"I wasn't alone. I had Tina and Smith and Wesson along." Juliette had a carry permit and, except when jogging, was generally armed. "There's a kayak rental place near here. I spotted it on the way back. Do you want to go out on Saturday?"

"Umm, if I do get free time, I'll likely go visit Arlo," Nadine said.

"I'll go!" said Tina.

Juliette looked surprised. "Really. Do you kayak?"

"No, but I can swim and I'm a fast learner."

Juliette nodded and gave Tina one of her most generous smiles. "All right then."

"How long until you get the DNA back from the sperm sample on Karnowski?" asked Nadine, back to business.

"Should have it in a day or so."

"Fast."

"FBI labs," said Juliette. "I'm getting spoiled. I'm anxious to see if they get a hit."

"Me too." To get a match would be amazing, but it wouldn't be the first time a serial was caught because of forensic evidence.

"You heading to the office?" asked Tina.

"Meeting with Nikki Darnell's parents first."

Nadine was itching to get to work building her psychological autopsy of the two known victims, seeking commonalities in behavior, physicality, and mental state, but first she wanted to meet Karnowski's boyfriend and Nikki's mother.

"See you later then," said Tina.

Juliette offered a wave and the pair headed toward their rooms on the first floor, which allowed pets.

Nadine veered toward the breakfast area, finding a new worker there setting out oranges, this one a white man about her height. She did not see the small woman who had been working yesterday, and wondered if the attendant had gotten into trouble for throwing away her breakfast. She headed toward the man to ask, but he veered through the swinging door to the kitchen at her approach.

Nadine grabbed a bowl of oatmeal, added milk and dried fruit, and collected a small plate of eggs.

In the dining area, she spotted Demko, who sat reading the paper and simultaneously munching on a bagel slathered with cream cheese and topped with walnuts.

She slipped in beside him and he pushed a cup of coffee in her direction. Then he leaned in and planted a kiss on her lips that made her drop her spoon.

"Good morning," he whispered and then drew back.

"I missed your text."

"It was late." He finished the bagel in three bites, showing strong white teeth. The sight did funny things to her breathing.

"I had a migraine."

"Again?" His expression now reflected concern.

"Yeah, stress reaction. I took my meds and they finally knocked me out."

She sipped the coffee, completely aware that they had not been alone together since she'd returned from DC. Though he was seated beside her, she missed him physically in a way that had her aching and distracted.

"You get any sleep?"

"Couple hours," he said.

"Oh, darn it!" She glanced toward the lobby. "I forgot that damn packet from Skogen upstairs."

"You saw him?"

She shook her head. "Left us policy manuals at the front desk."

He waved a hand. "Keep it."

She drained her coffee and glanced about, searching again for the little breakfast lady, Bibi, but could not find her. "What happened with the trail cam?"

"Sheriff and I waited for the FBI to get there. We left it on the tree, exactly as you found it."

"Skogen make the pickup?" she asked.

"One of his people. Don't get your hopes up. It's a dud. The SIM card is missing."

Her shoulders sagged. There would be no image of a killer dumping a victim.

"Maybe we'll pull some prints," he said, offering some hope. "Anyway, that's how I learned they'd notified Betters."

Hugo Betters was Rita Karnowski's boyfriend, the man they'd failed to reach last night.

"What? He's been notified?"

"Yeah."

Her frustrated exhalation fanned her coffee. She'd missed seeing Betters's initial reaction.

She growled out the words. "They didn't contact me."

"Might want to talk to Skogen about that," said Demko.

"Oh, I will." She drew out her phone and sent a text to Skogen.

"So tell me what you heard," she said, setting aside the device and turning to her eggs.

"Special Agent Coleman told me that she notified Karnowski's parents yesterday afternoon and caught her partner at his residence."

"When?"

"After we left. He'd gone from work to a pub for dinner."

She stirred her oatmeal, then tucked in. "So, you know where to find him today?"

He nodded. "Got the job site from Coleman. That could be our first stop."

"Sounds good." She finished the oatmeal and dropped the spoon in the bowl. "Thank you for coming with me. It means a lot to have you here."

He smiled. "You can thank me if I ever manage to get you alone."

Her head sank. "I'm sorry we missed each other last night."

"Me too."

Her phone chimed and she read the message.

"Skogen didn't think it necessary for me to be there. But wants me in on the formal interview."

"What do you think about that?"

"I'll tell him what I think in person."

His brows lifted and he gave a slow nod.

She set aside the phone. "So, first the job site of Karnowski's partner, then the meeting with the parents of Nikki Darnell?"

"Without any of Skogen's team?"

"Seems only fair."

Nadine read from the missing person's report as Demko drove. "'Rita Karnowski's partner, Hugo Betters, reported her missing on Saturday, March 20th, calling the rangers three hours after getting separated from her on a short hike.'" She lowered the report. "That's a long time."

"Wonder what he did for three hours?"

She made a sound in her throat and turned back to the report.

"Says he went back to his truck to grab their lunch." She scanned ahead and then read. "'Search and rescue teams struck out in the forest. Called it after thirty-six hours. Bodies were discovered Friday, March 26th, by a member of the parks' maintenance crew.'" She closed her laptop.

"Skogen didn't clear Betters," said Demko.

"But he's not in custody."

"I'd be checking his timeline. No arrest until I had solid evidence."

"Well, I look forward to our chat," said Nadine. "I'm particularly interested in why it took him three hours to call for help."

"Ditto. You buy his story that he left Rita on a hiking trail to go retrieve their lunch?"

"Doesn't quite fit, does it? And he reported that, when he returned, she had vanished. Why not pack the lunch in the first place? Or go back for the lunch together?"

"Why were they on a trail?" he asked.

She found that detail on the statement. "He reported that Rita wanted to take a nature walk after their kayak trip. Her remains were recovered miles from where she had been reported missing."

"They get a sample from him?" asked Demko.

"Yes. Voluntary. Comparing it to the semen found on Rita. Juliette expects results in another day or two."

"I could get used to that turnover."

"They also requested a sample from the man who found her."

"The maintenance guy? That's a good call."

"But he declined the request."

That got Demko's attention. "We should talk to him, too."

"Skogen has an interview scheduled for tomorrow."

"Get him a bottle of water. He leaves without it and you got your sample."

"I'll mention it to Skogen."

"Man won't give a sample, he's got a reason."

*

Hugo Betters was an electrician. They found him on the same job he had been subcontracting on before his girlfriend's disappearance. The site was easy to find just by following the sound of hammering. The framing of a new housing development was up on several concrete slabs. Other units already had plywood walls and roofing under way.

One of the contractors directed them. After introductions, Hugo agreed to speak to them. They moved through the empty house, currently just a shell and studs, to what would be the kitchen—it was farthest from the roofers and their hydraulic staple guns.

Despite the distance, the pounding was incessant.

Betters took one look at Demko and asked, "You cops?"

Nadine held her smile. "Yes. We are. This is Detective Demko and I'm FBI Special Agent Finch."

Inside, she started, realizing this was the very first time she had used her new title.

Betters gave her a once-over and said, "FBI told me about Rita yesterday."

"We're here to follow up on a few details."

She started with the easy questions and Betters seemed to relax. Only when she began asking for specifics did his outward cool begin to crack.

"Why did it take so long to get to your vehicle?"

"It was over a mile back."

"And you deemed it safe to leave Rita alone in the forest for the time it took to make that round trip?"

"She asked me to go." His face was red.

"And you complied?"

"Listen, what do you want me to say?"

Demko took that one. "We want you to explain why you didn't bring the lunch to begin with."

"Because we weren't going to eat there. We were supposed to eat at a park with picnic tables on the way home. But she insisted on this stupid trail. She's always doing that. Changing the plan, insisting on getting her…"

"Her… what?" asked Nadine.

"She can be childish."

"And it took you three hours to realize she was missing?"

"No."

"A one-mile hike round trip, to the car and back, should take…" Nadine turned to Demko.

"Thirty minutes. Forty tops."

"Let's say thirty minutes. Even if you searched for an hour, which would be doubtful," said Nadine, "what did you do with the other half hour?"

"I walked the entire trail. Listen, I told that other agent this."

"Where did you really go?" asked Nadine.

Betters clamped his mouth shut.

"You two argued. Rita was uncooperative. You left. Is that right?" Demko asked.

"No. I left to get lunch."

"I see. Wait here and don't leave until we give you the all-clear," said Demko and motioned to Nadine.

She followed him outside the construction site and stopped. "You are not seriously going to leave him in there. His story stinks."

"Got holes in it," he agreed.

"Then why did you leave him?"

"Give him a chance to do the right thing. Or not."

Demko motioned for her to follow him to the side of the house. "You think he'll run?"

"Or make a phone call, try and get someone to back up his alibi. What he won't do is wait."

"You think he did this to Rita?"

"I think he's lied to you about his whereabouts. That's enough for now. Call Skogen. Tell him to pick him up."

She did and explained the exchange while Demko watched the house.

"Why didn't you call? I could have sent one of my agents," said Skogen.

She ignored the question, having learned long ago that just because someone asks does not mean you have to answer.

"Would you like us to wait until one of the team comes to get him?"

"Yes."

Predictably, Betters rounded the outside of the structure and headed for his vehicle. Spotting them, he began to run.

Demko shot away from her like a hound after a hare, ordering Betters to halt—which he did not until he reached the door to his truck and saw Demko aiming his service pistol at him. Then he complied and Demko neatly handcuffed him.

He allowed Betters to sit up while they waited for the FBI.

"I was just getting a wire stripper," said Betters.

"Yeah, sure," said Demko.

An hour later, Hugo Betters was in custody and the forensics team was processing his truck. Meanwhile, she had rescheduled the meeting with the Millers so that she could sit in on an interview at the county sheriff's headquarters with Betters, who was amending his initial story.

For the interview, Demko waited outside, watching through the observation window. Inside, she sat in the corner, letting Skogen and one of his team handle the questioning.

"Tell us about the morning of the disappearance."

"What, again?"

"Yes, please."

Betters made a sound of frustration before launching into the events. "We'd spent the morning in the kayak. Her idea. A tandem, also her idea, so I could paddle, and she could watch for wildlife. It's hard work, paddling that thing, especially against the current. On our way out she insisted on a hike. Guess who carried the gear? Me, again. All she had was her water and binoculars. I had everything else. I told her I wanted to be home for the game. She said we'd only be out in the morning, but she kept adding things."

"What game?" asked Skogen.

"Tampa Bay Lightning were playing at home. My buddy has a seventy-five-inch television. Puck dropped at one p.m. But off we went on a hike."

Nadine interrupted. "You left her there."

The agents turned, their expressions echoing surprise. She kept her attention on Betters, his face now flushed and his eyes flashing as his frustration morphed to fury.

"She wouldn't come with me!"

The room went quiet. The agents turned back to Betters.

"You left her in the woods?" asked Skogen.

"She refused to leave with me. She knew I had to go or miss the first period, so I…"

"When did you change your mind and go back?" asked Skogen.

"When I got to I-4, I started to worry. She had her phone, but I had the wheels. I sent a text, which she ignored. I called and it went straight to voicemail."

This was the sort of detail they could verify once they had Skogen's team finish a digital forensics report.

"So when she wasn't at the trailhead, I checked the trail. I just knew she'd gotten a ride, but she wouldn't answer her phone. She does that. Sends me to voicemail when she's mad."

"What did you do next?"

"I went to her place. I called her sister. I called her friend. I even called her ex-boyfriend. Nothing." He rubbed his neck. "I still thought she was messing with me. That she'd achieved her aim, making me worry. Miss the game."

"But you called the rangers anyway."

"First I went back to the trailhead. Then, yes. I called."

And this, at last, Nadine believed. Rita might have been manipulative, but his feelings seemed genuine. And his explanation fit the timeline. Of course, they'd check it.

Betters pressed a hand to his forehead. "She was so stubborn." His hand fell to his side.

Nadine stood and let herself out.

Demko met her in the hall.

"He our guy?" he asked.

"Not sure. If it was just Rita, I'd be more inclined to think he was involved. But Nikki was first. And Betters has a solid alibi for that Saturday."

"Watching hockey," said Demko.

"In Tampa all weekend with his buddies. Besides, serials either begin with their intended victim, end with them, or never kill them at all and end up displacing their rage on similar victims. Killing his girlfriend second in a series makes no sense."

"People have staged murders to look like robberies, house fires, auto accidents. Maybe he killed her by accident and wants it to look like a serial killer."

"It's more likely that Darnell did that," said Nadine. "And Rita wasn't rich or planning to leave Betters for someone else, and she wasn't pregnant. So just break up with her and move on."

"Could have killed her in a rage and then tried to cover his tracks."

"No way—the cause of death is too similar to Nikki's. It was the same guy. Plus, how would he have known where Nikki had been left?"

Demko shrugged. "Saw her on a hike?"

"That was miles from where she went missing."

"Reportedly. We need to check the GPS on his truck and phone. See if he was where he said he was."

"True. But he doesn't like to hike. That's Rita's thing. He likes a recliner and a beer."

"Then what about Nikki's husband? She's rich."

"Roger Darnell? Why would he kill Rita?"

"Killed Nikki for the money. Killed Rita to throw authorities off track."

"And sent them into the river alive and bleeding to lure alligators, then pulled them back out? You think her husband did that?"

"He wouldn't be the first to kill other people to make his wife's murder seem to be the work of a madman. And he'd know where he'd dumped Nikki and could have put Rita nearby. Plus he stands to gain financially by her death."

"Not if her dad has any say. Still, she did have a trust fund and insurance policy. So there's motive."

"But he seems to have been right where he said on the day of his wife's disappearance."

"Well, his phone was anyway. No witnesses, receipts or anything tangible."

"Just leave the phone home?"

"Possibly. Or…" She shook her head. "Nope."

He waited.

"It's not Darnell or Betters," she said. "Have you seen anywhere near here that sells arrows?"

# CHAPTER SEVEN

She and Demko had left the Betters interview and driven to Orlando to meet with Clem and Caroline Miller. The exchange had yielded nothing useful beyond the parents' fury that, despite their cutting their daughter off, Nikki had married Roger a year ago.

There was only one disturbing detail, possibly a coincidence. Nikki had gone missing the day after their first wedding anniversary.

Nadine had now met Nikki's parents and both victims' partners. Neither partner seemed a viable suspect for crimes with this level of depravity.

Special Agent Skogen's team would be carefully checking their timelines and alibis. She could do nothing further on that account.

Now she needed to get out and get a feel for the area and see it as this hunter might. He had driven these roads, possibly stopped for gas or supplies.

She let Demko drive. He was taking her to a hunting supply place he'd spotted, but she'd asked him to stop anywhere he felt deserved a look. It turned out that was a lot.

In the course of the next three hours, they visited an insurance agent, a florist, an antique dealer and Curly Cutters hair salon. Demko talked, showed the photos of the victims and Nadine held Molly's leash and stood back to watch the behavior of the folks he spoke with. None had any information that Nadine found useful and she'd seen no obvious signs of stress or deception.

Nadine loaded Molly back in the rear seat and climbed into the front.

"Where next? The hunting place?"

"A vet's first. Then the gun shop and then an adventure outfitter."

He reversed out of the lot and turned them back toward Ocala National Forest.

They pulled into the veterinary office and she elected to wait in the car checking her in-box and replying to emails and texts from Tina.

When he returned, he was grinning.

Molly greeted his arrival to the cab with a lick on the cheek and received what Nadine would describe as a headlock, but the dog seemed content with the attention.

"What did I miss?"

"The vet has custody of a black Lab found wandering on a highway."

"You think it's Nikki's dog? Char?"

"She responded to her name."

"We have to call Darnell."

She phoned Skogen and relayed the find. He was sending someone to speak with the vet and check the dog before notifying Darnell.

She finished the call and tucked the phone away.

"I hope it's his dog." Small comfort was better than none.

"Next stop?"

"The shooting range and gun shop."

"Finally," she said. "Never been in one."

"I could pick you up a nice—"

"No."

"You need to carry protection."

She briefly closed her eyes, summoning the emotional energy needed to have this argument yet again.

"These are enough," she said, motioning to the Taser and pepper spray he knew she carried in her purse.

"They're not. A Taser is only good at close range and you have to get both contacts into the body."

"It worked for my mother."

The mention of her mother momentarily stopped him.

He was trying to protect her. She knew it and that thought crashed up against his dictatorial posture and the orders he issued as if she was one of his patrol officers. Or worse, as if he were her mother.

She needed to let Clint know that, although they had been dating exclusively for months, he was not her keeper.

"I'm not carrying anything that can kill someone."

"You should."

She would not allow ready access to something with such deadly irreversible implications. A little squeeze of a trigger and she was no better than the lunatics swinging from her family tree.

"Nadine?"

She shifted in her seat, facing him.

"Sleeping with me doesn't give you the right to make decisions for me, Demko."

His mouth dropped open a moment. She only called him Demko when on the job or, it seemed, when she was furious at him.

He lifted his gaze and pinned her, letting her see the hurt her words had caused before turning his attention back to the road.

"Now, see, I thought that a relationship meant looking out for each other."

That was a gut punch. She absorbed it and blew out a breath.

"Yes. It does."

His jaw muscles tightened as he stared straight ahead.

"You know, a relationship sometimes means compromise."

"My compromise is that you carry the gun and I carry my laptop."

The remainder of the drive to the gun shop passed in silence.

After they arrived, Nadine headed in first to see if the place was dog friendly.

Inside, she was struck with a blast of welcome cold air and the sight of various animal heads mounted on the walls, all staring down at her with glass eyes. Both the buffalo and the pronghorn wore bunny ear headbands, and the coyote held an Easter basket in its gaping jaws.

Festive, she thought and shuddered.

"Hey, there!" The cheerful voice came from behind the row of showcases along the far wall.

The sales associate was a middle-aged inked woman with jet-black hair and a tight, low-cut top that revealed a turquoise bra.

Nadine inquired about their dog policy.

"I love dogs. Bring him in. Leash, though, okay?"

She retrieved the pair, finding Molly squatting to pee and Demko on the phone.

"All clear," she said and returned.

The interior included rows of locked glass showcases, upright gun safes, regular safes and archery equipment. She narrowed her eyes on the arrows, relying on Juliette's belief that the punctures were small, thin, deep and created with a double-edged instrument atypical of even a double-edged blade.

While the sales associate lavished attention on Miss Molly, Clint made a loop of the store. He also paused before the arrows.

"You sell a lot of these?" he asked.

"Archery equipment? Sure. Quail season just closed. Deer season opens for archery and crossbow season in August. Then there's turkey and bobcat after that. No hunting now, though.

Mating season. Critters got to raise their young." She eyed him. "You need a permit?"

"Would you have a list of buyers?"

She straightened at this question. "I don't give out customers' information."

"We're working on a murder case."

Her expression hardened. "Even so." Then she called over her shoulder. "Dad! Get out here."

From the back of the gun shop came an elderly man with twin gray braids, wearing a black T-shirt advertising a country music festival. He had a cigarette clamped in the corner of his mouth.

The woman motioned her head toward them.

"Cops."

"Can I help you, Officer?" said the owner to Demko.

"We are trying to learn who might have purchased archery equipment from you in the last year."

"Long list. You got a warrant for this?"

"We don't," Demko said.

"Then I'll say good day and ask you to leave my shop."

"Your name?"

The owner lifted his chin. "Oliver Banderwall."

"Thank you, Mr. Banderwall, for your help."

They made a hasty exit.

"Banderwall?" she said.

Demko opened the computer fixed to his dashboard and started typing. A few minutes later, he shook his head.

"Yup. Mr. Banderwall. He has two daughters, June and Julie. Clean record. Veteran. Owns a Harley. No known criminal associates. No warnings for illegal sales. Seems to run a tight ship."

"Do you think our killer would buy arrows locally?"

"Might. Hard to say. But I'd mention this place to Skogen."

"How do you know he hasn't already been here?"

"Banderwall would have said so. Visit from the Feds leaves an impression."

Demko loaded Molly, and Nadine slipped back into the stifling hot vehicle.

"Clint? I'm sorry about the argument."

He took her hand. "I just want you safe."

"I know that."

He put them in gear and on they went.

"Outdoor adventure place?"

"Yes. It's the one where Karnowski and Betters rented the kayak."

The outfit he mentioned was inside the forest. Nadine read the reviews on Google as they pulled into the lot of Big Water Marina in Kerr City.

"Marina, kayak rentals, boat launch, eco-tours, bird-watching, fishing outings, uh-oh… bait, camping and hunting supplies."

"You want to come along or go explore?" he asked.

"Bit of both, I think."

They piled out and into the marina office and gift shop. The place was filled with useful items for boating, branded clothing and knickknacks. The area closest to the door seemed a camp store, with the sorts of foods you might enjoy while on a houseboat or RV.

Behind the glass counter stood a door to an inner office. Demko called a hello and a woman stepped out to greet them.

Her hair was stick straight, the color of wheat and hung beside her weathered face. Her smile deepened the lines bracketing her mouth. Nadine thought there were more than a few dark spots on her face that she might want to get looked at.

"Hey there, folks. Sorry, I didn't hear the bell."

"You the owner?" asked Demko.

"Me and the mister." She blinked benignly at them. "How can I help ya?"

"I'm Detective Clint Demko."

Her brows lifted. "Lou Anne Kilpatrick. What's this about?"

"Murder investigation."

Her eyes widened at that and her thin brow rose.

"We're speaking to all the businesses in the area. Not just yours."

Lou Anne nodded, seeming reassured by this.

"Seen in the paper about them two bodies found in the forest. Such a shame. Their poor families."

Demko went through his battery of inquiries. Asked about men traveling alone. Asking if she'd seen anyone that made her uncomfortable.

"No. Just the normal folks. Tourists, travelers, nature lovers and fishermen."

"One of the victims rented a kayak here the day she went missing," said Nadine.

The owner blinked and then said, "Oh, God."

Clearly, they'd beaten Skogen's team here. Nadine thought that would not be well received.

Demko continued his queries as she circled the store with Molly. Nadine eyed the bag of marshmallows, recalling Rosie mentioning a firepit table on the pool deck. Then she perused the collection of hunting knives and jackknives in a glass showcase. She saw no ammunition, firearms or archery equipment, but the corner was chock full of fishing gear, nets and a bubbler tank she assumed held live bait.

From Demko's questions she learned Lou Anne ran several types of tours per week and had three full-time employees, plus her husband and son. They were all here.

Finally he showed her the photos of Karnowski and Darnell.

Lou Anne pointed to Rita Karnowski. "She looks familiar. Might have seen her. You say she rented a kayak?"

"Tandem. Mid-March."

"Then I got a waiver. What's her name?"

"Karnowski. You have those waivers?" he asked.

She nodded and retrieved a stack.

"That's March."

He handed them to Nadine and asked for permission to speak to Lou Anne's people. She gave the okay.

"You'll find Simon out by the kayaks. He's my son."

Nadine found it curious that her smile faltered at the mention of her boy. She slipped on a pair of latex gloves and fingered through the stack of waivers.

"We have one naturalist, Lionel Decristofaro. He runs all the nature tours on the boat, the bird-watching outings and the nature walks. My husband is Roy. Anyone's guess where he might be, store, town, on the lake. Outdoors, that's all I ever know for sure. I'll call him on the radio if you can't track him down. Then there's Kelly Dietz, who takes morning kayak and paddleboard tours. She's part-time. Gotta be home before the kiddos, you know? And Jessie Useche who fixes anything with a motor and helps me here in the shop."

She glanced down to Molly, now lying beside Nadine's feet. "Uh, you want to buy that?"

Molly had somehow purloined a stuffed manatee from a lower bin without detection and now sat happily gnawing on its head.

"Oh, of course," said Demko. His hand went to his wallet again and he drew out a fifty-dollar bill.

"Detective Demko," said Nadine, holding up a waiver.

He met her gaze. "Karnowski?"

She nodded. Out came a large evidence bag. Nadine took custody of the evidence as Lou Anne called Jessie Useche in to take over so she could bring them around.

He was in his early thirties, with grease under his nails and on his jeans. He wore well-broken-in construction boots, a faded long-sleeved shirt and a worn cap advertising the marina.

He answered all questions but added nothing to the case. Lou Anne brought them out to see the naturalist next. Unlike Jessie, this man wore spotless tan clothing of light nylon and the sort of shirt that deflects the sun's harmful rays. His wide-brimmed hat and glasses covered much of his face, but Nadine noted he was average height, fit and mid-thirties. Around his neck hung the largest pair of binoculars she had ever seen, secured in a harness system, much like a reverse backpack.

As Clint spoke to him, a small, disheveled man made his way up from the boat launch. This employee wore frayed jean shorts that threatened to slide off his narrow waist and flat rear end. Sweat and lake water soaked his stained T-shirt, and he wore only flip-flops on his feet.

"Simon! Where you goin'?" Lou Anne's voice was sharp as cut glass.

Nadine gawked at the transformation between the jovial host who greeted them and this miniature tyrant now screeching at her son.

Simon skidded to a halt. "Um, break?"

His eyes held caution and his shoulders lifted toward his ears. Nadine frowned at the odd high tenor of his voice.

"You rinse all those kayaks?"

"Most of 'em."

Lou Anne stepped away. Nadine watched her berate the man, who looked close to forty, and send him scuttling back to the launch to drag the kayaks up from the lakeshore and onto the racks. Lou Anne supervised with hands on hips as he hosed down the crafts and then ordered him to put all the flotation vests in the shed.

Simon trudged through his chores, occasionally squeaking a reply to his overbearing mother. The scene reminded her of her own mother's outbursts as she screamed at her and Arlo over various offenses and she felt instantly sorry for Simon.

"She always on him like that?" asked Demko to the naturalist.

"Yeah. I told him he should quit, but he said he can't find another job. I mean, who would hire him?"

Nadine noted the worn sci-fi novel in Simon's back pocket.

"He average intelligence?" asked Demko, watching Simon.

"Yeah. Think so, but there's something off about him." Lionel's attention flicked to the lake. "Look at that!"

An osprey dove into the water, emerging with a fish.

"I'll bet she has chicks to feed. Nature's way."

"You a bow hunter?" asked Demko.

"Me? No. Never."

Demko finished up with Lionel who studied the photos of the known victims but did not recognize either. Nadine took Molly to a picnic table to watch as Demko interviewed Simon.

The man shifted restlessly, rubbed his neck and glanced away for rescue, but his mother had left for the office. He barely glanced at the photos. He was showering Nadine with signals of deception and projecting his unease.

They caught up with Roy before leaving. His wife had given him a heads-up. He seemed distracted, rushed and offered little.

Back in the vehicle, Demko turned to her.

"What do you think about Simon?"

"Odd guy. I'd run a background on all of them, but he's got loads of tells that speak of some issues."

"I agree."

She turned to watch Molly toss her manatee toy in the air and then dive behind the seats to retrieve it.

Demko was on his computer: "No priors on Useche, Dietz, Decristofaro or Mr. and Mrs. Kilpatrick. Useche is listed as a resident of Louisiana. The rest are Florida residents. All but Decristofaro and Useche have hunting and fishing licenses. Simon Kilpatrick has a failed attempt to enlist in the army and marines."

They made one more stop, at a bike rental and repair shop. The only interesting detail there was one employee with an outstanding warrant. Demko called that one into the sheriff's office and then headed toward Ocala.

Nadine now had two men who were providing many nonverbal cues of deception: Rita Karnowski's boyfriend, Hugo Betters; and the odd handyman and son of the owners of the marina, Simon Kilpatrick. Betters made her suspicious, but Simon gave off a different vibe. He reminded her of the runt of the litter, picked on by the rest of the pack.

"I forgot to tell you, last time I visited my mother, I mentioned you to her," he said.

Demko's comment jolted her from her musings as he casually dropped that bombshell in her lap.

"Did you?" she asked.

"She's anxious to meet you. I told her I'd try to talk you into a visit. Maybe Saturday?"

A visit to the high-security prison where Clint's mother was held—that also happened to hold Nadine's own mother—made the stress of meeting his parent all that more nerve-wracking.

"It's Arlo's weekend," she said, referring to her monthly visit to see her brother.

"Maybe next weekend." Demko cast her a long glance. "She's doing everything right. I don't think it's really necessary for her to serve her entire sentence."

"Except she planned your father's murder and he's still dead."

He scowled, the expression sending furrows across his forehead.

"My half brother did that. He threw her under the bus to get leniency."

She knew from doing some digging that his mother had given her eldest son, Connor, the cash to purchase the shotgun, but her boy had a prior for drugs and could not complete the transaction.

She also provided Connor with the key to the back door to his father's medical building.

In addition, prior to the homicide, Clint's mom had at least two affairs with men she tried to convince to kill her husband. Her motive was the two million insurance policy and over one million in assets.

Unfortunately, Clint had told her none of this.

"Clint. It's not healthy to allow your mom a pass on this or to level all of the blame on Connor." She knew Clint did not speak to, visit or write to his half brother. Connor Nesbitt had been twenty-four at the time of the crime. He and Arlo shared the same correctional facility.

Had their mothers met? she wondered.

Demko had legally changed his name after adoption by his dad's sister. He'd been born Caleb Nix. His sister, Carlie, born Caroline Nix, had done the same.

"She's a good person inside," he said.

She gave a long exhalation as she tried to gather her patience.

"What is wrong with loving my mother?"

"You can love her. My issue is with your unwillingness to assign her any portion of blame."

His face reddened and his grip on the wheel tightened.

"Do you think she was falsely convicted?" asked Nadine.

The pause stretched for more than a mile.

"I don't want to talk about it."

"Fine."

His voice turned sullen. "I'm not one of your patients."

"I realize that."

Molly left the window, where she had her entire head outside of the vehicle, and laid her chin on Demko's shoulder. He gave his dog a one-armed hug and a kiss.

After several minutes, Clint's grip on the wheel relaxed and the lines bracketing his mouth eased. Molly returned to the window.

How had the canine known that her master needed the dog's version of a hug? Nadine turned to watch the dog, jowls flapping, eyes half-closed and nose in the air.

Animals were so odd, intuitive in a way she couldn't comprehend.

"Listen, I'm sorry if I got defensive. I know what she did. I know she's manipulative. But she was a good mother to me and Carlie."

"Yes. I understand."

"And what about you? Is your relationship with your mom any better?"

A classic redirect, she thought, refusing to be sucked into this topic.

"Currently, I have no relationship with her. That's best for me for the time being."

He arched his brow but said nothing.

Nadine spied a Mexican market. "Hey, pull in."

He did and cut the engine. "You need something here?"

"Mexican Coke or Jarritos." She was so thirsty after their afternoon and wanted a drink. The Mexican Coca-Cola was made with real sugar and was simply the best. But the mandarin-orange-flavored soda was a close second.

He offered to go buy them something and she agreed to wait with Molly. Demko headed inside and she took his dog to the strip of grass and gravel so Molly could relieve herself. Afterward, they waited outside the market, in front of the windows, covered with Spanish advertisements. She suspected this was a place serving the migrant pickers that worked on the many farms and groves here.

One handprinted poster grabbed her attention.

The flyer taped to the window included a color photo of a smiling woman with light brown skin, long straight black hair, wearing bright red lipstick on her full mouth. She had a hand on her hip and gazed back at the photographer, her eyes full of mischief. The photo had obviously been touched up, removing imperfections along with personality to give the subject's skin an unnatural shimmer and making her eyes larger than normal. Below her image were three words.

*Desaparecida*
*Bianca Santander*

*Desaparecida*… as she puzzled the unfamiliar word, she knew. She was already on her feet and heading inside to find Demko.

They had another possible missing person.

# CHAPTER EIGHT

## FRIDAY

Demko met her for breakfast on Friday just before eight. Last night, something on an unrelated homicide investigation had pulled Demko from their dinner and she had not seen him again. They'd said good night via text, which was wholly unsatisfactory.

"Missed you last night," she said.

"Sorry. Did you get the waiver logged as evidence?"

"Gave it to Skogen's second."

"Is that Coleman?"

"Yes." She sipped her coffee.

"Listen, I ran a background check on that woman on the flyer from Belleview, Santander," he said.

"And?"

"Nothing. She doesn't exist," he said.

"What does that mean?"

"Illegal immigrant is the most likely explanation," he said.

"Is that why the cashier at the market wouldn't talk to us yesterday?"

"Possibly. I don't like it."

Neither did she.

"Did you mention it to Skogen?" asked Demko.

"Yes. We spoke by phone last night. He said he'd send someone over to Belleview to look into the disappearance."

"They won't speak to the Feds." He sighed. "I mentioned it to the sheriff."

"You think they'll speak to him?"

He shook his head. "I doubt it."

She picked at her oatmeal, wishing she'd chosen the bacon.

"How is the profile coming?"

"Moving along, now that I have the victims' identities and some of their timeline."

"You question Arnold yet?" he asked.

Barney Arnold was the parks' employee who discovered the bodies.

"He's coming in for questioning at nine. So I'll have a better idea after that interview."

"Should be interesting."

*

At the sheriff's department, Nadine asked Skogen if they had anything on the missing woman, Santander. Until she was located or her disappearance shown to be unrelated, her absence seemed more important than interviews with suspects.

"Who?" he asked.

"The Belleview poster. I mentioned about her—"

He interrupted. "Oh yeah, yeah. No one would speak to my agents."

"Did she turn up?"

"Unknown. The posters were taken down."

She frowned. "This might be connected."

"I can send my team again. But…"

"What?"

"She's Latina and our two victims were white. Seems unrelated."

"It's related until I know it isn't."

"What do you suggest?"

"Send a social worker. One who works with migrants and speaks Spanish."

"A little busy right now." He thumbed over his shoulder at the interrogation room.

"Okay. I'll do it." She lifted her phone.

"You coming in?"

"We'll observe from here," she said, the "we" referring to her and Detective Demko.

Skogen's eyes narrowed on her. But he strode away as Nadine called Tina, asking her to find a social worker who spoke Spanish and was willing to go to Belleview.

"I speak Spanish," said Tina.

"You can go with a social worker. Not alone."

"I'm on it."

Nadine gave Tina the details, tucking away her phone as Skogen entered the interrogation room accompanied by a sheriff and one of his team, Agent Layah Coleman.

Coleman, his second in command, was a tall, slender black woman with close-cropped hair. Today she wore a navy-blue suit with a tapered leg, accentuating her athletic form.

"You pissed off Skogen, not following him like a puppy," whispered Demko.

She had. "Not his hound."

He gave her hand a quick squeeze and cast her a warm smile. The tingle at his touch darted up her arm and she smiled back. It was finally Friday and she planned to be certain that she and Clint carved out some alone time.

In the interview room, Skogen took his seat facing Arnold.

"You check Arnold's priors?" Demko asked.

"Yes. DUIs don't bother me as much as the charges of indecent exposure."

"One including a sexual act," he said.

"Masturbation. Plea deal struck."

"Sexual offenders' registry?" asked Demko.

"Nope."

Nadine stared at the man. He was short, fit and dressed in his parks uniform, including a tan ball cap.

He began tapping his foot before the first question. Although he showed no other fidgeting, his stutter grew worse the more he was pressed to go over the details of the discovery.

Their request that he begin at the discovery and take them backward from that point flummoxed him.

"I told you b-before, she was lying th-there naked. I could see her perfect ass under the branches."

Nadine found this description of a corpse both odd and disturbing. She jotted the word *perfect* on her pad.

"You previously said the body you discovered was not covered with debris."

His eyes rolled up and to the left as he thought.

Nadine leaned forward, interest piqued.

Arnold shifted in his seat. "I mean under th-th-the tree's b-branches. She wasn't covered with nothing."

To Nadine this looked like a possible attempt to conceal his mistake. The use of a double negative could be seen as rendering the sentence a positive. A woman not covered by nothing was covered with something. Was that an unintentional blunder or just indicative of a poor education?

"Did you touch her body?" asked Skogen.

"No. I just nudged her a l-little to see if she was real."

So he did move her. By the blood pooling, Juliette noted that the second body had been repositioned after death. Postmortem, blood moved downward with gravity. The lividity—purplish discoloration on the skin—should occur at the lowest point, which in this case was the victim's side. Yet she was found on her stomach. Was that Arnold's doing? Nadine reminded herself to study those crime photos more closely.

"Where?"

"Her leg."

"You could see she wasn't bleeding from her wounds."

"Yeah. I was close enough to see that."

"How close?"

Close enough to ejaculate on the body? Nadine wondered.

"A few inches," said Arnold.

"Did you move her? Change her position at all?"

"I d-didn't do nothing."

Double negative again, thought Nadine.

She turned to the agent observing with them. "Ask him if he found her dead body arousing. Ask it exactly like that."

The agent left and, a moment later, entered the interview room relaying the question to Skogen. He nodded and asked her question.

Arnold's face turned scarlet and he slapped both hands on the desk.

Nadine smiled. It was a wonderful show of indignation and outrage. But he'd missed a step. His first reaction should have been shock, possibly horror or disgust. But Arnold shot straight to offense.

"Did they seize his computers yet?" she asked the agent who remained.

"No."

"Hmm." She'd bet her new plastic ID badge that there would be violent porn on his personal computer.

"He agree to a polygraph?" asked Demko.

"We haven't asked, but I would guess he'll decline."

Unfortunately, neither of those things made him a killer.

"You like him as a suspect?" the special agent asked Nadine.

"He's showing clear signs of deception."

"Skogen wants him under surveillance."

"I agree. See if he'll consent to a psych eval."

The agent nodded.

"You guys get a DNA sample?" asked Demko.

"He refused to provide one," said the agent.

The FBI didn't need permission to collect anything Arnold discarded in public and could check the DNA retrieved against the sperm recovered from Karnowski's remains. But a match would verify that he'd had contact with the body of one of the victims. Though not admissible in court, it would inform their investigation.

"He's under surveillance, we'll get something eventually."

Demko dropped her at the office, where she checked in with Tina about the missing woman.

"Did you find someone to go with you?" asked Nadine.

"I found a woman who works with Head Start and drove her down there. We only got back a few minutes ago."

"And?"

"We tracked down her brother. He told us he was supposed to pick her up after work, but his muffler fell off and he was afraid of getting pulled over, so she was planning on taking the bus. He said she called him in a panic on Tuesday around noon because an officer from Immigration stopped her and was taking her into custody."

"Immigration took her?" asked Nadine.

"That's what she told him."

"And they haven't heard from her since Tuesday? Is that normal?"

"The woman I was with said so. The family is working with an attorney. But she said sometimes they don't hear until after deportation."

"Hmm. See if you can find her."

"Yes, boss lady." Tina lingered. It was her first field assignment and she'd done well.

"Thank you, Tina. You keep this up and Clint will need to get you a badge."

She grinned and then spun, practically skipping out of the office.

Nadine settled at her desk. Skogen was right. Santander was undocumented and the disappearance was unrelated to their case.

Nadine returned to her suspect-based profile.

She believed these were stranger-attacks. The targets selected by some specific criteria. The victimization showed both a need to inflict pain and also an absence of feeling for the victims. Neither Hugo Betters nor Roger Darnell could be accused of lacking feelings for their partners. Betters displayed both irritation and worry, and Darnell certainly seemed to be grieving his wife's death, though she could not disregard that he stood to benefit financially because of it.

Meanwhile, the depersonalization, stripping the women, crippling and using them to lure predators, was more than horrifying, it was specific and baffling. A husband, even an enraged one, would act in passion. This seemed exactly the opposite. This more resembled indifference to the victim's pain and suffering. The inherent lack of sympathy, and the escalation from the neck wound to the back wound, made Nadine think this killer was progressing. Learning better ways to toy with his captives and linger over their deaths.

The killer chose to deposit his victims, in close proximity, in a place they were likely to be discovered.

Left on display.

Their unsub seemed intent on shocking the public or flaunting his victims to law enforcement. Perhaps both.

He appeared to be trying to gain someone's attention.

Meanwhile, Arnold did not know either Darnell or Karnowski. He was a good prospect. He had reason to be in the forest. He knew the trails intimately, had a history of sexual perversion, refused a polygraph, refused to provide a DNA sample and was flashing signs of deception.

She thought his psych eval would be fascinating if he was foolish enough to agree to one.

Nadine had researched similar crimes, teasing out commonalities in apprehended offenders, and had compiled a list. All were stranger crimes. A sizable percentage had priors for sexual offenses, a significant percentage had prior assaults against women. Curiously, driving records were universally spotless. These were careful hunters. Many also posed their victims naked in degrading positions, as was the case with Karnowski.

She put forth that this was a white male, living alone, intelligent, neat, employed, fascinated with porn pertaining to bondage and torture, narcissistic, possibly psychopathic, who had committed similar murders elsewhere. He would be unmarried, living alone, familiar with the forest, drove a truck with a cab. He would be average height and weight, neatly dressed, athletic, well-coordinated with archery and hunting experience.

She set aside her suspect profile. She'd come to the end of what she could accomplish on that for the moment.

With details on Darnell and Karnowski now pouring in, she thought a behavioral comparison of the victims was the next step. Untangling what specific actions, characteristics and physical details these two women shared might prove useful to the FBI in their hunt.

Rita Karnowski and Nikki Darnell both lived in the area, were familiar with the hiking trails they explored in the Ocala Forest, and both had a male partner. They each had a love for the natural world. Both were dumped in close proximity and appeared to have been tortured and killed in a similar way. But after searching the available information, Nadine had unearthed no other connection between the women.

She sat back and sighed. Stranger crimes were exceedingly difficult.

Both her phone and Tina's chimed with a group text from Juliette inviting them to happy hour in the hotel bar. She and Clint were having dinner together, but Nadine thought she could manage both.

"Oh, fun," Tina said. "I'll see you back there."

Tina headed out as Nadine closed her laptop and gathered her things.

Her team deserved a break.

She left her office, already anticipating the drink with Tina and Juliette. Afterward, she and Clint would share a nice meal and have some much-needed alone time.

Skogen intercepted her on her way out.

"We got a DNA sample from Barney Arnold."

"Oh, great. Voluntary?" she asked.

"No. Discarded cigar stub he'd been chewing on most of the afternoon."

"Wonderful. So it's at the lab?"

"Already there. A match will connect him to the body. We get that, we make an arrest."

Which then allowed them to collect a DNA sample, regardless of whether the DNA was relevant to the arrest. Otherwise, they'd need either a confession by Arnold, a witness or evidence connecting Arnold to the victim. Then they'd have to obtain a court order based on probable cause to mandate a sample.

"You think the DNA on the cigar will match the semen found on Rita Karnowski's body?"

"We'll see."

"Did he agree to the psych profile?"

"Declined."

She wasn't surprised, but still disappointed.

"You heading out?" he asked.

She didn't like the way he was lingering.

"Yes. Dinner with my team."

"Ah. Sounds nice." He headed back toward his office.

*

At the hotel, Rosie was back behind the counter and gave her a bright smile.

"Good evening, Dr. Finch."

"To you as well."

She glanced from reception to the two empty birdcages.

"Where's Petunia?" she asked.

"Happy hour out by the pool. She has a perch there."

"Jack-Jack?"

"Back in his room. Those two parrots are now besties. And Petunia is much quieter with Dr. Hartfield's bird here."

"Have you seen any of my team?"

"Also by the pool."

"Tiki bar?"

Rosie's bright smile widened. "That's right!"

Nadine cast her a wave and found the pool deck, but the instant she crossed the threshold, she was intercepted by Tina.

"Hey," said Nadine. "Where we sitting?"

"Um, hey." She just stood there zipping the crucifix about her neck back and forth on the gold chain.

Nadine picked up on Tina's obvious unease.

"Where's Juliette?" Nadine glanced to the crowded bar area decorated with surfboards and a thatched roof.

"Waiting." Tina thumbed over her shoulder but did not look back. "I wanted to speak to you before you… that is… Juliette said I needed to tell you…" Tina broke their gaze.

"Tell me what?"

She peeked through her lashes, like a naughty child. Both her hesitancy and flushed face put Nadine on guard.

"Listen, Dr. Finch. I have a confession."

# CHAPTER NINE

Nadine hated confessions and was guaranteed not to like whatever Tina said next. Had she spoken to a reporter?

"Yes?"

"I've been writing a prisoner."

Nadine's heart sank. Tina had been struggling with the urge to reconnect with her mother. Unfortunately, Tina's mother was a bad person with no moral compass who would certainly try to manipulate her.

"Your mom?" Nadine guessed.

"Your brother."

The shock of this ricocheted through Nadine like a rifle shot. "What?"

"I saw his email address and I wondered if he knew my mom's… the guy my mother worked with on…"

"The murder they committed?" Nadine furnished.

"Yeah."

"Why?"

"I wondered if Arlo could find out what this guy was like."

"And why, again? You're talking about a man who helped your mother bury an old woman alive. What more could you possibly need to know?"

Tina glanced down, breaking the eye contact.

"He was with my mom for a couple years. I thought he might be able to tell me more about what she was like. And maybe… maybe it was his idea. You know, he talked her into it."

Nadine recalled Tina was a teen when her mother was taken from her. She had guilt issues over the possibility that her mother had done this terrible thing in a twisted effort to provide for her little girl.

"Your mother abducted an elderly woman, lured her into her vehicle." Nadine knew this because she read every article available on Tina's mother in an effort to understand Tina herself better. "It was her idea to bury her alive and she was there digging the grave and covering a living human being with soil. Your mom does not get a pass on this, Tina, no matter how much you would like to believe she was somehow victimized."

"I just thought—"

"She spent the money from her victim's accounts."

"On an apartment for us. On food and…" Her words were choked by tears.

Nadine gathered her up. She knew that Tina's mother had bought lottery tickets, a new luxury sports car, clothing, makeup and tickets to one of the theme parks. Nadine could only imagine what Tina felt remembering that particular outing with her mom, whose sudden unexplained windfall would later be exposed to all.

"I'm sorry." Nadine rubbed her assistant's back.

Tina sniffed. "No. *I'm* sorry. It was stupid. I just wanted my mom to be… I don't know, the victim."

"That would be easier." She thought of Demko, still blaming his half brother for his father's murder.

Tina pulled back and used her fingertips to carefully wipe the mascara from under her eyes. She looked the picture of a forlorn waif. Was that why Nadine had taken her under her wing?

"How do you deal with it? What they did?" she asked.

Nadine pressed her lips together as the rage surged.

"By stopping people like them."

Looking at Tina was like looking in a mirror at a younger version of herself.

Nadine offered her a napkin from her bag and her assistant dabbed the moisture from her face.

"Tina, my brother is not a great resource for you. He's in prison for sexual assault."

"He told me."

"Did he also tell you it wasn't assault? It was rape. He accepted a deal in exchange for a guilty plea." Nadine struggled to keep her composure.

"But he's up for parole," said Tina.

Nadine hoped this was not heading in the direction she feared. Arlo was not going to form a relationship with her admin… Unless he already had. Arlo could be as manipulative as their mother, with whom Nadine had cut all ties.

Her mother had no way to contact her. But Nadine still corresponded with Arlo, and he still spoke to their mom. And now, it seemed, he also spoke to Tina Ruz.

"What does he want?" asked Nadine.

"Who?" asked Tina, but her cheeks flushed and she was rubbing her palms together like a woman trying to wash something away.

Tina hadn't made this confession out of guilt or remorse. She doubted it was even Juliette's urging.

So why? The answer settled heavily on her shoulders.

"My brother, Arlo. What did he ask you to do?"

"He asked me to tell you that there is something important in your email from him. He said he wrote you yesterday, but you didn't write back. He wants you to call him."

"I've been a little busy," Nadine said, regretting her words instantly, not so much because they were churlish, but because she didn't think her admin had a right to this kind of access to her mess of a family.

"Yes, I told him that," said Tina.

Just what kind of correspondence was this?

"It's something about your mother. That's all he told me. He's worried about you."

That seemed unlikely. But despite his faults, she loved her brother. That did not mean she trusted him.

"I'll check my mail."

"Now?"

Nadine made a face. Tina held her ground.

"All right, yes. Right now."

"Great. We'll be waiting at the bar."

Tina reversed course, speeding away as fast as she could without running.

Nadine perched on a lounge chair and drew out her phone.

There were two emails from Arlo. She read them in order. Afterward, she thumped back in her chair.

"Son of a bitch," she murmured.

Nadine's mother had gotten herself a biographer. Arlo had correctly concluded that Nadine would want to prepare herself for the inevitable intrusion of the writer's attempt to get an interview.

Which would *not* be happening.

Arlo had agreed to speak to the guy, because as he put it, "I have no reputation to protect and nothing but time on my hands." He ended by writing that he had something else he needed to speak to her about. Something "important" and he hoped to see her this weekend.

Nadine dashed off a quick message to Arlo, thanking him for the heads-up. She didn't like Arlo and Tina being pen pals, not only because such a relationship was bad for her assistant, but also because she really did not want Tina nosing around in her miserable childhood.

She knew it was a part of her. A terrible part, and running didn't seem to help as it kept jumping up to slap her in the face.

She'd get to the bottom of this. But she'd have to wait until tomorrow for visiting hours.

*

Juliette and Tina had already ventured out to the same pub as last night when Nadine headed upstairs to dress. Finally she and Clint were going to have an evening alone.

She took her time preparing, choosing her best underthings and a red dress, waving the flag before the bull.

He spotted her the moment she stepped into the reception area and answered his grin with a seductive smile.

He wore a blazer and tie. Had he realized this was the same outfit he had worn on the day they met?

"You look spectacular," he said and took her hands, leaning in to kiss her cheek. He straightened. "Nice perfume."

"And you smell… enticing," she said and then drew in another long breath of his cologne, loving the earthy aroma with a hint of spice.

He met her gaze; the intense contact made her body warm with liquid heat. Anticipation shimmered over her skin as she imagined finally having him alone.

"Did you pick a restaurant?" he asked.

"I did. It's not very far. The food rating is only average, but I think you'll enjoy the view."

"Lakeside?" he asked.

"No. It's got a view of your king-sized bed."

That sent his eyebrows high on his wide forehead. She giggled and ran a finger down his long nose.

"Ordering in," she said.

"Any time for appetizers?" His brow now wiggled suggestively.

"I haven't ordered yet," she said.

He offered his arm and escorted her back down the hall to his room. Upon opening the door, she found his room empty.

She turned to face Clint. "Where's Molly?"

"With the sitter." He looked sheepish, closing and locking the door. "I thought you might come back to my room and I wanted us to have some privacy."

She glanced about at the familiar toys strewn over the floor, including Molly's favorite, a pink flamingo, now missing a wing, and the manatee from Big Water Marina missing its flat paddle-like tail. Demko's shoes were all high up in the open closet, out of range of Molly. What she didn't see was a dog bed. "She sleeps with you, doesn't she?"

"Uh… Yeah."

"Well, it's my turn." Nadine laughed and then reached for him.

He drew her in, taking her mouth in a kiss that sizzled along her nerve endings. She came up breathless several moments later.

"Wow," he said, his breathing also labored. "Have I missed you!"

She ran her hands over his chest, feeling the reassuring strength of him and the absence of his Kevlar vest. She was separated from all that warm velvet skin by only a thin sheath of cotton.

His hands went behind her and pulled the zipper tab, opening her dress. She stepped back to allow the garment to fall, enjoying his expression as he took a long look at the black lace covering her breasts and clinging to her hips.

His jaw tightened and his Adam's apple bobbed.

"You're killing me," he said, shrugging out of his blazer and tossing it aside. Then he yanked off his tie, tugging it over his head, and fumbled with the buttons of his shirt.

Together they stripped him down to his boxers. One of his shoes struck the door as he lifted her into his arms and swept her up, tossing her onto the bed, where she bounced. She scooted backward before he landed beside her. He drew away her panties with his teeth and eager fingers as she released her bra. His boxers sailed past her and caught on the lampshade. He held her panties to his face and inhaled. The erotic sight made her skin stipple. Then he tossed them away.

The thrill of anticipation trickled over her skin. The waiting was done. He was all hers.

She reached. He stroked. They pressed together and apart and together again, unable to get close enough as they lifted their heads to gasp for air, struggling to contain the inferno of need roaring between them.

Clint retrieved a condom from the side table, tearing open the packaging. Nadine straddled his hips and rolled the condom over the beautiful erect length of him. Then she lowered herself over him.

They moved together, striving toward satisfaction. Their long absence and the need brought them to a swift plateau that burst first within her. She arched and he drove forward, holding her hips as he followed her over the edge. The waves of pleasure rippled outward, curling her toes.

She gasped and collapsed upon his slick body, sliding over warm flesh as he stroked the long muscles of her back. He lifted one arm and threw it across his eyes.

"That was amazing."

"We're amazing," she murmured.

Her body went slack as the lethargy stole through her. She closed her eyes, floating on the wave of contentment and savoring the sound of the steady thump of his slowing heartbeat.

Next came his snore and she smiled, pressing her palm to his chest to better feel the steady drum of his heart and each long intake of breath. She reached for the blankets, flipping them over their cooling bodies.

The growl of her stomach woke them both. She glanced at the clock beside the bed and saw she'd been asleep only twenty minutes or so. She chuckled at the sight of his boxers, dangling from the lamp finial.

"We better get you fed." He lifted her hand and kissed her palm.

He rolled to his feet and she growled her displeasure as he retrieved the menu and returned to bed. After a few minutes' discussion he called in their order and then placed the handset on the cradle.

"Forty minutes," he said.

"I could starve in that amount of time."

"Not if I distract you."

She smiled. "I don't think you're that good. I haven't eaten a thing in six hours."

"Is that a challenge?"

He did not wait for an answer but disappeared beneath the covers.

Nadine did not think about food again until her heart rate returned to resting and she focused on the hunt for her panties. She found them in the armchair and slipped them on.

"Would you like my robe?" he asked.

She accepted the offer. When the knock sounded at the door, Nadine was dressed in his striped robe and he wore only a tight cotton T-shirt and overlarge running shorts.

The porter set up in record time and left with a hefty tip in appreciation. Nadine did not even wait for Clint to return from locking the door before she had the plate covers off and her napkin on her lap.

She sat in the armchair before the table. Clint retrieved the desk chair and set it across from her.

Conversation ceased as they ate. She liked that he let her be quiet. A natural extrovert, Clint could have overwhelmed her. But he seemed to know that she required stillness to think and eat.

Sometime later, she wiped her mouth for the final time and sighed, leaning back. Nadine had left nothing on her plate but the onions that accompanied her steak.

"May I?" he asked, motioning toward her leavings.

She gestured him to help himself. He did, adding them to the remains of his baked potato.

"I'm so full," she complained.

As he finished, she fiddled with the shredded end of the robe tie. Molly's work, she suspected.

She glanced at the bed, wanting to return to the warmth of his body, but knowing she should head to her room. She didn't want to presume or to give him the idea that she planned to move in with him.

She told him about the correspondence between Arlo and Tina and about her mother securing a biographer.

"No wonder you're tense."

"Not anymore. My arms feel like noodles," she said.

"Glad to help." He carried the tray away and left it outside the door.

"Oh, one bit of good news. Not good exactly, I suppose. Anyway, Santander was picked up by Immigration." She told him what Tina had learned.

"That's too bad," he said. "But at least you can cross her off your list."

She made a humming sound in her throat and let her eyes drift closed.

"How's the offender profile coming?"

Nadine's eyes popped open.

"Full of holes." The kind that could only be filled by more evidence. More death.

"You know what you're doing."

She did. Because she thought like them. Understood them at a deep, visceral level. She could be good at this if she let that part of her out. That dangerous part she suppressed, trying to deprive it of oxygen with years of therapy.

All her breakthroughs came from standing in the place of a killer. In her mind, she had already done it, murdered both of those victims after their deaths. Thought about it, felt it, dreamed of it. She was like her mother, apart from one thing. She hadn't killed anyone.

Except in her mind.

"What have you got so far?"

"Offender is white, male, unmarried, athletic, employed and comfortable in the outdoors. Drives a truck with a cab."

He interrupted. "A cab?"

"He's a hunter. Hunters like SUVs and trucks, but he transported his victims, so…"

"…wouldn't want the bodies in the rear section surrounded by all those windows. Yeah, a truck with a cab. Okay."

She continued. "Hunting experience is likely. There's more. I'll forward it to you."

"Sounds a lot like Arnold. Our guy who found the bodies."

"Maybe. Oh, I almost forgot."

She told him about the DNA sample collected with Arnold's discarded cigar.

"I wonder if they'll find a match."

"We'll see. There's a lot we don't know about him yet."

"Like if he drives a truck." He made a face, then went on. "I can add one thing. I swung by Arnold's place this afternoon. He wasn't there, but I had a walk around. His backyard has about a dozen birdhouses in it."

"You promised to include me along on your field trips."

"Whenever possible." He took her hand and pressed a kiss onto her palm.

"Any hunting or fishing gear?"

"None evident. He lives in a mobile home. Windows were covered. Couldn't see inside. Outdoors is typical. Chairs. Rusty

BBQ grill and junk laying around. Just from the refusal to provide a sample, I'd move him into my suspects list."

"Skogen has. You know that if Juliette has the timeline right, Rita Karnowski might have been dumped only hours before Arnold found her."

"Or came back to visit her."

"It's possible."

If she wasn't so exhausted and so full, she'd pursue that tempting line of dark hair that curled above the collar of his shirt.

Clint took her hand and drew it to his mouth, dropping a kiss there. She leaned in, gave him the sort of kiss reserved for saying good night, and then swept the covers aside.

"Where you going?" he asked.

"I've got to look over my notes on Arnold and see if Juliette has the lab results yet." She moved about the bed, collecting her underthings and dress.

"It's nearly midnight."

She slipped into her panties and bra, then hesitated.

He reached. "Stay."

"Better not." She backed away, clutching her dress before her.

"Why?"

"Separate rooms for now. Okay?"

"Is it Molly?"

"No! I love your dog. But not so much in the bedroom."

"Nadine, we're good together, aren't we?"

"Great."

"Then why won't you spend the night?"

"Last time I did that, your house was surrounded by news crews trying to get a quote from the daughter of a killer."

"That's not the reason."

"I thought we agreed to go slow."

"It's been over half a year. That's pretty slow."

She gave him an imploring look.

Where did he think they needed to go, exactly?

Although she supposed it didn't matter. Any next step led to the steps she was unwilling to ever make.

She had no problem with Clint. The problem was her. She knew what she was. Because even if she could hold back the monster, she wasn't letting that genetic minefield loose in another generation.

She hadn't allowed them to have the talk about what they wanted, except that she knew Clint wanted them to "move forward" and "take the next step."

Did that mean he wanted common residence? Marriage? Kids?

What would he do when he discovered she didn't?

"I could come to your room."

She shook her head, hoping he didn't make her say no, yet again.

"Why, Nadine?"

"It's my private space. I need that."

"But you enjoy our time together."

"Very much. But we're here for a reason. Let's keep that our priority."

"My reason is that you're here."

That answer tugged at her heart and made her feel guilty all at once.

She kissed him and ducked into the bathroom to dress. When she emerged, he was also dressed.

"You don't need to walk me to my room." She was only one floor above him. Her team wasn't all together because the first floor of this wing was reserved for those traveling with pets.

He gave her a long stare and she said nothing more as he accompanied her in silence.

At her door, he leaned in and kissed her gently on the mouth. When she opened her eyes, she caught only a glimpse of him before the door closed.

"Lock it," he said from the hall.

So much for their romantic evening, she thought.

*

*Beautiful evening, he thought, returning to her after moonrise. But on seeing the empty cage, he momentarily feared she had somehow escaped. His instinct was to run. A detective had already spoken to his employer.*

*He waited, there in the brush. Were the FBI watching him right now? His gaze flashed to the black recesses beneath the tree canopy, beyond the reach of the moonlight.*

*Why hadn't he worn the forest ranger's uniform he'd stolen? Then he might succeed in bluffing his way out of here.*

*And then he saw her, much as he'd left her in the middle of the afternoon on Tuesday. He had not meant to be away so long. But he'd been so occupied with watching his real target and capturing the other one.*

*But she was there. He could see her in the silvery light. A lump of clay in his trap. Beside her was a hollow she'd dug between the bars filled with groundwater.*

*She'd been clever enough to take advantage of the downpours to make a mixture of mud to protect her skin from sun and the biting insects that hovered about her, searching for tiny cracks in her armor.*

*"Bibi!" he whispered. "Wake up."*

*She startled and rolled upright, shrieking as she clutched her calf. The movement caused the silver shaft of the arrow to glint. The scream made his skin tingle in excitement.*

*He smiled.*

*Her eyes went wide and white all the way around as he inched forward. She slid on her bottom in the opposite direction.*

*Why did they do that? He could reach her from anywhere. She was his plaything.*

*He circled the cage, lunging into the bars as she screamed and moaned. Delicious.*

*"You understand me?" he asked.*

*When she didn't answer, he reached through the bars and yanked her by her hair.*

*She screeched and twisted, trying to bite his arm. A cornered animal, trapped, but not helpless.*

*He shook her. "Do you?"*

*"Yes," she said, panting. "Let me go."*

*"Yes. I will. I will let you out and you will run."*

*He tugged her hair, forcing her up off her seat, and then dropped her.*

*Her expression registered a flicker of hope and then he lifted his crossbow.*

*"You understand?"*

*She gasped. Silvery tears ran down her cheeks. "No. I won't."*

*"Then I'll shoot you through the bars." He lifted the bow and aimed at her head.*

*"No. I run."*

*They always chose that, too. He released the locks and opened the cage, stepping back so that she had a clear path in the direction he wanted her to run, toward the water.*

*She cried as she tried to stand. The arrow, sun, rain, insects and days had softened her for him. She limped away and he pursued. If she moved to the right or left, he cut her off. But she was slow and the game grew tedious. He sighed in disappointment.*

*When she reached the shore of the lake, she paused to look back.*

*"In," he said.*

*"¡No sé nadar, me ahogaré!"*

*This time her hesitancy bore consequences. He aimed and released the arrow. The point protruded from her hip, striking bone. No spine injury for this one. She'd be able to feel them bite.*

*Bibi fell backward into the water and thrashed. When she managed to stand, he slipped the chain about her and clipped it tight. She tried to use it to drag herself from the water and he hit her opposite leg with another arrow. Down she went again. He glanced out over the water at the ripples.*

*The alligators sensed prey. He knew there were several fourteen-footers here and they were coming.*

*He waded in, taking a risk, and yanked his arrows from her. The one in her hip left its point behind, as he intended.*

*She struggled, gasped and cried. She called to God for help.*

*He moved to the shore to watch the other apex predators, knowing he was her god now.*

# CHAPTER TEN

## SATURDAY

In the morning, Nadine headed to Lawtey Correctional and Clint to Lowell Correctional, the women's prison where his mother was held. Arlo was expecting her, and she planned to speak to him about Tina and discourage the relationship.

She suffered through the indignities of the security screening and entered the visiting area, well inside the drab interior. Did every prison smell like mildew and bleach?

Once in the main gathering room, she perched on a stool at one of the many circular tables. The seats were fixed to the frame, because you couldn't throw a chair that was bolted down.

The prisoners entered through a metal door, transferring custody from the interior guard to the one beside the prisoner exit. She noted that this guard, though he clearly spent too much time lifting weights and guzzling protein shakes, greeted every prisoner by name.

It was only when she heard him say her brother's name that she recognized Arlo, and stood with her jaw swinging open. He looked so different than when she had visited last month. Then, his hair had been a wild tangle and he'd grown a scruffy beard that made him look more like Robinson Crusoe than the boy she remembered from their childhood.

This Arlo had short hair, a neatly trimmed mustache and wore round wire-rimmed glasses. She gaped.

"It's me, Dee-Dee." At least she recognized his smile.

"You're so polished up."

"I've been working on that. Trying to make an impression. I have another hearing coming up."

"Is that so?" He'd written her about that and all she could think was that he shouldn't get out. She believed in her heart that he was like them, the killers in her family. The only reason he was eligible for parole at all was the deal he received in exchange for a guilty plea. She knew what he'd done to his girlfriend at the time, and it might have been more if the neighbor had not heard the fight and called the cops. Mostly affable, he had an emotional firestorm lurking just below the surface.

Emotional damage from unresolved chronic trauma, family disruption and a psychologically unavailable parent, all resulted in rejection sensitivity and socially deviant moral reasoning justifying preemptive assault. Or that was what she would report, had she been asked to evaluate Arlo.

"Well, you are sure to make a good impression."

Arlo had been admitted into a program for inmates to train dogs over a year ago. Shortly afterward, she began to notice changes in his attitude and demeanor. He also seemed happier.

"Want something to eat?" she asked, turning toward the vending machines. She had brought small bills to buy food.

They walked together to the machines. He was several inches taller than she and muscular. This adult Arlo made her nervous and she missed the way they had been when they were kids, the two of them looking out for each other. He chose a cola and she selected water.

She worried over his release, dreaded it at a visceral level, fearing what he was becoming before his arrest. At the perceived threat of abandonment by his then girlfriend, Arlo had chosen a preemptive attack. He had been unable to handle the emotional rejection of even a possible breakup. And how much worse had his emotional difficulties become in the prison system?

She bought them each a breakfast pastry, slipped him fifty bucks, and they headed back to their table.

She handed him one pastry. "Happy Easter," she said.

"Hmm. Will be if it's my last in here," he said. "You get my message about Mom?"

"I wrote and told you that I did."

"Haven't had computer rights since yesterday. Anyway, she's plenty pissed at you for cutting her off."

"She sent a killer to encourage me to commit murder. What did she think would happen?" asked Nadine.

"I don't know, but she's really mad. She's got a biographer and I just know she's going to slice you up in her version of events."

The shiver traveled all the way from her tailbone to her face. Her mother had managed to send a serial killer after her from behind bars. Now she was writing a tell-all book. That could only be bad for Nadine.

"The guy writing for her contact you yet?" he asked.

"Not yet."

"He's aggressive. Persistent too."

"You've met?"

"Phone interview. I hung up."

Nadine waved her hand, making a show of dismissing his concern. Meanwhile, she was certain the barbed arrows her mother might launch with that book would draw blood.

"I'll handle it."

"Just be careful. She's dangerous when she gets like this."

"Okay. I'll be careful."

Nadine took the warning seriously. But really, her mother was dangerous at any time. Arleen Howler could no longer write her daughter, but she was far from helpless.

The pause lengthened. She thought of her main objective this visit.

"Listen, Arlo, about my assistant. I'm not sure you should be writing her."

"She wrote me."

"Yeah. But she's only twenty-two. I don't think a relationship is wise."

"I know she's too young for me, Dee-Dee. What are you afraid of?"

"I don't want her hurt."

His face flushed and the hand on the tabletop knotted into a fist.

"And you think I'll hurt her? I've told you. I've got it in control now. I don't let my emotions take over."

She smiled, certain that wasn't true.

"Great. So… no more emails?"

Correspondence of any sort was valuable to an inmate because contact with the outside world was precious.

"Fine. Be sure to tell her the same."

"Thanks."

He heaved a heavy sigh, then finished the soda in several long swallows as if anxious to get the taste of this place from his mouth. When he set the empty can between them, she had an idea. It was terrible, but there it was.

She could take that can and have a DNA sample to run with the others. She could see, once and for all, if Arlo had the killer code sequence she suspected ran through their family like a metastasizing cancer.

When he opened his pastry, she used her napkin to bring the can beside her water bottle.

"You're lucky, kiddo," he said. "Lucky to be able to walk out of here. I'd do anything to come with you."

"Soon."

"Here's hoping."

Rather than enjoy his pastry, he seemed to be choking it down.

"I could be in here, too, Arlo."

He regarded her a moment.

"You got reason to look over your shoulder?"

"No. But I used a knife on the first person I ever profiled."

"I read about that. Self-defense. It doesn't count."

"I'm not so sure about that. I have to think about it as part of my job. Murder, I mean. Really horrific murders."

"Thinking ain't doing."

The lump in her throat surprised her. Arlo still had her back.

"You're not like them."

Nadine looked at the empty soda can beside her water and suddenly found herself confessing about considering taking his DNA sample without his permission.

"So I'm a sneaky little turncoat."

"But you didn't take it. You told me. As for the DNA thing, go ahead and run it."

He was a convicted felon. She had little doubt of the results.

She hesitated. He pushed the can in her direction.

"I'll put it in writing for you. How's that? Sign a waiver." He reached across the table, breaking the rules on contact, and patted the top of her hand. "You could do anything, Dee-Dee. All of us could. But it only counts if you take actionable steps."

*Actionable steps.* Had Arlo been studying law?

"Like stealing a DNA sample?"

"Yeah. Like that. But technically, you only moved it."

"And told you."

"That part wasn't wise. Admission of guilt."

"Actionable steps, admission of guilt. You sound like a lawyer." He flushed.

"What?"

"I'm taking law classes. Already finished three semesters."

"That's great!"

"I can't ever practice. Not allowed to sit for the bar."

"I still think it's terrific."

He lifted his pastry and then set it down. "There's another reason I needed to see you. Something I couldn't put in writing."

He'd said as much in his email. She tried to hide her trepidation as she leaned in.

"Go on."

"Mom has friends in this prison. I'm afraid she might send one of them after me." Arlo's face was pale. "It's easy. Cheap, too. Lots of the inmates have nothing to lose. No chance of parole. Maybe do it for free. I know she writes some of them. I might get shivved in the shower or while I'm sleeping. It's not hard. The money you just gave me is enough to buy a hit."

"Oh, God, Arlo!"

"I want you to understand how simple it can be."

"But why would she send someone after you? I'm the one who cut her off. And you haven't done anything to her."

He gave her a look that made her question that assumption and revise her denial.

"I'm about to."

She leaned in again.

"You remember Mom telling you that she killed some guy by accident and used his truck to move him?"

Nadine sat back. Her suspicion was that this unnamed stranger might have been their dad. She'd told Arlo as much and now wondered if that had been a mistake.

"Of course."

"You said she told you that he owed her money. And you were right that Dad owed her child support. He never paid her, at least that's what she said."

Nadine had heard often in her childhood of her deadbeat dad who ran off with another woman.

"She said she hit him," said Arlo.

"With a shovel," she added. "Arleen told me that she used his truck to move him. Then buried the body somewhere near the St. Johns River. She wouldn't say exactly where."

"I could help find them."

"Them?"

"Yeah, plural." He gave her a hopeful look. "I think she killed them both."

"I don't understand."

"Dad and his girlfriend, Infinity. You look her up, Infinity Yanez. She's gone. I'll put money on it. Missing person. You understand?"

Nadine gaped. Her ears buzzed. She considered her options and then told Arlo what she already knew about the woman her father had left her mother for.

"I had the same thought about Mom and had someone look into it. Yanez has been missing since 1993."

"I knew it!" He pumped his fist as if scoring the winning goal.

"But I don't have a shred of proof that Mom had anything to do with it," she said.

"I might."

Her mouth was so dry. She wanted desperately to find their father. But not like this.

"What, Arlo?"

"I rode over to see Dad the day before he left."

"On your bike. You told me."

Arlo had been only eight at the time, but fairly independent for a kid that age. Certainly, Arleen hadn't reined him in.

"Yeah. I saw them, Dad and Infinity kissing, so I never got the nerve up to speak to him. They drove off in that black truck. I rode over the next day and he wasn't home, but his truck was there. It had a red sticker on the driver's-side windshield."

"What does that mean?" she asked.

"The state police have to check all cars and trucks on the shoulders of highways. They check for theft or injured drivers."

"How do you know that?"

"My van broke down and got red-tagged by a trooper."

"I see."

"If the car is unoccupied, they red-tag it. It's a big red sticker on the driver's-side window. Then they call it in."

She didn't understand.

"What has this got to do with your parole?"

"Mom used Dad's truck," said Arlo.

Last year, her mother had told her that she'd killed a man. That she'd used the victim's truck to move the body.

Arleen had failed to mention that victim was their father.

"Can you back up and explain about the sticker?" she asked.

"She drove them in his truck. Dad's truck. She parked on a shoulder somewhere that night and took those bodies into the woods and buried them. While she was gone, a trooper tagged Dad's truck. Just bad luck, really."

She nodded, following him now.

"If you could help me, find out who tagged that vehicle. They'd know where Mom took their bodies."

"But Mom said Dad left in that truck."

Arlo looked away. "They didn't. Mom had a friend; he knew a guy. They took the truck to a chop shop. I heard her talking about it and how much money she got."

Nadine blinked, absorbing the implications. Up until this point she'd only had suspicions as to what Arleen might have done to their dad. Now she had something more, a witness to a possible crime.

"That truck would have been red-tagged over twenty years ago. I'm not sure there will be any record."

"Check. Will you?"

"Yes. I will."

"If you can find something and I come forward about seeing that sticker, my lawyer said it could help them solve two murders and might get me early release."

And if he didn't, their mother could find out that her son had snitched on her. Was Arlo right that she'd try to teach him a lesson?

Nadine started sweating. If she helped Arlo and he succeeded, he might be on the outside sooner than planned and might pick up exactly where he had left off. But if he failed, he'd be stuck in here and their mother might send someone to hurt him.

"What do you think, Nadine? Will you help me?"

# CHAPTER ELEVEN

## MONDAY

When she removed the *Do Not Disturb* door hanger, she noted that the hotel service included delivery of the Orlando newspaper. Looking down at the pages, Nadine spotted an article about an upcoming book tour by her former boss. Dr. Margery Crean had worked with a ghostwriter to produce a tell-all book on the Copycat Killer.

"Is everyone writing a book?" she muttered.

She reminded herself that she was through hiding who she was. But that didn't mean she enjoyed standing naked in the spotlight.

Safely back inside, she tucked into the armchair and read the article while rain lashed her window. Crean, who had retired after their prime suspect shot her in the face last year, would be in Orlando on Friday to speak and sign copies of her book with the on-the-nose title: *The Copycat Killer*.

The AP photo of her former boss showed puckering pink scars on her left cheek and right lower lip. Nadine learned from Tina that Crean's upper palate had been destroyed and her reconstructive surgery was still ongoing.

Her phone chimed, alerting her to a text: Juliette asking if she saw the paper. Before she could answer, Demko's text arrived and then Tina's, both asking her the same thing.

She did not see Demko Saturday because he had left early to visit with his mom and then gone directly to his son, Christopher, in Miami.

She group-texted them all, then sent a DM to Juliette, asking her if she had time for the blood draw.

Thirty minutes later, showered and dressed, she headed to Juliette's room where the ME drew a vial of blood. Meanwhile, Jack-Jack, the cockatoo, did a serviceable imitation of the beeping used by a garbage truck backing up.

Nadine spotted a small Easter basket on Juliette's nightstand. Inside were the same chocolates Clint had left in a larger basket hanging from the door latch of her own room Saturday.

Juliette noted the direction of her gaze.

"Clint gave me that," she said. "When I was a kid, we had an egg hunt every year before church." Her smile and faraway look touched Nadine.

Unlike Tina, Clint or her, Juliette had been adopted as an infant into a normal, affluent home and only learned of her mother's crimes when she was no longer a child.

"When did you see him?" asked Nadine.

"Caught Demko at breakfast, Saturday. He came by to get his blood drawn and deliver the basket before he went to the prison. He gave me one like it to deliver to Tina."

"You got his blood draw?"

"Yes, and I took mine and Tina's on Friday night. Do we know how to party or what?" She laughed and then secured the cotton ball and Band-Aid to the puncture site before placing the vial in her mini refrigerator. "So we're all set."

"Almost. I need one more of those tests."

"Which one?"

"The same, only on this."

She handed over Arlo's soda can inside an evidence bag and the waiver, written on a napkin and witnessed by a guard.

Juliette rolled her eyes. "Fine. But I'll tell you again. You are not going to get any answers. Even if your result is positive, the association to violence is, well, it's not widely recognized and it's not like a diagnosis for a disease."

"Small study. Correlational at best. I understand."

"Do you?" Juliette eyed her suspiciously. "Did you know that an increased sales in ice cream is correlated to a spike in reported rapes?"

Nadine frowned. "What?"

"So, do you think it's the ice cream's fault or maybe it's because the weather is warmer, and more people are outside?"

"I understand a correlational relationship, Juliette."

Her friend looked unconvinced. Nadine was about to leave when the ME said, "How was your visit with Arlo?"

"I'll tell you later. It's a lot."

"Highlights?"

"He wants to offer evidence to a double homicide in exchange for early release, but if he doesn't get out, he'll have implicated our mom and is worried she might send someone to kill him."

Juliette whistled.

Her phone chimed with a text from Demko.

*@brkfast. Where r u?*

She said good-bye to Juliette, fired off a text and headed to the hotel's breakfast area.

Demko had settled at a table with a plate of sausage and biscuits and a mug of coffee for her.

"How was your Easter?" he asked.

"I went to church with Tina and Juliette, then back to work. Oh, and we all got your baskets. Thank you very much." She kissed him and he smiled.

"That's great."

With her father gone and her mother and brother both incarcerated, Nadine spent most holidays with her aunt Donna's family, never feeling quite at home. But yesterday Juliette and Tina had made her feel part of a family.

"How was your visit with Christopher?"

"Nice. Too old for an egg hunt, but I gave him a basket, too."

"The one you left me is huge! It was so much." She pushed a small box in his direction and then set the envelope beside it.

"What's this?"

"An Easter gift. One that Molly can't destroy. The envelope is from Skogen. The policy manual I told you about."

He opened the gift, a metal flip-style wallet, tested its use and then gave her a kiss.

"Thank you." He ignored the envelope. "Christopher was sorry you couldn't be there."

Nadine glanced down, breaking eye contact.

"Once he meets you, sees we're serious, it will be good. He's a sweet kid, Dee, and I really want you two to be friends."

She nodded, remaining silent. She feared that Christopher would not want her as a friend.

"Maybe next time?" he asked, pushing.

It seemed they'd only pressed pause on their last conversation.

"After we catch this one. Okay?" Nadine glanced up.

His mouth was tight.

She stood. "More coffee?"

"Why is it every time I mention getting more serious, you run?"

"I don't." She so did.

"You either take me to bed or change the subject. What are you afraid of?"

"Demko, can this conversation wait? We are here to catch a killer."

She realized she'd just proven his point.

He took her hand and brought it to his lips, then released her. "*I'm* here because you asked for my help."

"I know." His reminder made her recall her conversation with her brother. She settled back to her seat. "Speaking of help…"

Nadine explained about the red-tagged vehicle that had belonged to her father.

He went silent, seeming to consider for a moment. Was he deliberating allowing her to again table this topic or pondering the problem of a vehicle tagged more than a decade earlier? At last he sighed and folded his hands before him.

The former, she decided.

"That's a tough one. Let me call Willie Druckman."

"He's a trooper up here?"

"Orlando. That's the closest barracks. This is their territory, though."

He made the call and left a message for the highway patrolman to contact him. Then he rose.

"See you tonight." He walked toward reception and then out the front door. Beside his empty place at the table, the envelope from Skogen still sat.

At the office, she found Tina working. She paused to beam up at Nadine.

"I wish you could have joined us on the kayak trip yesterday. We saw otters and loads of turtles."

After Easter brunch, Nadine had skipped their outing in favor of work.

"Did you locate Bianca Santander with Immigration?" Nadine asked.

"Her attorney can't find her. She's not listed in the detainee locator. He's still looking."

"Is this normal?"

"It's illegal to withhold a detainee's location, but, yes, it happens."

"Keep on it."

Nadine tucked in behind her desk and opened her email.

"Holy cats!" she said.

Tina stopped working and came around her desk. "You've got one hundred forty-five new emails."

"From media. Look at this. Major networks and newspapers… is that the *Washington Post*?"

Did the press somehow know she was profiling this case? Or could the influx of emails be linked to Crean and her upcoming book?

"Open one," suggested Tina.

Nadine blew out a breath and did so. She scanned as Tina read over her shoulder. White cat hairs clung to the cuff of Tina's black sweater.

Most days she could handle the myriad of offers she received, but since her initial success as a profiler, and Crean's book tour apparently, her email box was slammed. Tina seemed to pick up on her disquiet.

"Do you want to be interviewed, provide a quote for their articles or appear on camera?"

"No way."

"Then let me answer them," said Tina.

"You got it."

Nadine forwarded them to Tina, who went silently to work as Nadine did the same.

Exactly at noon, Tina announced she was going to the grocery store deli for a sandwich.

"You want something?"

"No."

Forty minutes later, Tina returned with a cup of chicken noodle soup and a hard roll for Nadine.

"It's pouring out again."

"Really?" Nadine had no window to check. She glanced up to discover that Tina's hair was plastered to her head.

"Wow."

"Eat your soup before it gets cold."

She did and devoured the buttered roll in minutes.

Tina gave her a critical stare.

"What?"

"You are worse than Demko, forgetting to eat."

"Two meals a day are plenty."

"It isn't, though," said Tina.

The afternoon sped along as she filled in details on the victims and searched for commonalities.

Tina stepped out for more coffee, passing Skogen, who appeared in her doorway, a wide, self-satisfied grin on his face.

"We got a match on the DNA from Karnowski with the groundskeeper, Barney Arnold."

Nadine wasn't exactly surprised.

"That's great."

"He's in custody. Already amended his bullshit story. Now he's admitted to the sex act. Pervert found Karnowski's nude body arousing. He called it in and then, well, he had several minutes alone with the remains."

"To masturbate," said Nadine.

"It's not normal."

"Agreed. But masturbating doesn't mean he killed her. Where's the evidence for that?"

"I've got enough to charge and hold him. Get a search warrant issued and see what turns up. I'm heading over there now."

Skogen's team would confiscate Arnold's computer, laptop, tablet and phone. The tech team would use them to assemble a forensic digital profile. Gathering the data would be quick, since they had the devices. Sorting through it all would take several days, and that was a conservative estimate.

"I'll let you know what we get." Skogen raked a hand through his hair. "Nadine, I think we got him."

She felt a great weight lifted off her shoulders. If this was their guy, then they had succeeded in stopping the series in just two. That would be marvelous.

Nadine pushed aside the niggling worry. In many ways Arnold fit her profile. So why wasn't she relieved?

# CHAPTER TWELVE

## TUESDAY

Nadine glanced at the hotel clock beside Clint's bed, wishing she'd gone to her own room last night after they'd tangled the sheets.

Last night, she had slept in his bed and Molly had slept on the floor. Now, her bedfellow lay on his stomach.

Nadine drummed her fingers on the sheets. She'd been up since five, thinking, and wishing she had her laptop.

Arnold was a possible match for her profile. He was a loner with numerous priors for offenses involving sexual misconduct. He was white, single, fit, lived alone, hunted, knew the terrain, drove a truck with a cab and was at the scene only hours after the body of Rita Karnowski was dumped. But despite all that, as of last night, the FBI had no weapon, no indication of transport in Arnold's vehicle, and no souvenirs from either victim in his possession. There was nothing, in fact, to connect Arnold to the victims except the semen and his discovery of the bodies shortly after Karnowski's death.

They needed solid evidence. But that was not her job.

Skogen's team was on it. They would find proof he committed the murders.

Or they wouldn't.

Enough, she thought. It was nearly six. Close enough to the time to get up. She slipped from the bed, creeping around trying to find her clothing in the darkened room, with Molly following her, hoping to go out.

"Nadine?" Demko's voice was groggy.

"Taking Molly out. Be right back."

She shimmied into her dress and clipped Molly's leash to her collar. As she reached the corridor, her phone vibrated.

"Arnold's timeline doesn't work," said Skogen as she picked up.

"What?"

"Barney Arnold was in Montana with his brother fly-fishing from March 12th to March 21st. Confirmed."

Nadine knew that covered the two Saturdays their victims had been taken.

"All right."

"All right? You don't sound surprised," said Skogen.

She had known. It was why she couldn't sleep.

"I'm not. See you later on." Nadine ended the call.

The killer was still out there. She needed to get back to work.

*

At the office, one of Skogen's special agents delivered more bad news to Nadine.

"We have another missing woman. Details are on the file share." Nadine's stomach clenched.

Her name was Linda Tolan. Nadine found her a likely victim because, like Nikki Darnell and Rita Karnowski, her car was found on a trailhead.

Tolan was a single female from out of the area, reported missing by her sister on Sunday night when she tried and failed to reach her. Tolan, a wildlife photographer on assignment for a birding magazine, had disappeared sometime after the sisters' last contact on Wednesday afternoon. Like the first victim, Nikki Darnell, the abandoned vehicle was found by rangers shortly after the sheriff logged the call from Tolan's sister on Sunday. Park rangers had made a sweep of the trail but found nothing.

Tolan's car was well within Nadine's geo-profile's range for their unsub's hunting territory, so she recommended to Skogen that search and rescue expand the search area, not just to the trail, but to a 100-mile territory she had identified as within the statistical probability range of this killer.

She then called her team with the bad news. They now all knew the killer was still out there.

Midmorning, Tina appeared from the break room with fresh coffee.

"I found out why the office is so empty." She set the mug before Nadine. "They're all out looking for that missing person."

"Good."

"Drones, dogs and men, that's what the tech guy said."

"Do they need me?"

Tina laughed. "You aren't the go-to for this."

That was true, but it was difficult to sit indoors and wait for news while the search was under way.


At noon, Nadine tried and failed to reach either Skogen or Demko for an update. Cell service in the Ocala Forest was spotty or nonexistent and her calls went straight to voicemail.

At two in the afternoon, Tina burst into her office, coming to an abrupt stop before Nadine's desk.

"They got her," Tina said.

Nadine startled to her feet.

"They used your profile." Tina bounced up and down. "And the information from Tolan's sister. And search and rescue found a woman in a hog trap out there."

*A hog trap.* That sounded exactly right.

Nadine braced herself. "Dead?"

"No. She's alive!" Tina bounded forward, capturing Nadine's hands and shaking them in excitement. "Skogen said you saved her! Dr. Finch, you're a hero!"

At five in the afternoon, Nadine sat quietly in Tolan's hospital room as Skogen took a seat bedside in a vinyl chair.

Nadine recognized that Linda Tolan's rescue was a fortunate combination of data synthesis and luck. There was so much she didn't yet know about their killer.

Sadly, Skogen now thought she was some sort of oracle and she had not been able to convince him otherwise.

Their surviving victim was a painfully thin freckled Caucasian woman with long brown hair, streaked with gray, who had been confined in an animal cage in the forest since early Thursday morning.

Her face was covered with bug bites and she was sunburned with cracked and peeling lips. Her skin showed numerous scrapes and razor-thin crisscrossing lacerations on her face, neck and arms indicating her captor had likely dragged her.

Nadine took in Tolan's gaunt features and the dark circles beneath her bloodshot eyes. There was something vaguely familiar about this woman. The possibility sent an unwelcome prickle over her skin, as if a spider was crawling on her neck. Nadine used one hand to brush the feeling away.

Tolan was lucky. She'd survived over five days in a hog trap without food or water.

The preparation phase, Nadine thought.

In a faint and raspy voice, Linda told Skogen that she had been on assignment.

"My sister said that I drove up here on Wednesday and was staying until Sunday or until I got the summer tanager."

"The what?" asked Skogen.

"It's a songbird. A bright red songbird… winters in South and Central America, but it's here now." She paused, pressing a hand to her chest as she gasped, the air rasping as she exhaled. "Their song is wonderful." She pinched her eyes shut, lying still as she whispered. "I'm working on a story for a national magazine. The spring migration."

"Your sister told you this?"

"Well, I remembered the assignment. But not the drive down here or anything else until after the attack." Her brow knit and she folded her hands across her middle. "It's like a big fuzzy mess."

"Where did you stay?" asked Skogen.

Tolan shook her head. "A hotel? I don't know."

The FBI could run her credit cards and figure out where she had been. But it was troubling that Tolan didn't remember.

"Maybe my sister will know. She'll be here soon. I spoke to her this morning. But I don't remember much of our conversation."

Tolan's doctors described her condition as retrograde amnesia resulting from the head trauma. Whether her memory would return was anyone's guess.

Nadine knew it would be best for Tolan if it didn't. Some blank spots were better never filled in.

"Do you remember the capture?" Special Agent Skogen asked.

"I'm sorry. I don't." She rubbed the back of her head. "There's still a lump."

"What's your first memory?" asked Nadine.

"Waking up in that cage!" Tolan shivered. "I was so thirsty. There were two padlocks on the door, the kind with the key. And it rained. I drank all I could, but I was shivering. Couldn't get warm."

"What time of day was this?" asked Skogen.

"Before sunup."

Yesterday morning, Nadine remembered, she had awoken to rain and there was a violent storm midday. Had that cloudburst saved Tolan's life?

But if today was her first memory, that meant Tolan had lost the memories of five days of captivity. Nadine wondered if hypnosis might offer some answers.

"And you saw your captor?" asked Skogen.

"Not at first. I woke up naked and covered with mosquitoes. I freaked then, trying to get them off me. I was bleeding from my arms and back. The doctor said it looked like he beat me." She dragged the hospital gown down over her shoulder to show an example. "Then I saw I was in a cage. My head was splitting. I swear, it felt like my skull was fractured."

"When did you see the man?" asked Skogen, notepad out.

"I heard someone chuckling and turned to see this guy. He was laughing at me. I knew then what was happening. That he wouldn't help me. I could see it in his face. He was so happy to have me like that." She dropped her gaze as her breathing accelerated.

"You're safe, Linda," said Nadine, keeping her voice low and calm.

"What if he comes back?"

"These sorts of predators hunt in a territory. They don't target specific women," said Skogen.

Vague and not completely accurate, thought Nadine, but perhaps comforting. She said nothing to contradict but made a note to speak to Skogen. Lying to her might be best in the short term, but Tolan needed to up her guard.

"We have an artist coming to help you make a sketch of your attacker. It's very important that you try to remember all the details you can," said Skogen.

"You know what I do remember? My sister telling me not to go alone. But I was carrying, and I thought…" Her words trailed off. "He almost killed me."

Skogen spoke up. "Did you say you were carrying a firearm?"

"Pistol. Yes. In my camera bag." Her hands went up and her mouth dropped open. "My cameras! Did you find my cameras?"

"No. Just you, Ms. Tolan," said Coleman.

She was crying now. The loss of the cameras seemed to be her final blow.

Skogen redirected her.

"Do you know where that pistol is now?"

She gave him a bewildered look. Tears coursed down her cheeks. "With my lenses, I guess. It was all together in my bag. I don't know."

Her confusion appeared genuine and heartbreaking. Nadine glanced to Skogen, who seemed oblivious to Tolan's obvious distress. Was he so fixed on his investigation he was indifferent to what this woman had suffered?

"Is it registered?"

"The gun? Yes. Oh, yes. I took the class and everything."

Skogen sent one of the agents out to investigate the missing firearm.

Over the next hour, Skogen asked a series of questions, circled back a few times and came up with a vague description of a white man who wore large mirror glasses and a cap. Tolan described his clothing as the sort a hiker would wear. Light nylon shorts, athletic T-shirt and hiking boots.

In other words, not dressed as a hunter. That surprised Nadine, but then… his attire was perfect camouflage for a man hiding from other humans. He was average height, weight and size. He was male, likely white, tanned or possibly Latino, and dressed like every other hiker, kayaker and bird-watcher in the forest.

The only distinctive feature was his voice. Linda described it as feminine and higher in pitch than most men.

Nadine's mind went immediately to the man at the adventure outfitters. The one she had felt sorry for and who had an odd high tenor to his voice. Simon Kilpatrick, the underachieving man-child who couldn't find a job except at his parents' business.

"Agent Skogen, could I see you outside for a moment?"

They stepped into the hospital corridor together.

"We met someone with a high, female voice."


## WEDNESDAY

Nadine spent the morning with Linda Tolan, whose memories had not returned despite hypnosis. If the part of her brain that stored memories had suffered damage from the blow, the issue was not psychological repression but brain injury. Nadine feared that they would not retrieve any more useful information from this third victim.

Skogen's team had taken Simon Kilpatrick into custody last night. Most of his people had been at the wilderness outfitters all day executing the search warrant. She had arrived at the sheriff's office in the afternoon in time to sit in on much of the interview of Simon. He denied any involvement with either woman but appeared confused to Nadine but was cooperative. The interview ended when the Kilpatricks' attorney arrived just after 3 p.m.

"You get anything on the search warrant?" she asked Skogen.

"Nope. Nothing to hold him for. But he's a very strong suspect. This might be our guy. I'm going to question him again tomorrow with his attorney present."

She shook her head. "It isn't Simon."

"Well, forgive us if we make that determination."

"Our guy has an above average IQ," she said.

"What?"

"He's smart. Capable. Clever. And Simon is an underachiever."

"With a high voice."

Nadine raised her voice. "Anyone can change their voice."

He continued as if she had not spoken.

"Rita Karnowski's boyfriend rented the tandem kayak from Big Water Marina on Saturday, March 20th. Simon put their kayaks into the water."

She recognized the deadlock and moved on.

"Anything on Tolan's camera equipment or that gun?"

"All still missing. We have her weapon in the database. Fingers crossed we get a hit on that firearm."

Without it killing someone, she thought.

"I'm sorry the hypnosis didn't offer any further details," she said.

"Me as well. Oh, our crime techs have finished going over her vehicle," he said.

"Any prints?"

"Yes. Too many. They are sorting them now. You've seen the sketch?" Skogen referred to the rendering of the unsub Tolan had worked on with their sketch artist.

She shook her head and he pulled it up on his phone.

Sunglasses covered their unsub's eyes and brow. The cap covered much of his head. The jawline was distinctive, pointed, and his mouth was wide. This could be Simon, she thought.

Really it could be almost anyone.

"Not very helpful, I think."

"It's a start." He tucked away his phone. "Heading back to the office?"

She nodded, turning to go, and then faced Skogen again.

"One more thing," she said. "I recommend that the public be alerted to Linda Tolan's abduction so they can take precautions."

"Press conference scheduled in one hour. We want it on the front page."

She fidgeted with her thumbnail.

"You will not be in attendance, Dr. Finch. Confidential, as we agreed? My secret weapon."

*

Back at the office, Special Agent Coleman stopped by just after Nadine returned from the sheriff's.

"Heading over to the press conference now, but I wanted to alert you that Tolan was discharged."

"She won't be alone?"

"No. Her sister is driving her home to Jacksonville and staying for a few days."

Linda Tolan would need years of therapy, and even then, the attack and capture would change her forever. How could it not?

"Okay. See you tomorrow."

"Oh, and the items recovered from Tolan's vehicle are now on the file share. Have a look."

"Will do."

Coleman waved and headed out.

Nadine didn't think the contents of the vehicle would have much to add to her victim profile, but she scrolled down the list of the sort of things you would find in anyone's glove box. But one item stopped her.

A black-and-gold headband.

Her stomach pitched. She moved her mouse to open the PDF document that included photos and there it was. Her Versace headband, with a distinctive pattern of three bleach spots. It couldn't be a coincidence.

She felt it in the ice water now circulating in her bloodstream.

How could her headband have ended up inside Linda Tolan's vehicle?

"He knows I'm here."

# CHAPTER THIRTEEN

Nadine's first called was to Demko.

"I'll have the security office pull the tapes from last Wednesday night," he said. "Where's Skogen?"

"They're all at the press conference."

"Okay. I'm heading to the hotel. Meet me in the security office."

She was glad to have Demko be the one in charge. She trusted him, while Skogen had not earned that yet.

"Could you check the security footage on my floor?"

"Absolutely."

Before leaving the office, she left a message on Skogen's phone.

Delayed by traffic, Nadine arrived at the hotel at five to find both parrots in their cages eating from their food dishes. Rosie welcomed her from the front desk, checked to see if it was all right to let her back to the security offices and then escorted her. En route, Nadine's stomach gave a tremendous growl and Rosie laughed.

"Well, I'll bring you one of the cookies we have in the afternoon for guests."

"You have cookies?" Why was she just hearing about this now?

"Three to five every day. I mentioned them on check-in"

And there was her answer. She'd been exhausted on arrival and she never got back here until after five.

"Thanks, Rosie. I appreciate that."

Rosie knocked on the office door and Demko let her in, introducing her to the night guard.

"We found something," Demko said. "This is Wednesday evening, March 31st, the day you came back to the hotel with Juliette and Tina after we found the trail cam."

She recalled the crippling migraine and her late-night visit to reception to collect policy manuals that no one wanted or, likely, ever read.

For the next twenty minutes she looked at footage of her arrival to the room and then her departure, including her toppling into her neighbor's door the night of her migraine.

Demko glanced at her with a concerned expression and she shrugged.

"Lost my balance."

"Why?"

"Migraine."

Demko turned to the playback, pointing out that she was wearing the headband to reception and that the door across from hers opened when she made her initial exit. So she'd woken him twice.

The next series included her at the front desk, then waiting for the elevator, in the car and finally her exiting onto the second floor, envelope in hand.

"Why are you covering one eye?" asked Demko.

"Light sensitivity."

The camera picked up clearly that she had dropped the envelope into the bin while righting it. The door across from hers opened again when she was fumbling with the trash bin. The headband had slipped off her head but remained in her hair as she reached the corridor.

Nadine was glad there was no audio for the bit when her female neighbor had come out to shout at her. The woman snatched Nadine's key card and opened her door for her. She'd forgotten that part.

At this point Rosie returned with a cookie the size of a frozen potpie, distracting Nadine from the replay. She thanked Rosie and tucked into the cookie, closing her eyes at the taste of chocolate chips and brown sugar.

"There," he pointed. "Headband just fell."

Nadine's eyes snapped open. There lay the headband on the floor of the hallway directly between the two opposite doors.

"Here's the interesting part," said Demko. "The door opens again. But you can't see this guest. Now watch this."

The guard slowed the recording. Nadine watched her door close and something extend from the opposite door.

"What is that?" she asked.

"Golf umbrella," said the head of security. "We lend them to the guests. One in every closet."

The occupant used the umbrella to drag her headband into his room. Then the door closed.

Nadine placed a hand over her pounding heart. He'd taken it.

"Avoiding the cameras," said Demko.

"Who stayed in that room?" she asked.

"That's the trouble," said Demko.

"The room was vacant. No guest stayed there," said the guard. "I've got to call my boss."

"We checked the footage all the way to Sunday. No one came out of that room," said Demko.

"We walked the exterior," said the guard. "The window is missing and repaired with a sheet of Plexiglas and electrical tape. Whoever it was, went in and out through the second-floor window."

"How?" she asked.

"Ladder or from the roof with a pulley," said Demko.

"You have this recorded?" she asked.

"No cameras facing the building," he said. "They only show the lot. The approach must have been along the grass under the window. Outside the camera's view."

"It's him," she said.

*

Special Agent Jack Skogen arrived in the hotel security office with his digital forensics expert where she, Demko and the hotel's head of security waited. Demko filled them in on the headband and what they had found on the security footage.

"We think it would be wise to move you and your people to a new location. As a precaution," said Skogen. "In the meantime I've tightened security. Added undercover agents on-site and we have you and the hotel under surveillance."

"He won't be back. He got what he came for."

"Still."

She suffered through the long silence.

"The sketch artist will come by tomorrow at the field office to see you. Let me know when you two come up with a rendering."

"I will."

"We need a sample of hair to compare with the one found on the headband," said Skogen, evidence bag open.

Nadine ran her fingers through her hair, coming away with several strands, dropping them into the bag.

He sealed the bag. "I'll rush it."

She left the men and joined Tina and Juliette in the hotel restaurant, explaining what Demko had found over their meal.

Afterward, the three took Molly out for a short walk and then escorted Nadine to her room.

She did not sleep well.

THURSDAY

Back at the office the following day, Nadine did her best with the sketch artist. She wished she had not seen Linda Tolan's version, as it had crept into her mind and influenced her memories.

Afterward, Tina stopped in.

"They found Santander! She's in the Glades County Detention Center."

"Finally, some good news."

They shared a smile before Tina bombarded her with messages. The press mainly, requesting a quote responding to Dr. Crean's new release and her comments about Nadine's "deeper issues," plus a few important questions from the psychologist who had filled her position in Sarasota.

Before lunch she took a call from Juliette.

"I wanted to alert you."

Something in the tone of her voice triggered all Nadine's anxieties. She shot to her feet.

"I got a call from Dr. Kline. She received a possible drowning victim from up in Putnam County."

Her hammering heart made it difficult to hear and she wrapped her free arm around herself to stem the shivering.

"Where?"

"Recovered in Grass Lake outside Fort McCoy."

"We don't have any missing persons," she said, as if saying so out loud might make this death unconnected. Her voice held an unwelcome hysterical edge.

"Calm down, Nadine. It might be a simple drowning."

Don't jump to conclusions, she thought. But her mouth had turned to cotton, and the cold sweat increased her trembling.

"Yes. All right."

"We don't know much yet. There's significant decomposition, apparently."

"Age?"

"Under twenty-five is the ME's best guess."

"When is the autopsy?"

"Today or tomorrow."

"Let me know when you have more details."

"Yes. Will do."

Demko made a rare visit to Nadine's office at midday on Thursday and she filled him in on Juliette's news on the body recovery.

"ID?"

"No," she said.

"I'll go see what I can find."

"Sounds good."

"Listen, I heard back from Willie Druckman," he said, after Tina had left them.

"Who?"

"He's the trooper in Putnam County. The one I asked to look into that red-tagged vehicle for you and Arlo."

"Anything?"

"Yes. Druckman came up with several F150 pickup trucks, tagged that way during that year."

He offered her a photocopy.

"You going to contact Sean?" asked Demko.

Sean Torrin was the FBI's lead investigator on the Copycat Killer case who was now exploring several missing persons as potential victims of her mother. Unfortunately, Arleen had been uncooperative. But if Arleen had murdered their father, Nadine was ready and willing to get involved.

"Not yet," she said.

"Why not?"

"If I tell about the tag, I remove the usefulness of the information Arlo wants to barter for parole."

She pondered her dilemma. The morally right thing to do was to give this intel to Arlo's attorneys and help him get out early, as any sister should. But she could withhold it, destroying his chance of early release, because she feared he might present a threat to others. She was his sister. But also a trained psychologist. Either course held minefields.

"What's wrong?"

"I want to find my dad. I'm just not sure releasing Arlo is a good idea."

"You wouldn't be the one making that decision."

"I'd be the one aiding him."

"Nadine. He's your brother."

"You don't know him. He's got that darkness inside him."

"But keeping him in prison because of possibilities is wrong," said Demko.

For him, family came before society. But he didn't go to bed thinking of the lives his mother destroyed. Or did he?

When would Juliette have their DNA tests back? Knowing Arlo's results, and if he had the genes that predisposed a person to violence, might help her decide. In her heart, she feared the day of Arlo's release.

"I'll pass it on to him," she said and lifted her phone to write an email to Arlo.

*

*Linda Tolan left her home darkroom after eleven, holding the photo of the summer tanager that had nearly cost her life, taken much closer to home, thanks to her sister's willingness to stop on their return journey. Failing at sleep, she'd turned to work, hoping that the next time she lay down in bed it wouldn't be in a cold sweat as memories assaulted her like thrown bricks.*

*The photo of the cheerful, bright red songbird usually made her smile. But now, inexplicably, she found her hand trembling as the pain and confusion descended on her without warning.*

*"Flashback," she said. Linda had never had one, but she recognized the chill lifting the hairs on her neck and the twisting of her stomach.*

*She carried the wet image to the kitchen, determined to hold it together. Her appointment on Monday with a psychologist would help her sort out her emotions.*

The unfamiliar sound caused her to freeze. It was a clicking. She lifted her gaze from the image and saw a man standing in the hallway before her.

In his hand was a familiar pistol pointed at her. Her gaze flashed to his face.

He wore no sunglasses or hat now, but she recognized him instantly.

"No," she whispered and dropped the photo, backing toward her darkroom.

"We didn't finish our hunt, Linda."

She reached for the knob, but her numb fingers fumbled. She couldn't even feel them. Was she passing out?

"Come along, now, my little rabbit," he said, keeping the pistol aimed at her chest.

She knew what awaited her if he took her alive.

Instinct and terror washed through her and she ran at him, clasping the gun as he fired. The searing pain in her shoulder dropped her to her knees.

He grabbed her hair and yanked, then punched her in the face. She was vaguely aware of being lifted and wrapped in something. Her head ached and her stomach rolled. She was going to be sick.

It was him. He'd come back and this time she knew they would never find her in time.

# CHAPTER FOURTEEN

## FRIDAY

Special Agent Coleman surprised Nadine and Demko at breakfast in the hotel. Her expression of urgency brought Nadine to her feet.

"Come with me," she said.

They did, following her toward the waiting SUV.

Had another woman been captured?

"What's happened?" asked Demko.

"Jacksonville police logged a 911 call last night, possible gunshots." She held open the passenger door.

"Jacksonville?" said Demko.

Nadine knew before Coleman confirmed her suspicions. It was hard to hear past the buzzing in her ears.

"Police responded. Tolan's sister reported being awakened by a single shot before midnight on Thursday and discovered her sister missing. There was blood in the bedroom hallway."

"Linda Tolan," said Nadine.

"Yes. She's missing."

"You didn't give her protection?" said Demko, the accusation unmistakable.

Coleman looked away. "Deemed unnecessary."

Nadine gasped. Was this her fault? "I should have recommended…"

"We could have had him," said Demko simultaneously.

"Yes," agreed Coleman.

*

The Jacksonville police had Linda Tolan's boyfriend in custody. Agent Coleman headed north on Monday afternoon to interview him.

Nadine doubted he would be a suspect for long. As Friday afternoon inched along, she could not stop thinking about Linda Tolan. She was likely alive right now, naked and locked in an animal cage.

Again.

She'd provided a likely search area but was certain this monster would have moved to a new territory. She struggled to guess where.

The pressure to find Linda, and the knowledge that the task was just too much, squeezed the air from her lungs. She didn't think the roadblocks or any other measures by law enforcement would stop him. Not this time. He was already back in the terrain where he felt safest.

*Where?*

Demko was out looking with highway patrol, sheriff's office and local search and rescue. Nadine tried to picture where she would take Tolan. She rested her elbows on the desk and placed her hands over her eyes.

*Think!*

With her eyes closed she pictured Linda's recapture from the details provided.

Where was he now?

Safer to bring her somewhere out of the area. But that would spoil his fun and the game he was playing with law enforcement.

Had the killer brought Linda all the way back here? Yes, she thought. Definitely. He would teach her a lesson. Teach all of them how clever he was, how effective.

He wouldn't be denied his playthings. She could almost hear his thoughts.

*No, not playthings, prey. My game is always in season. I have lots of hunting grounds and I know these jungles better than anyone. They can't find her. They won't. I'll move deeper. Keep her long enough that she understands she's mine to do with as I like. How long will I make her wait?*

"He wants notoriety," Nadine said. "That's why the bodies were dumped on a busy trail. Bound to be discovered. Could have buried them. Left them in a remote place. But it's a performance."

"Dr. Finch? Who you talking to?"

Tina's voice brought her head snapping up.

"Myself. Did they find Linda?"

"No."

Nadine sagged.

"You have to eat." Tina held a Greek yogurt. "And Special Agent Wynns is here to see you."

Her admin was worried that she wasn't eating enough and had already brought her a sesame bagel, an apple and a bran muffin. She now added the yogurt and plastic spoon to the lineup on Nadine's desk.

Tina ushered in Special Agent Kirk Wynns, who was in charge of digital forensics. He had hazel eyes, a head of unmanageable red curls and a freckled complexion.

"Warrants were discharged for collection of the victims' phone records. My team assembled their devices. We've dumped all their data and made personal topology for everything they've run in the last ninety days. All three victims showed commonality of certain apps." He handed her a list, which she scanned, seeing the usual suspects that came with the phones and additional ones for weather, social media, travel, communication, banking, utilities. The list went on for two pages.

"We also ran a check on the use of these apps and discovered that two of the victims used ones for navigation shortly before their abductions."

Nadine sat up straight. Was the hunter using a lure to draw his victims into his chosen territory?

"Navigation to the trailheads?" she asked.

"No. Near them. Used GPS coordinates. They lead to nothing that I can see on Google Maps."

"That's odd. Isn't it?"

"I think so. Very exact. Like they were hunting for something."

"Which victims?"

"Darnell and Tolan."

"Not Karnowski?"

"No."

"Check her boyfriend's phone or his vehicle nav program. He was driving."

"We're doing that now. He's cooperating."

She studied the map he supplied. They'd have to know this was the woods. Nothing there. Just… what?

Remote locations. Private. What did he use to lure them in?

"Do any of you have a theory as to why they went to these locations?" asked Nadine.

"Unsure," said Wynns. "Still waiting for some of the details from their phones, but none of their families or coworkers know where these women were heading or why."

"Texts and alerts?" she asked.

"Not yet," said the agent. "Hopefully, sometime today."

"Do you have their phones?" asked Nadine, surprised.

"No. Digital footprint is all. It's good but not as complete as the actual phone."

Nadine smiled at him. "Knowing the site of capture is a huge step. Thank you."

The agent flushed. "I'll get you whatever else we turn up." He lifted a finger and then tapped at his phone. "One more thing. Coleman said we have a report on the bullet retrieved from Linda Tolan's apartment. Blood on the round is a match for Tolan and is the same caliber as her missing weapon."

"He used her own gun?" Nadine blinked in astonishment at the notion that this killer had stolen Tolan's gun and then fired it inside Linda's apartment. Careless… unless… it wasn't.

"No way to make a complete match without that weapon."

He'd used her gun. She was positive. He likely had an arsenal of hunting gear, including guns, but he'd chosen to use hers and leave a bullet behind.

"Thank you. I'll share all this with my team." She lifted the pages he'd provided.

She stared at the data sheets and maps feeling the pressure of minutes. They had to find Linda Tolan.

Tina stepped into her office immediately after Agent Wynns stepped out.

"Dr. Finch, Special Agent Skogen is on the line. He wants to speak to you."

"Okay."

Nadine took the call.

"He wanted us to know he would take her again!"

She'd never heard Skogen sound so angry.

"How do you know that?"

"The Orlando *Star* received an anonymous letter this morning. In it the sender takes credit for the first two murders."

"You sure it's from him?"

"Whoever wrote it said he'd take Tolan again."

This was going to terrify the public.

"Read it to me."

"Business-sized envelope says: 'FBI Agent Skogen.' Single folded sheet of paper, message is handwritten. He writes, 'Welcome to my hunting ground. So, you have collected my two little offerings. Wonderful to know you discovered my lures and have warned my quarry. It won't matter. They'll still come. I saw you at the press conference. But you left one of your pack behind. She's the one who found my little bird, isn't she? Well, I'll capture Lovely Linda again. Come and find her if you can.' That's it."

Nadine repressed the horror that clawed at her throat. She needed to think.

"I'm the member of the team left behind?"

"It seems that way."

She was already aware that this monster knew of her. Still, the letter shook her. Nadine cleared her throat, trying to summon her voice.

"You have the letter?"

"Our team is collecting it now."

"Where was it mailed?"

"Orlando."

"Video of sender?" she asked.

"Sent from a private shipping business. No camera."

"When?"

"FedEx delivery label says Thursday."

The day Linda was released from the hospital.

"He mentioned the press conference in the letter. He'll be following the media from here on out," said Skogen. "We can use that."

He was taunting the FBI. Reckless or overconfident? she wondered. The third possibility was that he was neither and his self-assurance was justified.

"Simon Kilpatrick was in custody most of Thursday," said Nadine.

"He couldn't have mailed the letter," said Skogen. "Didn't have time to get there before closing. So someone else mailed it for him, someone is just yanking our chain or—"

"Our killer mailed it," said Nadine, interrupting. "It fits. He's displayed his victims. Had direct contact with at least one member of your team. Mentioned the recapture of one of his victims before it happened and told you he's watching this investigation."

Skogen said nothing to this.

"Get me a copy of the letter."

"Yes. Will do."

Nadine ended the call, knowing two things. This killer was calling her out. And he wasn't going to stop until she stopped him.

She held their video call in her office. Both Juliette and Demko appeared virtually. She filled them in on the digital data collected so far.

Demko was interested in the GPS data and the slug recovered from Tolan's apartment. Juliette latched onto the common apps. All had grim demeanors, reflecting their worry over Tolan. Like her, Tina, Juliette and Demko felt the weight of hours and their continued failure to find her.

"How long do we have?" she asked.

Juliette confirmed Nadine's fears. "Based on all my findings, the time of death is three to four days after capture."

"So she's still alive?" asked Tina, wide-eyed as a baby fawn.

Nadine hoped so, but she knew, at this point, if Linda Tolan was not dead, she was wishing she were.

"We might find her," said Demko.

He'd been out with search and rescue since they'd learned of the abduction. The view of blue sky behind him told her that he still was.

"He might keep her until he has another," said Juliette. "It's what he did before."

Tina continued scribbling notes. She was turning out to be invaluable. Nadine had hired her out of pity and a feeling that they had too much in common for Tina not to be included in this odd inner circle. She'd underestimated her.

"Anything on the hair sample from the headband?" she asked Juliette. Nadine had put her in charge of all the physical evidence and she worked closely with both the ME, FBI lab technicians and Agent Wynns to keep track of it all.

"Hair samples are physically similar. Still awaiting DNA results. But those bleach stains. It's likely yours."

Nadine looked to Demko, sitting in his vehicle somewhere with a background of palmetto palms. "Anything to add?"

"No hits on Tolan's gun."

She turned to the communication from the killer.

"Skogen got me a photocopy of the letter sent to the papers." Nadine looked to Tina, who pulled up the document and shared her screen. They were silent for a few moments while they read this important bit of evidence.

Nadine looked down at the words on her copy, knowing he had written this, held the original paper in his hand and pressed a pen to the sheet to write his initial contact.

"Fingerprints?" asked Demko.

"None. And before you ask, it's a peel-off envelope. No DNA recovered."

Juliette's shoulders sank at this.

"Hunting ground, quarry, pack," said Demko. "Hunting terms."

"Pack seems more like a biologist," said Juliette.

"And offering sounds religious," added Tina. "And why call the two murdered women lures?"

"Lures to bring the FBI?" suggested Nadine. "We have not only his words but also his penmanship and the timing. He was bold enough to speak of a capture that he had not yet accomplished."

"Calling his shot," said Demko.

"What?" asked Nadine.

"Sports term," said Juliette. "Players in baseball and basketball sometimes signal their intentions. It shows bravado and a certain arrogance."

"Exactly," said Nadine. "Also, his grammar and punctuation are flawless. He's educated with a better than average mastery of the English language."

"Lefty," said Tina, her voice so soft, Nadine barely heard it.

"That's true," said Demko. "Lefties make their strokes from right to left. See here." He pointed to the top line of a capital *T* and the mark did seem to flow backward.

"He's printed this," said Juliette. "No cursive."

Nadine looked at the tight, neat lettering that sat in a perfectly straight line. "Thoughts and lettering are organized."

"Looks like he used a ruler or something. Straight as an arrow," said Tina and then sucked in a breath at the comparison.

Nadine had to get back to her profile and so she brought the meeting to a close. Tina and Juliette vanished.

Only then did she remember she hadn't asked Juliette about the autopsy on the body recovered in the lake.

Demko remained on the screen. It was clear from the angle that the phone was in the holder and he was driving.

"Arlo get that information on the red-tagged truck?"

"Sent it to his attorney. Arlo wrote to say thank you." Some part of her still worried she would regret helping him return to society.

He didn't sign off.

"What's up, Clint?"

"On my way back. I need to talk to Jack. He there?"

That would be bad. Up to now, the two alpha males had coexisted by occupying different spaces. Demko rarely came into the office, preferring to be out in the world, talking to law enforcement, helping with search and rescue and exploring the forest.

"Yes. Just a few minutes ago. About what?" she asked.

"Something I saw on the security tapes. Just a speculation that I'd like Jack to dispel."

"What exactly?" she asked.

"Let me find out if it's even a thing. Okay? Make sure he doesn't leave."

She didn't like where this was going, but she trusted him.

"Okay."

He disconnected and she stared at Tina.

"What's that about?" Tina asked.

"Something bad."

Demko appeared within the hour. Together they headed to Skogen's corner office, finding him behind his desk speaking to Agent Wynns.

"Demko," said Skogen by way of a greeting. Even the single word seemed a challenge.

"I've been over the hotel security tape of the second-floor corridor several times," said Demko.

Skogen's microtwitch set off alarm bells in Nadine. She'd studied body language extensively. Skogen was off balance.

"Security tape?" he asked, as if confused. Repeating the question gave him time to think and he was doing that now, judging from the upward angle of his gaze.

"Yes. The woman who came out to complain to Nadine about the noise in the hallway looks a lot like Linda Tolan."

# CHAPTER FIFTEEN

Nadine staggered back a step, but Demko caught her elbow and kept her from stumbling. She was no longer reading Jack's expressions and body language because the implications of what Demko suggested struck her like a thrown bucket of ice water.

"What are you saying? That I met her?" she asked, facing Demko and interrupting.

"That's what I'm trying to find out," said Demko and turned to Skogen.

Both Jack's hands were up before him, palms out, in a classic gesture of halt. Then he extended his arms, pushing the problem back at them.

"Look. We didn't think it was wise to bring this to Dr. Finch at this time."

"Why the hell not?" she asked, her voice sharp, accusatory. "How am I to create profiles if you withhold data?"

"We didn't want to alarm you with it. Things like this can rattle a person and we need your head in the game."

"So you put her in danger," said Demko.

"No. We have undercover agents on her floor, yours as well, and embedded in the hotel."

"How long have you known?" Demko asked.

"Digital forensics on Tolan's phone recovered her hotel registration. We made the connection yesterday."

Demko's hands went to his hips, his fingers just before the service weapon clipped to his belt.

"I want the adjoining room," said Demko.

"Occupied by our—"

"I want the adjoining room," he repeated.

Skogen sighed. "We'll work that out."

The tingling shuddered over her skin as she prepared for a dash to the bathroom if her stomach continued to pitch.

"Was the woman Nadine met in the hallway Linda Tolan?"

Skogen's voice held resignation. "Tolan stayed on her floor. She had the room next to Nadine reserved until Sunday. And, yes, Nadine and she spoke in the hallway the night before Tolan's abduction."

"Important detail. Don't you think? Because it means this killer might not have been targeting Tolan but was focusing in on your profiler."

Skogen pressed his lips together and said nothing.

Nadine's eye began to twitch. She pressed her hand to the spasm that continued to pulse.

"But you already knew that. Didn't you? And you are using her as bait."


Demko escorted Nadine back to her office, where Tina took over care and support. Demko headed back to confront Skogen. They took it behind the closed door of Agent Skogen's office, but the barrier wasn't thick enough to completely block their raised voices. She listened as she sipped the water from the mini bottle Tina had fetched.

"You sure you're going to be okay?" asked Tina. She hovered before Nadine and pressed a hand to her own throat, eyes wide as golf balls.

"Yes," said Nadine. If she kept her eyes closed, she could hear better and did not have to see Tina pacing.

"Your color is not good."

"Thanks for that."

There was no mistaking Demko's approach. He charged down the hall like an attacking grizzly. Tina flattened against the cabinets to avoid him. He drew up short before Nadine's desk.

"Come on," said Demko.

Tina stepped between him and her. "I'm not sure that's a great idea."

Nadine's eyes widened in astonishment that Tina would confront Demko when he was in such an agitated state. It showed either a monumental disregard for her own safety or outrageous courage.

"She's still white as a sheet," said Tina.

Demko ignored her as he might a troublesome moth flapping about him. He kept his gaze fixed on Nadine.

"Get whatever you need. We aren't coming back here today."

"Where are we going?"

"It's after six. I'm taking you for something to eat," he said.

"Clint, I have work to do on my profile. Linda's still out there. We have to find her."

He looked to Tina. "Did she eat lunch?"

Tina shook her head.

Demko turned back to Nadine. "Bring your laptop."

She did, along with her purse and briefcase.

"See you later, Tina."

She nodded, worrying her hands together as Nadine preceded Demko out of the office.

At his SUV, he opened her door and helped her into her seat, then climbed behind the wheel. They set off in silence. She was happy for the few moments to compose herself and he seemed to need the time to lower his blood pressure.

Clint spoke first. "Withholding that kind of evidence is reckless."

"Might have allowed me to sleep better not knowing."

He glanced in her direction and back at the road. "You don't really think that."

"No. I don't. It's always better to know and prepare."

They drove away from Ocala and into the national forest, their headlights casting out before them, chasing back the darkness. The trees loomed on both sides of the road, seeming to close in about her.

Nadine pressed a hand over her pounding heart.

"He wrote that letter to you and he's watching you."

"It's why Skogen used me as bait."

"I could kill him for that."

She glanced his way, noting his clamped jaw. He looked fully capable of making good on that threat. She was glad they were driving away from the temporary office.

"I wish it had worked," she whispered. "That we'd caught him."

But they both knew it might have worked in the opposite manner, with Nadine now locked in a hog trap deep in the dark, dank woods. Her stomach knotted.

"We'll catch him. But not that way."

She nodded, drawing on his confidence.

"Nadine, he knows that the FBI has a profiler. He stole your headband and put it in Tolan's vehicle. He's trying to figure out who you are. That's why he's watching the hotel. Likely, he's watching the FBI field office. He would have seen all of us. Now he has to fill in the pieces. Linda Tolan was just in the wrong place at the wrong time. If she had chosen a different hotel, she might still be alive."

"Or if she hadn't yelled at me."

He stilled and glanced at her. "You think that?"

"I don't know. Possibly."

"Why?"

"Because he could have taken me as easily as he took her." The truth of that froze the marrow in her bones. "But he didn't."

"No. He followed her into the Ocala Forest and took her there."

"Did he? Or did he lure her there?"

"How?"

She shook her head, unsure. "It's just a feeling. The others followed GPS coordinates to nowhere. We need to see if Linda Tolan did the same."

Her lips were still tingling. A sure sign that either her circulatory system or endocrine system had gone into protective mode.

*

Demko drove them to a marina with a dining room that overlooked the St. Johns River.

He ordered wine and they shared their appetizers—gator bites, deep fried and served with Thai chili sauce, and a smoked fish dip with saltines. The speed with which the food disappeared bore evidence that they were both starving.

The server arrived with jambalaya for him and the blackened mahi dinner for her.

Demko lifted the bottle of red wine, offering to refill her glass.

"No, thanks."

He shrugged, refilling his. Their interactions felt forced to Nadine. Something was happening between them and it made her uneasy.

They finished their meal and settled the bill, heading out.

Demko checked his phone, retrieving a message. "Hotel vacated the room beside yours. Looks like Skogen is good for something."

Once back at the hotel, he escorted her to her room.

"I've got to move my gear."

"I'll unlock the door between our rooms. Come in after you settle in."

*

Nadine changed out of her dress. She was in her nightshirt and matching shorts when Molly rushed forward to greet her, tail wagging. His dog was permitted on the floor by request of the FBI and Nadine was glad to have the canine nearby.

She found Clint in their mutual doorway. He gave his dog a few minutes and then called her back to his room.

"You going to work?" he asked.

"Too tired."

Demko seemed hesitant and their conversation faltered.

He did not step into her room. A new uncomfortable tension radiated between them. It made her nervous. His expression showed concern.

She'd made it a thing that he didn't stay over in her place, but he wasn't inviting her to his.

Was he waiting for her to invite him to cross the threshold?

Impasse. Stalemate.

She knew one thing; a stalled relationship was one that was destined to end. Only that scared her more than moving forward.

"Why don't you come in?"

He blew out a breath.

"Well, you're not breaking up with me because no woman would do that in her bedroom."

"Breaking up! Is that what you thought?"

"Nadine, we can barely carry on a conversation if it isn't work related. And every time I mention our relationship you change the subject. I guess I'm confused about what it is you want."

Nadine saw it all ahead of her. Their conversation about the relationship and where it was heading. His desires for them to take the next logical step. She still did not know what that step was because she had never allowed him to finish this conversation. She assumed it meant living together or possibly something that looked like an engagement. She saw the inevitable fight that would follow when she shot him down yet again.

He stared at her with earnest blue eyes and a hopeful expression. She felt the push and pull within her as she struggled against her fears. She glanced away and heard him sigh.

She crossed the distance between them, reaching up and stroking his cheek. His eyes drifted closed and he tilted his face into her palm. She lifted onto her toes and pressed her lips to his. He deepened the kiss as she threaded her fingers through his hair, pressing closer.

It wasn't fair to use her body as a diversion, but she needed his touch and thought he needed hers. There would be time for fighting tomorrow. But right now she needed comfort, solace and his mouth on hers.

The sound he made deep in his throat was a growl of primal need. She felt the answering heat rising inside her.

She tugged at his shirt, fumbling with the buttons. He stepped back into his room, dragging the garment up and over his head, tossing it away. She stripped out of her clothing and reached for his belt. He unclipped his weapon and badge, setting them on his side table, then dropped his khakis, kicking them aside.

They tumbled to the bed together. Her need made her frantic. She wanted to be closer to him, needed to feel the friction in the glide. She rolled on top of him in a frenzied dash to their fulfillment.

Afterward, they lay on their backs staring at the ceiling as the air-conditioning cooled the sweat from their feverish bodies and their heartbeats slowed. The next time was an unhurried sensual exploration. She was now well acquainted with the tempting hollows and hard planes of his chest and stomach. She loved stroking the perfect musculature of his torso.

This time when they fell into satisfied lethargy, he wrapped her in his arms, holding her tight to his chest, and stroked her hair.

He coiled one strand about his index finger and stared lazily down at her.

"It's not enough. I still want more."

She made a humming sound in her throat. "After a little rest."

"I'm not talking about the sex. Did you realize we are in your bed? That's a first."

She opened one eye to glance about, perceiving her earlier olive branch as a potential tactical error.

"So we are."

"That means you can't sneak off the minute I get too close."

"You're pretty close." She smiled up at him, hoping he would be disarmed by humor. He did not smile, and her heart gave a panicked jolt. She glanced toward the door connecting their rooms.

"I need something beyond a physical relationship, Nadine. I'm wondering if that is more than you are capable of giving me."

"Is that some sort of a threat?"

Demko dragged his index finger over her bare shoulder and kissed her forehead. "Why do you always see me, us, as a threat?"

"Because I don't want to lose you, but I'm not ready to 'move on.'" She made air quotes.

"Move on to someone else?" he asked.

"No, for us to move on. Can't we just keep things as they are?"

He gave a slow shake of his head, his smile a tragedy.

"Not unless you explain it to me."

She sat up. He let her go. Did he expect her to flee? The urge to disappear into the bathroom was almost too much to resist. Instead she scooted sideways so she could face him.

"My mom manipulated both me and my brother as kids. She withheld affection. She exploited us, controlled our behavior with bribery, threats and lies to keep us quiet and afraid. My therapist says my unwillingness to allow people too close comes from—"

He cut her off. "I don't want to know what your therapist said. I want to know how you feel about me."

"I think I just showed you how I feel."

"We've never had any issues in the bedroom, Nadine. I've never manipulated you and I never will. Is that really the issue?"

Nadine gnawed on her lower lip. He waited and waited and finally rolled from the bed and retrieved his trousers and drew them on. He didn't say anything as he reached for his service weapon and shield, but she knew. She was losing him and that scared her more than what might happen if she told him the truth.

"Wait," she said.

"For what?" He sounded so weary.

She scooped up her T-shirt and dragged it over her head. Then she grasped his hands and led him back to sit with her on the end of the bed.

"It's not just the past. It's the future."

He lifted a brow. "Go on."

Here it was. What she'd been afraid to say to him, all this time.

"I'm afraid of what you want and where it may lead us. I'm afraid that the next level and moving forward means a commitment. I'm afraid you want to get married again, and afraid you might want to have more kids." She felt as if she might throw up.

Instead of admitting that was what he was seeking, he said, "And that's a problem for you because…"

"I'm terrified that I'm not even capable of real intimacy or personal connections. I'm desperately afraid that my mother's influence has crippled me, prevented any true feelings of empathy."

Words were tumbling, one on another, rolling and sliding like a car on loose gravel.

"What if I have it? The killer code, that gene sequence correlated to extreme violence? What if I'm like *her* or if I could become like her? What if I'm like my great-grandfather who killed a guy in a bar fight? My grandfather who ran over his boss with a forklift and broke his neck. My brother—"

He gave her hands a little tug.

"None of them are you. And I hate to break it to you, but you've already formed interpersonal connections with Juliette and Tina and me. You are fully capable of relationships. You are fully capable of loving me. And you have empathy, too much empathy. It's why you are so good at this job. You empathize with everyone: the victims, the victims' families, the law enforcement professionals and the killer. You understand their minds in a way that is unique."

"Because I'm like them."

"I don't think that's why."

"We'll find out when I get that blood work."

"That stupid blood test? That's just an indicator of a higher percentage of violent behavior. *Your* violent behavior is what saved my life when the Copycat Killer attacked me. It was appropriate violence, necessary violence. You can do this, Nadine, the profiling, us, all of it. I believe in you."

She wanted to fall into his arms and hug him. She wanted to leave the conversation there, but she owed him the entire explanation. So she drew a long breath and blew it away, trying to verbalize her deepest dread in a quiet trembling voice.

"It's not just about me. I'm not just afraid of what *I* might do. I'm afraid of…" She'd nearly said it aloud but checked herself, editing her words. She had been about to say that she was afraid of what their kids might do, of what they might become because of the mix of poison her genes would inject into their being. Instead she edited, saying, "I'd be a terrible mother."

He released her hands and drew back. His brow furrowed and he looked stunned.

"That's a little fatalistic. Isn't it?"

"Is it?"

"I had no idea that's how you felt." He shifted his position, inching away from her.

"Isn't that where you want to take this?"

"Yes, but I think you'd be a terrific mom. But if you don't want kids, we can… we'll talk about it. We can…"

He couldn't think of a future for them that did not include children. And it was all clear to her. Clint did want all the things that scared her most profoundly. A wife, a family.

He was pacing now, like a trapped animal.

He stopped and looked at her with such a pained expression. It was finally hitting him that she might not be the one, and that killed her. She wanted to be the one. She wanted to share her life with this man. But her unwillingness to bear his children could be a deal breaker, even if she kept the real reasons for that choice hidden. It had, at least, temporarily stunned him speechless.

She had thought that it was unfair of her to keep him when she couldn't be all he wanted. But now she feared he might be thinking along the same lines. He might be preparing to end this right now.

So she did what she always did. She stalled.

"Clint, you need to give me some space to get this investigation going. I have to stop this killer and I need all my defenses up."

And this time, he seemed glad to agree. Happy to put their relationship on pause while he processed all she had told him and then, let her go.

Nadine reached out her hand and he took it, allowing her to draw him back to bed.

She couldn't help the thought that this might be the last time.

# CHAPTER SIXTEEN

## SATURDAY

She and Demko met in the lobby, after they'd ended up sleeping in their separate rooms, and drove the route along the trail Linda would have taken from the hotel, just after sunup the day she was first captured. He was unusually quiet. She felt herself losing him. Up until now she had been holding him at arm's length. Now he seemed ready to let go.

With their personal life in tatters, she turned to the case, studying the data provided by the FBI, as he drove. She now knew, thanks to digital forensics, and Tolan agreeing to let them access her phone while in the hospital, that all three victims had entered GPS coordinates. "Only Karnowski was accompanied. Darnell and Tolan plugged in coordinates and Karnowski did the same using her boyfriend's onboard nav system."

She had already seen the body dump for Karnowski and Darnell. Now she wanted to see the trail where Linda Tolan had been taken.

Nadine glanced down at her screen. "Tolan entered the GPS location at four fifty-five a.m." She returned her attention to Demko. "What's your take on where they were each headed?"

He grimaced. "Would be helpful to see the direct messages and alerts."

"Should have them soon."

"The most likely scenario is a drug deal or meeting someone for sex. Especially at that time."

"I'll look for that sort of app on the data sheet. But these are remote locations for either of those. Also, no one likes to get naked in these woods. The bugs are too vicious."

"That's why they invented backseats and air-conditioning."

She recalled missing an illicit affair in her last profile because the two meeting for sex were divorced and she hadn't considered that they were still sleeping together.

"I suppose this is somewhat of a halfway point between the east and west coasts. The parking area gives a natural place to meet."

"Exchange of goods. Something they bought online?" suggested Demko.

She'd have to check for sites like craigslist and eBay. The FBI could do that for her.

"A woman would have to be crazy to come all the way out here to do such a thing alone. Stupid dangerous. None of these women were stupid."

But all of them were still dead. She feared that also included Tolan.

They followed Tolan's route to the trailhead for the Yearling.

Nadine stared at the gap in the split-rail fence and the hollow in the undergrowth marking the path.

"Do you think this is named for the book?" she asked, staring up at the wooden sign that marked the start of a five-mile loop.

"What book?"

"*The Yearling* by Marjorie Kinnan Rawlings?"

Demko shook his head. "No clue."

He collected two water bottles from the cooler in the rear section and shoved one in the back pocket on each side of his khakis.

"You haven't read it?"

"No. You have?"

"Yes, of course. It's about a young boy who nurses a fawn. Mandatory reading in school."

She paused to stare across the lot and onto the sandy patch that disappeared through the pines and live oaks.

Together they exited the vehicle and walked toward the trail.

"The FBI has already been all over her route," he said.

"I know. I just want to get a feel for the place. GPS coordinates can only take me so far." She paused at sighting the yellow crime scene tape strung across the trail, surprised at this reminder of the initial abduction.

"Haven't they cleared the scene yet?" she asked.

"I would have thought so."

"They should have, because they didn't find anything."

He snorted. "But since Skogen has decided to withhold evidence, it's impossible to say."

"Thank you for defending me."

She squared her shoulders, preparing to follow Linda Tolan's route.

He laced his fingers with hers. Together they ducked under the yellow tape and walked into the forest.

"You tell me when you'd like to turn around," he said.

She nodded as they strolled side by side in the dappled sunlight. The temperature beneath the canopy of trees was a good ten degrees cooler than out in the sunshine. There was a dampness to the ground and the musty smell of rotting things. It did not take long for the bugs to find them. Demko offered her the spray.

"How would this look at five-thirty in the morning?" she asked.

"Predawn. Dark."

"Would she carry a flashlight?"

"She might."

"That would make her easier to spot." She scanned the treetops. "Early morning is the best time to spot animals, isn't it?"

"Birds, anyway."

"Summer tanager," said Nadine.

They continued on as she pictured Linda, carrying her photographic equipment. Holding a light, fiddling with the camera as she listened for the bird song, looking at the lacework of branches. What did that songbird sound like?

Nadine heard many birds but could not tell one from another. Tolan could have.

He nodded and then looked back on the trail, again. He had stopped more than once to scan behind them.

The breeze picked up, blowing sand into her eyes. She knew the signs. They were in for a thunderstorm. The trees made it difficult to see the sky, hard to know where the clouds were building into thunderheads, but the wind told her it came from the east.

"Better turn back," she said.

On the return, Demko did not hold her hand and stayed slightly ahead of her.

She was looking at the sky when Demko grasped her hand and drew her off the trail.

"What's—"

He lifted a finger to his lips.

She flattened against the tree trunk, suddenly terrified. Demko's hand went to his pistol and he rocked the weapon from its holster, bringing it up before him. The gesture did not reassure.

"Someone's following us," he said softly.

"A hiker?" she suggested, clutching at the safest explanation.

He shook his head. "Trail's closed."

She listened but heard nothing.

"He moved off the trail when we got near. Hiding over there." He gestured with his chin.

"You can't shoot someone for hiding."

He snorted. "We'll see."

She tugged his sleeve, silently imploring him to stay.

He glanced down at her. "Stay here."

In a moment he was gone, running in a semicircle across the trail and out of sight.

The sharp bark of Demko's voice made Nadine jump.

"Police! Hands where I can see them. Now!"

She heard a muffled reply but could make out nothing of what the person he was shouting at was saying.

"On the ground. Hands out to the sides. Do it!"

Nadine peeked out from behind the tree. From her vantage she could see Demko standing, gun held in two hands and pointed at the back of a man's head. His target sprawled before him on the ground. There was something large and black in his right hand. It looked like the kind of automatic weapon she had seen during her FBI training.

She crept forward and heard Demko instructing him to sit up.

"Who are you?" he asked.

As she inched closer, she saw that the object beside the man was something more dangerous than an automatic weapon. It was a camera with a giant zoom lens.

She'd looked into a lens like that before. Twice, actually. Once after her mother's arrest and throughout her trial. The second time was a year and a half ago when the media discovered who she was and that she was profiling the copycat killer while sleeping with the lead detective, Demko. Sweat beaded on her upper lip. Her heart pounded in her throat.

The man retrieved his wallet from his front pocket. The ball cap on his head and the lowered tilt of his chin kept her from seeing his face, but she did see the flaxen ponytail thrusting from the gap in the back of the hat. He wore tan and olive-green clothing that seemed designed to allow him to disappear into the landscape.

Demko accepted the offered ID before beginning a string of profanities. He glanced in her direction holding the credential so she could see it read PRESS. Her stomach dropped.

If this fellow knew who they were, it would certainly end up in the papers.

"Why are you following us?" asked Demko.

"FBI press release said that we have a serial killer stalking the hiking trails in the Ocala Forest."

"You thought I was the killer?" asked Demko.

The man shifted uncomfortably in the leafy debris.

"You're a cop. I know a cop car when I see one. Figured you to have something to do with the case so… What's your name, Officer?"

"You tell me. You're the reporter."

Nadine had reached the trail and was approaching the pair outside the line of sight of the seated man. Demko spotted her and gave a nearly imperceptible shake of his head; then he waved her off. She stood frozen for just a moment and then realized he was telling her to return down the trail alone. She gave her head a definitive shake. She was not going anywhere in this forest by herself.

His lips pursed and he glared at her before returning his attention to the seated man, who was now looking over his shoulder at her.

"Who's your partner?" asked the reporter.

Demko said nothing as Nadine moved off the trail and again out of sight.

If he figured out who she was, her anonymity was blown. The media would set up their tarpaulins and the three-ring circus would commence. Nadine hated the spotlight. It made her sick to her stomach and reminded her of all of the terrible parts of her life. It took her right back to the courthouse in the three days she testified against her mother.

She wiped the sweat from her lip.

Nadine wanted many things in her life. Notoriety she had already, and hated it. She did not want to be some celebrity profiler with her own talk show. She wanted to be left alone with the luxury of an ordinary life.

She saw the chances of that fading with the day's sunlight.

"If you're arresting me, you have to give me your name," said the reporter.

She turned back just in time to see Demko looming over him. She hoped he wasn't going to do anything that would get him fired. She opened her mouth to warn him, then realized she was about to say his name and closed it again.

"Let me get out my phone so I can record this conversation."

Demko was staring at her now. He motioned her back toward the trailhead and this time she went.

"Pull up the clock app." That was Demko's voice, a command, followed by a pause. "Start the timer." Another pause. "You leave this spot before ten minutes and I will arrest you. Understand?"

"On what charge?"

"Trespass and obstructing a police officer. You crossed under the crime tape, buddy."

This was met with silence.

"Ten minutes," said Demko.

A moment later, Demko emerged onto the trail carrying both the man's wallet and his camera. He captured her elbow, bustling her along.

From behind them came the shout from the trespasser.

"You can't take those!"

She glanced back over her shoulder to see the man standing in the underbrush clutching his phone.

"He's right," she said, referring to the reporter's equipment.

Demko paused to check the camera and removed the flash card.

"Hey! That's my property. I'm reporting this!"

"I'd expect nothing less from a reporter," Demko mumbled as he set the camera on the trail. He removed the press badge from the man's wallet. Then he dropped the wallet beside the camera and turned to Nadine.

"This is bad," she said.

"I'll say. Thought we might have found him. Instead we get punked by some reporter." He glanced at the identification. "Timothy Murphy. Orlando *Star*."

"It's happening again." She hoped the dizziness was from the heat, but that didn't explain the sharp pangs in her stomach or the dread collecting within her heart.

Nadine had gained nothing to help find Linda Tolan from their outing, and despite the FBI and search and rescue's efforts, Tolan remained missing and Nadine feared she was dead.

Downhearted, she sat in the SUV as Demko drove, checking her messages, hoping for a miracle.

She found an email from Arlo asking her to call him today between eleven and twelve, when he would be waiting by the prison's communal phone banks. She glanced at the time, realizing it was already a few minutes after noon, but she placed the call.

The phone rang once and then was answered by an unfamiliar male. She asked for her brother and then waited as the inmate answering, from the phone bank in the prison, handed the receiver to him.

"Hey, Arlo. What's up?"

"I was afraid you didn't get my email," Arlo said.

"Just read it. Sorry I'm late."

"It's okay. Thanks for the red-tag information."

"Oh, you're welcome."

"My attorney called that FBI guy you worked with."

"Torrin?"

"Yeah. He was pretty hyped about it, I guess. Said that this might close a cold case. May just get me out of here."

It was what she had hoped and feared. Arlo on the outside. The unknown future. But she forced herself to tell him that his news was wonderful. Because she could think of little worse than knowing your sister did not have your back.

"Is that why you wanted me to call?" It didn't seem like reason enough. A thank you could wait for her regular visit.

There was no answer.

"Arlo?"

"The Copycat Killer managed to get a message to me."

"How?"

"Mailed from the Sarasota jail, I think."

Nadine's skin itched.

"Wants us to write to each other and asked about you, wanted your new address."

"Did you write back?" she asked.

"You think I would? That asshole shot you."

She smiled at that. After all these years, Arlo still came to her rescue.

"I just wanted you aware that this maniac is still… consumed by you. Thinking about you. Be careful."

Her stomach twisted, but she managed to hold her tight smile. "Always."

"See you soon?"

"Count on it."

They said their good-byes and she tucked away her phone.

At the hotel she learned that Skogen had a place rented for her team. Somewhere the killer didn't know about. Tina told her that they could move in immediately.

They checked out together, moving to a turnkey town house in a gated community. Skogen's team escorted them to ensure they were not followed.

It did not take Tina or Juliette long to recognize the tension vibrating between her and Demko.

Juliette pulled her aside as they were retrieving their luggage from their vehicles.

"What's going on?" she asked.

"It's nothing. We just had a tiny disagreement."

Juliette gave her a skeptical look. "Doesn't seem tiny."

Nadine lowered her largest suitcase to the ground and extended the handle. Then she grabbed the carry-on. It thumped to the pavement. She really needed to get that brick out of her luggage.

Beside her, Juliette shouldered a large duffel and grabbed her fishing pole.

"Okay. I won't pry. But I'm here if you want to talk."

"We're all here. Aren't we?"

April Rupp, the owner of the adjoining town house and their new landlady, stepped out on her landing for the fifth time since handing over the keys to Demko.

It annoyed Nadine that Mrs. Rupp had decided that Demko was the leader of this group. The woman was chatty, and Nadine suspected she used her front gardens as a means to gossip with neighbors.

The woman wore oversized sunglasses and her broad-brimmed hat made it impossible to see anything of her hair. She had an athletic figure and Nadine judged her to be in her mid-sixties. From the snatches of conversation she overheard, Rupp was from South Carolina's Lowcountry, was recently widowed and lived with two elderly dogs and one new kitten. She had brought her dogs out to meet Molly, and all three seemed to be getting along in a blur of sniffing and tail wags.

Nadine had left it to Demko, the presumed leader, to furnish the information he wished without revealing anything that could not be blathered about the neighborhood. The agreed-upon story was that they had a short-term contract with the state, surveying infrastructure.

Nadine thought Juliette extremely brave to put Jack-Jack's cage on the landing so that the dogs could get acquainted with the cockatoo. But when Radar, Mrs. Rupp's dachshund, got too close, Jack-Jack nipped his nose, and Nadine recognized she'd underestimated the bird, who did not need defending. Radar yipped and retreated.

Tina wisely carried her gray-and-white tabby cat, Muffin, into the room that she and Juliette decided to share so that the study with the sleeper sofa could be used as a work area for all of them.

Nadine left the unpacking for later and hooked her laptop to the Ethernet in the study, diving back into her work, interrupted around suppertime by the enticing aroma of fried food.

In the kitchen, she discovered Clint setting out paper plates and Tina and Juliette unpacking containers as Molly watched the proceedings with interest.

Nadine thought that communal living might not be so bad after all.

"Mrs. Rupp stopped by again. Brought brownies," said Tina.

"She said, 'The normal kind'!" Juliette laughed. "Gave her a chance to snoop around. Took me almost twenty minutes to get her out the door. She's harder to get rid of than bedbugs."

Despite everything, despite the fact they were only all here because a killer was directly trying to access Nadine, she felt oddly safe and happy with her friends about her. The fact that the town house had a security system didn't hurt.

Although things were smooth on her living situation, the strain continued with Demko. Tina and Juliette did their best to ignore the tension.

They were all keenly aware that another day had passed with no sign of Linda Tolan.

The badly decomposed body, found in the water outside Fort McCoy, remained unidentified, but no women had gone missing.

Juliette had told her that a backlog at the ME's office had pushed the autopsy until next week.

Her team members were not the only ones frustrated. Skogen and his team seemed to think she could magically identify their unsub from the information they'd collected.

"It's like having a family," said Tina, passing the brownies and bringing Nadine out of her thoughts.

Her comment struck Nadine hard. None of them had normal families. All were complicated: Nadine and Demko adopted by aunts, Juliette adopted by the same DA who convicted her mother, and Tina spending her teen years in foster care.

After the brownies had made their rounds, Juliette passed out what looked like a DNA bar graph to each of them.

"What's this?" asked Tina.

But Nadine knew. It was the enzyme sequence testing that would show if they had the genes that might indicate a predisposition to violence and murder. Juliette already had their results.

"How'd you get this so fast?" asked Demko.

"Polytech is close by and I went to school with a guy that works there."

Polytech was at least ninety minutes away, but Juliette had obviously found the time. Nadine realized that with the initial victims' bodies now released to their families for burial, Juliette might not have very much to do.

"These are our tests?" squeaked Tina, studying the printout. "What does it say?"

"Let me preface this by saying the relationship between violent offenses and this sequence is in dispute by experts," said Juliette.

Tina gave her a blank look.

"Researchers don't agree because the study's subject pool was exceedingly small and from an all-male prison population. So please don't place too much weight on the results."

"What are the results?" asked Nadine.

Juliette read from a sheet of copy paper. "Juliette Hartfield, positive." She glanced at them. "That means, yes, I have this sequence." She returned her attention to the sheet. "Arlo Howler, positive."

Nadine sucked in a breath. Demko scowled at Nadine.

"He gave permission," she said.

Juliette continued. "Clinton Demko, negative. Tina Ruz, negative."

Tina sagged, head down. Demko turned his worried expression on Nadine.

"Nadine Finch, positive." Juliette lowered the page.

"Fifty-fifty," murmured Demko. "Me, no. You, yes."

Nadine's head sank. Both she and Arlo had the gene repeats. Both carried the genetic marker for violence.

Juliette placed a hand on Nadine's knee. "You're a good person, Nadine. Don't let this make you doubt that for a minute. These really don't mean anything."

But it did matter. She never believed she could be completely good.


Nadine's phone vibrated with a text. She'd been sitting alone in her room, processing her thoughts around the gene sequencing. It confirmed all her worst fears. And what could it mean for her and Demko?

She returned to her friends, still seated at the kitchen table, to read them the text.

"Skogen wrote: 'Orlando *Star* asked me to confirm that Dr. Nadine Finch is our lead profiler.'"

The word was out. And there was no more hiding for Nadine.

# CHAPTER SEVENTEEN

## SUNDAY

Nadine was the lead headline the following day. Skogen had given no comment. But the paper had confirmation from an anonymous source. The article highlighted her role in the capture of the Copycat Killer, her mother's horrific crimes and even gave a summary of the conviction of her murderous grandfather.

Alone at the kitchen dinette, Nadine studied the newspaper article on her laptop in their new residence. Both Tina and Juliette were out jogging, so she had a few moments' peace before heading up to Lawtey to visit Arlo.

Nadine had not planned to visit him this weekend, but their recent phone conversation had changed her mind.

She had nearly completed reading and her second cup of coffee when there was a hammering on the front door. Muffin, who, she had not realized, was in the room, shot off the adjacent chair and darted out, and she followed.

Demko pounded down the hall in his gym shorts.

"Don't answer that!" He hurried past her to the foyer. At the entry, he pushed Molly away with his leg and held his pistol behind his back as he opened the door.

She had expected reporters, but it was Mrs. Rupp, dressed in jean shorts and a floral top. Without her hat and sunglasses,

Nadine noted, her face showed a deep tan that made her sun-damaged skin look weathered as old wood.

She gripped the Saturday paper in her hand.

"I had no idea you were FBI or what you all were tied up in. Had I known, I never would have sublet this place."

"Sorry you're unhappy," said Demko. He stepped out onto the stoop. "But I believe you signed the agreement."

"I want you out. The lot of you." She aimed the paper at Nadine, who now stood in the doorway.

Across the cul-de-sac, beyond the parked cars, a man paused to watch the scene as his Jack Russell terrier sniffed at a mailbox. Nadine glanced back to Demko.

"Unfortunately, we have a legally binding contract," said Demko.

"We'll see about that. I'm calling my lawyer."

"You do that. Have a nice day."

Rupp was not finished, but Demko motioned Nadine inside and then closed and locked the door.

Demko turned to her. "She's going to call the newspapers. Guaranteed."

"They'll come here. Camp out front. And if they know where I am, so will he." Her words sounded frantic, disjointed. Nadine clutched her empty coffee mug feeling the tears welling up. "The case has stalled and we haven't found Linda Tolan. By now, she's probably dead."

"Come here," he ordered.

She did and he folded her into his strong arms. Molly jumped up, trying to lick Nadine's face.

Nadine was still crying when her phone began ringing.

"They got my number," she said, drawing back, certain it was a reporter. But a check showed it was Skogen. She took the call. "What's up?"

"I wanted to alert you that the Putnam County Sheriff's Office has informed me that your brother, Arlo Howler, helped his officers identify the possible search location of two missing persons in a cold case. He pinpointed a search area within the National Forest."

"What? When?"

"Yesterday afternoon sometime. A search is under way. I'm just learning about this."

Nadine flipped the call to speaker so Demko could hear.

"So my brother was out of prison yesterday?"

"Yes."

Nadine pressed her free hand flat against her chest, feeling the drumbeat of her heart. "I spoke to him at noon on Saturday. He didn't mention anything."

"Because they wouldn't have given a prisoner advanced notice."

That did make sense.

"But why wasn't I told?"

"No alert to family, either. I only found out because Special Agent Coleman spotted them setting up a search and rescue operation. She called me and they just got back to us."

Nadine groaned and Demko stepped up beside her, cupping the phone, and her hand, in his.

"They found something. Sheriff's office is calling in anthropologists from the museum up in Tampa. He is requesting that your ME come out. But they can't reach her by phone."

"She's running."

"Okay. Have her call me."

"Are you going?" she asked.

"Me? Why? It's unrelated. Graves are over two decades old."

Skogen ended their conversation. Then Nadine thumped to her seat at the dinette. Her stomach twisted tight as a boa constrictor.

"I think they just found my father."

*

Juliette told Nadine that the grave site was near the St. Johns River outside DeLand. Closest access road was County Road 42. Arlo had identified a primitive camping area in the Ocala Forest called River Forest. She knew the place instantly and the connection between this location and a double murder sent every hair follicle of her body lifting.

Her mother used to take them there to fish and one of her victims had been found in the river here.

Arleen sometimes drove them along a remote access road paralleling the river's course. Nadine recalled the hiss of the sand spraying the wheel wells as her mother took the rutted road at high speed and in high spirits. The reason for her gaiety now made Nadine's skin prickle.

The site just off the road was close to their trailer in DeLand, remote enough to be quiet, but public enough to draw the sort of folks that liked to avoid paying for camping and enjoyed illegally hunting alligators at night. Nadine knew that anything dropped in that murky water rotted or was eaten in short order.

"Truck was red-tagged on Route 42, here," said Demko, pointing at the map on satellite view.

Nadine zoomed in on the donuts. The evidence was still there, a brilliant white sand oxbow cut into the emerald green foliage. "Is this where you're heading?" she asked Juliette.

"They just said they'd meet me where River Forest Boulevard crosses the electric lines."

Nadine pointed. "The turnoff is back here. If you get to the power lines, you missed it. Look on the left. The whole thing is unpaved."

"If you know the route, maybe I'll follow you," said Juliette.

Nadine and Demko rode together and Juliette shadowed in her Subaru wagon. The ease with which Nadine found the utility trail was disquieting. At 10:40 a.m., they pulled up behind a sheriff's vehicle and two from the Florida Museum of Natural History.

Juliette found a sheriff's deputy, who agreed to escort them. Deadman's Circle looked much as it always had, a large near-perfect ring of sparkling white sand, the center of which was all scrub grass.

Leaving the climate-controlled air-conditioning and stepping out into the blazing sun gave Nadine an instant headache. They were met by a forest ranger and second sheriff's deputy. They followed the deputy along a narrow gash, recently cut through the undergrowth in the palmetto fronds. Nadine knew that the stem of each leaf held a saw blade of jagged barbs capable of slicing skin and snagging clothing. No one would travel far in this dense foliage without both a machete and a very good reason.

Had Arlo walked this way just recently? Had her mother? She looked in the sand for Arlo's footprints but saw just a jumble of many.

She noted the new cuts on the palmettos and also the old ones, higher up, the branches that were missing from a long-ago traveler. Arlo had taught her how to find the animal trails, to make passing through simpler. She paused to finger a gash in the trunk of a palm at eye level. No animal made this, at least, not a four-legged one. Air currents rippled across her neck and she could sense her mother.

Nadine continued after Demko and Juliette.

They did not have far to travel. She came up short, nearly bumping into Demko's back.

Three men stood in an excavated pit some three feet deep.

Was this her father's grave?

"Why dig here?" she asked Demko.

He had his hands on his hips. "Dunno."

Juliette left them, speaking to a woman who was kneeling on a blue tarp and placing a long bone with others.

Nadine gravitated toward the tarp upon which two skeletons were taking shape. One was completely bone. The other had some sort of desiccated flesh and tendon still connected on several joints. One of the hands seemed to be wearing a shriveled skin glove and there were patches of hair on the skull.

Her nose wrinkled at the grisly sight. She wondered what her mother would think, seeing her work. But she knew. This aberration would delight her. She'd be thrilled to see even a photo of this carnage.

Juliette returned to them.

"They've got most of the pieces already."

"How did they know where to dig?" Nadine asked.

The woman on the tarp peeked up from beneath a large canvas hat.

"A tip from a convicted felon gave us this animal trail. From there we searched for changes in vegetation. The foliage over this spot was obviously different. Then we found the depression."

"You use probes to detect gases?" asked Juliette.

"Didn't need to. We have ground-penetrating radar. Got it from a grant to study Native American shell mounds," said the scientist.

Juliette gave a low whistle. "Nice."

"The soil is clearly discolored, so after we got down a foot or so, we knew we had something." She beamed up at them, like a dog presenting a dead possum to its owner.

Nadine's instinct was to back away. Instead she looked beyond the woman to the bodies.

"Dr. Burton," said Juliette. "These are members of my team. Detective Clint Demko, and this is our team leader, Dr. Nadine Finch." She turned to them. "Dr. Burton is an anthropologist from the Florida Museum of Natural History."

The scientist scrambled to her feet and wiped her hands on her thighs, removing much of the soil and sand before extending her hand to Nadine.

"Oh, gosh. Dr. Finch, it's an honor. Call me Claire. Do these two have some connection with the missing women?"

Nadine clasped her hand, which was damp with sweat, before releasing it to find her palm coated with sand.

"Not at all. This one is personal. The convict that gave you that tip was my brother. One of these remains could be among my mother's victims. The male, if you find one, might also be my father."

The woman's brows lifted in shock. She opened her mouth as if to ask a follow-up, glanced at Juliette's face and then reconsidered. Juliette would answer the inevitable questions. Nadine was grateful.

Right now the heat and the heavy air made breathing difficult.

Dr. Burton left them for the pit and Nadine tried not to notice her relaying the arrival of a celebrity.

Demko leaned in, nudging her. "Think they'll ask you to sign one of their trowels?"

She tried and failed to hold a smile.

"You all right?"

In answer she shook her head. Demko stepped nearer. The three of them stared down at the human remains spread out on the tarp like some dreadful picnic.

Juliette leaned in. "You see, that one was buried in the soil. This one might have been wrapped in something like a canvas tarp. It affects the decomposition." She pointed, her voice animated with excitement. "Oh look! A belt buckle."

Nadine stared at the larger skeleton that peered out at her through empty eye sockets.

"I'm just going to go have a chat with the anthropologists," said Juliette, sensing Nadine's mood, and hurried off.

"How can anyone enjoy this sort of work?" asked Nadine.

Demko snorted. "One might say the same thing about your job."

"That's true."

"Hell of a way to spend a weekend."

They stood for a long while watching the anthropologists carefully excavating the grave site.

"You think it's him?" Demko asked.

"Location seems right. Age of the skeleton, too, maybe, though I'm no expert." The heat and humidity drained Nadine. Sweat soaked her clothing and ran between her breasts. She attributed the nausea flipping her stomach to the heat and not to images of her mother dragging these two bodies into the woods.

How many times had Nadine and her family visited the River Forest camp area? The real reason for her mother's fondness for this site sickened her. Her stomach rolled, sloshing the coffee, churning it to acid.

She stared at the larger skull, noting a missing tooth and several fillings in the lower jaw. She turned her head, twisting for a better look without having to step closer.

"Is there something wrong with the eye socket?" she asked.

"You mean besides the crushed skull?" he asked. "Looks like someone hit him with an ax."

"Shovel," she said. "That's what she told me."

He glanced at her.

"Remind me what your mother told you?"

"Something about a guy who owed her money. Wouldn't pay up and they argued. She hit him with a shovel. She claims it was an accident, but who swings a shovel at someone's head not expecting to kill them?"

"Just said, 'a guy'?"

"Yeah. I told you I had suspicions about the possibility of this being our missing father. She said he abandoned us. Ran off with someone. She was lying. She's always lying. I should have known that, even then."

She tried and failed to control her ragged breathing as she faced the truth. Her father was really gone.

"Let me check in with Juliette and tell her we're leaving."

While she waited, one of the anthropologists approached, placing a green vinyl sandal on the tarp beside the smaller skeleton.

The footwear looked nearly new except for the dirt and sand clinging to the crevices.

Nadine stared at the object, puzzled at its pristine condition.

"Man-made materials," he said, pointing. "Vinyl doesn't break down with bacteria or rain. The elements never touched it. Take years for it to rot."

"Hmm," said Nadine.

"You're Dr. Finch," he said.

She nodded.

"I understand you might be a relation," he said. "I'm sorry for your loss. I hope this might bring you some closure."

She frowned. As if that were even possible.

He shoved his dirty hands in his pockets and rocked forward and back. Nadine cast him a questioning look.

"Yes. Right. Well, the thing is I've been sent over to ask if you would be willing to provide a—"

"Don't tell me. A DNA sample?"

"Yes. Exactly."

Nadine pressed a hand to her forehead and said, "Why not?"

He drew on a latex glove, offered a swab and she brushed it inside her gum before handing it back.

When Nadine's phone rang, she nearly jumped out of her skin. A glance told her that it was Skogen. They must have added a cell phone tower somewhere close by because service here used to be hit and miss.

"Hello, Jack."

"Listen, we now have new data from the three known victims' phones. We now have a complete list of common apps. I'm sending it to you. We flagged all the ones that had notifications switched on."

"I need to see the text messages and direct messages."

"Yes. I should have it on the file share soon."

"Anything else?"

"No. You?"

"Have you figured out yet how my involvement was leaked to the press?" She suspected that the reporter, who had followed them into the woods, might have figured out who they were.

"Not yet. Believe me, I'm giving it my full attention. I'm going to find whoever did this."

"And do what?"

He paused. Was he shocked that she wanted to know exactly what he planned to do to the person on his team who leaked her identity to the press? He shouldn't be. In many ways she was, after all, her mother's daughter.

"I said I'd handle it."

The sound she made in the back of her throat revealed dissatisfaction with that answer.

"I'm sending you the data I mentioned. Let us know if you have any questions."

"Yup. I've got to go. Phone battery," she said, keeping the lie short before signaling to Demko that she was ready, and walking away on the single-file trail.

They had missed lunch and she'd sweated so much that her head pounded, and her leg muscles trembled. Around them, the shadows loomed, and lizards scurried, hopping out of their way.

Her relief at reaching the road was short-lived as the late-afternoon sun had lost none of its potency. Leaving the leafy canopy, she found the air ten degrees warmer and the glare of sun on the sand made her squint.

Her phone bleeped an alert. She glanced down, seeing the text from Skogen. He'd sent her a link to the data.

"I need something to drink and a Wi-Fi connection."

Demko found both at a grill on the St. Johns. They sat at a table by the window overlooking the moorings for the houseboats. From the ceiling hung pendant lights and colorful Styrofoam floats from crab traps. There was plenty of beer on tap and specialty drinks, including a tempting Bacardi rum bucket, bright blue, with plenty of crushed ice, served in a plastic sand pail, but she ordered water.

Weekend or not, she was on the job.

They had landed at the grill squarely between lunch and dinner and only a few patrons still lingered over their meals.

They ordered as Nadine itched to reach for her laptop.

Instead she took a moment to look out at the gently flowing wide river.

Lunch arrived. The aroma of fried clams and hush puppies made her mouth water. After lunch she booted up her laptop as Demko sipped his iced tea and scribbled notes on his pad.

She studied the inventory of purchased apps shared by all three victims. It was a long list that included games, banking, entertainment and weather programs. They all shared several apps for airlines, hotels and social media. She glanced at the navigation apps, knowing some of the women had used these to plot the route to their own deaths. The list included data from Rita Karnowski's boyfriend's phone and vehicle. Nadine noted that Betters used his onboard vehicle navigation system to find that trail's parking area. But what had drawn them to these locations?

She skimmed down the list, focusing on the apps set to deliver notifications. Several she didn't recognize.

Nadine paused as two drew her notice. One was a sky guide used to identify stars, set to send alerts and shared by all three women, but it was unlikely that they would have used this during the day.

The second one was for bird-watching. It grabbed her attention for three reasons: it was shared by Darnell, Karnowski and Tolan, notifications for each was switched on—and she and Juliette both also had this application. Was this the reason these women ventured off into remote locations?

Bird-watching?

Linda Tolan was photographing birds for a magazine.

She needed to find out if any of the victims had received notifications from this or any other app the day of their disappearances.

Nadine retrieved her phone and checked her settings. She had the notifications on the bird-watching app switched off. But Juliette's was switched on.

If Juliette were to review her old notifications, would any match those used by the victims?

*Juliette!*

Nadine pulled up Juliette's number from her list of recent calls. "What's up?" asked Demko.

She explained as she placed the call.

"Might be a coincidence," he said. But his expression said she was onto something.

"You think so?"

"I think I'd proceed as if you figured it out, until I knew otherwise."

The phone call flipped to voicemail.

"Damn it!" She lowered her phone. "No answer. We have to warn Juliette."

# CHAPTER EIGHTEEN

## MONDAY

The knock on her door woke Nadine to daylight. She stared at an unfamiliar ceiling fan, trying to orient herself. Morning, the town house, Monday and she was back in goddamned Central Florida.

Yesterday they'd delivered the message to Juliette not to follow any bird notifications and the Bureau was collecting alerts now.

There was another series of taps on her door. She groaned and rolled, grasping her phone as the tapping came again.

"Nadine?" It was Demko's voice.

"Yes. I'm up." She wasn't because she'd tried to use her phone to stop his knocking.

"Can I come in?" he asked.

She threw back the covers and swung her bare feet to the vinyl flooring, forcing herself vertical. She raked a hand through her hair and tugged down her cotton nightshirt so that it covered her.

"Yes, come in."

The door creaked open and he peered inside. They'd agreed to keep separate rooms, mainly not to irritate Tina and Juliette. Neither she nor Demko was a quiet lover. She flushed at the view of him, shirtless, in a pair of low-slung gym shorts. Demko half-dressed was a better wake-up than any alarm. He seemed momentarily stunned at finding her wearing nothing but a thin veil of cotton that barely reached her thighs.

Molly pushed past Demko and greeted her, tail wagging as she pranced. Nadine patted her shoulder and she retreated out the door.

"What time is it?" she asked.

"After eight."

"What?" She reached for her phone and found it dead. She stared at the black screen in confusion.

"Power outage. Did you hear the storm last night?"

She shook her head and retrieved her battery charger, plugging in her device and seeing the charging icon appear.

"I got a call from Skogen, trying to reach you. He's with the District 5 ME. They have another body."

Her heart jackhammered in her chest. "Is it Tolan?"

"Unknown. I've got to find Juliette, she's out on a run."

"Not alone?"

"Tina and security. The female special agent. What's her name?"

"Coleman."

"Right." He left her.

Nadine finished in the bathroom and dressed. Her phone rang and she scooped it up. The display showed only a 5 percent charge and that Skogen was calling.

"Where are you?" Skogen asked, loud enough that she had to hold the phone away from her ear.

"Sorry." She offered no explanation. "What's up?"

"Boater found a body."

"Tolan?"

"Possibly. Body is female, found in Silver Glen Springs State Park."

She knew the natural springs. The limestone opening poured millions of gallons of freshwater a day from the aquifer, creating a lagoon as clear as the Caribbean Sea. She and Arlo had swum there often, trying to breach the submerged opening, only to be pushed back out by the force of water. The sandbar just beyond created a destination and natural docking spot for the many houseboats on the river. The spring created a quarter-mile pool that flowed into Lake George.

Now she pictured the idyllic destination with a body pushed by that same constant current.

"We're on the way."


The state park was as Nadine remembered it as a kid, except for all the sheriff's boats, where Skogen and Juliette, who'd gone on ahead, waited. Skogen scowled at Demko's arrival but did not prevent him from boarding the vessel, held steady by one of the rangers.

Allie Lowe, a Marion County sheriff, ferried them to the crime scene. She was a striking middle-aged woman, with a uniform so pristine she looked like an advertisement to join the force.

The body lay on the far side of the lagoon, pushed up a channel as far as the current could convey it to tangle in the tall reeds. The corpse looked more like a movie prop than the remains of a human being.

Sheriff Lowe idled the engine, angling them toward shore.

"We believe someone dropped it from the camping area and the spring's flow pushed it there," she said, indicating the developing crime scene.

They beached and stepped from the vessel to stand together on the shore, where they had a clear view of the remains.

"How long has it been in the water?" asked Demko.

"Unknown," said Lowe, at the same time as Juliette said, "Not long."

Dr. Kline and Juliette waded into knee-deep water for the extraction.

"I want you and Juliette to be present at the autopsy. I've asked the district ME to push it."

The extraction took much of the morning. Skogen remained with Nadine as she waited anxiously to hear if this was Linda Tolan.

At last the District 5 ME returned, wet from the waist down, with bits of debris on her pants.

"Okay, body is gone, so we can head back to District 5. You can meet us there."

"Is it Tolan?"

"This one has implant dentures. Tolan didn't. So, no. Not her."

Nadine's shoulders sagged. It wasn't Linda.

But then, who was it?

Nadine and Juliette headed to the morgue, while Demko remained at the scene. Dr. Kline sat at her computer monitor, glanced to the door and removed her glasses.

"There you are." She rose and led them out. "Busy day."

They paused to don their PPE and then entered the autopsy room. At first glance the room might have appeared to be an operating theater except for a few key differences. The surgical tools were the same. The industrial sink and coiled hose and hanging stainless-steel scale were not.

Here, none of the machinery was associated with monitoring vital signs and, though the tables were stainless steel, each had a lip and trough to catch fluids. Nadine had the darkly bizarre thought that this made them resemble huge turkey platters.

Beyond double doors sat the refrigerator in which the grim queue likely formed.

Kline seemed not to notice Nadine's disquiet as her gaze flicked around and settled on a bone saw.

They paused at one of three tables between two bodies. On the right was the bloated female recovered this morning from the natural springs. On the left was a blackened, grotesque, nightmarish partial remains.

"Is that the recent unidentified female?" Nadine could tell nothing, not even the sex of this badly decomposed body.

"Yes. From Grass Lake up in Fort McCoy. Possible drowning. With Dr. Hartfield's help, we might get them both done today."

Juliette nodded.

"But we'll tackle this one first." Kline pointed to the remains recovered from Silver Glen Springs.

Nadine stayed well back, but still the smell of rot overwhelmed, and her eyes watered. Juliette offered Vicks VapoRub and Nadine applied a dab of the greasy gel beneath her nose. It helped.

The body stretched in perfect stillness before them. Nadine stared down at the naked body of a woman that seemed to have been approaching her senior years, judging from the hair color. Despite herself, she looked for some movement.

She shivered in the icy room and wished she had a sweater.

Kline and Juliette spoke as they conducted a superficial exam of the body. The face was bloated, unrecognizable to Nadine.

"These wounds are unusual," said Juliette.

Nadine noted the deep gashes at the ankles.

"Seeing the incision on her neck in the water, I thought it might be a suicide, but it's clear she didn't do this," said Kline.

"How long has she been dead?" asked Nadine.

"Oh, less than twenty-four hours."

This wasn't Linda, so who was it?

Juliette looked to Nadine.

"Do we have any missing persons for older females?"

Nadine shook her head. "We don't."

Kline directed their attention to the ankles of the corpse.

"I believe that she might have been hanging at some point, possibly from a snare. The wire cut deep." Kline lifted a leg with a gloved hand. "Right through the tendons. See?"

Nadine wished she hadn't. The stench in here made her cover her mouth, muffling her words.

"Did you say, a snare?"

Nadine's experience with snares was that they were used on small animals, like rabbits and squirrels.

"Yes. Have a look at the soles of her feet." Kline moved to the end of the table. "The lacerations tell me she was running barefoot. That accounts for these as well." She motioned to the many thin slices on the body's lower legs.

"You think she was running naked through the woods?"

"Looks that way. This is a first for me and that is saying something." She lifted one of the arms and rotated it. "Have a look at this."

Nadine did and icy tendrils slithered about her heart. The wound was a puncture. The body's hands were still bagged, to preserve possible physical evidence, but they did not obscure the thin slice on the upper arm.

"More of them here," said Juliette, pointing a finger at three small wounds on the upper thigh.

"Like the others. Exit wounds. Entry is on the posterior thigh. She's got more on her back."

Nadine blanched. "How many more?"

"Still counting. Arrows again," said Kline. "If there's one in the body, we'll spot it on X-ray."

The killer had left an arrow point behind in the bodies of both Darnell and Karnowski. She'd seen them. Usually this type of arrow screwed into a plastic housing in the shaft. But these points had the threads filed away, so that when the shaft was removed, the point remained. It was no accident. He'd intentionally planted these projectiles inside his victims.

"Spine injury?" asked Nadine.

Kline glanced up at her through the clear plastic face shield. "We'll see."

The smell was so bad she could taste it at the back of her throat. Nadine tried to picture this woman's death.

It seemed to Nadine that someone had sent this woman running naked through the thick tropical underbrush and shot her from the back multiple times. Was that before or after catching her in the snare? A running target was more challenging. A swinging one perhaps more enticing because you could see her face.

"Could you determine if she was snared while alive?"

"Definitely. The bruising alone and the tissue damage."

Nadine folded one arm about her and used the opposite hand to pinch her nose with her thumb and index finger to block the stench. Breathing through her mouth was only slightly better.

Then she closed her eyes. She could see this woman, running for her life. Tripping and falling and scrambling to her feet, unaware she was being herded along.

Nadine pictured her plight. Her pink body darting in and out of palmettos. The rustle of the wide fronds and the rasp of her heavy breathing, punctuated by her weeping. She would have taken the animal trail, of course. Easier to run.

*I let her get just far enough ahead to feel she might escape. It's so much sweeter that way. Do I shoot her now or wait until she's helpless? If I shoot her now, she might fall and not get up. I want to see my snare.*

*Patience. I follow, stalking with my bow gripped tight. Waiting. Just a few more steps…*

"Dr. Finch?"

Her eyes snapped open. Both women stared at her.

"Are you all right?"

"Yes. Why?"

"You were making a sound. I thought you might be feeling ill."

"I'm fine."

A tapping caused them to turn. Skogen stood in the observation area, gesturing to Nadine.

She nodded at Kline and Juliette and stepped out to talk to him. His face was grim.

"We got another call from the Orlando *Star*. They've got a new letter we believe is from our boy."

Outside, warm sunshine drove away the chill, but the stink continued to linger in her nostrils. She used a napkin to wipe away the Vicks.

"He's calling himself 'the Huntsman,'" said Skogen.

She glanced up at him. "Appropriate."

His expression was giving her a really bad vibe, like he knew something, and she wasn't going to like it.

"What's going on?" she asked.

"He's issued a challenge."

"To whom?" But even as she said it, she already knew the answer. Icy tendrils threaded down her spine.

"To you."

"Where's the letter?" She needed to read it. See his exact words.

"It's actually a greeting card, this time. That reporter, Murphy, read it to me over the phone."

"What did it say, exactly?"

"He mentioned three new victims."

Her voice rasped as horror gripped her throat. "Three?"

"He said so. We just picked one up at Silver Glen Springs. And he cited that location in the card. But he also referred to Lake Bryant and Grass Lake."

"We don't have three missing persons. Only one. Only Linda Tolan." She rushed on, rejecting the possibility.

"I know. I have a team up at the other sites now with search and rescue."

She barely registered this as her mind raced. Three victims. "He said three?"

Skogen nodded.

Was their unsub bluffing? No. This killer didn't bluff. He'd killed three more women. The horror of that settled heavy in her stomach. Nadine thought she might be ill.

Her heart gave a panicky little flutter of recognition as she recalled just moments ago looking at the blackened skin on the partial remains right now awaiting autopsy. The body had been recovered from Grass Lake. A possible drowning victim, the ME had said.

"We found a body in Grass Lake," Nadine said, explaining it to Skogen.

"So you think the possible drowning victim is one of the three?"

"I don't know." She pressed a hand to the top of her head. "Yes. Yes, I do. But it's not Linda Tolan. She's been eliminated. They don't match." She had out her phone, dialing Juliette.

"Tolan might be in Lake Bryant. That would make the three."

Her heart pounded as unease prickled across her neck. The call to Juliette continued to ring. Her friend was performing an autopsy. Nadine would have to leave a message or send someone to tell her the partial might be a victim.

"He's issued a challenge to you directly, Nadine. He asked why you didn't recognize any of them."

"Recognize them?" The unease now sent hot darts of fear through her heart. "Agent Skogen! Why should I recognize them?"


They pulled into the lot of the Orlando *Star* fifty minutes later, leaving Skogen's vehicle, followed by Nadine's new security detail.

Nadine's mind spun like a crashing plane. Did she know the victims?

She had not attempted to recognize either body because she never expected even a chance encounter with any of his victims. But she'd met Linda Tolan *before* her abduction, at the hotel. Had she met others?

He was indicating that she had. Which confirmed that he wasn't just targeting those women. He was targeting her.

"I've got to keep the *Star* from publishing that damn letter," said Skogen. "Let's go."

Juliette's text chimed on Nadine's phone and she glanced down at the screen, pausing before the building entrance.

*Arrow point in hip of partial #1, Grass Lake vic. ID made on vic #2, Silver Glens Springs. Call me.*

"Just a minute," she said to Skogen and called her friend.

Before she could say a word, Juliette broke in.

"Nadine, it's April Rupp. They made a positive ID."

Nadine gasped and pressed her hand to her forehead. Cold sweat beaded there.

"What?" barked Skogen.

She plugged her ear to block out Skogen and focus on Juliette.

"We know her! Our landlady! Nadine, I called Clint. He says this is bad. This is personal."

She'd seen their landlady only yesterday morning. The woman had been angry that they had not disclosed they were FBI. Could that bloated, unrecognizable corpse they'd dragged from the weeds really be April Rupp? The warm springwater had sped decomposition, making her unrecognizable but, yes, it could be.

Nadine wrestled with accepting that someone she knew was so suddenly gone, when the fear began seeping in. She knew her. She knew April Rupp and she knew Linda Tolan.

"We didn't have Mrs. Rupp listed missing," said Nadine, as if that would make this any less true.

"I know. Clint's checking."

Nadine had met two of the missing. Skogen was right. This was not a coincidence. Then what, exactly, was it?

"The arrowpoint in the partial?"

"Yeah. I got your message it might be connected. The arrow point confirms. Do we know her, too?"

"Call Tina. Ask her to confirm that Bianca Santander is being held in the Glades County Detention Center."

"Okay. Right now."

"Then call me back."

Clint's call came in as she was speaking to Juliette.

"What's happening?" asked Skogen as his phone began ringing. A glance showed Special Agent Coleman calling.

He took his call as Nadine took Demko's.

She heard Skogen say, "Who?"

"Clint?" she said into her phone.

"Did Juliette get to you first?"

"Yes. She said that it's Mrs. Rupp."

"Where are you?"

She told him about the letter and that they were in Orlando now.

"Did you say three victims?"

"Yes. And that I should have recognized them. Clint, I never thought to even try to recognize them."

"You couldn't. Not after they were out that long in the heat." He scrubbed his mouth with his palm. "This is because of that damn leak. It put you front and center before this madman." He spit out the words like venom.

"But I met Tolan before the leak."

This was met with silence. She swallowed the lump in her throat and listened to snatches of Skogen's call.

The sound of Clint's rapid breathing did not reassure.

"How does he know you didn't recognize them?"

That thought was equally disturbing.

"I don't know."

"He's watching you. Possibly us."

She thought of the security tape of the hotel corridor and the man she had seen, but the camera had not, and shivered.

"So Linda Tolan is connected to you. Rupp is connected. Who is the third?"

"The partial remains?" she asked.

"From Grass Lake?"

"Juliette said there is an arrow point in her hip."

"Our guy?"

"Yes."

"What do you think?"

"I don't know. But I asked Juliette to check with Tina about the woman from the poster." Her voice sounded so breathless.

"Bianca Santander? She's still in detention."

"I know, but… No one else is missing."

"That we know of. Demko never found Rupp listed as missing. Besides, you don't know Santander."

She turned to see Skogen staring at her. His mouth was hard set. The grim expression only increased her panic.

"Are you with Skogen?" asked Demko.

"Yes."

"I mean right with him?" he asked.

"Yes. And the security detail is here."

"Stay with him. Don't let him go anywhere without you until I get there."

"Yes."

"Right with him. Promise me."

"Yes. I promise."

She ended the call and pivoted to face Special Agent Skogen. "What?" she asked.

His words and voice were somber as a shroud. "The Huntsman just made this a contest between you and him."

Nadine began to shake. Skogen moved closer. He reached out as if to pull her into an embrace and she stepped back.

She didn't need comfort, not from him. She needed answers.

Nadine turned to the entrance. "Let's get that letter."


Two hours later, Nadine was back at the office. Special Agent Vea had dropped the new communication from the Huntsman to the FBI evidence lab in Orlando and she was waiting for a digital copy.

On her arrival Tina gave her a chef's salad and a bottle of green tea.

"Green tea?" she asked.

"You need the antioxidants," said Tina.

She needed a sedative.

"Thank you. Where's Demko?"

"Up in Marion County with the sheriff searching Lake Bryant for remains."

"What about the detention center? Do they still have Santander?"

Tina's shoulders sank.

"No. They never had her. Her attorney told me it was a mistake. The wrong person. Same name."

Nadine's stomach flipped. "She's still missing?"

Her assistant nodded, looking close to tears.

"Call Juliette. Tell her this. Ask that social worker to contact the family and get something to identify her. Scars, tattoos, dental records. Something. Then get that to Juliette."

"I can contact the family. I have her brother's number." Tina sped away.

Nadine dove into her work. She knew no other way than to focus all her anxiety and panic than to pinpoint it onto her profile.

It was clear that Darnell and Karnowski had been lured into the forest. But had Linda Tolan been lured or had the Huntsman followed her from the hotel? In either case, their unsub's method had clearly changed when Tolan had escaped. He'd taken her from her home. He'd presumably taken April Rupp from her yard.

What had made him change his method?

She stared at the names and dates and places as an idea began to form, a new pattern and the important date where the entire thing pivoted, Tuesday, March 30th, the day she had arrived in Ocala.

In the outer office, she heard Tina on the phone speaking in rapid Spanish. A moment later, she rushed in.

Nadine gave Tina her full attention. The sinking feeling was back in her stomach.

"What?"

"I reached the brother of Bianca Santander. His sister worked two jobs. Housecleaning and breakfast attendant at a hotel."

Apprehension rippled over Nadine on a current of air.

"Which hotel?"

"The one where we all stayed."

Nadine's heart clenched as she thought of the small, anxious woman at the breakfast area on her very first day at the hotel.

*Bibi.*

# CHAPTER NINETEEN

Nadine sucked in a breath as Tina continued.

"Her brother gave me the name of the dentist they use."

"Call Juliette. Give her the name."

Tina's eyes brimmed with tears. "You might have met her, too!"

"I… I, yes. I remember a small woman in the breakfast area my first day here. But we don't know for sure that it's her."

Tina gulped.

Nadine was on her feet. "Call Juliette."

She headed for Skogen's office.

There she found him with Special Agent Wynns hunched over a computer monitor reviewing security footage.

Wynns glanced up at her.

"Dr. Finch?" he said, causing Skogen to glance up.

She told them what Tina had discovered, about the arrow point in the hip of their Jane Doe. Finally she relayed the interaction she'd had with Santander at breakfast.

"When?" asked Vea.

"It was Tuesday, March 30th, just after eight a.m."

She'd covered for the woman with her boss after Santander had accidentally discarded Nadine's uneaten breakfast. And Linda Tolan had shouted at her, so had Mrs. Rupp. Had these slights doomed them? It seemed unlikely but the notion was taking root.

"Pull up March 30th," said Skogen, lifting his phone and speaking to Special Agent Vea, instructing him to contact the hotel to verify employment for Santander.

Nadine waited, watching as they began.

They found the footage and she pointed.

"There. That's me."

Strange to see the scene played out again from a different perspective.

"That's Bibi." She pointed again.

"Bibi?"

"That's what her boss called her."

"Okay. We got it."

She hovered and then left them, pausing midway to her office. Poor woman. She thought of the partial remains, unrecognizable.

Was that Bibi?

Nadine covered her face and let the tears come.

"Hey, hey. Come here."

She glanced up to find Clint Demko closing in, his gaze sweeping over her. She said nothing, just lifted her arms, seeking what she needed most.

Demko drew her in. He held tight, resting his chin on the top of her head. She sagged, letting him take some of her weight. He did so easily.

He rubbed her back, his hands confident and soothing as they moved rhythmically up and down. His breath warmed the top of her head. She pressed her cheek to his chest, feeling the Kevlar vest and inhaling the comforting scent of sandalwood.

"I thought you were in Marion County," she said.

"Wanted to check on you."

She kept her eyes closed and her cheek pressed to him as he rocked her.

"We'll get this guy, too, Nadine. We'll put him away so he can't touch you or anyone else."

She nodded. That was what she wanted, why she was here.

"He's watching me."

"You're his opponent. He's a hunter, so he likes games. This will make him easier to catch."

He didn't pull away until she stepped back.

"How did you hear?"

"Juliette and Tina."

He rested his hands on her shoulders, gazing straight into her eyes.

"We'll get him, Dee. We will."

She nodded, struggling with the knot corded in her throat.

His hands dropped away. The warmth of his touch lingered, and she no longer felt lost. She felt determined.

"I have so much work to do."

He smiled, as if he suddenly had her back.

"Have you seen the card we picked up yet?" she asked.

He shook his head.

"I have a copy."

They walked to her office.

Nadine retrieved the copy of the greeting card sent by the Huntsman that she'd received from Skogen and passed it to him, trying and failing to control her pounding heart. This card was personal, sent to her.

Demko accepted the double-sided color copy of an open greeting card. The back of the card was blank except for the product details and bar code. On the front, there was an illustration of an owl and the caption read: *Happy Birthday!*

He flipped the page to read the interior. The printed message read, *Hope your birthday is a HOOT!* On the blank side of the card was the familiar tight cursive lettering.

"Trace evidence?" asked Demko.

"I don't know. The lab has the original."

Demko scanned the message that she had already memorized.

Dear Dr. Finch,

I've lured three intruders from our home territory, removing them to Lake Bryant, Grass Lake and Silver Glen Springs.

Clearing the field for you.

I hope my display is not wasted and wonder at why you didn't recognize my little birds. I hope you similarly don't disappoint.

I look forward to your thoughts on my manifesto coming soon.

The Huntsman

When he glanced up, his expression gave away nothing.

"Before you ask," said Nadine. "Marion County Sheriff and Skogen's guys are searching Lake Bryant for Linda Tolan's remains. It's one thousand acres, so…"

It might be a while.

"Listen, Nadine, he's targeting you. Skogen assigned Axel to coordinate your protection."

Special Agent Axel Vea was a big, light-skinned black man with hair shaved to nothing, who, Clint had told her, was a former army ranger.

"Good choice."

"I know you like your privacy, but from here until we catch this guy, you're going to have company. Constant company. Axel has more agents coming in specifically for protection detail. And we will be moving again."

Nadine could not contain the groan.

"It's a necessity. April Rupp's disappearance demonstrates that he knows where you are staying. Because of that, Coleman is canvassing the neighborhood, speaking to neighbors who may have seen April Rupp. She sent me a text that the television news crews are set up on the street before the town house."

Nadine pressed a hand to her forehead as the weariness pushed down upon her shoulders.

"What about our stuff?"

"The FBI is moving everything to a safe house. Undisclosed location. Protective detail when travel is necessary. We're going to be working out of that house for a while. You won't be coming here, either. Videoconferencing and the agents coming to you when necessary."

House arrest, she thought.

"What about Juliette and Tina?"

"They'll have an individual agent assigned to their protection. Juliette will attend autopsies virtually and no running for a while. Tina will set up your new office in the safe house."

"What about you?"

"I've refused protective detail."

*

By 8 p.m. Nadine was situated in an innocuous home in a gated community. The structure was a single level, U-shaped, with a split-bedroom plan, so the master suite was isolated from the other bedrooms by the common area. The exterior sported Bermuda shades that added privacy. Nadine thought the caged inground pool might be some consolation for the Bureau canceling Tina and Juliette's morning runs.

She had commandeered the master suite, as it had a sitting room, which she planned to use as her office. The actual office would be shared by the team. The furnishings were new, a nautical collection in cream and navy with accents of coral and yellow. High ceilings, cream-colored tile and marble countertops gave Nadine a peek at how the other half lives.

Juliette had phoned to deliver the bad news. The dental records of Bianca Santander were a match for their Jane Doe.

They now had five victims.

Tina, and her new protective detail of one very capable-looking female agent, had shuttled the contents of the office to this residence and completed the setup as Nadine grabbed several hours of uninterrupted think time with her laptop in her new sitting area.

It was helping. She saw no personal connection between herself and Nikki Darnell or Rita Karnowski. But had a brief contact with Santander, Tolan and Rupp. Linda Tolan was interesting because their killer had used a lure *after* she had made contact with Nadine, which meant he must have known what Tolan was doing in Ocala. The reason for the travels to the forest for Tolan, Karnowski and Darnell had become obvious when the notifications on their phones were unlocked.

All three of these victims had received similar alerts from the same app.

Darnell had been lured to a remote parking area by the possibility of seeing a magnolia warbler, which Nadine now knew was a small songbird with yellow-and-black markings.

Karnowski was interesting. She did not have a bird-watching app. But Agent Wynns had found an alert on the phone of Hugo Betters, Karnowski's boyfriend. He had confirmed that this alert caused Rita to demand they take their fateful hike. Rita's commune with nature included sitting with his binoculars in the area where a painted bunting had been reported. How had the killer known Betters had this app unless he had targeted them earlier?

Nadine believed that Karnowski had been lured by the Huntsman. Betters reported that there were many other kayaks on the river that day. Was one of them their killer? Had he followed them to the nature trail?

She called Skogen to set up another interview with Rita's boyfriend via Zoom.

Bianca Santander's disappearance was especially troubling because she had been taken and killed well before Nadine's involvement with this case had appeared in the news. Though her remains were the most recently recovered, she had died before Linda Tolan. That meant that the Huntsman learned of her arrival on Nadine's first day here. But how?

Watching the FBI field office? Staking out the hotels in town? By chance? She didn't know. She did know that Bianca's cell phone was not able to use apps and she had no interest in bird-watching. She had been taken outside the hotel after her shift ended and before her brother could pick her up.

Linda Tolan had told the FBI that she had been seeking a summer tanager as part of an assignment for wildlife photography.

Nadine checked the list of notifications and there it was, the summer tanager alert on the morning she was abducted.

The question was, did the Huntsman follow Tolan from the hotel because of the altercation with Nadine, send out a notification for this scarlet songbird seeking a random target, making her capture a coincidence, or had he somehow known this was the bait that would bring Linda to him?

Nadine tended toward believing that final possibility.

The last known victim, April Rupp, did not use the bird app or receive notifications that brought her into the forest. In fact, she did not own a smartphone. This woman was targeted, like Santander, for her relationship to Nadine, hunted and abducted. The leak of her identity in the papers corresponded with their move from the hotel and the capture of Rupp.

She reminded herself to ask Jack how he was doing in identifying their leak.

Nadine now had a direction and emerging portrait of a killer seeking notoriety, baiting the authorities and relishing his game. But was she any closer to identifying him?

The gentle tapping on her closed bedroom door drew Nadine back to her surroundings.

"Come in," she said.

"Jeez! This place is huge. Where are you?"

She recognized Juliette's voice, coming from the bedroom area.

"Walk past the bed and through the archway."

Juliette wandered into the sitting area, glancing about before taking a seat on the navy-tone couch facing the coral stone fireplace.

"It's like a Tommy Bahama store threw up in here."

"Yeah, but I need a desk, chair and Ethernet connection," said Nadine.

"I heard Tina working on that. You'll have a desk tomorrow."

"Amazing. How are the critters?"

"Demko took Molly with him. I'm not sure where he is, but she's the first one to try out the pool. Tina's cat is still hiding but under a different bed, now. I swear I've seen that thing maybe twice."

"And Jack-Jack?" asked Nadine, inquiring about Juliette's perpetual two-year-old feathered dependent.

"He's in the kitchen with some mango slices. Tina's watching him."

Nadine shifted and her stomach muscles tightened, preparing for the real reason for her friend's visit.

"What's up?" Nadine asked.

"Well, you heard about the dental records."

Nadine nodded.

"Beyond that, the lab made a DNA match for your hair and the headband they recovered in Tolan's car. That means you had a face-to-face with our guy."

Disquieting did not begin to cover the electric bolt of anxiety prickling through her. It was one thing to suspect and another to know.

"I figured. Wish I could remember what he looked like."

"No luck with the sketch artist?"

"I hardly noticed him. Actually tried not to look at him out of embarrassment from waking him."

Juliette heaved a sigh. It was an opportunity lost. Nadine vowed to be vigilant, note her surroundings, and all the men she spotted from here on out.

She suddenly recalled the man walking the small dog that day she had been outside with Mrs. Rupp. Could that have been the same man as at the hotel?

Nadine thought it possible and jotted a note to discuss it with Demko.

"What else?" she asked, returning her attention to Juliette.

"They found Tolan's remains in Lake Bryant. Kline made a positive ID. Autopsy tomorrow, but on visual inspection, it looks like the others."

Nadine heaved a sigh. "This might be my fault."

"It's not. It's our perp's fault. Don't forget it."

The room grew so quiet Nadine could hear the hum of the fan's motor.

"Anything else?"

Juliette's hesitation did nothing to calm her nerves. Her friend sat forward, resting her elbows on her knees, her hands clasped before her, studying the ground. When she met Nadine's eyes, her expression was grim and her mouth pressed tight.

"We also got a hit on the DNA on one of the bodies recovered from the River Forest area."

Nadine's momentary confusion was erased when she switched gears from their current case to the cold case. Juliette was referring to the human remains that her brother had helped authorities discover. Two bodies, one male and one female.

Whatever Juliette was about to tell her, Nadine knew it was bad. Did that mean they had not found her father or that they had?

"We got a hit from the DNA database. The results show a familial match to your brother, Arlo. Parent–child."

Nadine nodded. "So you found our father."

"It's Dennis Howler. Yes. In addition to the DNA match, we have medical records indicating a fractured wrist and collarbone. Also a match. The female skeletal remains belong to Infinity Yanez. Identification through dental records."

Nadine let the news sink in that her absent father had not abandoned them as she'd long believed. He had been torn from their family.

Her hopes of having a nice, normal father collapsed.

The next realization struck like a slap. She and Demko now had something else in common. Both their mothers had murdered their dads.

"Another lie," she murmured.

"What?" asked Juliette.

"My mother. All this time, even knowing what I do, I believed her when she told me he ran out on us."

"Don't beat yourself up. And I'm sorry, Nadine. Truly sorry for your loss."

All her stupid tiny hopes that someday he might come back for her were snuffed out. Arleen had killed any chance of that, along with Dennis.

"I have to tell my aunt Donna."

"I can send an agent or the ME from her district."

"No. I'll tell her." Nadine used both hands to wipe away the unwanted tears. "Are they looking at my mother for the murders?"

Juliette nodded.

"Thank you for telling me," said Nadine.

Juliette's look was filled with anxiety. She cleared her throat and swallowed. Nadine lifted a brow, waiting for the other shoe to fall, and pushed herself deep into the padded backrest.

"There's one more thing. We ran your DNA from the swab you provided against Dennis Howler." Juliette leaned forward and placed a hand on hers. "Nadine, you're not a match."

"What? How is that possible?"

"Because Arlo is only your half brother."

The buzzing was back in her mind, the kicked hornet's nest making it difficult for her to think. Her lips went numb and her fingertips tingled.

"If Dennis Howler isn't my father, then who is?"

# CHAPTER TWENTY

## TUESDAY

Nadine sat at the kitchen's marble island. Since learning that Dennis Howler had left Arleen around the time she'd given birth to a daughter—Nadine herself—she had puzzled at the timing.

Now she had more reason to believe her birth was the trigger. Nadine pictured the scene. Howler knowing he had been in the service when his wife, Arleen, had gotten pregnant. Nadine needed to check his military records to verify her suspicion that Howler would have known he could not be the father of the child his wife carried.

She wondered what her chances were of getting a straight answer from her mother on the identity of her real father.

Did Arleen even know?

As she pondered that conundrum, all last night, Nadine had called her aunt Donna. She'd seemed to take the news in her stride, telling her that she'd come to acceptance that her brother was gone long ago. Her aunt would see about collecting Dennis Howler's remains and make arrangements.

Nadine hadn't told her aunt that Dennis Howler wasn't her father, not out of fear of what Aunt Donna would say but because she wanted to have that conversation face-to-face. She knew her aunt loved her, but would that change when she learned that

Nadine was not her brother's child? The uncertainty gnawed with sharp teeth against the backbone of her aunt's support and unconditional love.

And with that truth now sinking in, Nadine again wondered if her real dad might be out there, missing her, as she missed him.

"What's going on in there?" Demko asked.

He was leaning against the counter with a full mug of coffee. How long had he been here?

Nadine glanced about, reengaging with her surroundings. "What?"

"You're scowling."

She dropped her gaze to her lap and the cuticle she had dragged loose of all but the last attachment. She yanked it away. The sting of raw flesh was somehow soothing.

"Did you speak to Juliette?" Nadine asked.

"About?"

She told him everything, starting with the familial DNA match of the male remains to Arlo and the negative finding for her, about her theories and hopes and fears.

"And you've held this in all day?" he asked.

"It's embarrassing."

"Also disconcerting. The ground keeps shifting under your feet, Dee."

"Do you think my mother would tell me the truth, if I asked her?"

He made a face, wincing. "From what you've said, she's seriously upset with you."

"That's an understatement. I cut off her money and all communication. Arlo said she's raging. He also said the Copycat Killer contacted him somehow to ask about me."

"Why am I just hearing this?"

"Because the Copycat Killer is in jail and can't get to me. But…"

"What?"

"Arlo told me to watch my back."

Demko took her hand and lifted it, brushing her knuckles with a kiss. "That's my job."

They shared a smile, but the melancholy lingered.

"Maybe Arlo would be a better source."

"He was only five when my dad split." Nadine rubbed her forehead. "I mean, when Dennis Howler was murdered. I'm still getting used to that." She dragged her hand over her mouth before continuing.

"He was old enough to remember if there was someone steady around."

"Could have been a one-nighter."

"I suppose."

The conversation lulled until she picked it up again.

"So my father's skull, it was crushed. And according to Arleen, she hit the guy who owed her money. Now I discover that guy was my dad. I mean the man I thought was my dad. This is so confusing. I'd like to drive up to the correctional facility tomorrow. Maybe see Arlo afterward."

"You don't go anywhere without your security detail."

She groaned. "I already forgot."

"Speaking of forgetting: Special Agent Wynns told me that they've taken down that birding app. No more notifications to lure potential victims in his territory. Let's see how our unsub feels about that."

"He's moved on. Not using that bait any longer, but I'm sure he'll let me know. I'm anxious to see what the forensic document expert has to say about our greeting card and note."

"Yeah. Me too."

She told him about the guy she'd seen the day Mrs. Rupp had appeared on their doorstep shouting.

"You get a good look?"

"Not really. Better of the dog. It was a Jack Russell terrier."

"I'll see if any of the neighbors have one or saw him."

Nadine pressed her thumb to the raw skin at the base of her index fingernail bed to stanch the blood welling at her cuticle.

He drained the remains of his mug.

"Do you think I'm the reason he left?"

"Nadine, don't do that."

She lowered her head.

"We have no missing persons. So take a half day and go up there."

"You think so?"

"Yes. Go ask Arleen about your real dad. But remember, whatever she says may be a lie."

## WEDNESDAY

Nadine drove with her FBI security agent to Lowell Correctional. The agent accompanied her through the indignities of the intake process for visitors, which was identical to Lawtey's and included metal detectors and a pat down. Once in the visitor area, the agent peeled away, keeping her eyes on Nadine and in proximity, without drawing notice. They'd even arranged an inmate for the agent to sit with in a mock visit.

Nadine waited by the prearranged table for Arleen to appear. This time she'd brought only twenty dollars in small bills because she'd be damned if her mother would get one dime from her that she didn't use in the vending machines during their visit. Nadine had dressed with intention to most resemble the attire her mother once wore, so she entered the gathering spot in jeans, boots and a loose T-shirt, covered with a plaid cotton shirt, unbuttoned, with the sleeves torn off. Her hair was down and she wore no makeup. Looking at herself in the mirror before departure, she was unsettled by the resemblance to her mother's younger self.

Nadine had not seen Arleen since August, before closing her first case, some eight months ago. After discovering that Arleen had aided the Copycat Killer with those monstrous crimes, Nadine had also stopped sending money to Arleen's account. That alone was bound to incite her mother's fury.

She'd had time to prepare for this encounter but still felt outmatched, David facing Goliath without even a single rock. Sweat slicked her palms as she scrubbed them over her face and sucked in a breath, readying herself.

Arleen was among the first of the inmates to enter the visiting area. She glanced about, her face a hard mask of thinly veiled fury. Her focus pinned her daughter and her eyes narrowed dangerously, taking aim. Then she marched toward Nadine, who had decided to remain standing near the biggest guard she could find for this reunion.

Her mother had lost weight, Nadine realized. The pale blue uniform now hung on her and the neck of the T-shirt gaped, revealing bladelike collarbones.

"Well, there she is. La-dee-fuckin'-da. The prodigal child returns. Still digging into my business?"

"Hello, Arleen."

She snorted. "You want to take a seat or you plannin' some half-assed duel?"

Nadine motioned to the preselected table and waited for Arleen to settle into one of the round stools with her back to the agent guarding Nadine.

The general setup of the room reminded Nadine of any institutional cafeteria. But instead of the aroma of pizza and French fries, this room stank of unwashed bodies, mildew and desperation. They certainly weren't wasting any money on air-conditioning. The room must have been eighty degrees.

"If you're here to try and stop me from publishing, you can go spit."

Nadine sat across the table from her mother, keeping her hands on her lap and out of Arleen's reach.

"I'm not."

"But you heard about the book. Right? I've got *whole* chapters on you. My only daughter. The one I protected from my little ventures and I don't know how many of my men. And how does she repay me? Still have the knife in my back." Arleen thumbed over her shoulder at the imaginary blade.

She had practiced what she planned to say. And been very clear in her mind about what details she would share with Arleen, and which she would retain. Now it all jumbled together like the pieces of a jigsaw puzzle. She wiped the sweat from her brow.

She did not wish to do anything that would jeopardize Arlo's deal with the parole board. Neither did she want to put Arlo and Arlene at odds. They would be soon enough, because their mother would be livid to learn he had stolen her chance to avoid execution. Arleen's attorney had offered a deal. She'd identify her victims in exchange for reducing her death penalty sentence to life in prison. Arlo's deal threatened that. The less time her mother had to prepare, the better.

"I'm working on a new case," said Nadine.

Arleen shrugged and flattened a hand on the table. "That mean you can afford to buy me something to eat?"

Nadine rose and headed for the vending machines, following her mother's instructions as to what she wanted. Not one healthy choice among them. No wonder her mother's teeth were rotting away. Several were already missing.

They headed back to their table past the other guests and inmates. Nadine noted the eyes turned in their direction, and conversations whispered at their passing. She was certain they were quite the celebrities. The notorious serial killer and the daughter who turned her in to authorities. Nadine knew that the one thing that inmates hated more than the guards was a snitch.

Her mind flashed to Arlo again. How to protect him, and still get the information she needed.

"You want me to send a few sample chapters from the book? I'd let you have some say if you was to start putting money back in my account."

It occurred to her that by law Arleen could profit nothing from any book deal. How frustrating that must be. Nadine pressed her lips tight and considered her words.

"Awful hard to pay for what you need on the thirty-two cents an hour they pay me to fold laundry."

"I don't want to see the biography. I don't want to see sample chapters."

Munching on her chocolate bar, Arleen's eyes narrowed as she regarded her daughter. Trying to puzzle out the reason for her visit and how she could leverage it to her advantage.

"So what *do* you want?"

"Anthropologists from the Florida Museum of Natural History were exploring remains of a Native American fishing camp and they uncovered a body. Two, actually."

Arleen stopped chewing. The glob of chocolate made one cheek stick out.

"Where about?" she asked, her words garbled by the food.

"Putnam County."

Her mother shifted on her seat.

"Ocala Forest."

Arleen lowered the remains of the chocolate bar to the table.

Nadine leaned forward. "River Forest."

"I'll be damned."

"No doubt," Nadine said. "Male and female skeletal remains."

To this bit of news, Arleen smiled broadly, showing melted chocolate clinging between her remaining teeth. Nadine suppressed a shudder.

"You know anything about that?"

Arleen made a respectable attempt at looking offended. "Why should I?"

"Because someone hit the male with a shovel and fractured his skull. You once told me you hit a man with a shovel, accidentally killing him. And the age of the skeletons match." Nadine had no doubt that the blow had not been accidental, but she gave her mother this potential out, hoping she might reveal the truth. Nadine still had not decided if she should disclose that the identity of the man was known. But she could not figure a way to ask about her parentage without doing so.

Arleen shrugged. "That could be anybody."

Nadine lost her temper. "It *could* be anybody. But it's not. It's Dennis Howler. They've made a positive ID."

Arleen's brows shot up.

"It's my father." Nadine watched her mother closely. She was rewarded by the clearest expression of *duping delight* she had ever witnessed. The completely inappropriate grin was wide and gone in a flash, the leaked expression derived from the twisted pleasure Arleen derived by deceiving her daughter.

Now came the conundrum. Clearly, Arleen knew that Dennis Howler was not her father. But she had no reason to tell Nadine the truth. Should Nadine reveal that she knew as well, on the slim chance that her mother would volunteer the information she sought?

"Well, what do you know?" said Arleen, lifting the chocolate bar once more and taking a vicious bite. Then she laughed.

"You want to tell me about that?" asked Nadine.

"Why should I?"

And she had her answer. Arleen and she were solid adversaries. The only way she got information was by paying for it.

"They ID the other body?" asked Arleen.

"You know who it is." Nadine suddenly felt exhausted.

Meanwhile, Arleen looked energized. Her eyes sparkled. Even her posture had changed.

"They're going to come at me for this one. Blame it on the ex-wife. Figures." Rather than seeming upset, Arleen revved up. "They want me to plead, they'll have to make me a sweet deal. Keep that hypodermic needle and shove it up their own ass."

Arleen had been unsuccessfully attempting to negotiate a reduced sentence from lethal injection to life imprisonment for years. Nadine realized that the state's desire to close this new cold case might be an opportunity for both Arlo *and* Arleen. The idea sickened her. She often wondered how much better her life would be after her mother's departure from this world. It made her a terrible daughter. But perhaps a good person.

"How'd they know it's him?"

"I don't know. But they've asked me for a DNA sample."

Arleen's eyes widened. She looked suddenly worried. "Don't they got Arlo's DNA on file?"

"I suppose. Either way. No difference. Right?"

Arleen's eyes narrowed as she tried to gauge what Nadine knew against what she was prepared to tell her.

If they didn't use Arlo's DNA but Nadine's, there would be no match. And Arleen's hopes for a deal would dissolve like ice on a hot sidewalk.

Finally Arleen shrugged. "Right. No difference."

And there was that smirk again. *Duping delight* at her daughter's expense. She would not be asking her most pressing question because Arleen had no intention of revealing the identity of her real father.

"You have anything else to tell me about this?" asked Nadine, giving her mother one last chance.

"You want answers? You can buy a copy of my book 'cause I just added a chapter."

Nadine rose and left, pursued by her mother's laughter.

*

Two hours after arrival, she had cleared security at Lowell Federal Institution and drove her new shadow to Lawtey, to visit Arlo. They stopped only to grab some takeout, which Nadine now regretted as the fast food roiled in her stomach like the contents of an Amish butter churn.

She reached the visiting area with her gloom continuing to cling like wet clothing. Her companion stood with the three guards in the observation office, behind the shatterproof window, her steady gaze on Nadine, who headed inside and sat, glancing from the cracked concrete floor to the greenish cinder-block walls, waiting for Arlo. Many of the inmates sat at the other round tables, already chatting with their guests. Several of the tables had checkerboards printed on the laminated surface. She wondered if there were any checkers. She knew only that she had never seen any.

Beyond the guard booth, a bank of seven payphones waited. These were the sort that used credit cards rather than money. Above the seating area an L-shaped catwalk hung. Armed guards stood along the metal railings staring down on them like expectant vultures.

Her mood improved only at seeing Arlo. He grinned and threw open his arms. They were permitted a three-second hug.

Arlo stepped back, beaming. "There she is!"

He motioned her to an empty table she'd already claimed, and they sat in adjacent seats rather than on opposite sides as her mother and she always did.

"You look well."

"Yeah. Feel good. Working out and waiting to hear from my lawyer. He thinks I got a reasonable shot at early release."

Nadine felt guilty bringing Arlo more troubles. He certainly deserved some good news.

"You were out in the forest recently," she said.

"Yeah. Sure was. They wouldn't let me contact you. Obvious reasons, I guess. Wouldn't want me escaping into the woods." He laughed at that. "I think I was pretty close to wherever she buried Dad. She used to stop on that damned circle all the freakin' time. Smoke and talk about Dad, what a piece of shit he was and how we were all better off without him."

"They found him, Arlo. Thanks to you."

Elation lifted his features. "They did? My attorney didn't tell me."

"Not public yet."

"This is good news, only…"

Was it now occurring to him that he'd been right? That their father was really gone and was never coming back?

"You wish you were wrong?"

"I guess I hoped that he was out there and just smart enough to get clear of our mom. Always wished he'd come back for us when he got settled. Stupid."

"It isn't. I used to want the same thing."

They shared a long silent stare and the sorrow at being right. Finally Arlo let his head hang. She waited for him to digest the bitter pill she'd given him. It didn't take long. Arlo was strong that way. When he lifted his head, his eyes were misty.

"So Dad never ran off. He's been here all along."

"Yes," she said. "They made a positive ID."

"My lawyer said if we can show a murder, my testimony against Mom can be leveraged for my release."

"Mom's planning to use a confession to the crimes in exchange for a sentence change to life in prison."

"How does she know?" he asked.

"I told her today."

"Well, shit." Arlo thought about that for a while. "She's free to try. We all do what we gotta. Where was he?"

Nadine told him all about it. About her visit to the grave site and what she had seen. When she finished, Arlo was scowling.

"What?" she asked.

"Spill," he said, gesturing with his fingers for her to hand over whatever was troubling her.

Her big brother might be a danger to society, but he had always had her back.

She told him everything. About the DNA match to him, the identity of the other body, that Dennis Howler was murdered with a blow to the head. He listened as she babbled on, a tumbling brook of information, about the soil and second body and green sandal, finishing with the news that he and she had different fathers. Dennis Howler was not hers.

He took her hand beneath the table. "I'm sorry, Dee-Dee. Sorry we were right about where he's been. Sorry that this just means more questions for you."

She wiped the tears from her face with her free hand. "Did you know?"

The guard behind her barked from atop the catwalk. "No physical contact!"

Arlo drew his hand back. She huddled, sad and hollow, needing a hug now more than ever in her life.

"Did you?" she asked.

"I didn't. But…"

"What?" she asked.

"Dee-Dee, you don't look anything like him. And you and me… our faces are a completely different shape." He pointed at his cheeks. "You got no dimples. No cleft chin and my hair is curly."

"And you have his hazel eyes."

"How could you remember that?"

"From the two photos you rescued before the bonfire."

"Oh, right. You have them?"

She nodded.

He inhaled and then blew away a breath. "So now what?"

"I guess I'd like to join Aunt Donna when she buries your dad." Her chin sank to her chest. "Arlo, Donna isn't my aunt anymore."

"She'll always be your aunt."

"She took me in, helped me through college. I have to pay her back."

"You don't owe her, Dee-Dee. Family is more than blood."

She nodded, understanding but not accepting his belief, but praying Aunt Donna would feel the same.

"And on the burial, how about wait on that? I'd like to be there."

"Sure. No hurry." Nadine wrung her hands under the table. "Arlo? Any idea who my dad is?"

## THURSDAY

Yesterday they had run background checks on each dark-haired male between twenty and forty-five, and had identified which had hunting and fishing licenses in any of the three counties targeted in her geographic map.

Last night Nadine worked from the safe house, reviewing the database on the server that included each available photo, criminal records, wants and warrants and known associates for all the men that Demko and Skogen's team had provided that fit her criteria in her suspect profile.

This morning she was at it again, sitting with her computer and coffee at the dining room table when Demko appeared holding an open laptop.

"I was going over surveillance footage with the digital forensics agent. We want you to see something."

She couldn't imagine what this was because despite scouring the hotel security recordings from the time of her arrival, they had made no progress on identifying the Huntsman among the guests. They knew he had been in the room opposite hers, but they also knew he'd gained entry through the window.

Demko set his open laptop on the table before her. Agent Wynns offered a good morning from the screen via video call. Demko explained that he had asked about any personnel who had recently quit or left employment at the hotel. There was only one. A man who had worked midnight to seven at the bell stand and had left with no notice.

"Then we found this." Wynns shared his screen, running the security video clip of a man in a bellman's uniform in the breakfast area the morning after Nadine arrived.

"Who is he?"

"Unknown. Manager initially identified him as one of his people. Originally named this man as the employee who had left. Trouble is, this is the morning *after* he failed to show for his shift. And employees that we've spoken to do not recognize this person," said Wynns.

She studied the footage of the man, who kept his head down. "Is that him?"

Demko nodded. "We have video of him leaving the hotel after Santander. She heads to the bus stop on Wednesday after her shift. He approaches her, wearing a uniform of some kind, then accompanies her back to his pickup truck." He met her gaze. "His truck has a white cab."

"Plates?"

"Nope. Got the make and model, though."

"Is the bellman, the one who left without notice, dead?"

"We're checking."

"Why are you just seeing this now? You've been over this surveillance footage again and again."

"There was nothing suspicious about a woman getting into a vehicle at a bus stop."

Nadine pressed her hands to her forehead.

"How did he know that you'd call me to profile?" she asked. "How did he know I'd stay at that hotel?"

"Serial killer in your mother's home territory. You just finishing your training at BAU and your recent success with the Copycat case," said Agent Wynns. "Seems a logical leap."

"Timing is perfect," added Demko.

Her gut had told her that the Huntsman had been watching her the morning she had not finished her breakfast. Had witnessed the interaction between her and the breakfast attendant, Bianca Santander.

Now they had proof.

*

Nadine arrived at the sheriff's office at nine-thirty in the morning with her escort and was shown into the interview room.

Despite her vague description, Skogen and Demko had homed in on several of the males from the database.

Two in particular. One was an employee at the gun shop that Demko and she had visited, because Skogen's attempt to question the man caused him to immediately lawyer up. Skogen would be speaking to him this afternoon in the presence of his attorney.

The second man, Simon Kilpatrick, had agreed to come in for another interview this morning.

Nadine didn't like the son of the owners of the outdoor adventure outfit for their unsub because, unless he was playing them, he seemed incapable of orchestrating such a plot. He had already been interviewed, and had been in custody when the first letter from the killer had been mailed. Despite her opinion, they'd obtained his phone and Simon had furnished the password, which rather proved her point.

She sat in on the interview. Simon was smallish, muscular, approximately thirty years in age and had a definite lisp and a high voice.

The longer she listened to him, the more convinced she was, yet again, that he wasn't smart enough to pull this off. Regardless of a high IQ, he didn't have the façade of normalcy necessary to operate successfully as a killer.

The interview went sideways when Skogen asked for permission to release Simon's medical records. He refused and asked for his parents, a request that Skogen denied. Simon had then asked if he was under arrest and when Skogen replied that he was not, their suspect kicked over a chair and departed without his phone.

As Skogen left to see a judge about gaining permission to release Kilpatrick's medical records, Nadine went to meet Demko for a debrief.


Clint had stopped at a food truck that he said had the best Korean barbecue he'd ever tasted and brought her beef tacos with caramelized kimchi and *sriracha* mango, topped with shredded purple cabbage, and a dish of pot stickers on the side. The fusion of foods was amazing.

They sat at a picnic table behind the sheriff's office under the shade of an enormous old oak beneath fluttering Spanish moss. The day was dry and clear with a pleasant breeze from the north driving off the humidity.

Molly found a branch and flopped down to chew on it as they focused on their meal. Her protection kept her in view, sitting on a bench near the door.

Midway through their meal, Skogen returned with the judicial order.

"Medical records should be up on the file share soon," he said, heading past them and disappearing inside.

A few minutes later, a jeep pulled into the lot and a gaunt young man exited, smoking and pacing until the arrival of a gray

Mercedes. He met the occupant at his driver's side and the two men began a conversation.

"Who's that?" asked Nadine.

"The guy from the gun shop. I'm guessing the other is his attorney."

Nadine eyed the potential suspect. His olive-green tank top made it easy to see how painfully thin he was.

Demko studied him as well. "Not him," he said as the two passed them and entered the station.

She turned to face him. "How do you know?"

Demko finished his last pork dumpling. "Santander got into a pickup truck. This guy drives a jeep."

"Could have used someone else's vehicle."

"True. But the driver had a medium build and wore short sleeves. His arms were visible."

"No tattoos," she said as the realization struck.

"And that one has a full sleeve on his left arm."

She nodded and sipped the remains of her water as Demko finished his last taco.

"I canvassed the neighborhood back at that town house. No one owns a Jack Russell terrier," said Demko. "But animal control recorded one recovered tied to a mailbox two streets over."

"Is it okay?"

"Yeah. Has a microchip. The owner's been contacted. The interesting part is that the collar and leash were missing. Whoever it was secured the dog to the post with a lightweight chain and clip."

"You think I saw him again?"

"Very possible. I gave the information to Skogen."

"Why use a chain?"

"Let us know it was him, maybe."

They shared a long silence as Nadine thought of the chain marks found on the torso of both Nikki Darnell and Rita Karnowski.

"Prints?" she asked at last.

He shook his head. "Special Agent Vea said maybe they'll get DNA."

She very much doubted that.

"Did they find the guy from the hotel? The one who left without notice?"

Demko gave her a grave look and shook his head. Clearly, he thought the man was dead.

She lowered her gaze and it fell upon Molly, who had fallen asleep with the stick still in her mouth.

"I heard from Arlo's attorney," she said.

Demko lifted his eyebrows.

"He told me that the DA is willing to recommend early release, but that's no guarantee. They're going to charge my mom with two more counts of homicide. She's denying it, of course."

Demko used the napkin briskly on his hands and wadded it into a ball before tossing it into the empty paper container before him.

"She's trying to leverage a confession for a reduced sentence."

"Wouldn't you?"

She conceded that point. "I checked the timelines. Dennis Howler would have been in the army when my mother got pregnant with me."

Demko nodded.

"It could be anyone. And Arleen won't tell me." Nadine sighed. "If she even knows." She'd already shared with Demko her conversation with Arleen and the one with Arlo, including her brother's promise to try and remember any men who had been with Arleen when he was five. It was a lot to ask for many reasons, among them that he'd been so young and that there had been so many men.

"You going to look for him? Your dad?"

"I was thinking of doing that DNA thing. Maybe get lucky and find a stepsister or cousin or something."

Demko scrunched up his face.

"Or find one and get unlucky," he murmured.

"What does that mean?"

"Nadine, you've taken considerable pains to distance yourself from members of your family. And with good reason. Do you really want to know who your dad is, or is this one of those sleeping dogs?"

There was a myriad of possibilities. Her father was someone her mom knew back when she was drinking too much, hopping from dead-end job to dead-end job and murdering couples. It was doubtful that he would resemble one of those sitcom dads she'd latched onto as a kid. More likely the DNA match would be an unknown unsub wanted by authorities.

"You're probably right. It's just… It's a hole in my personal history."

"Like being adopted."

"Yeah."

"Just think about it. Carefully."

Her computer chirped. Nadine checked the alert and found the first of Simon's medical records had appeared.

*

Everything Nadine saw in Kilpatrick's medical records was deeply troubling. Simon exhibited a hatred of women. His inability to follow orders from a female officer resulted in his discharge from the military. Psychological reports delineated Kilpatrick's hatred of his mother stemming from her constant belittlement, which Nadine had witnessed firsthand.

As she scanned the clinical notes, she discovered that each of Simon's known attempts to engage in a sexual relationship had been universally humiliating. She was surprised to see he had a higher-than-average IQ, but despite that, his low self-esteem had driven him to a suicide attempt with a bizarre contraption designed to shoot arrows at him. It was this detail that caused Nadine to request that Skogen detain him.

Even worse, both she and Demko agreed that he resembled the man captured on the hotel's security cameras the morning of Santander's abduction. Yet she'd dismissed him as a suspect. Had that mistake cost April Rupp and Linda Tolan their lives?

Could Simon have left custody and gotten to Linda that same night?

His parents reported taking him directly home and that he did not leave that evening. They also had the statement from the naturalist and handyman who reported seeing him at the marina late that afternoon.

Simon Kilpatrick was a solid suspect who ticked all the boxes. Smart, with a history of women troubles, failed military service, psychological problems, depression and a suicide attempt. He also was known to have met at least one of the victims. Textbook, she thought, and frowned.

Perhaps too perfect a fit?

Nadine requested that Special Agent Coleman make the arrest because she wanted to see how Simon reacted to a female agent detaining him. The arrest didn't take long and Coleman arrived with the Putnam County sheriff with Simon in custody. Nadine met them at the county jail just after 3 p.m. Simon had resisted arrest, fought and made a run for it, nearly escaping into the woods before one of the sheriffs and Special Agent Coleman brought him down.

"You were right," said Coleman. "He hates women telling him what to do. Dr. Finch, I think we got him."

*

Simon Kilpatrick did not confess to the crimes but was being held without bond as the arrows in his possession were compared to the wounds found on the victims.

Demko stood with Nadine beside the observation window. Beyond, Simon sat with the sheriff and Special Agent Skogen.

"You think he's our guy?" Demko asked.

"Not convinced. You?"

He shook his head.

Simon fit her description, but not her profile. She'd always insisted on that, ever since he'd first been arrested. Since the man in the room across from her in the hotel did not speak, she did not know if he had a high voice like Kilpatrick, but was nearly certain it had not been Simon. This guy had been predatory, and Simon was not.

Wait a minute. He *had* spoken. Tolan had complained that Nadine's banging had awoken her twice, and he'd said something like, "So help her and go to bed."

Nadine shuddered as she recalled the cold, fixed stare. She had looked at him. But what had she seen? What had she heard?

"What's wrong?" he asked.

She told him. "He didn't have a noticeable accent. And his voice was not unusually high, as Linda Tolan had said."

"Not Simon?"

"I don't think so."

"Better let Skogen know," he said.

A few minutes later, Skogen emerged from the interrogation room and passed her a sheet of white paper onto which Simon had copied several of the lines from the greeting card.

Demko glanced at the page. "He's a righty."

Nadine was no expert, but Simon's handwriting did not resemble the writing on the two communications in the least.

She was missing something. She scowled at the niggling annoyance stemming from knowing an obvious detail was right in front of her but still outside her conscious mind. It aggravated like a splinter under the skin.

"It's not him," she said to the special agent.

"Because?"

She told him about the voice of the man in the hotel. Skogen continued to shake his head, unwilling to consider that this might not be their guy.

"He's too perfect. The psych background, the arrows, the hatred of women, the outdoor experience and the proximity to your second victim."

"Rita Karnowski kayaked there before she went missing."

"Our guy is smart and he's invisible. I looked right at him, twice, and don't remember a single defining characteristic. Simon, on the other hand, caught my attention almost instantly."

She returned the paper. "Did you look at this handwriting sample?"

Skogen rubbed his neck. "Someone else could have written them for him."

"Really? Who?"

"His mom?"

She shook her head. "It's not him."

The stalemate ended with Nadine retreating down the hallway ready to head back to the safe house. She was waiting with Demko for her protection detail when Skogen tracked her down again. She turned, bracing for another battle.

"The *Star* called. They have a new message. It's a manifesto of some kind, but the cover letter is one line. Coleman is on her way to retrieve the packet now."

Her eyes widened.

"Kilpatrick could have sent it before he was picked up," he said.

She shook her head, rejecting the notion. "What is the one line?"

"'She says her name is Jo.'"

She blinked at him. "He has another one."

# CHAPTER TWENTY-ONE

The missing woman was Josephine Summerville, known as Jo. Her car had been tagged yesterday by a Putnam County sheriff. Her vehicle appeared to have been rear-ended. The minor fender-bender likely sent her to the shoulder. Thanks to the cover letter they'd received and Demko, who alerted the sheriff's office that there might be a woman missing named Jo, the patrolman remembered seeing the name on the vehicle's registration and called the Feds. Further digging showed that Summerville's golden Lab, Captain, was found on a hiking trail on the eastern side of the forest the same day. Attempts by the forest department to contact her failed. This initiated a search, but they had found nothing as of 4:45 p.m. today, Thursday, when the latest communication arrived priority mail at the Orlando *Star* escalating the search.

This contact was unlike the others. Beyond the one-sentence cover letter was a seven-page typed manifesto. She read it in the conference room, surrounded by Special Agents Skogen, Coleman and Vea.

"He mentioned in the birthday card he was writing a manifesto," said Vea.

This seemed like dogma, she thought, scanning.

...believe in the power of an apex predator. We do not submit to your laws. All men must follow but one law—the law of nature. Kill or be killed. Survive to adulthood, establish home territory and defend it from all rivals. Murder is a convention of men. Predators understand that killing ensures the success of the species. We are all links in a chain of survival. An animal must show strength to attract a mate, win the right to breed, defend against rivals, raise offspring and ...

She set the statement aside.

"Who is 'we'?" she asked.

"What?" asked Skogen.

"'*We* do not submit...' Odd, don't you think? And if he was defending territory, why kill women, who weren't a threat to his territory in the first place?"

Vea cast her a blank look and Skogen shook his head.

"How do we know he wrote this?" asked Nadine.

"This came along, too. Final page." Coleman laid down the sheet. "It's a copy and I'm no expert, but I'd say the writing is a match."

She recognized the handwriting instantly. The prickling awareness grew to an ear-buzzing rush of blood as she read his demands.

Dear Dr. Finch,

Another bird removed from your territory. If you want a catch and release, read the enclosed pages aloud for me on the local network. I want to see your face... again. You have three days.

I'll be watching.

The Huntsman

Nadine's attempts to swallow failed. Her throat felt lined with chalk.

"You still think Simon Kilpatrick is our man?" she asked.

"We're holding him on the possibility he's working with someone," said Skogen.

She shook her head. "He's not."

"You're probably right." He turned to Special Agent Coleman. "Arrange an additional security detail for Dr. Finch." He turned back to her. "Seems this is a battle of wits between you two."

"What do you want to do?" she asked.

"I'd like to hear your suggestions," said Skogen.

"Well, I think our best chance at recovering Jo Summerville alive is to do as he asks. I need to go on TV and read all this out." She lifted the pages. The convoluted message made little sense. She'd be spending some quality time with it, that much was certain.

"He might kill her anyway," said Coleman, looking grim.

"What is the downside of doing what he asks?" asked Vea.

They all looked to Skogen, a scowl etched his brow. "Makes us look weak. Makes him more important, gives him a platform and notoriety. Scares the public."

"Dr. Finch could go on air and call him a lunatic. Say we don't negotiate with killers. Call him a monster and hint that we already know who he is and are close to an arrest," said Coleman. "Flush him out."

"I think that's a mistake," said Nadine.

"Why? He's challenging you. Questioning your abilities."

"I'm not sure it's a challenge, exactly," she said. "But I believe the threat to Jo Summerville is real."

"Then what? Cave to his demands?" asked Vea.

She blew away a long breath. "I'm not sure. I need to think."

Skogen pointed at an imaginary wristwatch, tapping his wrist. "Tick-tock."

FRIDAY

Nadine had spent much of her adult life dodging cameras and avoiding interviews. Now it seemed she would appear live on television to read the ravings of a psychopath. Check that. Possible psychopath.

Much of the diatribe involved natural selection as seen through humanity's bloody history. Survival of the fittest. The struggle to persist. Rival males battling for territory and females. The importance of hunting in modern-day life as applied to civilization. The need to rid "our race" of the weak in order to create a stronger gene pool. With only a very few tweaks this would be an excellent justification for ethnic cleansing. It turned her stomach to even read the words silently. She could not imagine reading them aloud. But she would. In a few hours, to be exact, because after much discussion, debate and argument, Nadine convinced the team that Jo Summerville's best chance for survival would be for her to go live with this damn thing.

The hunt for her had yielded nothing. The community organized search parties as the authorities continued their quest for the missing woman.

This was the first time their killer had given them the opportunity to recover one of his victims. She didn't mean to squander it.

The worry that he was lying undercut her confidence.

Demko reminded her that the Huntsman was not infallible. He had, in fact, lost Linda, because of Nadine's correct targeting of his territory. Unfortunately, they had not protected her from the second attack.

It was two in the morning and Nadine had given up hopes of sleep. She heard the agents assigned to their protection having a conversation in the living room beyond the master suite. Their laughter drifted through the closed door. Demko had moved a day bed into the seating area. But he slept in her bed. He'd gotten used to her nightly prowling and no longer woke when she sat at her desk with her laptop.

Since the latest letter, she'd been under house arrest, which was fine because she could barely think at the office. Too many interruptions. But now, in the dead of night, she had think time.

Nadine slipped on her noise-canceling headphones and opened her laptop. For the next two hours she re-read every scrap of evidence, every report and her profiles.

When she finished, she had more questions than answers. Gazing at the photo of Jo Summerville, she wondered, did she know this woman? She looked vaguely familiar. Pulling up everything about her on the file-share platform, she made a chilling discovery.

Although Jo worked full-time as a receptionist in an urgent care place, her taxes showed other sources of income. Summerville had a vendor's license for selling antiques with a listed income of $1,200 for the previous year. And she had earned $6,000 working part-time at their favorite gastropub.

"He's been following me," she whispered to the glowing blue screen. "Attacking women on the periphery of my inner circle."

How long until he worked up to Tina, Juliette or Agent Coleman?

*He's showing me how close he can get without my knowing.*

She snatched up his manifesto and re-read the section on camouflage and stealth. Now she wondered if this was less a declaration of his beliefs than an attempt to connect with her and explain or justify his attacks. Did he think that she would understand him because of her connection to an infamous serial killer?

And then another thought struck. Was this his home territory or had he chosen this location because it had been *her mother's* home territory? The chill lifted every hair on the back of her neck and she felt certain she was right.

She stared at the screen, speaking to it as if it were the killer.

"Where were you hunting before this? Where's your home territory?"

She came to another conclusion. This man would not release Jo Summerville. That was not part of his game. He had taken a risk to recapture Linda because she had the audacity to escape him. He would not be making that mistake again.

So why have her read this on air? Was it entertaining for him to have control of her?

Nadine thought about the women in the periphery of her circle and the ones closest to her heart. They all had only one thing in common. Her.

*Was* this a battle of wits or something more? Skogen believed the Huntsman was goading her. That did not quite fit the pattern that was emerging.

At four in the morning, the light began to change. Weariness settled over her and she thought that she could at last sleep. Nadine drew off her nightshirt and tossed it beside the bed. But once she crawled beneath the covers and snuggled up close to Demko's warm solid body, she found herself thinking of other activities.

Demko roused to make a humming sound in the back of his throat. He stroked her shoulder and arm and tugged her close. Both of them slept naked, allowing a wonderful pressing of flesh to flesh.

"Can't sleep?" His voice was gravel.

"Hmmm. Not sleepy."

"You need to rest," he said.

"I know," she whispered.

His hand slipped down her back, cupping her bottom. He turned his head, and she lifted her chin, angling to meet his kiss.

Mouths met and opened. Their tongues began a slow dance of arousal. Even after she had pushed aside all his efforts to move their relationship forward, and stalled and hesitated, he did not withhold what she needed most, the underpinning comfort of his body. As he rolled her on top of him, Nadine understood how much she needed him and how very fortunate she was.

She paused, reaching for the side table and retrieving a condom. He waited as she tore the package and rolled the contraceptive over his erection. Then she straddled him, hungry to take what he offered.

They moved in opposition as they deepened the kiss. She relished the liquid heat and friction, the way his body moved with hers. Her thoughts and worries faded like the sounds of the night creatures at the approach of dawn. All her attention now focused on reaching satisfaction. It was close and he knew how to coax her body to yield.

Her release began with a rippling wave, cresting and crashing into a curling torrent. She threw herself upright upon him, arching back as the pleasure rippled outward, staring down at him, her mouth open and her eyes wide. He gripped her hips. His face showed the strain of a man waiting for his woman's release. Their gazes locked. She groaned as the waves ebbed, feeling him vibrate with the tension to remain still, to hold on just a moment longer.

She lifted and then rocked her hips down on him. He cried out and arched, his eyes pinched closed as his expression mixed pain and ecstasy. The erotic sight and the surging of his body brought her a second release.

Nadine collapsed on his slick chest. He withdrew and pulled her to his side. They panted, staring at the ceiling and the orange light of dawn creeping along the edge of the closed blinds.

"You're so good at that," she murmured.

"*We're* good together. Amazing."

She lifted a hand to his chest and her head to his shoulder. Then she closed her eyes. He settled against the pillows as the light stole between the slats of the venetian blinds.

She needed to tell him about her connection to Jo Summerville and her belief that this killer was circling her like a wolf.

"Not a game," she murmured and forced her eyes open.

But Demko's snore told her that this would have to wait a bit. Nadine's body stilled with her slowing heartbeat and she melted into slumber.


The aggressive buzzing of Demko's phone alarm woke her in what seemed only a moment later but was actually six-thirty in the morning.

She was dizzy from lack of sleep and her body ached in all the right places. Something important, she needed to remember. What was it?

Demko flicked off the alarm. She groaned.

"How late were you up?"

"Till four."

"Oh, Dee. You should rest."

"Can't. Got stuff."

She retrieved her nightshirt, sat on the edge of the bed, and dragged it on. When her head popped through the opening, she discovered Demko on her side of the bed on both knees.

"Lose something?" she asked.

"I hope not," he replied and cast her a lopsided grin. He didn't move and she frowned, sensing something was happening but too dim-witted to work it out until he lifted his hand. In the center of his large, calloused palm was a small black velvet box.

The meaning of this crashed in on her like a falling anvil.

Her mouth dropped open as he lifted the lid. Inside the jewelry box was a gold solitaire ring, the square-cut diamond glittering in the morning light like a thousand rainbows.

His timing was *way* off, she thought.

What she said was: "I haven't even brushed my teeth yet."

He made a sound that might have been a chuckle.

"I know you have concerns about moving forward. I wanted you to understand what the next step looks like for me. This is it."

She stared down at the glittering offering, speechless, as he continued.

"I wanted to do this before you went to DC and then again when you came back and every Friday night since you stepped off that plane. I've been carrying this ring in my pocket for months waiting for the perfect time. Finally it struck me. There's never going to be one. What we do, our jobs, shows us very graphically that life is uncertain. So I'm not waiting any longer. Waiting is a mistake."

She understood that. And he was right, this case alone showed her not to take even one minute for granted.

Nadine's heart hammered so hard in her chest she thought it might break a rib. Her breathing came in short rasping gasps.

*Was this really happening?*

"We're a good team," said Demko.

"If we are such a good team, why did our last case end up with me getting shot and you getting brain surgery?" she asked.

"It was just a clot," he said, waving away her objection.

"On your brain!"

He cleared his throat and tried again.

"Nadine, I love you. I've been in love with you since the first moment I saw you in the lobby of the police station."

Nadine thought she might hyperventilate.

Demko took her hand. "I want you to be my wife, Dee. I want you to believe in the possibility of a life together. I know you have fears."

"I'm terrified."

"I'm asking you to be braver than those doubts and give us the chance to be happy."

"I don't know what to say."

She watched the disappointment flash across his face. He wanted her to say yes. A resounding yes, with no doubts or misgivings.

"He might target you." She'd brought this killer into the center of his proposal. She lowered her head as the shame and guilt took hold.

"There'll be another one after that and after that. It's what you do, Dee. It's your calling. I'm okay with that. But I want to be here beside you. You need me to have your back. I'd do that anyway."

"I know you would."

"Then stop resisting the happiness that is right here for us. You deserve this, Dee. We both do."

Did she? She wasn't as certain. Some of that darkness lived within, it was why she could do this job. Because the shadow of her mother's crimes fell long over her.

He waited. She stared as her heart banged in her throat. Her skin grew damp. His mouth pressed to a grim line and he nodded.

"Keep the ring. Think about it. I'm sorry I didn't do this right, with flowers and champagne."

"I hate champagne."

"I know." He did laugh then. "Here."

He closed the box and pressed it into her hand. "I love you."

He held the ring box tight in both hands over her heart.

"Clint? It's all right, taking a little time?"

His smile was sad and showed the weariness of the world. But he said, "Of course."

"I'm just worried about this case." She didn't want his life jeopardized because of her. She didn't want to bring this killer to this man she loved. Clint wanted to protect her. She wanted to do the same for him.

Her heart ached as joy and sorrow thrashed against each other, two dying fish in a barrel.

"Can we keep this a secret for now?"

His voice was incredulous. "I'm not telling anyone I proposed to a woman who asked to think about it."

She gaped, understanding the punch she'd given his male ego.

He smiled, leaned in to kiss her and rose to his feet.

"You're a thinker. I get it. Just don't think too long because it's a decision of the heart. Now get dressed or you'll be late to the studio."

"Studio!" It all came flooding back to her.

She clutched his hand and explained the connection she had uncovered between her and the latest missing woman. When she finished, he pointed at her phone.

"Call Skogen."

Then he headed to the bathroom as she reached for her phone and remembered the engagement ring. She paused alone in the bedroom and opened the box, drawing out the circle of gold to admire the raised setting and the white diamond. Then she slipped the ring on her left finger. It was a perfect fit.

But was she a perfect fit for Demko?

They'd have to have a conversation, the one she dreaded. The reason she had not wept and cried and instantly said yes. He deserved to know what he was giving up by marrying her.

She returned the ring to the box and slipped it into her nightstand. Then she called Skogen.


Special Agent Jack Skogen arrived to pick Nadine up forty minutes later. Her hair was still wet from the shower, but she'd finished her makeup and one cup of coffee. They pulled up at the television studio at eight in the morning. She was to appear on the ten o'clock news broadcast.

Upon arrival at the studio she discovered that her makeup was all wrong for the cameras and lights. Their makeup artist took over. Nadine watched as she was transformed. Meanwhile, the chrysalises in her stomach emerged.

Her message would air on the morning news. Skogen insisted on pre-recording so that Nadine would be away from the studio at broadcast. Coleman would be here, surveilling for possible appearances of the Huntsman.

The timing of her piece was under three minutes. They seated her and attached a microphone, threading the wire up under her shirt. The director told her to watch for the red light as she counted in.

She focused on the director's hand as he counted.

"Five, four…" Then went silent as his fingers continued to count down, ending by pointing at her. The red light glowed. They were recording.

The moths in her belly settled and she faced the glass eye of the camera, suddenly numb.

"I'm Dr. Nadine Finch, the FBI profiler working on the Huntsman case. He has forwarded this manifesto and a request that I read it on air."

Then her eyes were on the page as she read the now-familiar words with a flat, emotionless affectation. Would he watch it?

"'…To procreate, all living things must attract a mate by displays of strength and cunning, proving themselves strong enough to reproduce, defend their territory against rivals and protect their offspring. To exist past their own life they may pray on weaker members of their race, reject inferior beings, and seek to breed with a suitable female. It is the right of every living creature to ensure their survival by all means. This is the way of life. Fair warning, The Huntsman.'"

She finished the last sentence, the last word, and glanced up, staring at the cold glass eye of the lens.

"And we're at break," said the director.

Nadine rose, forgetting the mic as a woman rushed in to help her detach.

Skogen beamed at her. "That was perfect. Just the right amount of a hostage-reading-demands vibe."

"I'm not a hostage."

"No. Of course not."

It was an odd thing to say.

"Now we wait for word from your boy."

"He's not my boy," she said, more disgruntled by the minute. How long before the major networks picked up the story of Arleen Howler's daughter reading a killer's rant on television? How long before it was up on YouTube and she was a GIF or meme? She felt dirty and the makeup itched.

She headed to a dressing room to wash off the mask. It was not until she cupped the cold water on her scrubbed face that she realized she was sobbing.

Damn them all for making her do this and damn this hunter for fixing his deadly aim on her. There was more than one way to kill a person, she realized.

Sometimes all it took was a very bright spotlight.

An ant on the sidewalk, under the pinpoint light of a magnifying glass, knew that much.

She needed the focus on him. Not her. How this affected her didn't matter if they caught him.

Several serial killers were apprehended because they had fixed on a single person associated with the investigation and opened communications. The Zodiac picked a district attorney. Son of Sam chose a newspaper reporter. The BTK Killer selected a television studio and the lead investigator.

She reassured herself that such contact led to captures. Except with Jack the Ripper. He'd contacted the papers, or so it was believed. But the Ripper had never been stopped. Some thought he'd just moved to Chicago.

Nadine toweled off her face and used her lip gloss. Then she pulled herself together and downed a second antidepressant.

She studied herself in the mirror, thinking about Jo Summerville as she met her own stare.

"He's not going to release her. But if he does, he's not capturing her again."

There was a knock on the door. Skogen's voice was muffled by the barrier.

"He got your message. Floral arrangement just arrived at the studio for you. The card is from your… the Huntsman."

She swung open the door and extended her hand for the card.

He passed her the note, now tucked in an evidence bag.

"Any way to trace this?" she asked.

"Delivery guy is detained. Coleman is on his way to the florist."

She nodded and glanced at the message, seeing a series of numbers. It took only a moment for her to decipher them.

"Is this geographic coordinates?"

"Yes. Vea and the sheriff are en route."

"Where?"

"River Forest in Ocala."

The bag slipped from her fingers. Had he left Jo Summerville at the site of Dennis Howler's grave?

Skogen retrieved the evidence and they rushed from the studio and headed to the forest. When they arrived at River Forest camp, they were directed to the search already in progress with dogs, but Nadine knew a faster way.

"Come on," she said, motioning Skogen back to the vehicle.

He glanced in the direction of the search party and then followed. From the foliage came the bloodhounds' bay. In only a few moments, they reached Deadman's Circle. Storm clouds billowed as a cold current of air shook the trees, making the palmetto fronds rattle.

The dogs were on the scent, but she didn't need them. She knew exactly where she'd find Jo Summerville. Nadine walked to the animal trail, using her hand to push aside the palmetto and spiderwebs as she ran to the unmarked grave, beating the dogs to the clearing. Skogen was at her heels.

It takes an hour for spiders to weave a web. Her mind tossed the information into her conscious thoughts, alerting her that no one had traveled this path recently.

"Where are you going?"

He drew up short at the site before them.

There, pinned to the tree with rope and arrows, just beyond the disturbed earth of Dennis Howler's unmarked grave, was Jo Summerville.

Nadine stepped forward, raising a cloud of flies that had darkened the woman's eyes and gaping mouth, now filled with what looked like cooked rice, but was, Nadine knew, blowfly eggs.

Maggots wriggled from the open wounds covering her lower legs.

"Dead," said Skogen. "Son of a lying bitch!"

Nadine leaned in to read the note over Jo's heart, pinned to the woman's naked chest by an arrow, and read aloud.

"'I have complied with our bargain, releasing my captive.'"

"Bastard." Skogen ground out the word between clenched teeth.

Semantics; releasing her did not mean he would release her alive. Death was a kind of release, she mused.

Nadine stared at the woman, the friendly vivacious bartender from their favorite spot. Rage boiled, rising within her like hot wax. This was more than a game of wits. This was a mission and she would not stop until he was in a cage like the animal he was.

"I need to release Kilpatrick," said Skogen.

"I need to speak to my team."

Nadine saw something, a twitch at the corner of the woman's eye. A shadow, from the ever-changing light dancing across the open patch in the forest, or the wind moving the corpse?

She leaned closer, thinking, *Please don't be alive.*

She spoke, raising her voice to be heard above the wind. "Jo? Jo Summerville?"

The woman opened her eyes, choking as she stared directly at Nadine.

# CHAPTER TWENTY-TWO

Jo Summerville died en route to the hospital. Mercifully, thought Nadine.

She remained at the site of the homicide with Skogen as he processed the scene. Axel Vea and Layah Coleman arrived, followed by men and women from both the Orlando and Maitland FBI field offices.

Crime scene photographers and techs came and went. Jo's body, now at the hospital, would soon be in the hands of the medical examiner and Juliette had gone to help expedite that release.

The day stretched into the evening. The rain came in torrents, further hindering the investigation and soaking Nadine. The insects, deterred by the wind and rain, returned in force after the storm, driving Nadine into the vehicle until the repellent could be located. As the gloom was giving over to true dark, Demko arrived and took her to the safe house.

Nadine sat in the SUV, too tired to hold her head up, her forehead now cradled in the palm of her hand as Demko drove.

"He did as he promised. He released her alive," she murmured.

"Knowing that she wouldn't survive her injuries. He cheated," Demko said.

"Serial killer," she reminded.

He made a humming sound. She had not meant to sleep but must have dozed because she woke with a start as Demko pulled into an Applebee's. The FBI protection unit pulled in beside them.

"Be right back," said Demko.

Nadine watched him go, then nodded to the agent before fiddling with the radio, settling on NPR and a discussion of the red tide, algae bloom and the implication to fish. The topic seemed safe and she rested her head back, closing her eyes.

Demko must have called in an order because he was back within minutes. She had not thought she was the least bit hungry; in fact, she thought she'd never want to eat again after seeing Summerville's final moments. But the aroma of fried food and seared beef roused her appetite. Her stomach growled in anticipation.

Back at the safe house, Molly greeted her, joyful as always to see them. Nadine showered, and emerged feeling half human to share a meal with Demko and Tina. Juliette had not yet returned and she suspected was engaged in an autopsy with the regional ME. Demko put her meal in the refrigerator.

After the leftovers were cleared away, Demko kissed her good night and she dragged herself off to bed. Before turning off the light, she reached in the drawer of the side table and spotted the ring box. It was still there.

She had a half thought it wouldn't be. That his proposal was all a dream. Nadine opened the box and slipped the ring onto her finger again, wishing that marriage forecast happiness and a family instead of uncertainty. She needed to have a heart-to-heart with Demko. Until then, she couldn't accept his ring.

But, oh, how she wanted to! She clutched her left hand in a fist and pressed it to her heart, cradling it with the other, like the infant she longed for and knew she would never have.

The lump rose in her throat and she sagged onto her pillow. She was lucky, she told herself. She had a wonderful man who loved her enough to wish to spend his life with her. A man who understood her in a way that no one else ever had.

For him, their future was bright and clear. He could conceive of no other outcome. But for her, their future was uncertain and strewn with dark prospects. A game of genetic Russian roulette.

And this ring meant she'd have to explain the gamble they would be taking. Then, if he still wanted her, she'd marry him.

Nadine glanced down at the ring, flashing with brilliant white shards of light. Then she squeezed her eyes closed and let the tears leak onto her pillow.

## SATURDAY

Nadine woke with the lamp on her side table still on in the hours before dawn. As was becoming her custom, she moved to the seating area and her desk, flipped on the lamp and roused her desktop. She turned to her profile and hesitated. Then she wrote down the conjecture that had stirred in her mind for days. Putting it down in black and white only made her more certain that she was correct. There was a sick rightness about her theory. And the danger howling straight at her like a tropical storm.

The chilling panic gripping her throat with icy fingers made her more certain. Explaining this, speaking her theory out loud, would be difficult. She hoped to only do so once.

Nadine closed her laptop and noticed the diamond engagement ring she had all but forgotten she wore. She slipped it back in the box, promising to speak to Demko as soon as possible. After that, the decision would be his.

She waited until eight that morning to text her team. Then she fired a group message off to Skogen and his people, summoning them for a meeting at the safe house. She did not expect them to be done processing the scene, but they surprised her. Skogen, Coleman, Vea and Wynns arrived at nine that morning, joining her people at the large rectangular glass table.

"I just released Simon Kilpatrick, the prick. His mommy picked him up." Skogen snorted out of his nose as if expelling an unpleasant odor and looked to Nadine. "So we're all here."

All eyes turned to her. She felt a rush of blood in her face and the tingling awareness lifted the hairs on her forearms. She dragged in a breath and summoned the courage she needed.

"The Huntsman's manifesto was all about hunting, stealth and camouflage. Hiding in plain sight, just out of the notice of his prey."

"We've all read it," said Skogen.

Demko glared at him across the glass surface.

"Yes, and it was also filled with references to domain, building and protecting a territory from all competitors. He referenced the birds. Breeding pairs chasing others of their species from their territory."

Skogen lifted an open hand as if he did not understand her point. She needed to be very clear. Leave nothing to interpretation.

"I have a theory that he did not target these women until after he established his territory. He chose this area and then he used the birding app to lure birders, waiting for likely victims to arrive. It's unclear why he felt the need to clear the area of only female trespassers. But he seems to be attempting to prove himself worthy by clearing women from it."

"That makes no sense," said Coleman, spinning rhythmically back and forth on her counter stool.

Skogen said, "Worthy of what exactly?"

"Of being a provider, a protector. I'm not sure. But he was showcasing his skill as a hunter. He chose this area, the place where my mother killed those women, then killed and displayed them to draw attention. *My attention.* He initially selected his targets at random because he was not trying to lure them. He was trying to lure *me.*"

Demko rose to his feet, shoving the chair backward. He lifted his hands from the glass surface, and she watched the heat outlines evaporate.

"That's not it," he said, leaning in, hands pressed flat to the glass surface. But he'd gone pale.

He thought it possible, terrifying, but possible. No one else objected, though both Juliette and Tina gaped at her.

"Unsubs often watch investigations. Even insinuate themselves into them," said Skogen.

She shook her head. "Not the investigation. Me."

"Explain," said Skogen.

"First he chose this region. Intentionally because it was Arleen Howler's territory. Then he made two kills designed to bring me here. Once he had accomplished that, he selected females with whom I had contact. I only once spoke to Bianca Santander. Linda Tolan and I had a confrontation in the hotel hallway. She clearly made herself a rival. April Rupp may have as well because we argued outside the rental when she learned we were FBI tied up in this case. Demko was there. And Jo Summerville greeted us every time that we went out to supper as a team."

Tina gasped. Juliette looked stunned.

"She was a hostess," said Nadine. "Check her taxes. She worked at the gastropub. My team ate there often."

"Our favorite spot," mumbled Tina.

Tina started to shake. Special Agent Coleman stepped forward to press a hand to her shoulder and Tina seemed to pull herself together.

"Santander, Tolan, Rupp and Summerville belonged to my outer circle. But he's moving inward, toward me."

Skogen's digital forensic expert, Special Agent Wynns, spoke up. "She's right."

The pause stretched as each considered her theory.

"Following that logic," said Special Agent Coleman, "he might attack any of the females in this room."

"Yes. I believe that's true. Eventually."

Demko thudded back to his seat.

"We all need protective details," said Juliette.

"Agreed," said Nadine.

"He was targeting you before the leak?" asked Skogen.

"That's my theory. He's showing me how competent he is as a hunter. How capable of securing a territory."

"How did he even know you were here?" asked Juliette. "How did he know where you were staying?"

Nadine shook her head. "I don't know."

She used her thumb to rub the spot where the engagement ring had been.

"Why?" asked Demko.

"Because he thinks we're the same. I'm the child of a killer. Whatever motivates him to kill, he thinks he and I are alike. This is not his home territory. We need to go over the database again looking for people who have moved into the area within the last year."

Wynns nodded. "I'm on it."

He reached in his bag, retrieved his laptop and powered up.

"If I'm right, he's done this before or something similar elsewhere. We need to find that series. Look for other cases like this one," said Nadine.

"We need to surveil other possible targets," said Skogen. "Nadine, you need to give us a list of any other women with whom you've had casual contact in this area."

"I'll work with her on that list," said Coleman.

Even considering the limited time here, she thought that would be quite a list. Her mind started popping names and faces. The medical examiner for District 5, the cheerful receptionist at the hotel, the tattooed daughter of the gun shop owner. She nodded, momentarily flattened by the enormity of the task.

"He's been targeting you from the beginning," said Demko. His shoulders dropped.

"Yes. I think so. Maybe since my name appeared in the media with the last case. That might be when he moved to this location."

Wynns scribbled something on the notepad beside his laptop.

"I understand why he'd pick you," said Demko. "But I don't understand what he wants with you. Is he planning to do to you what he did to those other women?"

"No. Mating ritual. A bonded pair," she said, using the words from the manifesto and expecting one or more of them to laugh. None did.

"What?" asked Coleman.

She knew what she would say next was narcissistic in the extreme. It was a character flaw she had struggled with. But that did not make her conclusions any less true.

"He's cleared my home territory. Impressing me with his displays of his victims. He's moving closer. He's not trying to outwit me. Has never been trying to outwit me. He's trying to intrigue me."

"We need more protection," said Demko.

"Yes and no," she said. "If I'm right, I'm your logical decoy. He wants me and he'll come after me. Especially if he senses another male in his territory."

Demko and Skogen faced off across the table.

"You're a profiler. Not an investigator. You've never done undercover work," said Demko.

"I won't be undercover. I'll be myself."

"You don't even carry a gun, for Christ's sake."

She regarded him, silently begging him to trust her. She needed to stop this killer. This was the logical way. Then she turned her attention to Special Agent Jack Skogen.

"Jack carries a gun. What do you say, Jack? Care to help me trap this bird?"

Demko was on his feet again, clearly realizing what she intended.

"Act as your 'bonded pair'?" asked Jack.

She nodded. "That's what I'm suggesting."

"I'm not going to let you act as bait," growled Demko. "This is a terrible idea."

Jack ignored Clint and seemed to be weighing his options.

"Since we have a leak, only the people in this room can know about this. To everyone else, Nadine and I need to appear to be a real couple."

"If he's been following your first case, he'll have seen in the news that we were together last year," said Demko.

She shrugged. "We'll make it clear that I've moved on."

Demko gripped the seatback and thumped his chair. He stormed from the table, pausing in the doorway.

"Nadine. Could we have a word?" Then he continued out.

She looked from one silent staring face to the next. Tina and Juliette had her back. Coleman's look was assessing. Skogen's agents shifted uncomfortably. Only Jack smiled, seeming to enjoy Clint's outburst.

"Excuse me," she said.

She passed her security detail en route to the master bedroom. There she found Demko pacing from the seating area to the bed, with Molly trotting along. Did he know he was marching from the symbolic place of her work to the symbolic place of their relationship?

"You're upset," she said, clarifying the obvious. She knew that much. Was it because she'd placed herself in danger by volunteering as bait or because he was angry that he was not acting the part of her love interest? She took a guess.

"If it's because I asked Skogen to act as the decoy, it's his investigation. You're here to assist. And I don't want you being a target." There, she'd covered both possibilities. Now she just needed to get him talking to see which one had him storming from the table.

He paused and stared at her, still as carved marble. Molly sat, eyes on her master. Now Nadine was the one shifting from side to side.

"Say something."

"Is that what you think? That I'm a jealous child, unwilling to let another man near you? That I have so little faith in you, or in us, that I'd rant and cling?"

Cross that off the list.

"My idea is unconventional. But many serials have been caught because they established a relationship with someone connected with the case."

He lowered his chin, dangerously. If this had been her mother, she would already have been shouting, threatening and menacing. But Clint just stared at her, looking as if she had struck him.

"I'm not happy to have you act as a decoy. But I believe you might be right. This may be our best chance at catching this bastard."

"Then I'm confused." She was bewildered by his red face, yet calm tone. His entire approach was so different to either Arleen's or Arlo's. Both of them were volatile as nitroglycerin and apt to go off into a rage with the slightest nudge.

"I can see that."

He stood before her, arms now relaxed at his side. His shoulders dropped and he took a long breath. She held hers as he released his.

"Nadine, are we a couple?"

She cocked her head, not understanding the question.

"I'm asking. Do you think of us as a couple or have I misjudged this relationship entirely?"

"Of course we're a couple." She was more confused than ever.

"Couples make major decisions together. They discuss things. They work things out and come to a compromise or some consensus. At the bare minimum, I would have expected you to mention this to me before throwing it out to a committee. This is a decision that affects us both. Do you not see that?"

Now that he mentioned it, it did seem obvious. She had blindsided him and embarrassed him by not giving him even the barest heads-up.

"I'm sorry. Yes. I should have done that."

"If we are together, then this isn't just about you. It's about us."

She stepped forward. He retreated. For someone who was trained to read other people's emotions and understand relationships, she was certainly blowing hers. It was like a blindness with Clint.

"This hurt me, Nadine. You understand?"

"I should have consulted you. I'm not used to… I've been on my own for a while. I just… I blew it. Please forgive me."

She wanted to make excuses. Blame the stress related to catching this killer. Blame her upbringing or anyone else that was conveniently at hand. It was exactly what her mother would have done. Take no responsibility for her actions. Blame every mistake on others. And that was why she kept silent, refusing to go there.

"It's my fault," she said. "How do I make this right?"

"You can't. Done is done, as they say. But what you *can* do is make sure there are no repeats. I'll do the same. From here on, we talk about things, especially decisions that involve risk."

"Yes. Yes, of course."

Then he took her hand and lifted it to his lips, brushing a kiss on her knuckles.

"Don't shut me out, Nadine."

"I won't."

Forgiveness, she realized, and a second chance. He'd given her both, simply at her word that she'd do better.

She glanced at the nightstand where her ring hid. The object seemed to be drawing her like iron to a magnet. She wanted to slip it on. Tell him she would marry him, that she longed to marry him. But they needed to have another conversation first.

"Clint?"

He released her, giving her a gentle smile. "You better get back out there."

He left her. She took a few moments to summon her courage, then returned to the meeting, slipping into her place to review the preliminary list of locations she had frequented, and begin to compile a list of women with whom she had had casual contact.

One of Skogen's people left to organize security teams on the top ten potential targets.

Finally Wynns briefed them on cold cases. Two drew Nadine's interest. One was a series of four missing persons dumped in a wildlife area near New Orleans. The cases were over a year old. Each woman had vanished from wetland trails in the Barataria Preserve. No bodies had ever been recovered.

"Because he didn't want them found," she said.

The second cold case was a single murder of a white female ornithologist whose body was discovered tied to a tree in a Delaware state forest.

"Mode of death?" asked Skogen.

"Unknown," said Coleman. "There wasn't much left of her. The ME was unable to determine if there were soft tissue injuries such as lacerations or punctures."

"How long after her disappearance was she recovered?" asked Skogen.

"She disappeared in May and was not discovered until September."

Nadine glanced at the tabletop. Four months. The elements, predation by animals and insect infestation, she assumed, removed most of the evidence leaving nothing but bone and sinew.

"Clothed?" she asked.

Special Agent Wynns met her stare. "I don't know. Let me find out."

"Jack," said Nadine, "see if any of our list of male contacts lived in Delaware or Louisiana."

# CHAPTER TWENTY-THREE

## SUNDAY

*After Nadine had read his words, the FBI announced a press confer-ence. He knew they'd found Summerville. The scanners told him that much. A call to the news confirmed that she had not survived.*

*He sat down to watch the FBI's four-thirty press briefing. He'd had to bail on the afternoon workload to see this. His boss was not happy. Not that he cared. She was lucky to have him, didn't deserve him and certainly did not pay him enough for his qualifications.*

*He could have turned on the set in the office and watched there. But he wanted privacy. He knew he would rewatch it many times, focusing on every detail of Nadine's face. He'd taken notice of what she wore and how she tried to hide her feminine willowy beauty beneath the façade of professional attire. She had a natural appeal with a rosy complexion and tempting features. Symmetrical. And they had so much in common. He could hardly wait to have the conversations with her that he had had in his mind. Soon, he promised himself.*

*He was proud that his work had now gained national attention. The broadcaster introduced the clip from the FBI press briefing.*

*He pounded his fist on the arm of the chair in anticipation. The players were already in position. FBI lead investigator, Jack Skogen, stood at the podium looking calm and in control, which he was not. She stood behind and to his left.*

*Nadine Finch wore her hair up in a bun. She looked pale except for the lipstick. He leaned in. The color was a soft pink, the near-identical match to the satin blouse she wore beneath the navy blazer.*

*Skogen spoke about the newest victim, Jo Summerville. He smiled at the memory of securing her dying body to a sturdy oak at the foot of Nadine's father's grave.*

*He had been there. At the dig, dressed as a forest ranger, and spoken to several of the patrolmen. From one of the anthropologists, who needed frequent smoke breaks, he learned what was happening but had not ventured to the dig site until after they had finished.*

*He had had his prey trapped in that small cage so long that her lower half had begun to shut down, shunting blood to her core so that her feet and ankles turned purple and her toes turned black. When the maggots appeared on her feet, he knew he had to act quickly. He'd moved her to her display area before dawn. She had been mainly deadweight at that point. Unable to struggle, semiconscious. The arrows had roused her and he had enjoyed watching her squirm along with the maggots. They were both the same. Inferior species.*

*It was a shame he couldn't stay to watch. He'd left after a long backward glance, fixing the image in his mind.*

*Moving his attention back to the screen, he watched Skogen clear his throat before speaking.*

*"We have recovered the remains of Jo Summerville. The Huntsman failed to honor his agreement to release her alive because he is without honor."*

*"She was alive when I left her," he muttered.*

*"He is a despicable, heinous murderer of innocent women and a liar without integrity."*

*"I'm not a liar. I did as I promised. It's your fault she died."*

*Skogen introduced Nadine.*

*And then he noticed something else. His eyes narrowed as he moved to the edge of the chair, leaning so far forward that he nearly toppled onto the carpet.*

*Was she gazing at Skogen?*

*She was! She wasn't just staring at him—she was fawning. Batting her eyes as she cast him an adoring smile.*

*His insides clenched and he set his teeth together as he watched them.*

*"I'd like our lead forensic psychologist to give the public a few characteristics that might help us catch this killer." Then the FBI agent turned toward Nadine and extended his hand.*

*She slipped her palm against his and held his gaze as he made a disgusting show of escorting her to the podium. There he retained her hand a little too long before finally releasing her and stepping back. Nadine cast Skogen a seductive smile before turning to the camera.*

*He shot to his feet.*

*"No!" he bellowed. "No! She's not interested in him. She's mine. She knows she's mine."*

*He gripped the remote, glaring at the rival male who stood just behind Nadine. Maybe it was his imagination. He rewound the live broadcast and watched again. This time when Skogen dared touch Nadine, he bellowed, the sound shaking the room.*

*Rage built and then pounded through his bloodstream, drenching him in sweat. He lowered his chin, targeting this challenger. He would not lose her to that inferior male.*

*Nadine spoke into the microphones.*

*"His condition is called compensatory narcissism. This disorder leads him to strike at others before they have a chance to strike at him. He can do this because he believes that societal rules do not apply to him."*

*Nadine was now looking at the camera.*

*"In other words, a coward attacking solitary women, while believing these attacks should foster in us a sense of admiration at his cleverness."*

*His jaw gaped and his skin prickled. How could she not understand?*

"*He has no capacity for empathy or for love. But thinks himself deserving of both. No. Not deserving*—entitled, *when he is, in fact, a cold, calculating, arrogant, remorseless killer.*"

*Rage bubbled through him. He lowered his chin.* "*I suppose that makes me like looking in a mirror,*" *he said to the screen.* "*We're the same. I know it. You know it.*"

*Nadine finished. Skogen placed an arm around her shoulders as he switched positions with her. As Nadine turned, Skogen rested his hand momentarily at the nape of her neck.*

*He switched off the television and hurled the remote. It collided with the wall, expelling its batteries.*

*He'd watch it again later when he got himself back under control. Right now, while the lead investigator and two of his agents were conducting a press conference, he would continue clearing the area of troublesome females. He had an itch to hurt someone and had already targeted his next victim. Her shift started in just a few minutes and she was a woman of habits. He grabbed his keys, determined to make this one suffer for everything he'd suffered today.*

"*Damn her. He's not the superior male. Why can't she see? He's not for her. She can't choose him.*"

*He drove to his camp, deep in the forest, and gathered his supplies. His bow and arrows, skinning knife and the spike strip. He'd use this device on the highway to puncture her tires. When she stopped, he'd take her.*

*He caught the flutter of white at his periphery and paused to admire the ghost orchid that he'd collected by skinning the bark from the tree where it had clung. This prized plant was so rare that most people would never see one. Just as they would never see the giant sphinx moth responsible for pollinating them. The flower's feathery petals sparkled white, pristine and perfect. He thought the name frog orchid less poetic but a good one, as the long labellum resembled the legs of a frog. The plant had tolerated the move, thriving for months already because he recognized what it needed to flourish, just as he understood what all creatures needed to survive.*

*Or to perish.*

*He headed out, to lay the trap. He knew her vehicle. It was a simple matter to lay the strip. If he spotted a different car, he'd drag it off with monofilament fishing line. This stretch of road, between her work in Silver Springs and her trailer, was remote and little traveled, especially at this hour when most folks had already made it home for supper. But hers was the night shift.*

*Rosie reported to work at 8 p.m. She was never late, and her car passed this stretch between 7:31 p.m. and 7:39 p.m.*

*The woman was slim and athletic. He imagined seeing her naked, staked to the ground before him, and his mouth watered. That tingle and zing of excitement zipped through him.*

*He'd take Rosie and then he'd move to Nadine's pretty, doe-eyed assistant, Tina Ruz. Oh, the sounds she'd make when he released his first arrow into her pink flesh.*

*The ATV started up with a twist of the key and he roared toward the road, anxious to catch his next bird.*

*

Nadine stood beside Skogen as he fielded questions from the press. She admitted that he was excellent at this piece of his job, leveraging the media to help them narrow the search. She was, however, painfully aware that their offices would soon be flooded with tips that led nowhere, false leads and contacts by some profoundly disturbed individuals. His people would sift through them like a pan full of mud and rock to extract the gold.

When one of the reporters asked if the two of them were involved, Skogen's smile made her squirm.

"Actually, we were together prior to Dr. Finch's completion of her FBI training."

When the questions became repetitive, Skogen called a halt, thanking the media for their attendance.

Coleman and Vea preceded them as Skogen escorted Nadine with an arm resting familiarly around her waist, hand cupping her hip. She smiled up at him, resisting the urge to shake loose. When they stepped through the doorway and the door closed behind them, she glanced expectantly at him, but he didn't remove his hand from around her waist. Instead he drew her closer.

"What do you think?" he asked.

She stepped away, frowning. "It went well."

"I would assume that there will be some media in the lobby and outside the hotel. I think we should hold hands as we leave the building," he said.

She nodded her consent.

He was correct. Several of the reporters lingered in the lobby snapping their picture as they exited hand in hand.

Outside, they emerged into a thunderstorm, waiting beneath cover for their cars. Their driver emerged with an umbrella, which Skogen used to cover them both, holding her at his side with one hand as he extended the umbrella up high enough to allow photographers to catch their exit.

She respected Skogen but did not enjoy his touch, his scent or his overconfident smile. However, she thought he made an excellent target for the Huntsman.

That afternoon, Jack Skogen stopped at the safe house to check in. Tina alerted her and she found Jack in the kitchen accepting a cup of coffee from her assistant.

"Did you see the list Wynns forwarded?" he asked Nadine.

"Yes." She slid onto one of the four stools at the kitchen island. There, Nadine opened her laptop and pulled up the document.

Tina set the mug before Skogen and took her leave. Nadine resisted the urge to call her back and then felt foolish at the impulse.

"Any word on the missing bellman?" she asked.

"No."

Skogen lifted the mug and then came to stand beside her.

Kurt Wynns had narrowed their existing list of male contacts down to thirty-two Caucasian males who had moved into the area within the last seven months.

"Any live in Louisiana or Delaware?" she asked.

"Wynns is running their IDs now for previous addresses. He'll send it along. You have anything else on the profiles?"

"I've narrowed the range based on the last victim's capture and recovery. You're sure she was taken from the pub where she worked?"

"Her car is still in the lot."

"Okay. And I've added it and the recovery site."

"Great." He looked over her shoulder at her map, leaning in too close. He could have looked at this at the office. A Zoom meeting would have sufficed, and she would not now have his breath fanning her neck or his scent invading her nostrils.

"Could you let me know what this updated profile adds to our current target region?" He placed a hand beside her laptop keyboard, inches from hers as he leaned in. Nadine cast a sideward glance at his hand, and the dusting of dark hair on his knuckles. Was he hitting on her?

"My team found something else. We wanted to alert you."

She turned to face him.

"Someone placed a tracking device on your vehicle."

Her heart gave a jolt as she straightened.

"What? When?"

"Unknown. It's been there awhile. Wynns went over it after you suggested that our target might have been watching you. It's likely how he knew you had arrived and where you were staying."

She was now glad that her vehicle had remained parked at the FBI field office since they'd moved to the safe house.

"The other vehicles?"

"Checked and cleared. It was only you. You were right again, Nadine." His appreciative smile made her uncomfortable.

Jack's phone buzzed and he glanced at the screen, then took the call.

"Skogen," he said and then paused. "Where?" More silence as he listened. "Hold on." Jack flipped the call to speaker. "Say that again."

"I said, one of the surveillance teams stopped an assault. Victim is Rosie Napper." That was Axel Vea's voice.

Rosie was the cheery desk clerk at their initial hotel. She worked nights and Nadine had spoken to her often.

"Did we get him?" asked Skogen.

"Negative. Suspect fled from Route 314 south of Salt Springs in an ATV into the forest. They're in pursuit."

Skogen was up and out before Nadine had time to close her laptop. He paused in the doorway, gripping the frame.

"Come on."

Skogen stood with Nadine on the shoulder of Route 314. On either side of the road, just beyond the trimmed grass, stood the dark wall of foliage marking the wilderness of the national forest. From somewhere within came the ominous howl of a coyote, sending a shiver up Nadine's spine.

Behind them, Nadine's protective team waited inside their SUV. Before them an FBI special agent, whom Nadine recognized from Orlando, emerged from a sedan. He met them at the shoulder.

"What have we got?" asked Skogen.

"Napper is en route to the sheriff's headquarters. No injuries. Her would-be attacker used a spike strip to rupture her tires."

He pointed to the chunks of rubber illuminated in their headlights and strewn across the road; beyond were the skid marks where Rosie had obviously tried to steer her car to the shoulder. "Pursuit car was within sight. Napper saw the attacker drag the strip off the road with a rope or something in her rearview. He was approaching Napper's vehicle when support pulled in behind her and scared him off."

"Our guys?"

"Sheriff's deputy."

"Damn it."

Before arrival, Skogen had a chopper in the air, dogs en route and roadblocks up.

"The ATV?"

"Abandoned in the woods."

"Is he on foot?" asked Skogen.

"Unknown."

"Show me."

"Two-mile hike," said the agent.

"Let's go," said Skogen.

"I'll wait with my security," said Nadine.

She was not leaving her protective detail to march into the forest at night, in the dark, with two agents—or ten, for that matter.

"You should wait, too," she said to Skogen.

He frowned at her and then seemed to belatedly recall that they were both now bait in the trap they set.

"Okay."

Coleman, Vea and the agent out of Orlando headed into the woods with flashlights. It shocked Nadine how quickly all traces of the trio disappeared.

"I'd like to speak to Rosie Napper," she said.

She followed Skogen back to his vehicle and he drove them to the highway patrol headquarters in Ocala.

Rosie waited in the office, sitting glumly beside a metal desk. Nadine barely recognized her, she looked so small and downcast.

Unfortunately, Rosie had little to share in the way of details. She had gotten a very good look at the ATV, less so of the driver. The man had straddled the all-terrain vehicle in the darkness of the forest. His headlamp and the headlight prevented her from seeing him at all. When the security arrived, he'd reversed into the trees.

She and Skogen remained with her until Demko appeared, and Nadine left Rosie to speak with him.

"Seems you were right, again," he said. "He's targeting women around you."

"She needs more protection. He'll come back for her."

They stood in silence, both recalling the fate of poor Linda Tolan.

"I'll speak to Wynns. He's the only one not in the forest."

"Did they find him?"

"His camp. It's temporary, according to Coleman. She's the only one who picked up my call. They got the ATV by a creek. Running the serial number now."

"He took a boat."

"That's what they're thinking. He'd be on the St. Johns in minutes."

"My mom used a kayak sometimes. No evidence trail."

"He might already be outside our perimeter."

"Or he lives inside it."

"Tomorrow I'm going back to canvass the businesses around Salt Springs. This guy works in the area. I met him or I've missed him. I need to search again," said Demko.

"And find the bellman."

"Yes."

They made it back to the safe house a little after midnight. Demko left her in her room with a kiss.

"You could stay," she said, feeling exposed and needy and embarrassed.

He shook his head. "You're exhausted."

"Is that the reason?" she asked, feeling this was punishment.

"Mostly," he said. "You asked for time."

She had and he was giving it to her. Their relationship, already complicated before his proposal, now seemed as unstable as a home poised beside a deepening Florida sinkhole. Everything had changed between them since his proposal. She was afraid that moving forward would mean losing him.

He left her alone in the master suite.

She sat on the bed and opened the drawer of the nightstand, drawing out the engagement ring box. The diamond sparkled with promise and she slipped it on again, wishing things could go back to how they had been. Recognizing they never would.


MONDAY

The following morning Nadine met Tina in the kitchen, accepting the coffee she offered.

"Thanks. What's happening?"

"They haven't found him. They're processing evidence at his camp. Been there all night. The ATV was rented with a stolen card. Juliette left a few minutes ago. Back to the ME's office for the Summerville autopsy." Tina shuddered.

"Where's Clint?" she asked.

"He took Wynns's list and said he was running leads. Wanted to speak to Lou Anne Kilpatrick again."

"Simon's mother?"

Tina nodded.

"Why?"

Her assistant shrugged. "Toast or a corn muffin?"

"Muffin." She retrieved her phone and sent Demko a text asking him where he was. Then she sipped her coffee and waited. By the time she'd finished, she was frowning at her silent phone. "Out of range?" she muttered.

There were plenty of places in this region that lacked cell phone service. Still, the disquiet remained as they went to work in the home office.

Agent Wynns connected with her midmorning with a video call. Kirk had a new database to offer. It included all the men between twenty and forty-five who applied for a hunting license. There were several hundred names. Nadine stared at the screen share.

"But this eliminates anyone who has lived here long enough to renew their driver's license," he said, "and this"—he hit something from the sort function—"includes only Caucasians who have brown or black hair."

"How many names?" she asked.

"Fifty-seven."

"All right. Thank you. Did you compare it to the list of men who moved into the area within the last year?"

He hit a button and half the names disappeared.

"What about their previous addresses?"

"None from Delaware or Louisiana."

"Any live or work in our target area?"

"Seven."

She studied the list for any familiar names. "Okay. Thanks. Did you give this to Clint?"

"He's got it."

"Great."

"Also, the brass is on their way. Supervisory Special Agent Gabriella Carter is arriving sometime today."

"Okay." Nadine didn't know if that was good or bad but suspected the latter. "Anything else?"

"Skogen got the handwriting report. He asked me to forward it to you. It's in your in-box."

Wynns disconnected and Nadine navigated to her email in-box. Ignoring the other messages, she opened Skogen's forwarded email.

The report concluded that the handwritten documents were original, not copies, and that the writing was placed there mechanically. The details were not terribly helpful. The expert believed the card and letter were both written by the same person and that this person's "chain code–based features indicated a male affectation." So it was likely a man.

She closed the email that shed nothing new on the investigation.

Tina went for more coffee and Nadine tried Demko again. Then she left him a voicemail.

She had just lifted the coffee to her lips when another video call came through from Agent Wynns. If this kept up, she was moving back to the room and silencing her phone.

Nadine cast Tina an impatient look, relaying her annoyance at this latest interruption. Tina's smile was knowing, well aware of Nadine's need for quiet to work.

"Yes, Kirk."

"Just got a voicemail forwarded from the Orlando office. You need to hear this."

Something in his voice sent her heart pounding in her throat. She rose to her feet, sensing disaster.

"What is it?" she said. *Was Demko safe? Had the Huntsman captured Juliette?*

She gripped the laptop, lifting it from the countertop, her eyes fixed to the screen.

"Ready?" he asked.

She wasn't. "Yes."

"Okay, listen." A moment later, he started the recording, and she heard a high male voice.

"Nadine, I've got your partner. He's going to die, slowly. But first I'll torture him one day for each time he dared to touch you. You won't see him again, but I look forward to our first meeting."

Nadine's heart struck in her throat like the clapper to a bell.

"He's got Clint!"

# CHAPTER TWENTY-FOUR

For the next ten minutes, Nadine slowly lost her mind as she paced from the master bedroom to her office. Meanwhile, Tina, seated at her desk, tried and failed to alert the team.

"I can't reach any of them," said Tina.

Nadine's mind was a confused tangle as the shock and relief interfered with reason. There was something she needed to… *think*. She pressed both hands to her temples trying to focus. The Huntsman said he had her partner.

*Her decoy partner!*

Nadine rocketed to her feet.

"Skogen! Did he mean Skogen?"

Tina stared at her, mouth gaping as Nadine's mind cleared. The Huntsman had Skogen or he had Demko.

"Call highway patrol and the sheriff's offices."

Tina lifted her phone and went to work.

When Nadine's phone rang a few minutes later, she nearly jumped out of her pumps. It was Juliette's number. She sagged in relief and took the call.

"Nadine? What's going on? I've got troopers in my autopsy observation area. Are you okay?"

"Did you get my message?" she asked. Her voice had risen an octave and sounded shrill.

"No. Phone was off. What happened?"

Nadine told her about the message from the Huntsman and that she needed to come in.

"Can I finish up here?"

"How long?"

"Twenty minutes."

"Tell the troopers to wait. Have them escort you from the building and to the safe house."

"Okay. Did you reach Demko?"

Nadine's throat closed. "No," she rasped.

"Oh, my God. I'm coming, Dee." Juliette ended the call.

Nadine sank to her seat, cradling her forehead in her palm, letting the fear escape in the hot tears that rolled down her cheeks.

Tina hovered, uncertain what to do.

She didn't want it to be Demko or Skogen. But her heart ached for Clint and the fear that blasted through her nervous system was all for him. The effort of controlling her sobs took everything she had. She would not let this monster harm him or steal their future. This was her fault for bringing him here.

Why did it take this to recognized that she wanted a life with Clint? She needed him back. She squeezed her eyes shut praying it was a bluff and knowing it was not. The Huntsman had one of them.

She brushed away the tears. Time for that when she saw him safe. Held him in her arms and…

*What if he was already dead?*

No, she was not falling into that pit of *what ifs*… it was a quagmire that would only keep her from doing her job.

Agent Wynns phoned again. Tina huddled close to listen as she put the call on speaker.

"I reached Coleman. Vea's been shot."

"What?" How could that be? "What's his condition?" she asked.

"Stable. Layah said that they were checking a houseboat on the St. Johns. Looking for the Huntsman, and the occupants fired at them. They engaged and killed the shooter. Axel took a round in the neck."

"The neck!" Nadine's hand went to her abdomen and the place that held the scar from her own bullet wound.

"Did they find them?"

"It was a meth lab."

She wrinkled her brow in confusion. "A what? So… unrelated?"

"Yes. Bad luck on both parts."

She pressed one hand to her mouth as she exhaled, trying to hold it together.

"Clint?"

"Nothing. We're looking," said Coleman.

"Skogen? Do you know his whereabouts?"

"Unable to reach him. We'll keep trying."

Wynns disconnected and Nadine called Demko again, leaving another voicemail. She was just ending the call when Demko strolled into the bedroom.

"Hey, there you are," he said to Nadine.

Nadine leapt to her feet, the tears streaming down her face, and threw herself into his arms. Her knees gave way and he wrapped her tight, holding her against the wonderful solid wall of his body. She inhaled the sweet scent of sandalwood and sweat. *Thank God.*

She buried her face in his neck and sobbed. He lowered her into the chair in the bedroom. Then he sank to one knee at her feet. She held tighter, locking her arms around his neck like an inexperienced wrestler, refusing to let go.

"Hey, there. What's wrong?" He rubbed her back and gradually she released her grip and allowed him to ease away. He held her upper arms and stared at her wet face as she cupped his jaw in both hands and gulped air.

"Where have you been?" she said, her words a croak.

"Running leads at outdoor adventure outfits operating in the forest." He pulled back and looked from Tina, also weeping, to his escort agent and back to Nadine.

"Why didn't you call? I left messages! You didn't—"

He interrupted. "My battery died. What happened?"

Tina explained about the phone call while Nadine tried to pull herself together.

Demko lifted her chin with the pad of his index finger. "You thought it was me."

She nodded. The relief over his miraculous return set off a shudder and another round of tears. And now she trembled and sobbed, face planted in her hands.

"I'm here. Hey. Easy now. Breathe." He stroked her head and then moved his broad hand in a circular pattern in the center of her back. "It's all right."

"It isn't. This means he has Skogen," she whispered.

Clint snatched up her phone. "I'm calling Coleman."

Nadine stopped him and then caught him up, telling him about Axel, the meth lab, Skogen being missing and that Skogen's supervisor, Gabriella Carter, was en route from DC.

She had just finished her explanation when Juliette burst into the bedroom. The two women hugged, triggering Nadine's tears again.

"He's safe," said Nadine.

Juliette lifted an arm to hug Demko. Tina hugged them both and the four of them held each other until Demko broke away.

"We look like a rugby scrum," he muttered.

Her team was all here. All safe.

But she felt a chasm open in her stomach as she remembered that Skogen was in horrific danger.

"Call Coleman. Tell her it's Skogen," she said to Tina.

"Or he's bluffing," said Demko.

Nadine wished that were true, but every instinct told her that the Huntsman did not bluff or make threats. He had Agent Jack Skogen and they needed to find him fast.

Supervisory Special Agent Gabriella Carter appeared on the conference screen before them as they all took their seats. The woman had a cap of short black hair, brown skin and a military bearing. Her lips were stained a burgundy color and her mouth was drawn into a tight line.

"Dr. Finch. Agent Wynns has briefed me." She turned her head. "Wynns just heard from Florida Highway Patrol. They've located Agent Skogen's vehicle at a marina south of DeLand and have secured the scene. His protective detail is dead and Skogen is missing."

Nadine swallowed. This confirmed it. The Huntsman had Jack.

Carter turned her head again. "Coleman, how is Agent Vea?"

"Stable. Bullet passed through muscle at the base of his neck. Blood loss was significant."

"I'm sure." Carter scanned the room. "We have an abducted agent and one dead. We need to mobilize every law enforcement agency in the state and find Skogen. Get Skogen's photo and description to media outlets, and I mean now. I want alerts to every cell phone in three counties."

Nadine raised her hand as if she were back in elementary school. Something about this woman intimidated the heck out of her.

"We have a leak. Someone released my name to the media. I don't want that leak to jeopardize this operation."

The supervisory special agent cocked her head and gave Nadine a disappointed look.

"Special Agent Jack Skogen was the leak. He released information on you to the media when the investigation stalled, hoping to engage the unsub."

Nadine's jaw dropped open and she gaped, turning to Demko.

"Well, it worked," said Demko, his tone relaying banked fury. "We got his attention. And he got our lead investigator."

# CHAPTER TWENTY-FIVE

*Jack returned to his senses, trying to remember why he was on the ground. His head throbbed. Had he fallen? He raised his hands to check for injury and saw silver duct tape secured his wrists before him.*

*A shiver of apprehension trickled down his spine as he thought of Jo Summerville strung to a tree like a rotting carcass. He remained motionless, moving only his eyes. He was lying on his side along the roots of a large tree. Blood dripped across his forehead and pooled against his cheek.*

*He heard only the wind—and then the sound of footsteps. Jack closed his eyes and forced his body to relax. Through veiled lashes he watched a person squat beside him.*

*"Wakey, wakey." The voice was male, and the words punctuated with a tapping at his cheek.*

*Jack lunged, taking his opponent to his back. The man's eyes startled wide with astonishment. Jack used his bound wrists to strike the man's jaw.*

*Blood sprayed across the ground.*

*The downed man lifted a hand in surrender. "Hey, relax. I was trying to help. Thought you were drunk."*

*Jack had both fists raised above his head. He hesitated.*

*"I'm a federal officer," he said and felt something brush his leg.*

*An instant later, his muscles spasmed and he toppled to his side. The man beneath him scrambled up and the cramping abated. Jack pushed himself up to sitting and this time saw the electric baton wielded by his opponent as it contacted his leg. Instant pain and cramping followed. His body seized, no longer able to follow his brain's command. A moment later, the world went dark.*

*He came to, on his back, staring up at an opening between a web of tree branches. The gray-green Spanish moss hung limp over them against a cloudy sky. His first attempt to move met with resistance.*

*Jack lifted his head and glanced about. His wrists and ankles were now tied with leather straps. Each tether was anchored to a metal stake driven into the damp ground. He wore only his trousers. His shirt, shoes, socks and slacks had been stripped away, leaving him in only his boxers. Where was his gun—his phone?*

*His breathing accelerated as he recognized that he was staked spread-eagled. He tugged at the bindings and found them fast.*

*Helpless. Sweat poured down his chest as fear locked his aching joints. His hesitation might have cost him everything.*

*He listened for some sign of human activity. He'd been on the short trail from the archery range, heading for his vehicle when…*

*Cattle prod. It had to be.*

*Jack flexed his leg and found it ached, as if he'd suffered the worst cramp of his life.*

*A breeze rippled through the trees, fluttering the sheets of moss. The quiet and the peace were illusions. He needed to get free before whoever did this to him came back.*

*He tested the bonds again, wondering if he could yank one of the stakes from the earth. Given time, he might.*

*Then he heard the scraping sound. Rhythmic. Familiar. It took only a moment to find his captor. The man sat on a stump six feet behind Jack's head, whittling. Beyond him stood a weathered, windowless shack. Someone had tacked a huge gator skin to the graying boards. Long ago, judging from the rusty nails. The man thumbed over his shoulder to the hide.*

"Gonna tack you up there when I'm through. Leave you as a gift for posterity." He checked his work, rubbing a thumb over the pointed tip of the sliver of wood. "You'll probably end up in an FBI textbook of what not to do when confronting a predator."

Jack's stomach twitched as the man stood and sidled forward. If he had seen him before, he did not recall. The man was clean-shaven, dressed in camouflage, laced military-style boots and wearing a red cap. There was a pistol fixed in a leather holster at his hip and fastened to a nylon belt around his waist. Jack made him at five-seven, one-sixty. Slim, athletic and maybe thirty-five. He had the gaunt cheeks and rasping voice of a habitual smoker. Dark hair and eyes.

In other words, he looked unremarkable.

"Got me memorized yet?" His captor folded the blade and tucked it away. "Did you see I'm missing the tip of this finger?" He held up his right hand, indicating his index finger. "Shrimping accident. Winch. Unfortunately, you won't have a chance to give that description to anyone." He thumbed at the gator skin again and smiled.

"You should let me go. Kidnapping a federal agent—"

"Hush now, or I'll muzzle you." He didn't raise his voice. The calm was chilling.

"You're the Huntsman?"

He doffed his hat and then tugged it back in place.

"And you are the man who dared to touch my intended." He squatted beside Jack. His eyes blazed, intent, as his smile broadened, curving into a terrible mockery of contentment. Anticipation, Jack thought. The look of a cat the moment before…

He pounced, capturing Jack's left hand, and pinning it to the ground.

Jack struggled, in an ineffective attempt to escape. The Huntsman slipped the sharpened wedge of wood under Jack's nail and shoved.

The pain exploded up his arm and Jack screamed.

The agony finally receded to a pulsing throb and he could think once more. He looked at his left hand. Blood trickled around the *wooden shiv rammed beneath his index fingernail. Jack glanced back, finding the huntsman again sitting on his stump, whittling a new sliver of wood.*

*

Nadine and her team sat with Agents Coleman and Wynns in the safe house on the video call with Skogen's supervisor.

Nadine closed her gaping mouth, still wrestling with the revelation that Jack had released her name to the media after promising to keep her involvement private. He'd betrayed her to get his investigation moving. And he'd succeeded, but at great personal cost.

From the monitor, Agent Gabriella Carter fixed her attention on Clint.

"Detective Demko, right?" asked Carter. "I've heard a lot about you."

"None of it good, I'd imagine."

"Little. But it seems you are the closest we have to a liaison with local law enforcement, so I'm putting you in charge of that."

"I don't work for the agency," Demko reminded.

"I'm making you a special agent, effective immediately."

Special Agent Carter scanned Nadine's group.

"We're landing. I'll be there in eighteen minutes."


## TUESDAY

From then on, everything happened very quickly.

The FBI took Nadine's phone and gave her a replacement. The substitute worked, but the FBI now had the ability to record all incoming calls and listen in real time. Agent Wynns told her she'd never know the difference. Even the cover was identical.

Unfortunately, as the afternoon dragged to evening, they still had not located Skogen, and, at Tina's insistence, Nadine had finally dragged herself to bed.

So when the phone rang at 12:01 a.m. on Tuesday, it startled Nadine from a sound sleep.

The disorientation lasted only a moment and she had the phone in her hand before the third ring. Her first thought was that it was Demko with word on Skogen. She had tried to get Demko to stay with her but, as liaison with local law enforcement in the hunt for a missing FBI field supervisor, he had too much to do and left as soon as he was assured that she, Tina and Juliette were secure in the safe house.

She lifted her new device and checked the caller ID: *SKOGEN*.

Her heart rate tripled as she pushed herself to a seat, frozen as the phone rang again. The Huntsman had Jack Skogen. So he also had Jack Skogen's phone.

Nadine swallowed, her mouth now a salt mine, clogging her throat.

"Hello?" she whispered.

"Dearest one." The male voice was unfamiliar, high-pitched and unnatural. "I hope I didn't wake you."

"Yes. I was asleep."

"That doesn't bode well for your fiancé, Jack. He'll be grieved to know he is so easily forgotten."

"Do you have him?"

"Of course."

"Why?"

"He touched you. That means he belongs to me." The sound he made rippled in his throat like a purr of pleasure. "For a while longer."

"Don't hurt him."

"Too late for that."

"If you give him back, we'll…" She struggled for some bargaining chip.

"You'll what?" His voice contorted, as if he were an actor playing some part.

"We won't press charges for his abduction."

He laughed.

Nadine's heart slammed against her ribs. Were they listening? Tracing the call?

"You can do better."

"Why don't you use your real voice?"

Another chuckle.

"What do you want?" Even as she said this, she understood her mistake.

"Hmmm. Beyond the sound of your sweet voice?" His heavy breathing gave her chills. "I want *you*, Nadine. But you know that."

Her skin went damp in a cold sweat, and icy tendrils constricted her throat.

"I'll release him alive only if you agree to come to me tomorrow by noon. If you fail to appear, I'll skin Agent Skogen alive and tack his hide on my wall."

"Where?"

"So quick to trade your life for his? Heroic, my love."

"You aren't going to kill me."

"How do you know?"

"Because we're the same. It's why you want me."

He chuckled. "Very good, my little huntress. Very good. Already we understand each other. And this one? He's not for you. Too predictable. Too moral. Too one-dimensional and far too weak. He's bound by all those rules that don't apply to ones like us."

"Tell me where."


She had been off the phone only moments when her security detail had charged in. They hustled her out of bed and debriefed her, sending Nadine back to her room after two in the morning.

Once alone, she called Clint and, bless him, he picked up on the first ring.

"What's wrong?"

The hour of the call accounted for the alarm in his voice.

She told him. No one from the FBI had alerted him that they'd had contact with their unsub.

"He's lying again," she said. "He won't let him go."

She knew this because she understood him. The Huntsman believed Jack Skogen had been with her. There would be no pardon from that sin.

"Does he think to take us both?" she asked.

"He'll never do it. You'll have better protection than the president. Did they tell you their plan?"

"What do you think?"

"That'd be a negative."

"Right in one," she said. "Where are you?"

"Four forty-one at a roadblock."

"I don't think he's using the roads."

"We are also stopping marine traffic."

Nadine turned the engagement ring on her finger, so it caught the light. Wearing this at night had become a habit. It reminded her of the future that she and Clint might share if she were brave and he were understanding.

"When are you coming back?" she asked.

This was met with silence.

"Clint?"

"Nadine, you know what he'll do to him. I have to try to find Skogen." He blew away a breath. "I told him tempting the Huntsman was a terrible idea."

"Yes. You did."

What was the Huntsman's plan? Was he going to grab her and keep them both? Would he make her watch Jack's death? Now that sounded so much like what her mother had done that it had her drawing the covers up over her knees.

"I need to speak to you," she said, noting the quaver in her voice.

"I'll be there in the morning. Try and get some sleep."

"I sleep better when you're here."

"Me too."

He disconnected and she watched her phone flip back to the factory-set home screen, realizing belatedly that the FBI had been listening to their call, in real time.

She curled in a ball, pressing her left hand into her right, feeling the precious metal against her palm. Then she rose from the bed and dragged on her robe. The agents stood as she entered the center of the house.

"Just getting Molly," she said.

She found Demko's dog asleep on his bed. Instead of bringing his companion back to her room, she crawled under the covers beside Molly.

The dog groaned and then placed her head on Nadine's stomach. She rested a hand on the dog's shoulder, listening to her soft snore. Sometime after the sky turned gray, she melted into exhaustion, sliding away to troubled dreams.

The gentle rap on the door brought her awake.

"Dr. Finch? We need you," said a female voice.

She slipped her legs over the side of the bed and headed after Molly. One of their security detail took the boxer out and she continued to her room where she slipped the engagement ring back off her finger and returned it to the box. Each morning she was more reluctant to let go of her ring, the physical reminder of Clint's love.

Tina's cat appeared from the hall to lounge in the patch of sunlight on the plush carpet. Nadine stepped over her on the way out.

When she appeared in the kitchen, it was to find two women sitting at the table with Tina and Agent Coleman. With a jolt she recognized Gabriella Carter, Skogen's supervisor. Nadine nodded a hello.

Carter had brown skin, was tall, curvy and cast an imposing figure in a pinstriped fitted suit. Her shoulder-length hair, styled in corkscrew curls around her face, did not soften her forbidding expression. The director motioned to the other newcomer, who wore a navy-blue suit, peach-colored blouse and a familiar necklace. Now that she thought about it, Nadine recognized both the suit and the blouse as well. Because they were hers.

The woman rose and Nadine noted that she was small, with dark brown hair, tugged back in a ponytail at the nape of her neck, exactly as Nadine now wore her hair.

The female faced Nadine and she recognized other similarities. The shape of her face, her pale complexion, height and weight, even the makeup all matched. But not the eyes. Her eyes were not hazel but gray.

"Dr. Finch, I'd like to introduce you to Agent Taplin. Samantha will be your body double for today's operation."

"My what?"

"She's taking your place," said Tina. "We're staying here while Taplin heads to the Marion Sovereign Building on Magnolia."

The peeling white elephant was once the tallest in the city, an anchor in the older section of town. A hotel in the 1880s, it survived through transformation into an office complex and sat on the next block to the new, imposing concrete-and-glass complex of the Marion County Judicial Center, built over the original courthouse. That massive complex stretched over three blocks and held who knew how many court security officers, police and correction officers. The location seemed an odd choice, but her indignation at being left behind overwhelmed her puzzlement.

She was an FBI agent, too.

"Oh no she isn't," she stormed.

"We aren't letting you go on this operation."

"Why not? He expects to see me."

"You don't have the appropriate training for this sort of field operation."

She pressed her mouth tight, trying to think how to convince them. This was a mistake. He'd seen her more than once, up close. He'd been following the last case and likely watched the press conference. But her belief that the body double would fail accounted for only part of her disquiet.

It was the site. It didn't fit.

The Huntsman had picked downtown Ocala. The historic district could not have been more unlike the national forest, plus this location simplified the FBI's operation. Surely, he'd realize this.

"He'll know. If you want him, it has to be me."

Director Carter shook her head. "Nonnegotiable."

The pause stretched as Nadine refused to back down.

The doppelganger stepped between them, facing Nadine.

"Dr. Finch, I'm so pleased to meet you. I'm a fan."

She offered her hand. Nadine took it and found another difference. The woman was clearly in top physical condition judging from her bone-crushing handshake.

Carter took the opportunity to step away from the confrontation.

"I'd like to spend some time with you this morning, getting to know your mannerisms, how you walk, sit and so on." The woman had a hard New York accent.

Nadine stepped back as annoyance crept up past the indignation.

"Are those my clothes?" she asked Agent Taplin.

"Why, yes. Your assistant collected them for me this morning from your room."

Because she'd been sleeping in Clint's room.

"The operation is only three hours away," Tina said. "She needed to get prepped. I helped her with the makeup."

Nadine gaped.

"Not your makeup," Tina assured her. "Mmm, let me get you some coffee."

Nadine studied the light makeup and familiar lip stain on Samantha Taplin. She felt stupid that she had not known there would be a body double until she remembered that she could not read minds.

Director Carter motioned Nadine to a seat and the two began peppering Nadine with questions. Over the next hour, Nadine performed such difficult tasks as walking, sitting and speaking, while her doppelganger practiced.

"Where's your gun?" asked Nadine.

"Which one? I have three," said Taplin.

Nadine did not think the Huntsman would be fooled. This woman was too bold and brimming with confidence. A standout, where Nadine preferred the role of observer and entered the spotlight only as a last resort. But Taplin seemed destined for press conferences and commendations. An attention-getter.

During the morning together, the woman's accent faded, replaced with Nadine's, as she picked up the same intonation, cadence and tone.

Agent Taplin left wearing Nadine's sunglasses with one of the security detail, before eleven. As she watched her go, Nadine felt sick to her stomach. She knew it wouldn't work, but there was nothing she could have said to convince Agent Carter otherwise.

"What do we do now?" she asked.

"Anything you like. Try to relax, Dr. Finch. You seem tense," replied Carter.

"What if he calls me again?"

"He won't. Agent Wynns is seeing to that. Calls intended for you will be routed to Agent Taplin for now. If all goes well, we will have him in custody in a few hours."

*

The hours passed and none of the agents returned.

Demko arrived back that evening. She and Tina saw him fed before he dragged himself off to bed for a few hours. Molly joined him, curling up with her jaw resting on his feet.

Nadine returned to the main room to find Muffin walking across the buffet. From the kitchen came Tina's voice.

"Yes, I'll get her." She rushed from the room, coming up short when she spotted Nadine. "The exchange failed. Something went wrong."

"Do they have Jack?" asked Nadine. She pressed both hands over her heart, trying to stem the frantic beating. What had gone wrong?

Would he kill Jack?

"No. He never showed. They've been waiting for hours. But nothing."

"He still has Jack."

Tina extended her phone. "Carter wants to speak to you."

She took the phone. "This is Nadine."

"Dr. Finch, I'm sure your assistant told you."

"Where's Jack?"

"We don't have him. The target either backed out or this was some part of his game. Do you have any opinion?"

"Neither the time nor the place seems appropriate. His captures have all taken place in the forest or at the perimeter. Yet this meet was urban. Even worse, there is no way to escape with a hostage from the Marion Sovereign Building. And no cover on 1st Street or Magnolia for a getaway. He wouldn't have cover and you would have taken the higher ground."

"We had snipers in place on the Judicial Center and surrounding buildings."

"He would never have been able to get away from you."

"That's true. Dr. Finch, this input would have been helpful during the planning."

"And I look forward to being included in that planning going forward."

The silence was as close as she'd ever get to an apology.

"Noted," said Carter. "Operation is shutting down."

"How is Agent Vea?"

"Out of ICU. Prognosis is good."

"May I see him?"

"No. Too dangerous at this time."

Nadine heard muffled voices.

"Hold on a moment." She picked up more side conversation before Carter returned to the call. "Wynns has a call for you. Patching it through now. Pick it up, Nadine, it's the Huntsman."

# CHAPTER TWENTY-SIX

Even expecting the call, the ring from the phone clenched in her hand made Nadine jump. Tina stared at her, wide-eyed, clutching her cat.

Nadine cleared her throat and answered.

"This is Dr. Finch," she said. Her voice relayed calm, a technique she had learned when dealing with her mother's manic behavior. But inside, her blood roared, pounding in her temples like a battering ram.

"Nadine. So good to hear your voice. Did you have a pleasant afternoon?"

"I waited for you."

"But not alone. That was a condition. And a body double." The pause stretched. "Disappointing."

"You weren't going to show up in any case."

"True. I'm not an urban hunter."

"Then what was the point?"

"To let your handlers know it won't work. It has to be you. Only you."

"I want to speak to Jack."

"I'm sure," he said and chuckled. "Unfortunately, I'm not addressing your desires but mine. You disappointed me. Jack will be paying for that disappointment."

"Don't you hurt him."

"Or what? You are in no position to rescue him. You were, earlier today. But you decided to bring an army. Was all that FBI or did you also have locals? I've never seen so many sheriff's vehicles in Ocala before."

"So you were there."

"Of course."

And yet, none of the agents had spotted him.

"Where?"

"Let's just say when you are watching an eagle, you choose the second highest tree."

"Because the eagle takes the highest?"

"Very good. Especially for someone who spends so little time out of doors."

Was she supposed to keep him talking? There had been no time for instructions.

"Your fiancé is a strong man. I'll give him that. But he won't take much more. I don't want us beginning on the wrong foot, so I'll give you a last chance, Nadine. But you must come alone."

"Where? When?"

"Tomorrow night. Eleven p.m. You'll be in a kayak, alone on the St. Johns."

"There are gators in those waters. They are active at night."

"So stay in the kayak."

"I've never even been in a kayak."

"You have all morning to practice. Drift downriver from the marina where your mother worked. I'll find you. I look forward to meeting you privately."

That scenario gave her a chill that wrapped right around her neck to her jaw.

"I want Jack alive. No tricks."

"One more chance, Nadine. And no more body doubles. If you don't show, I'll kill him and send you his heart."

*

Nadine crawled into bed after midnight. The operation had moved to their field headquarters. After lengthy discussion, and over Demko's objections, Nadine had agreed to go in person down the river, at night, in a kayak. She needed to practice kayaking in the dark.

The FBI had obtained three kayaks and Juliette and a Navy SEAL had taken her out to practice on a portion of the river temporarily closed to all boat traffic.

She had as much confidence in her ability to maneuver the watercraft as she did in her ability to walk on water. Chances were high that, despite the training, she'd likely flip over. She'd flipped it today and knew that once she went in the river, she was not climbing out onto a tippy, brightly colored, plastic log.

The FBI had decided that "alone" would mean she made the journey by herself. But there would be Navy SEALs in the water and snipers in the trees from DeLand to Blue Hole State Park.

Sore muscles and exhaustion did not help Nadine fall asleep. Demko's objections and images of Jack Skogen undergoing torture kept flashing through her mind's eye.

When Demko had seen her on the verge of tears, he had ordered her to bed, promising to take up the argument in the morning.

Nadine sat on the coverlet, flicked on the light on the nightstand and opened the velvet box. Then she went through her nightly ritual of slipping the engagement ring on her finger.

Tomorrow, before they left for the river, she'd voice her concerns to Clint about what their child might become. If he still wanted her after that, she'd keep his ring and marry him.

Something moved beneath the bed. Nadine yipped and scrabbled in the bedside drawer for the Mace. Now kneeling on the bed, she held the open container and prepared to scream for all she was worth when a furry arm darted out from beneath the coverlet and batted at her discarded socks, sending one skittering across the laminate flooring.

"Muffin! You nearly gave me a stroke."

She put down the Mace and lifted the remaining sock. Then she crawled off the bed and dangled it just out of reach of the feline. Muffin's paw appeared again, swiping at the moving target. Finally the cat darted out from beneath the bed.

Nadine lifted the cat and held her against her chest. She stroked the soft fur and cooed.

"How did you get in here?"

Muffin rubbed her head against Nadine's neck and purred.

"You are a bad kitty, scaring me."

She smiled, closing her eyes as she held the comforting ball of fluff. Suddenly she understood why Tina allowed this unmanageable feline to have the run of the place.

"You're all right, Muffin," she whispered and rocked back and forth. The cat draped over her chest and shoulder.

Nadine spun in a slow circle and froze.

Before her stood a man, dressed in black from his head to his feet with only his eyes showing. Black grease covered his face.

Adrenaline flooded her system, speeding her heart rate and lifting the hairs on her head.

"Nadine, I've so looked forward to our meeting," he said, his voice low and holding the slightest foreign accent. He lifted some sort of straw to his lips and his cheeks puffed out.

Nadine's lungs and feet seemed to have switched off and she found herself frozen, unable to run or scream as terror lashed at her vocal cords. She threw the cat as she dove, rolling over the bed. She landed on the opposite side on the floor. Something stabbed at her neck, burning like a hornet's sting.

She lifted her hand, probing, and plucked out a dart. She stared at the thing. It had a red pom-pom on the end. But it was going blurry. She blinked, trying to focus.

Someone had stamped on the brakes in her body. Her heart rate slowed. Her eyelids drooped. She needed to scream and filled her lungs to do so when he was there beside her, gloved hand pressed to her mouth. She inhaled the acrid smell of sweat and grease. Her muscles turned to jelly and she sagged. He drew back his hand.

The familiar zipping sound of adhesive tape being torn preceded the tape being slapped across her mouth.

He smiled and stroked her cheek with a gloved hand. "You rest now and I'll get us home."


Nadine woke to discover she was on her side, trapped in a plastic container. From the jostling, she believed she was in a vehicle, traveling over rough road. How much time had passed?

Nadine thrashed inside her tiny prison, howling through whatever covered her mouth. She banged back and forth against the enclosure. Was it a coffin?

Not a coffin. She howled, the sound a sad mewling cry, muffled by the tape across her mouth. Tears leaked from her eyes, gliding down her sweat-damp cheeks. Back and forth she rocked, lifting her knees to crash against the walls of her enclosure.

How long she raged and thrashed in the dark, she did not know. But exhaustion took her at last. The dryness in her throat and the throbbing at her temples told her dehydration had begun.

She lay her head down on the hard floor of the container. She needed to think.

*Stop moving. Figure out what to do next.*

Did they even know she was missing?

How had he gotten past the cameras, protective detail, and security system? How had he even found the safe house?

Nadine's heart slammed against her rib cage.

They'd followed Agent Wynns or Juliette. Or Jack had told him. She was certain and knew that, under torture, she would have done the same.

She struggled to control her breathing. Looking back wouldn't help her. She needed to look forward.

Gradually her senses reengaged.

The air smelled of plastic and the temperature here was so hot and humid that sweat poured from her body and puddled beneath her.

She thumped back and forth in her tiny cage and discovered several things. First, her wrists and ankles were bound with duct tape and secured together, placing her in an awkward position with her arms and legs tugged behind her so she was stretched like a bow. Second, she had both a gag in her mouth and tape across her face. And finally, someone had drilled airholes in the top of the container. By craning her neck, she could see the stars. She could also see that the holes were drilled in precise rows and columns as if punctured by machine or by a very orderly individual.

She tried and failed to topple the container. Craning her neck again, she noted that some of the holes were obscured, suggesting some kind of a strap secured her container in place. Listening attentively, she determined that she was in the open rear section of a truck. The familiar hum told her they traveled over pavement. She could determine nothing from the stars. But she could discern when they were passed by a vehicle heading in the opposite direction from the momentary light that flooded into the top of the container. From this she saw the box was black and the top yellow.

Some part of her brain recognized that this was useless information, since she could not pass any of it on to those who would be searching for her.

How long of a head start would he have? She knew the shift change happened at 1 p.m. and 1 a.m. She would assume that the

Huntsman made his entry during the brief time when the alarm was off for agents to leave and their relief to arrive. Entry sensors were also disabled when any of her team came and went or when one of the agents took Molly out.

So her abductor could have arrived at 1 p.m. and waited in her room, or had entered at the same time that Wynns returned from the field office, or when Juliette returned from her autopsy, or when Demko left to pursue leads.

Nadine's heart sank. There were dozens of times during the day that the security entry systems were disabled.

Security cameras were monitored both on-site and off-site so even if one of the agents was not at his computer monitoring the cameras, the off-site location should have registered motion and video of her abduction.

She knew it was close to 1 a.m. when she'd been taken and that Demko had not returned to the safe house.

Perhaps he would check on her and find her bed empty? But she feared this was not the case. Since she'd asked for time to consider his proposal, she and Demko had not shared a bed.

She wiggled her fingers and felt the engagement ring. She blew away a breath, uncertain as to why this discovery brought her any measure of relief.

If her capture had gone undetected, then it would likely be Tina who first noticed her absence sometime tomorrow morning after seven.

Seven hours. How far could a man get in six hours?

By truck, he'd be well out of the state. Somewhere in Georgia or Alabama by sunrise.

He'd made her a promise. Then he'd broken into her bedroom and taken her. Had he released Jack?

She might never know. But experience had taught her not to expect honesty from a psychopath.

The vehicle slowed and Nadine's heart hammered in her throat. But then she felt the motion of a turn and acceleration as the vehicle sped. The swerve and sound of a car horn told her that they were now on some highway.

She glanced up in hopes of seeing streetlights. Instead she noted that the stars had disappeared. Was morning approaching?

The answer came soon after with a flash of light followed by the familiar rumble of thunder. When the rain began, she tipped her head toward the holes, feeling the sweet relief of cool raindrops. The gag and tape prevented her from drinking any of the water.

Lightning flashed, changing her world to brilliant white for just an instant. She knew from Arlo that if she slowly counted one Mississippi, two Mississippi, until she heard the thunder, she could gauge the distance of the strike. Four Mississippis for every mile.

On the next flash of lightning she counted.

*One Mississippi…* Crash!

She closed her eyes and hunched. And quickly discovered she had a new problem. Already there was over an inch of rain in her plastic prison. The downpour continued to beat on the lid in a deafening drum and the water slowly dripped in.

She could drown in here. Nadine began to kick and wiggle. Now if she rested her cheek on the container floor, her nose was underwater.

Nadine screamed into the gag, craning her neck to keep her nose from the rising water.

The rain that had once been a sweet respite from the heat and humidity now soaked her clothing and drenched her hair. The violent shivering began. Only the gag kept her teeth from chattering.

She managed to roll to her back and inch her head up the side of the container enough that only her jaw was submerged. She blinked against the bite of the rain stinging her closed lids, trying to steady her breathing as the panic tore at her throat.

Meanwhile, the voice in her head screeched.

*They'll never find me in time.*

She was going to drown right here in this plastic tub.

# CHAPTER TWENTY-SEVEN

Tina tapped on the door to Nadine's room. Her boss's alarm had been sounding for twenty minutes. She tapped again, louder this time.

"Dr. Finch? It's past seven a.m." She listened, ear pressed to the door, and thought she heard a scratching. "Nadine?"

Tina eased open the door. Muffin slipped out of the crack and wove her way around her owner's legs, making a racket.

"Muffin!" She stooped to scoop up the cat. "How did you get in there?" Tina lifted the boneless feline and looked into her bright green eyes. The last time she had seen her cat was when she had let her out at 5 p.m. "You had me worried sick. I thought you were out all night."

Tina had called for Muffin from the front and back doors several times last evening. But Muffin did not reappear. It was the first occasion that her cat had gone missing and Tina was certain a coyote had gotten her.

She eased Muffin to the floor and the cat trotted off toward the kitchen, sending an urgent meow back at her pet parent.

"Muffin, if you could work that can opener, you'd have no use for me at all." Tina peered back into the room and found Nadine's bed empty and the covers dragged partially onto the floor. The first inklings of alarm sounded in her mind as she stepped into the room.

"Dr. Finch?"

She charged to the empty seating area, reversed course and ran to the master bath. The door lay open and the room vacant. Running now, she charged to the walk-in closet and then searched under the bed. Scrambling to her feet, she shouted.

"Dr. Finch!"

The pounding of footsteps preceded the arrival of the FBI security agent assigned to the morning detail.

"What's wrong?"

"She's gone! Dr. Finch. I can't find her." Tina pressed a hand to her chest, gasping now for air as the panic gripped her heart.

"Is she in the kitchen?"

Tina locked her fists in her hair and shouted at the agent. "She's gone! Do something!"

The agent left her to search the bathroom, walk-in closet, and returned to look under the bed. Meanwhile, Tina had her phone out and was texting Demko, who was out walking Molly.

The agent moved to the window and pulled back the venetian blind. His hand went to his service pistol.

"Call Director Carter now."

As Tina placed the call, he yanked up the blind revealing a large square cut from the lower glass of the window, which now stood open. The matching pieces of the contact alarm, now detached from the wall, sat on the marble sill.

"Director Carter? This is Tina Ruz. Nadine is missing. Someone broke into her room."

The front door banged open and Demko charged down the hall, pistol held out and down as he raced toward her. Tina had never seen this wide-eyed look of panic.

"Where's Nadine?"

*

"You've got to be kidding me," said Special Agent Coleman as she stood in the backyard with Agent Wynns staring at the metal cable threading from the neighbor's ancient oak to the roof of the safe house.

"I'm not. He sailed right to the roof, over our perimeter alarm, on a zipline and used that second one to slip right back over. His cable is three feet above line of sight for the cameras."

"How'd he get from the roof to her window?"

"Looks like he dropped down from the eave."

"I thought we had motion sensors."

"Inside, yes. Outside cameras, one agent on duty and motion on the top of the walls."

"Which he never touched."

"Correct," said Wynns.

"Entry sensors?"

"Were off to let the dog out at ten-thirty p.m. and again at shift change. Looks like he cut a hole in the glass big enough to climb through, removed the contact alarm and then took her out the open window."

"One a.m.," said Coleman. "How'd he find the safe house?"

"We are working on that. Possibly he followed the ME back from one of the autopsies, or one of the agents from the press conference to the field office and from there back to this location."

"Or Skogen told him."

"Also a possibility."

"So she's been missing for seven hours," said Wynns.

"Yes."

*

Nadine's mouth barely breached the waterline as the rain now poured off something above her and cascaded into the container, trapping her under a waterfall. She'd finished thrashing but rejected her imminent end, focusing on her next breath. She was surviving this because each minute she kept her head above water was another minute they had to find her.

He'd stop soon because he'd need to get to a safe location and buckle down while the FBI's search ramped up. His only chance was to be off the roads before she was discovered missing.

She had no idea what time it was. But she did know morning was closer with each breath. She had managed to work her hands from behind her back to behind her knees. This allowed her to roll to her back. She tucked her knees against her chest and scooted up until her head touched the lid. Further pushing did not dislodge the top. So she concentrated on holding her knees to her chest to preserve body heat and on keeping her nose out of the water.

Nadine ignored the signs that her core temperature was dropping. Unfortunately, Juliette had once told her about some of her experiences in New Hampshire during her residency. They'd had people who fell through thin ice, slid off snow-covered roads and froze to death inside their vehicles. But the one Juliette obsessed on was a young girl who had been hiking out ahead of her family and taken a wrong turn. By the time the parents realized she was not on the correct trail and walked out to get help, the temperature had dropped to fifty degrees with a light mist. Not cold, but cold enough. The girl had died of exposure despite the temperature being well above freezing.

"Because she was wet and because she never took shelter."

Nadine couldn't feel her hands or feet. They didn't hurt anymore, but they *should* hurt. The thought of gangrene sent the first shiver over her in hours. Her teeth no longer tapped against the gag, and she felt warmer.

Perhaps hugging her knees was working?

She opened her eyes and realized the rain no longer dripped into her watery tomb. The sky seemed dark gray, lighter than the interior. Morning was nearing. He'd stop. He'd help her.

But would he?

If she was right, he meant to possess her. Not kill her.

But what if she was wrong?

*Where's Jack?* Had he left the agent behind or killed him?

She thought of the moment she'd seen the Huntsman in her room and dropped the cat.

Her opinion of Muffin had changed again. Nadine decided there was a reason there are no guard cats.

Useless piece of fluff. Molly would never have let that happen. She'd have… licked the intruder's face and brought him her chewy toy, she thought. But at least Nadine would have known he was there.

The truck swerved again and then slowed to a stop. Nadine sucked in a breath and held it as the water sloshed over her nose. The vehicle turned and continued at a much slower pace. She knew exactly when they reached the jeep trail from the number of ruts.

Nadine refused to drown on the last few miles. Then she slipped from the wall and back to her side. Submerged.

She thrashed. Holding her breath as pinpricks of light exploded behind her closed eyelids. Her legs no longer responded to her commands. Her arms were useless.

*I'm sorry, Clint,* she thought as she fought against the urge to breathe. Her life was now measured in heartbeats and the seconds she could resist her body's hungry demands for oxygen.

The tub slid, scraping the solid surface beneath her. Light flooded in as the lid fell away. Nadine turned her head to see a blurry form and then the tub crashed to its side, spilling the water and disgorging Nadine onto the ground.

"Nadine!" His frantic voice seemed far away.

She gagged. Unable to draw enough air through her nose.

He roughly tore the tape from her mouth and yanked away the gag. Just in time, as she spewed water and the contents of her stomach. Coughing and sputtering.

"I'm so sorry. The airholes. I didn't realize. I should have put a hole in the bottom."

Nadine continued to choke and gag as he rubbed her back.

"You're freezing," he said.

He left her there. Nadine's neck ached. The rest of her body seemed carved of wood.

Her captor returned, wrapping her in a blanket and hoisting her into his arms. Only then did she realize she was not in a truck but in the bottom of a flat-bottomed boat, towed behind a pickup truck. She glanced around, the adrenaline now surging through her, waking her brain from its stupor.

This might be her only chance to see her surroundings.

Everything she observed only deepened her terror. They were in deep forest on an elevated jeep trail, under the canopy of interlocking branches with broad rounded leaves. Not oak, she realized, so she was no longer in Central Florida. A glance at the roots of the trees gave her the answer. They arched over each other like croquet wickets gone mad, covering the ground in a wild tangle that terminated in glistening silver water. Mangrove trees. One of the few plants that could survive the salt water of inlets, bays and the mouths of Florida's rivers. With the change of tide, the roots would vanish, submerging with everything but the elevated road. Beside the jeep trail, and just above the tideline, scrub palmetto squatted.

Nadine craned her neck.

Low tide. But which coast?

The Gulf of Mexico or the Atlantic? Or it could be the Florida Everglades. One and a half million acres of wetlands, the river of grass that was exactly the opposite direction that the authorities would assume he had gone. They'd be closing roads and airports to the north, shutting off arteries leading out of the state. They'd be searching vehicles at roadblocks. And she'd be lost in one of the most inaccessible places in the entire state.

A mangrove forest.

She knew such places were unlike any other forest on earth because between their trunks and the mud below, the tidal water constantly flowed. It was possible to walk from branch to branch, but you would never touch the ground because there was no ground. Only the brackish water. Where the tidal surge flowed fast, channels formed through the trees. But in still waters, like these, the passage had to be laboriously cleared. These trees were so special, so important, that damaging them was illegal.

But someone had cut these—recently.

The three-foot-wide tunnel before her showed that. And here on an empty coastal road, she knew this aquatic corridor was not part of any park service trail. The nearly imperceptible break in the foliage would be invisible to motorists. But she saw it and it terrified her. Once he took them through this fissure, the dark maw would swallow her up.

She recalled her Florida history. The indigenous people, the Seminole, were the only tribe in the country who had never signed a peace treaty because the US military could not find them in the Everglades to force a surrender. Their guns had rusted, and their wool and cotton clothing were torn to ribbons by the sawgrass. Meanwhile, the Seminole persisted, retreating like the Russians in winter ahead of the German army. They had only to wait.

The Huntsman lowered her into the bottom of the boat and left her there as a feast for the mosquitoes, returning in short order carrying something that taxed his strength, judging from the grunting and heavy tread.

Jack.

She craned her neck to see Agent Skogen limp in the arms of their captor. He set the unconscious FBI agent beside her in the boat, banging Jack's head on the seat. The aluminum vibrated, but the agent did not move.

He left them, disappearing toward the truck.

She nudged Jack with her shoulder, jostling him, in an awkward attempt to rouse him.

The truck engine turned over and they rolled backward. The steep angle caused a surging wave of panic as the boat tipped and rolled down the embankment.

Both she and Jack skidded to the stern, halted by the metal seat. The splash told her that the carrier beneath them rolled through tidal water.

The Huntsman disconnected the boat from the carrier and shoved the craft off and into the mangrove tunnel. In a moment her captor stood, knee-deep beside the boat.

"There's my girl. You gave me a fright." He stroked her cheek. "You're cold as an ice pop. I'm going to wrap you next to that sack of shit. Maybe he's still good for something. You can steal his body heat."

He set her on a foam mat, rolling her to her stomach. He lifted her arms, stretching them painfully. A zipping sound preceded her release as her kidnapper cut through the tape binding her wrists.

"Get the blood back in those hands." The Huntsman rubbed her arms, setting off an agony of pins and needles.

She cried out in pain.

"Hurts? That's good. Blood's coming back." He yanked her hands before her.

She moved her thumb and felt the engagement ring Clint had given her. She spun the ring, so the diamond pressed to her palm as he again bound her wrists together before her.

Finally their captor rolled her half on top of Jack's limp body and tossed a blanket over the pair of them. The hissing of a spray and the odor of bug repellent followed.

"That'll keep most of them off you. You hang on. We'll be there in a little while."

He left them again. The sound of the truck engine revving and the wheels spinning in loose sand followed. She didn't hear the clatter of the boat trailer rattling up the incline. Had their abductor left it here in the passage?

He was moving the vehicle, leaving them secreted in the tidal tunnel.

"Jack." She nudged his shoulder, wiggling against him.

He had not bothered to tie the agent and that worried her. Either Jack had a fever, or she was freezing. Either way, his skin burned against hers.

This might be the only time they were alone, and Jack didn't even perceive that she was there.

"Jack! Wake up right now!"

He stirred. Muttering something.

"It's Nadine. Do you hear me?"

More mumbling.

The truck engine halted. Nadine stilled, lying motionless beneath the rough wool blanket, listening. Minutes stretched before she perceived the slosh of the Huntsman returning to them. The small craft rocked as their captor climbed aboard and sat in the seat inches from her head. The scrape of a pole and the ripple of water against the boat told her they were in motion.

The scratch of the mangrove branches on the aluminum hull revealed that the fit of the craft in the passage was tight. How invisible would such an aperture become after only a day or two? Soon, the flattened vegetation on the shoulder would rise, the tracks of the trailer hitch in the mud would vanish with the tide and they were as lost as if they had strayed into the Amazon rain forest.

How had he hidden the truck? He'd have to, she was certain, or his vehicle might be reported abandoned. Was it even his?

Nadine rested her cheek on Jack's chest, listening to the beat of his heart. If Jack was to survive, it would depend on her.

The slosh of the water on the boat lulled her. Exhaustion tugged relentlessly. But she feared that sleep would lead her to unconsciousness, then death. And she was not done fighting yet.

The sound of the motor turning over and then accelerating shook her from her stupor. The ache in her back and hip pulsed with her heart. Soon, lying still in the bottom of the boat became impossible as larger waves tossed them. Were they going out in the ocean in this thing?

Water sloshed over the gunwales, soaking her again. The understanding that she did not feel cold troubled her as much as her throbbing back. Again and again, the boat lifted and slapped down.

Now her stomach heaved, completely taking her mind off her back. She recalled that she hated boats because of her seasick stomach.

For the next eternity, Nadine squeezed her eyes shut and tried every trick she knew to keep from vomiting on poor Jack.

Finally the rocking eased. Her stomach continued to pitch even after their captor cut the motor and paddled them through still water. The buzz of insects returned. The wind died.

At last they came to a stop, still floating, she was certain. The boat rocked and banged against something as their captain left the vessel.

He tugged the blanket off her and she struggled with the urgency to sit up.

"I'm going to be sick."

He plucked her from the boat, leaving Jack behind, and held her as her legs gave way. He eased her to the rough plank docking and tugged back her hair as her stomach released its meager contents. His touch only made her more desperate to vomit. She heaved until her throat burned and her mouth filled with the taste of bile.

He drew a bandana out and wiped her mouth.

"You always get seasick?"

She nodded.

"I'll have to get you something for that."

Why? she wondered. Were they going somewhere else in that damned metal coffin?

She groaned and he eased her to her knees. Nadine let her cheek rest on the worn wood. In the dim gray light of morning, she peered at a shack constructed of vertical boards so old the lumber had turned gray and moss clung to the wood with the lichen. Where was Jack?

She craned her neck, spotting him, now a motionless lump beneath the dirty blanket.

"You're freezing. Seems that sack of shit isn't even good as a handwarmer."

He easily swept her up into his arms and strode inside. The darkness blinded her. Gradually her eyes adjusted, and she recognized a woodstove and a cot. A small table stood beside the stove with two ancient chairs. Curls of peeling paint clung to the wooden legs. On the center of the table sat a plant in a rusted tin can set on a chunk of firewood. She blinked at the feathery white bloom, recognizing it instantly, though never having seen one in person.

A ghost orchid. The rarest bloom in the entire state, some thought in the world. The long lower petals were two feet in length and slightly twisted.

"Started that one for you over a year ago," he said.

So she'd been right. He'd planned this for at least a year, targeting her. The chill now crept into her heart.

"You like it? Folks say you can't keep them. But you can if the conditions are right. It's a white frog orchid."

"Ghost orchid," she said, momentarily marveling at its beauty. The endangered bloom belonged fixed to a tree somewhere deep in the glades, beyond the reach of man.

Was that where she was now?

He lowered her to the cot and opened the grate on the stove. He'd set the makings for a fire. A carefully arranged pyramid of wood captured dry kindling at the center. The man had his back to her as he struck the match.

The clothing he wore was unremarkable, a blue T-shirt and loose-fitting jeans. His mesh ball cap sported a camouflage pattern and his worn work boots were wet, with bits of grass and fern clinging to his pant legs.

With the fire crackling, he turned to her. Her eyes widened as he withdrew a knife from the leather carrier on his belt. Then he sliced the tethers connecting her hands and feet.

"Got to get you warmed up." He tugged her from the cot.

She fought him but was too weak as he cut away her wet T-shirt and tossed it aside. She slept in only that shirt and so she was now naked.

He straightened to stare.

"My God, Nadine. You're beautiful." He grasped her torso and she stilled as a new panic flooded her, choking her so she could not breathe.

His hands slid down her sides, stopping at the flare of her hips, nodding in approval.

"Perfect," he said. "I knew you would be."

Then his thumb grazed over the pink, puckered scar left by the bullet from the last killer she'd profiled. Her skin crawled and screamed with disgust.

"To think something so small could have taken you from me," he mused.

He straightened, releasing her. Nadine inched back.

Then he tugged off his shirt and joined her on the cot. She rolled away, giving him her back, but he easily dragged her against him.

"I need to warm you."

"Let me go," she said.

The stubble on his chin scratched against her temple as he shook his head.

"Lay still or I'll tie you again."

She forced herself to be still. She was weakened from the journey and could barely feel her limbs.

He dragged a down sleeping bag over them. Gradually the feeling returned to her arms. Her skin stippled and the trembling began. She jerked and shook as he held her. When the feeling returned to her feet and hands, she cried out. The slightest movement brought excruciating pain.

"You'll be all right. You're little, but strong. Folks underestimate you, I'll bet."

As the sensation returned, she developed an insatiable thirst. The dryness in her mouth made her tongue stick to the roof of her mouth.

She needed to think how to play this. Making demands and threats was useless. All she knew for certain was that he didn't want her dead—yet. Beyond that, all she had was theories. Time to get some answers.

"Are you feeling better?" he asked.

"Thirsty," she said, her voice a mere whisper.

He rolled to his feet and retrieved a jug, pulled the cork stopper and poured from it into a tin cup.

Inside her mind, a siren of warning blared. This was the Huntsman. He'd killed six women and now he had her. Her breathing came in shuddering gasps as fear pricked at her skin like nettles.

"I'm sorry it's not cold. No refrigeration out here, I'm afraid." His back was to her.

It gave her the moment she needed to grab her composure and wrestle it to the surface. He would not respond to weakness and cowering. No predator did.

Nadine had lived with a killer before. If she could negotiate that as a child, how much better equipped was she now?

He turned, holding the cup and paused, meeting her gaze. She forced her expression to curiosity, banishing the disgust in favor of a haughty affectation. He was an interesting specimen, a patient already in custody that she'd been asked to evaluate.

She took her first good look at him. He was as normal and unexceptional as she would have anticipated. This was the sort of man one would glimpse and immediately dismiss as inconsequential. He was not big or handsome. Neither was he small or ugly.

She'd guessed he was five-seven and less than 170 pounds, slim, with heavy muscle on his bare chest and torso. His golden-brown skin glistened with moisture, making him seem oiled. Wavy brown hair curled from under his cap. He lifted his bright green eyes and pinned her with a look, then a smile.

Something niggled. She knew him, had seen him before. When? Where?

Then it came to her. Clint had been questioning Simon Kilpatrick at the outdoor adventure place. And she had spoken to this man. Their killer, and she'd had no inkling. The trickle of uncertainty slid down her spine.

This was one of the naturalists at Big River Adventures. They'd chatted about bird-watching. She'd feigned interest.

"We've spoken before. Haven't we... Lionel?"

He beamed. "You remember. I'm flattered. That's so nice."

He set the water on the table and assisted her to a sitting position. She pulled the sleeping bag up to cover herself.

"I need a shirt," she said.

"I don't think so."

"I'm freezing," she said.

He ignored her, retrieving the water and holding it to her lips. She glared at him as she drank, draining the contents.

"Where are we?"

"This is a hunting cabin used by some locals. I've leased it for the season."

"Everglades?" she asked.

He shook his head.

"Where?"

"Nadine, you can't leave. You can't signal for help. So why do you need to know?"

"If all that is true, why not tell me?" She waited, worried to push further by asking if he was afraid to tell her. Best not to poke too hard.

He smiled. "We're north of Tampa. It's a spot you've never heard of. A place that everyone hurries by to get to their destination because it's no place at all."

"Why me?"

"Don't you know? I'd be surprised if you didn't work it out."

"It was never a game of wits," she said, tossing out one of her assumptions.

He stroked her cheek. "Though I do admire your wits."

It was so hard not to make demands. Not to scream and beg and threaten. She gritted her teeth and tried to think.

"You promised to release Jack."

His expression hardened and he rolled his eyes. "Yes. And you promised to come willingly."

They faced off. Nadine's eyes narrowed. Despite being half-dead, she still had something he wanted—her compliance.

"I can still offer you that deal," she said.

"I have you already."

"You don't. What you have is a captive. But you want more than that."

Now his eyes narrowed. "I *do* want more."

"Well then?"

His eyes now glimmered with clear anticipation. "What are you offering?"

"I'll go with you, willingly, if you release Jack to a location where he will survive and receive proper medical care—"

"Done."

"I'm not."

He glared and she met the beady frigidity of his eyes.

"And you prove that he survived to receive care and you promise not to return at a later time to kill him."

"Like little Linda." He smiled at the fond memory of the death of Linda Tolan.

The hairs on her neck lifted. Here was the face of the killer, unmasked. Her skin prickled, but she held her expression blank.

"You love him," he said.

She said nothing to this, uncertain if revealing the ploy would further jeopardize Jack. If she told him, would he leave Skogen or kill him?

Nadine needed to decide how to play this and she needed to do that quickly. She narrowed her eyes on him, showing her displeasure without challenging his fantasies.

"Answer me!" he growled.

"He was the best I could do, until now."

He gaped and then laughed. "'Until now.'"

She didn't respond.

"If that's true, why do you care what happens to him?"

"Because he's part of my team and that makes him my responsibility."

He stared at her with those bottle-green eyes as she struggled with her rising heart rate, feeling blood pound in the vessels at her neck.

She waited through his deliberation, stone-faced, while her stomach twisted and her heart thrashed against her sternum.

At last he said, "I make no guarantee against sepsis or other infections that might kill him after delivery."

"Understood." How badly was Jack injured?

"A deal then. Your compliance for his release in a location where he will be discovered alive and no return to kill him at a later date."

"I need to see him."

Jack had been left outside in the boat. Who knew how dehydrated or fevered he was by now?

"Soon. First, we need to chat."

She paused, desperate to get to Jack and check his condition, but recognizing the opportunity presented by the unsub's willingness to talk. The more she knew of him, the better equipped she'd be to survive.

"You work for the Kilpatrick family. Tour guide."

"Naturalist. Birds are my specialty. You can learn a great deal from birds."

"Like how to use a bird-watching app to lure women to you?"

"Yes. I used that method. Rare-bird sightings. I prefer trapping to hunting. It requires patience, but that patience is rewarding. I killed several that way recently in Miami. Only there I used a dating app."

"And in the Barataria Preserve outside New Orleans?"

He grinned. "Louisiana girls are sweet. Love the accent."

"Unlike yours," she said.

"None of them were my equal. But then I read about you." He squatted before her, stroking her cheek.

She tried not to flinch but didn't succeed. She closed her eyes as his fingers danced down her neck and clasped her throat.

"Open your eyes."

She didn't and he squeezed.

Nadine met his gaze.

"That's better." His hand remained at her throat as he spoke. "The great-granddaughter of a killer, granddaughter of a killer and daughter of the most successful female serial killer ever captured. You are the ghost orchid, Nadine. The grasshopper sparrow among finches. After I found you, I moved, set up business in your mother's territory but with a difference. I let the world see them, my kills."

Like a cat depositing a dead bird on an owner's doormat, Nadine thought.

"I knew the deaths of these women would draw you to me. It's important to use the right bait. And for you, that's the irresistible sight of brutal, untimely death."

She pressed her lips tight, scowling, because he'd been correct.

"My wish was to entice the rarest of all females, the profiler with a serial-killer mother."

"You changed tactics once I got here."

"Yes. I had your attention and like any eligible male, I switched to my courtship dance. Driving rival females from our territory."

"Killing them."

He shrugged as if the distinction was inconsequential.

Nadine was certain that she didn't want confirmation on her next question. But she asked anyway.

"Why?"

"Because you are the perfect woman, unique in all the world. Worthy to be my mate and bear my children. They'll be like us, Nadine. Perfect hunters."

Nadine sucked in a breath as her body went cold. The very possibility that she found most repellant was the reason he had taken her.

It was her fear of being the mother to a psychopathic killer that had kept her from accepting Demko's ring. Deep rooted in her mind was the terror that whatever had gone wrong in her grandparents, mother and brother threaded through her DNA like a defective gene.

"If I refuse?" she asked.

"Then the deal is off, and I finish Jack. I'll still keep you. But you won't be my wife."

The tone of his voice was so clinical and matter-of-fact, it froze her heart, sending ice crystals piercing muscle.

"Be my bride, Nadine." He was on one knee before her, asking her to commit, after nearly drowning her and while her hands and feet were still bound.

She tucked her thumb over her engagement ring, praying he would not take her hand.

"I'm not agreeing to anything until you prove you're capable of caring for me." She lifted her chin, looking down her nose at him. "Your handling of me last night leaves me with serious doubts."

"I'll see to your needs."

"Really? Because I'm hungry and tired and cold."

He stood and returned with a flannel shirt. He cut the binding securing her wrists. It took him a little time to drag her up before him and slip her arms into the garment. Then he taped her hands before her again and buttoned the shirt.

"I need to see Jack."

He crouched before her. "Good. I'm anxious for you to see him. It's some of my best work."

What had this monster done?

# CHAPTER TWENTY-EIGHT

Three hours after the discovery of Nadine's abduction, Clint Demko left his vehicle in the lot. The FBI had begun their manhunt and he knew there was no organization better for that task. He also knew they did not need or want his help.

But they were searching thoroughfares. And *he* knew that whoever had taken Nadine would be off the road, hunkered down and waiting for the search to slow. It would be a waiting game. Could they find Nadine before time and resources ran out and the search halted?

He knew something else from what Nadine had told him. Chances were high that they'd already met this killer. If so, then their unsub would be absent from work today. That meant he needed to recanvass every single business and speak to each person he had interviewed until he discovered who among the hundreds of contacts had disappeared.

Tina had told him that the Bureau's attempts to track Nadine's new phone had failed. Presumably it was off or had no charge. Either way, finding her would not be that easy.

If the Huntsman decided to stash Nadine close to where she was taken, he might be back at work. In that case, Demko needed to figure out which one had been up all night and check if any employees were missing. Tina made calls while he headed out because he couldn't ignore the possibility that someone might lie to cover for the Huntsman.

His first stop was the gun shop on the north side of the park. Throughout the day he worked from one establishment to the next. By late afternoon, he reached Big Water Marina in Kerr City. The first person he located was Kelly Dietz, the woman who worked only mornings. It was late in the day for her to still be here.

She was hosing down the kayaks with freshwater, washing away the mud and grass.

"Detective, how are you?"

"I thought you worked mornings."

"Yeah. That's right. Good memory. But we're short-staffed today."

The skin on his neck prickled. "Is that so?"

"Lionel was a no-show for his afternoon tour."

"Decristofaro?"

"Yes."

"He do that often?"

"No. Never."

Clint narrowed his eyes. "Anybody check on him?"

She puffed out her cheeks and then blew away her frustration. "No idea."

"You know where he lives?"

"Nope. But Jessie might. And Lou Anne, of course."

"Anyone else missing?"

"Missing? He's just out sick."

"I see." He turned and headed toward the office. Until he had eyes on Lionel Decristofaro, the man was missing and had just moved to the top of his list.

He tried to remember anything he could about the man and had to check his notes to jog his memory. Then he remembered what Nadine had told him the day she'd raced off to confront the Copycat Killer to save a young woman.

High-functioning sociopaths and psychopaths are hard to catch because they are intelligent and fully capable of operating without drawing notice. They have the ability to "fake good," appearing to possess the complete range of human emotions. But it was an act. They met only their own needs and easily disregarded the needs of others to meet theirs.

Demko reached the office where he found the owner, Lou Anne Kilpatrick, studying her computer monitor.

"Be right with you," she said, without looking up.

"How long has Decristofaro worked here?"

"Only a few months. Been in the US awhile, I guess, but he just became a US citizen."

"From where?"

*

The Huntsman cut the bonds from Nadine's feet first and then her hands. She rubbed her wrists, still sticky from the tape adhesive. She held her thumbnail against her engagement ring, hiding it as best she could. When he put his knife away, she switched the ring to her opposite hand.

"I know you agreed to be cooperative. But in case you have other ideas, you have no shoes and no bug protection and are on an island. This time of year, without bug suits or spray the insects will torment you until you reach the water where the riptide will sweep you out to sea."

She coughed against the smoke filling the cabin. For an outdoorsman, he certainly didn't understand how a flue worked.

"And the bugs are worse at night. Much worse."

"They aren't biting me now?"

"I put sage on the fire. Smoke and scent keeps them off. I got us a mosquito net, too. No fire during the day. Too much chance of being spotted."

Nadine immediately set her mind to work on how to set a daytime blaze.

"Where's Jack?"

"I'll get him."

His smile gave her chills, but she kept her chin up until he stepped out of the cabin. The instant he left the shack, she hobbled to the cupboards. She found a rusted cast-iron skillet and a dented aluminum pot filled with mouse droppings, several tobacco tins and a rodent nest.

She turned to the stove, searching for a fire poker, but found nothing but stacked wood. Nadine wondered if a chunk of cypress would make a serviceable club.

One thing she knew for certain. She was not running blindly into a tangle of mangrove roots or trying to swim out of here. She was a weak swimmer, at best.

That left her one option. Stay alive until she had more options.

The banging of his feet on the rickety dock signaled his return. She hobbled back to the cot and sat. The door swung open and he stepped in, Jack thrown over his shoulder like a large bag of dog food.

He squatted before the stove and rolled Jack to his back before the fire. Nadine got her first good look at the agent and did not recognize him.

Involuntarily, she sucked in air.

"Not so pretty now. Is he?"

Jack's purple face was dotted with welts from insect bites. His cracked lips, puffy swollen eyes and the dried blood turned his face into a ghastly mask of infection and pain.

She rose, resisting the urge to rush to his side weeping. That route would serve nothing. This was a hunter. He did not value weakness, and emotional attachment to Jack would only provoke her captor.

"Do you think the nails will grow back?" he asked, his tone conversational.

Nadine directed her attention to the hand that the Huntsman now held for her perusal. The tips of his bloody fingers were raw pulp.

She narrowed her eyes in banked fury. "How do I know that's Jack?"

Now he was the one gaping. "That's Agent Jack Skogen."

Nadine shrugged. "Prove it."

He tried and failed to rouse the agent. Finally he growled and turned to one of his packs, withdrawing a medical kit and a syringe. An injection later and Jack roused, roaring as he sat up, frantically blinking his eyes and turning his head.

"What's your name?" asked the Huntsman.

"Jack Skogen."

"Where do you work, Jack?"

"Federal agent. FBI. You need to call the police, right now."

He couldn't see. That much was clear. Had he been blinded?

"Satisfied?" asked Lionel.

"No."

Jack turned his head in her direction, swaying. "Nadine?"

"Yes, Jack. It's me."

"He has you, too?" His voice had changed, turning flat with defeat.

She met Lionel's intent green eyes. "Not yet, he doesn't."

Lionel kicked Jack, who sprawled onto the floor. He crossed the distance between them in two strides.

He wasn't a big man, but he was bigger and stronger than she was. He grabbed her by the shoulders and lifted her, thudding her against the wall so hard it shook dust from the rafters.

"You do as I say."

"Do I? That's not how this works."

He dropped her and caught her before she fell, pinning her to the wall with one hand, now clasped around her throat.

"I could kill you right now."

She lifted her chin, playing the card that had worked with her mother. Self-interest. That was what moved such monsters to action or restraint.

"You won't."

"Why is that?" he growled.

"I can't bear your children if I'm dead."

He leaned forward, his mouth beside her ear. "True. And I want you willing."

"You can't have either if he dies."

His grip tightened and she gasped, the air just barely enough. "You *do* love him."

She shook her head, unable to speak. Strong fingers eased back. She gasped, grabbing greedy breaths of air.

Two things were clear. Decristofaro didn't believe her prior declaration that Jack was the best that she could do. That meant Jack's life was still in peril.

"I saw you together." His voice low with fury.

She needed to convince him that Jack was not, and had never been, a love interest. The simplest way was the truth. She debated the wisdom of making that revelation until he released her and fixed on the real target of his rage.

Nadine raised her voice, redirecting him away from Jack. "Because that's what I wanted."

He turned back.

She pointed at Skogen. "It was *my* idea to introduce a love interest. His to play that part. I told him it was a horrible idea. But *he* wouldn't listen."

Lionel released her and she rocked, keeping herself upright only because of the wall behind her.

"It *was* a horrible idea." He turned to look at Skogen. "An act?" Then he glared at her. "You're lying."

"I'm not."

"Prove it," he said, repeating her earlier challenge.

She assumed an affectation of disdain as she counted off the reasons on her left hand, keeping the right hidden.

"He's ex-military. I hate that. He's a bully. He won't take my advice or listen to my suggestions. He excludes me from important briefings. And most important of all, he allowed himself to be captured."

"So did you."

"Did I?"

His brow furrowed.

"Or was I expecting you?"

"I captured you."

She stepped forward. "You did. Snatched me right out from under their noses. I would have loved to see their faces in the morning when they discovered what you had done. You're everything that one is not. Brave, daring, smart and ruthless."

"I'm all of that."

"The complete package."

"Like your mother," he said, smiling.

"Like my grandfather. I wish you could have met him."

"He was like us?" The eagerness in his expression made her stomach heave all over again.

"Yes. Like us."

He grasped her by the back of the neck and yanked her to him, sweeping down to claim a kiss.

Nadine stifled the cry of disgust, managing only to keep herself from resisting.

When he pulled away, he glanced back to Jack, who appeared to have lost consciousness again. Nadine allowed herself to shudder in revulsion.

"Why not just let me roll him into the water. They'll never find him."

"You made a deal," she reminded.

"But if you don't care for him, why do you care what happens to him?"

"He's FBI. They'll never stop looking for him, and if he dies, they'll never stop looking for us. Don't you want to be clear of them?"

"Oh, we will be. Where we're going, they can't touch us."

"Where's that?"

*

"He's not taking her north out of the state. He's heading south," said Demko. "He's a naturalized citizen. Born in Cuba."

FBI Director Gabriella Carter eyed him like a fly in her ceviche.

"You have zero evidence on which direction our suspect is taking. Or proof that Decristofaro is the Huntsman."

"He hasn't been at work in two days!"

"I'll have an agent look into it. Happy?"

"I've done that. He's not at his residence. She's still missing and you have no leads, no suspects and no progress. We need to move operations to block him from taking her out of the country."

"I assure you, we have all airports covered."

"He's not flying. He's in a boat. A small one."

"Detective Demko, you need to leave this to the professionals."

"Exactly." He spun and stormed from the field office.

In the outer lobby, Tina Ruz and Juliette Hartfield waited.

"And?" asked Juliette.

"They're not moving operations."

"What!" said Tina. "What'll we do?"

"I'm going to pull every string I can find with the US Coast Guard while driving toward the coast."

"I'm coming with you," said the two women in unison.

An hour later, a startled vet had taken custody of a bird, a cat and a dog, while their three human owners piled into his SUV.

"Which coast?" asked Juliette.

*

The Huntsman had told Nadine he was taking her out of the country. His father had fled Cuba in the mid-1990s, escaping in a homemade raft to Miami with Lionel and his older brother, leaving his pregnant wife behind because the journey was too dangerous. Since then, his father had been unable to secure his wife and daughter's escape. Lionel planned to return to reunite with his family—the mother he had not seen since he was a child, and the sister he never knew.

Miami was, in fact, closer to Cuba than it was the state capital in Tallahassee. Decristofaro had a shrimp boat in Crystal River, north of Tampa. He'd told her they'd work their way down to the Keys, as innocuous as a tractor trailer on any highway. From Key West, the island of Cuba lay only ninety miles south. Nadine's courage slipped as she realized that, if Lionel succeeded, Demko would never find her.

He'd left her here, taking the flat-bottomed boat, as he made final arrangements. Nadine did not waste time verifying they were on an island because she feared that Jack's condition was worse than Lionel had indicated.

She washed Jack's wounds and the open sores blanketing his back. The bruising on his stomach caused her to suspect internal bleeding.

The Huntsman had taken the medical kit and lighter.

She sat with Jack's head in her lap. Trickling water from a rag into his mouth, trying to get him to swallow. Her diamond ring flashed in the morning sunlight, streaming through the cracks in the planking.

Why hadn't she told Clint yes! She'd been so full of fears of what *might* be, that she'd overlooked what *could* be. She wanted a future with Demko. She wanted to be his wife, and that meant she needed to be as fearless as her mother, without the crazy. She needed to survive this and tell Clint she would be his bride. If he loved her, he'd understand what had held her back and forgive her for her hesitancy.

She could not change where she came from. She could not change who had brought her into this world or the many relations in her life who had turned to darkness. But she had survived them, and if she could survive this, she could choose her future. She wanted that future with Clint. She wanted it enough to fight with everything she had to win the right to live with him as his wife.

They could make this work. They could share a life together. All she had to do was get Jack to understand where Lionel was taking her, and then keep Lionel from killing him. If Jack could survive to tell Clint, she knew Demko would never stop looking for her.

"Jack. Please wake up."

How long until he returned?

Nadine soaked the dirt and debris from Jack's tortured hands. Then she dabbed them dry and began wrapping them with strips she'd torn from her ruined nightshirt.

An idea struck her. She left him to pluck some leaves from the trees beside the dock. Then she returned to Jack and tucked the vegetation within the layers of fabric bandages on his hands. If they found him, they'd have something of this place as well.

Jack groaned, clearly in pain, and his eyelids fluttered.

"Jack!"

He moaned.

"Jack! Can you hear me? It's Nadine. He's taking me to Cuba. Do you hear me?"

His lips were moving. Was he trying to speak to her? She lowered her ear to his mouth but could make no sense of his mutterings.

"He's taking me down the Gulf Coast. Crystal River to Key West to Cuba." She said it again. Repeating it over and over. But it was useless. He was delirious. His mind shattered and his body pushed beyond its limits.

She tried again to get him to drink, holding the cup to his mouth as the liquid ran down his chin. But this time, he swallowed. Then again.

"Jack! It's Nadine." She started again, repeating her words, hoping he'd understand.

Her ring flashed again, a rainbow of hope in the dismal cabin. The idea struck her.

She slipped the ring from her finger and worked it onto Jack's larger one, pushing it down his little finger as far as possible. The engagement ring stopped between the first and second knuckle.

Nadine then used a bit of charcoal from the fire to write "Keys to Cuba" on his palm. Finally she finished wrapping his hands, turning them into mitts, praying that Demko would find his ring and use it to find her.

*

The team had made a pit stop. Demko stood outside a Wawa gas station on I-4, waiting for Juliette and Tina, when his phone rang. His heart lurched at the caller ID. The call was coming from the replacement phone issued to Nadine during the body-double operation. The FBI had tried but been unsuccessful tracking the device.

"Nadine?"

"Naw, buddy. I just got her phone." The male voice had a distinctive Southern drawl.

"Who is this?"

"That don't matter. I got a message for you from the guy wit' Nadine. Said you's a friend of his."

"Where are you?"

"I'm at a truck stop on I-95 outside Lumberton. Some guy paid me six hundred bucks to call you from here. Said Nadine stole your phone and you'd want it back."

"Where's Nadine?"

"Don't know. Just saw the fella. Give me your phone and passcode. I'm running my rig up to Richmond. I'll leave the phone right here at the counter." He gave Demko the exit number and name of the refueling station.

"Where did he give you the phone?"

"Lauderdale. Listen, buddy, I got to burn rubber. We good?"

"No, sir. We are not good. I'm a Homicide detective and Nadine is a federal agent and a kidnap victim."

Juliette had reappeared during this conversation and was already on her phone contacting Director Carter.

"Aw, shit!"

"The man who gave you this phone is wanted for multiple homicides in Florida and Nadine is his captive. You need to stay where you are until the FBI arrives to speak to you."

"Hell with that."

"You are a witness. I'm ordering you to—"

The call ended.

"Shit!" He turned to Juliette. "He hung up."

She handed him her phone and he relayed what had happened to Carter. After the conversation, he handed back her phone.

"Are we heading in the wrong direction?" asked Juliette.

"Possibly. Or he wants the FBI to think he's traveling northeast."

"Well, the opposite is south and west. This way." She pointed at the highway.

Tina spoke from behind him, making him jump. The woman was quiet as her cat. She held a sack of boiled peanuts and a Mountain Dew. The electric green liquid reminded Demko of radiator fluid.

"Someone found Nadine's phone?"

Juliette filled her in and Demko's phone rang again.

"I can track her phone again, now we know it's on," said Tina. "I have all her passwords."

"Do that," said Demko.

Tina went to work. "Yup. There it is."

# CHAPTER TWENTY-NINE

The Huntsman had taken Jack at midday, leaving Nadine locked in a hog trap with bug spray, food and water. He had not returned until the following afternoon. At twilight, they'd crossed the inlet back to the tangle of mangroves. There he'd floated the craft onto the trailer and hauled it, and her, from the murky swamp.

Once back at the truck, Lionel gave Nadine a phone and let her make the call to Apalachee Hospital on speaker.

"Yes, I just learned that my fiancé was taken to your ER."

"Would you like me to check for you?" The hospital's operator had a nice matronly voice and a hint of Brooklyn in her accent.

"Yes."

"Might not be in the system yet. Name?"

"Jack Skogen."

"Let's see. We have…" The woman went silent. "Who did you say this is?"

She looked to Decristofaro, who nodded.

"Dr. Nadine Finch. Is he there?"

"Yes. He is. Could you hold for a moment?"

Decristofaro took the phone and carefully ended the call. Then he dropped it to the pavement and crushed it under his boot. Extracting the SIM card, he snapped it into two pieces and threw them in the water.

"He's there," said Lionel.

"But I don't know he's alive."

"Best I can do. Now let's go."

Here in the mangrove forest, no glint of electric lights penetrated the blackness. Tree frogs trilled and insects buzzed while the occasional brown bat swooped overhead. You did not have to venture far in Florida to find wild places. Everyone knew that Florida had thousands of miles of white-sand beaches. But it also had thousands of acres of mangrove forests and saltwater marshes. Where they flourished, few people resided.

"You left him at the hospital?" she asked.

"I left him where he'd be found."

"Where?"

"Inside someone's car at a motel near Tallahassee. Set off the alarm to make sure they found him quick."

Had he been caught on surveillance camera?

"What kind of motel?"

"The kind nobody with money ever sees. Hourly rates. Privacy for the customers." He pointed at the ruined phone. "But that, they can track."

He motioned her forward with the electric prod. She rounded the vehicle, halting at the passenger-side door.

"Well. Climb in."

Had the FBI found her engagement ring yet?

*

Gabriella Carter called Demko a little after one in the morning.

"We've recovered Jack Skogen," she said.

"Alive?"

"Yes. He's in a medical facility in Tallahassee."

He asked for the address.

"Nadine?"

"No sign."

"I'm on my way."

The drive to Tallahassee took less than the four hours; it might have taken longer if he hadn't used the lights and driven 120 miles per hour on I-4 with an escort from highway patrol.

Juliette sat in the front with one arm braced on the dashboard and the other clutching the handgrip.

"You know that won't help you if we crash," he said.

"I know it."

Behind them, Tina was so quiet he almost forgot she was there.

At the hospital, they were escorted to the visitors' waiting area outside the ICU and found Axel Vea. It was the first time they'd seen him since he'd taken a bullet. The only indication of his near-fatal shooting was the white gauze taped to his neck.

"Agent Vea." Juliette gave him a hug. "How are you?"

"Better than Jack." He made a face. "We have to catch this guy."

"You've seen Skogen?" asked Demko.

The corners of Vea's mouth turned down and he nodded. "It's bad."

"Is he awake?" asked Juliette.

Vea shook his head. "Sedated."

Juliette peeled away to speak to the ICU nurses, ID in hand. There were places in a hospital that a board-certified physician could access that were closed to police.

"We think they're heading north because of the location of her phone," said Vea.

"Or he wants us to think he's heading north," said Demko. "Coleman and Carter think he's taking her out of the state."

"We discussed that possibility," Vea said.

"Did you locate the trucker in Lumberton?"

"Yeah. He's useless. Took the money from some guy in a hoodie. Phone was off and he didn't turn it on until he called you. Apparently, you're the first one listed in her favorites."

"The phone. Wynns has it. From what I understand, it was switched off the night Nadine was taken."

"By him?"

"Likely. On again at Lumberton."

"Prints?"

"You must be dreaming."

"DNA?"

"Yes. But Wynns doesn't think he used it. So we aren't hopeful."

"Did you find anything new on him?"

"Yes, thanks to you. Suspect is Lionel Decristofaro. Search of his residence uncovered hunting supplies, bow and arrows, traps and two uniforms."

"The missing bellman?"

"Used his uniform. Coleman found the bellman in Orlando working off the books at another hotel. He's also undocumented. Decristofaro threatened him, made him quit the day Finch arrived. Admitted to giving Decristofaro his uniform."

"He's okay?"

Vea nodded. "Second uniform is from the forest service, a ranger. We're checking with them, but believe it is stolen."

Demko thought of all the rangers he had spoken to, comparing them in his mind to Decristofaro. A guy at the scene when they recovered the remains of April Rupp came to mind.

"You don't have him?"

"No. He's still missing."

"Background, priors?"

"No priors," said Vea. "He listed his permanent residence as Miami. We've sent our people there. Carter likes him for our unsub."

"He matches Nadine's description. Slight build. Dark hair."

"Yes. We're hopeful that Skogen can provide more details. We have a photo of Decristofaro to show him."

"When?"

"That's up to the doctor."

"Can I see him?"

"Of course," said Vea.

They reached the protective detail at the door and Vea cleared them through, accompanying Demko and Tina to Skogen's curtained enclosure, where they paused at the foot of the bed.

The man lying there was unrecognizable. The swollen purple skin of his face reminded Clint of the reaction after being stung by hornets. He looked more corpselike than many corpses Demko had seen.

That made him check the machines to see if the agent was breathing.

The apparatus blipped and beeped, showing oxygen levels, respiration, heart rate and blood pressure. Clint watched the line of Skogen's heartbeat move across the green screen. Then he pinned his attention on Jack. An oxygen tube threaded over his pillow and fixed around his face. Tape held the intravenous line on the top of his bandaged right hand.

"Anything on the scene where he was recovered?" asked Demko.

"We've got crime techs there. They haven't found anything to help us locate Nadine."

"His clothing?" asked Demko.

"Boxers and bandages on his hands. They think it was strips from a T-shirt."

"Nadine's nightshirt?"

"Possibly. The strips were stuffed with green leaves."

"What kind of leaves?"

Axel shook his head. "Our techs have them."

"Got photos yet?" asked Demko.

Vea opened his device checking. "Yup. Already loaded."

He pulled up the images and held the cell phone so all three of them could view the screen. Then Vea scrolled from one image to the next.

Demko checked each image, seeing evidence bags filled with elliptical green leaves and vegetative debris. Another showed soiled fabric strips. Vea slowly swiped from one image to the next.

"Stop," Demko said. "Go back one."

Tina moved closer and Vea retrieved the photo.

"Zoom in."

Vea did, using his fingers to enlarge the image. Something flashed in the strips of dirt and rotting vegetation.

And then he recognized it. A chill rippled over him as Clint peered at the image of a familiar square-cut diamond set in a band of gold.

"Is that—" said Tina.

Vea interrupted. "It's an engagement ring. Recovered from Jack Skogen's fifth finger, right hand."

"That isn't a ring," said Tina. "It's an *engagement* ring."

"Nadine's ring," said Demko. "The one I gave her."

Had she been wearing this when he took her?

Tina rested a fist on her hip and glared at Demko. "Why didn't either of you tell me?"

*

Nadine settled into the passenger seat. Should she be grateful that he did not carry her in that dreaded plastic tub again? Perhaps her near drowning had taught him a lesson.

She knew that the highways had cameras. Could the FBI spot her at night in this seat? She didn't know, but the glimmer of that possibility gave her hope.

Decristofaro stood blocking the open passenger door.

"The boat is in Crystal River?" She prayed he'd given her the correct information on the long shot that they found Jack and he could remember her message.

He nodded. "We'll head out with the others tomorrow and then drop our nets, trawling south. That way we look just like the rest of them shrimpers up and down the coast."

"And then Cuba?"

"From the Tortugas. Easy as frying catfish. You'll love it there. The climate is like Florida and the people are nice, even to Americans. You're so smart, you'll have no trouble learning Spanish. We'll be so happy there." He bounced with excitement.

Nadine glanced at the door, checking to see what kind of lock she'd need to release before she rolled out of his truck.

Something pricked her neck.

She slapped her hand over the injury, her eyes flashing to him, in time to see him withdrawing a hypodermic needle.

"What was that?"

In answer he dropped the needle on the ground and lifted his opposite hand. Upon it was a realistic mask of a bald white man with a goatee.

He tugged the mask over her head. The odor of latex filled her nostrils, and she lifted her hands to tug the thing away. But her arms were leaden, refusing to lift more than a few inches from her lap.

"That's for any surveillance cameras. Just two men driving south."

Lionel reached across her, clipping the seat belt.

"Enjoy your rest because I'm certain you are not going to enjoy the shrimp boat." He patted her knee. "I know you promised to be cooperative. But my experience with women shows that they are most compliant when unconscious, afraid for their lives or dead."

\*

Dr. Juliette Hartfield returned to Demko, standing with him at the bedside of Jack Skogen.

"He's in bad shape," she said. "Internal injuries, a high fever, pneumonia and a collapsed lung. He's on massive antibiotics."

"Will he live?"

"His prognosis is good, barring infection."

"Sedated?"

"Yes. Midazolam, four hours ago. Should be wearing off soon."

"How soon?"

"Usually lasts one to six hours."

One of the nurses arrived to change the bandages on Jack's hands. Demko winced to see Jack's ruined nail beds and red oozing pulp where his fingernails should have been.

"He was tortured," said Demko.

Juliette gasped and covered her mouth. As a pathologist, this woman had seen the very worst that could happen to the human body. But all her clients were out of their misery, while Jack was not.

"Why is he sedated?" he asked the nurse.

"Help keep him calm and out of pain." The nurse finished the dressing and departed.

Demko showed Juliette the image of the ring that Vea had forwarded.

"What's that?"

"It's the engagement ring I gave Nadine when I proposed."

Juliette gasped. "What? She didn't tell me that!" Juliette's excitement turned to irritation. "Why didn't she tell me? It's beautiful. Such a perfect choice—"

"Juliette. Focus. It's got blood on it," said Demko.

Her expression turned somber as he described how and where the ring was found.

"How did the ring get on his hand?"

Demko shook his head. "I assume Nadine was wearing it the night she was taken. So did she give it to Skogen as a message? Or did Decristofaro take it from Nadine and leave it on Skogen?"

"Maybe Jack will tell us," said Juliette.

Demko met Juliette's gaze and for an instant he saw the dangerous flicker of her mother in her eyes. Her mom had murdered all Juliette's siblings, shooting them at close range.

"What did you have in mind?" he asked, steeling himself. He wanted Nadine back, regardless of the risks.

"I could lose my license," said Juliette.

"Nadine could lose her life."

Juliette drew a deep breath and straightened. Then she rummaged in her satchel and lifted a nasal spray from her medical kit.

"What's that?" asked Demko.

"Naloxone. It's a stimulant."

"Narcan?"

He knew it, of course. Had used it more than once on addicts who OD'd on heroin.

He stayed her hand. "Will it harm Skogen?"

"No. Should work in less than a minute. He's going to be in terrible pain."

He hesitated. Uncertain.

"Nadine is out there," said Juliette.

"And they've got our only witness sedated," said Demko.

"She'd do it for us. I know her. She'd break rules. She wouldn't stop. And he'd want this, too. He'll want us to get the guy who did this to him."

Juliette removed the oxygen cannula, placed the spray nozzle in Skogen's nose and pressed. Almost instantly, Skogen's puffy eyelids began to flutter and he groaned. Juliette replaced the oxygen.

"Get Vea," Demko ordered. "I need him as witness to anything he says."

Juliette hurried out.

Demko leaned over Skogen.

"Jack! It's Clint Demko. Where is he taking Nadine?"

"Nadine?"

"Yes. Nadine."

"He took us," muttered Jack.

"Who did?"

"Decristofaro," he said, confirming the identity of their suspect. "He took us."

"Yes. Where is he taking Nadine?"

The nurse appeared. "He's awake? I'll get something for him."

Demko ignored him. Concentrating on Skogen.

"Jack! We have to find Nadine."

He lifted Jack's hand. Jack moaned, his eyes blinked open to slits.

"Did she give you a gold ring? What did she say?"

Vea arrived, standing by Jack.

"He's awake?" he asked.

The nurse returned with Juliette and a needle. Vea lifted a hand. "Wait."

"Did you see Nadine?" Demko asked.

"Nadine? Yes. Dreaming." He garbled his words, mumbling as if asleep. "She... dreamed of her... and... we are going to..." Skogen gave a long groan of agony. "It hurts."

"He needs to be sedated," said the nurse.

"Step back," ordered Vea.

The young man did, instantly, and hurried away. "I'm calling my supervisor."

"And where, Jack? Where are they going?"

"Manatees. Warm water," said Jack. "River water."

Vea flicked his gaze to Clint. "He's hallucinating."

"Freshwater. Crystal clear water," murmured Jack.

Vea drew out his phone, placing a call.

Demko leaned over Skogen.

"Is it Clearwater?" he asked.

Jack shook his head. "River. Key. Cuba. Tell Demko. River, Key, Cuba."

Vea was on the phone with Carter. He could hear the woman's voice.

"He mentioned Clearwater," said Vea. "Yes. I'll alert the Tampa field office. They can begin a search there." He paused. "Yes. On my way."

"It's not Clearwater," said Clint.

The nurse returned. "I've called security. You are all to leave now!"

Clint backed up, allowing the nurse to move in beside Skogen. "What are you giving him?" asked Juliette.

The nurse replied and Juliette lifted her head, nodding at Clint. "That should help," said Juliette.

The nurse withdrew a needle from the fleshy part of Skogen's hip, but he still moaned in agony.

Vea continued his conversation. "Hold on." Then he spoke to Demko. "We have roadblocks up on A1A to Key West. Tampa office is checking Clearwater."

"He said they're on a river. Clearwater isn't a river. It's a city on a barrier island. Beachfront."

"There is no river that leads to Key West," said Vea.

"But if they're on a boat, they'd be on the coast."

Which coast? Manatees winter in all Florida's rivers. And then he understood what Jack was saying. *Not crystal clear water. Crystal water.*

"He said, 'River. Key. Cuba.' They're not in Key West or Clearwater. And he won't show in Jacksonville. He dropped Skogen in Tallahassee and drove back to Nadine. From there they'd take a boat to Key West."

"From Clearwater," said Vea.

"No. Not Clearwater. They're leaving from Crystal River." Demko explained to Agent Vea. "It's famous for manatee spotting. It's got crystal clear water because of the spring. And Decristofaro had time to drive from there to Tallahassee and back in one night. We need to check all boats leaving from Crystal River."

Juliette leaned over Jack Skogen, his body already easing into the bed.

"Thank you. We're going to get Nadine now. You rest and heal."

Vea and Demko left the ICU together, picking up Tina, who fell in behind them. Vea tucked away his phone and faced them.

"The hospital recorded a conversation from Dr. Finch," said Special Agent Vea. "She called eight hours ago to ask about Jack."

Demko frowned. "What? Where?"

"Pinged a cell tower in Citrus Springs."

"Where?" asked Tina.

"Between Ocala and the Gulf," said Vea. "We also got a call from the Tallahassee *Sun Times*. They fielded a call from someone claiming to be the Huntsman. He's offering to release Nadine for the sum of two hundred thousand dollars."

# CHAPTER THIRTY

Demko gaped. Whatever he'd expected, it wasn't a ransom request. Nadine believed that this serial killer had intentionally lured her to Ocala with his initial victims and then systematically killed women in her outer circle. What had she said? It wasn't a game of wits but a mating ritual. This didn't fit.

"No."

"No?" said Vea.

"He doesn't want money. He wants time. It's a diversion."

"Well, unfortunately, we can't make that gamble when he has one of our own."

"He's trying to distract you. Divide your resources."

"You won't mind if we negotiate for her safe release?" Vea's tone and expression were both sarcastic.

"He's not going to give her back. We have to take her."

Vea stopped walking.

Demko faced him. "Are you sending a team to Crystal River?"

"Unknown. Director Carter and I are flying to Jacksonville."

"Special Agent Wynns and Coleman?"

"Already in Key West."

"What about Crystal River?" asked Demko.

"Tampa field office will cover it."

"You said they were in Clearwater."

"We'll send a team north. Meanwhile, the Huntsman wants to make the exchange in Jacksonville."

Demko shook his head. "He won't show up."

Vea rested his hands on his hips. "Listen, Detective, I know you care about Nadine. So how about you step aside and let us do our jobs."

"He's just buying time to take her where you can't get her."

"Cuba?"

"Yes."

Axel shook his head and continued away. They watched Agent Vea disappear down the hallway.

Demko glanced to Tina.

"Can you get us to Crystal River?"

"I'm on it," she said, drawing out her phone.

"Where's Juliette?" he asked, realizing she wasn't behind them.

"She's coming." Tina's head was down as she worked her phone.

Juliette returned and the three reached the hospital main entrance.

"I booked a private charter here to Crystal River." Tina studied her phone. "They can take three people. Flight takes seventy-five minutes. They're waiting."

They loaded back into Demko's vehicle. In the rearview, Tina tapped away on her phone, now plugged into a jack in the backseat. Demko radioed to FHP and they reached the entrance to the private airfield twelve minutes later.

"You're a wonder," said Juliette to Tina.

Tina lowered her gaze and flushed. "Thanks. I'd never been in a plane before."

"Never?" asked Juliette. "This is your first job, right?"

"Working for Sarasota was my first. Now I'm a private assistant." Her chin went up and an expression of pride beamed, then flickered. "We have to find her."

"Agreed." Juliette reached over the seat and offered her hand to squeeze Tina's. "You took a chance on Nadine. Gave up that other position?"

She nodded. "I'd follow her anywhere. We have to get her back."

Juliette nodded. "Yes. We do."

Their flight took them to Crystal River Airport, a small private airfield so near the river it seemed they were about to land on the water.

"I rented us a car," said Tina as they clambered from the rickety aircraft. "Should be waiting."

She motioned to the parking area and they hurried toward the vehicles in a light rain.

"I found out about those leaves in the bandages. They're from a mangrove tree. Salt water," said Juliette. "They only grow in salt water. She's on the coast."

"Why didn't he kill Skogen?" asked Demko.

"Nadine arranged that," said Tina.

"And what did she have to bargain for his life?" Juliette asked Tina.

"Her own."

Demko blinked at her, knowing Tina was right.

"Her cooperation. She must have agreed to cooperate," said Demko. "At least until she knew he was safe."

Tina was back on her phone, a cylindrical charger now fastened to the port by a short magenta power cord.

He stopped at their rental.

"Minivan?" he said to Tina with all the disgust he could muster.

"It was that or a convertible."

He sighed and hit the lock release. The side door slid open and Tina crawled into the back as Juliette took shotgun.

"You have any place special to check?" asked Juliette.

"Marinas," said Clint.

"That's a long list," said Tina, tapping her phone.

"Then let's get going."

*

Decristofaro hustled Nadine onto the deck of a boat in darkness. She was groggy from the drugs he'd injected and barely able to walk.

"Who's this?" asked the fisherman standing on the deck in bright orange trousers, held up over his T-shirt with wide suspenders.

"This is my wife." He turned to her. "Nadine, this is my big brother, Leonard."

"You didn't say you were bringing a woman."

"Relax. It's fine," said Lionel.

"He kidnapped me," said Nadine, her words slurred.

"What did she say?"

"Nothing. I'll bring her below deck. She gets seasick."

"Give her a bucket," Leonard shouted after them.

Nadine's struggle was ineffective. Her muscles still would not cooperate, and Lionel overpowered her easily, carrying her below decks. The cramped compartment in the pointed prow of the boat had two sleeping platforms that came together in a point like a V. The red vinyl pads were cracked and stank of rotting fish and mold. Her stomach heaved.

"You keep quiet down here. If you don't, I'll have to kill Leonard. And that will be on you." He pointed at her nose.

She had no doubt he would kill his brother.

"You could leave me behind. You could get away."

"Oh, I plan to. And you and I are going to make that first baby right here." He pointed at the vinyl pad. "Right now, I got to either convince Leonard you were kidding or shoot him full of tranquilizers. Then I need some ice. Have to cool you down first. I'll be back."

Ice? The door banged shut. She rolled to her side, trying to think past the sedative.

Why ice?

Men who used ice to cool a woman's body were more comfortable having sex with the dead.

This time she shivered for a different reason.

\*

The night sped toward dawn as Tina compiled a list and they began their search to the north, working southward. The sky turned steel gray as they checked with the harbormasters and spoke to the charter boat captains, asking if they'd seen anyone new here lately.

With no leads, they returned to the minivan and headed to another marina, which held private boats, as the sun lifted over the horizon, gilding the shiny exterior of the vessels still in their moorings. Inside the cab, Tina asked Clint to have a look at her computer.

"What's this?"

"Social media feed," she said.

"I thought the Bureau checked that. Decristofaro doesn't have any accounts."

"That's true, but his older brother, Leonard Jr., does. He and Decristofaro Sr. are in business together." She tilted the screen toward him giving him a view of two men, arms about each other's shoulders, dressed in the high-bibbed pants and suspenders worn by commercial fishermen.

"Where are they?" asked Demko.

"Louisiana. They're shrimpers."

"You think he's on a shrimp boat?" he asked.

"I think the son of a shrimper knows about shrimping."

"Where do they dock?" he asked.

"All over the Gulf of Mexico," said Tina. "Tampa has a shrimp dock. He could sell their catch but…"

"What?" he asked.

"The closest place for commercial fishermen to fuel up is here in Crystal River."

"She's on a shrimp boat," said Demko. "We need to find out the name of his family's boat."

Demko spoke to the owner of the commercial marina a little after seven in the morning. The docks were empty except for the piles of ropes and nets, shipping containers and dollies.

Demko ran up the empty dock, his footsteps pounding on the wood decking. Behind him, a paunchy man stepped from the office, on the concrete pier.

"Son, this is private property," he said.

"Where are all the shrimp boats?" asked Demko.

"They leave at three in the morning. Dawn and dusk are the best time for catching shrimp."

Demko raked a hand through his hair and retraced his path.

"I'm Detective Clinton Demko. And you are?"

The man adjusted his belt, tugging his trousers up farther on his extended belly. Dressed in a workman's shirt and jeans, only the man's age distinguished him from the two men coiling rope farther down the pier.

"I'm Andy McGrail. This here dock and boat repair belongs to me and my boys."

"You have any boats here last night from Louisiana?"

"Yes, indeed. What's this about?"

"Kidnapping."

McGrail's hands slid from his hips. "Kidnapping?"

"Yes. A federal officer."

"You best come into the office."

They followed him, pausing before a crowded counter littered with papers and logbooks. A huge rubber shrimp acted as a paperweight, despite having lost one of its antenna.

McGrail checked a log. "Thought so." He glanced up to Demko. "You got some identification?"

Demko provided it.

"Sarasota. You're a bit out of your territory."

"I'm on a federal task force. You know about the serial killer in Ocala?"

He nodded. "Been following the story. My missus is obsessed with it."

"He might be on one of those shrimp boats. Louisiana?" Demko said, repeating his query.

"Yes. We had a shrimper out of there. Docked two nights. That's unusual, unless something needs fixing. Then add to that, he didn't motor out of here until after four in the morning."

"This morning?" asked Demko.

"That's right."

"Four hours ago," said Juliette.

"What's the name of the boat?" asked Demko.

"Let's see," said McGrail.

"It's *Miss Faro*," said Tina, turning her phone to show the Instagram feed of Leonard Decristofaro.

"All these boys are like family. Talk to each other on the radio, know each other for years, though mostly they never actually meet. Heck, we got shrimpers from Texas, Louisiana, Alabama, all over the Gulf Coast. They'll know where to find *Miss Faro*." McGrail lifted his radio. "You want me to call this boat?"

"No!" Demko stayed his hand. "Don't want him to know someone is looking for them."

"Okay. No radio," said McGrail, placing the handset back on the cradle.

"How far out could a boat that size get?"

"Little ones like that?" He motioned to Tina's social media stream and the image of *Miss Faro*. "Sixty miles offshore. International waters. Course, they go slow when they've got the butterfly nets out, say two knots."

"And you saw them at four?"

McGrail nodded.

"How many on board?"

"Two or three men, I think. One real little. Had something wrong with his head."

"What?"

"Looked… I don't know. Misshaped, shiny."

"Mr. McGrath, could that have been a woman wearing something, like a mask?"

He scratched his knuckles over the white whiskers coming in on his cheek.

"Now that you mention it. The walk, the size… maybe."

"How far could that boat get by now?" asked Juliette.

"Top speed on a boat like that? Sixteen knots. Don't figure they'd push much faster. Older trawler, you know."

"In miles?" asked Juliette.

"Twenty an hour," supplied Tina.

"Correct, in calm seas, like this." He waved toward the window. "But they'd have their towing booms out and bags in the water."

"So we're looking for a shrimper not shrimping," said Demko. "We need a boat and captain. Something that can catch that shrimper and someone who knows how to operate a boat."

"I got friends who run fishing charters out of Sarasota," said Juliette. "I'll call around."

"No. I'll call Sarasota PD," said Demko, referring to his own department some one hundred miles south. "They've got a marine unit. They'll find us a vessel."

"With a Zodiac and scuba gear," said Juliette.

"I don't know how to scuba," said Demko.

"I do," said Juliette.

"Shouldn't we call the coast guard?" asked Tina.

"Decristofaro sees the coast guard and he'll kill her and dump her in the Gulf."

# CHAPTER THIRTY-ONE

The chopper swept them from Crystal River to Sarasota where, with the help of the Sarasota Marine unit, they had a charter fishing boat waiting for them. With luck they'd be just ahead of the shrimper. The thirty-five-foot offshore fishing boat had three outboard motors and four hundred gallons of fuel. Better yet, the captain was a narcotics detective who headed the marine patrol and his copilot was an experienced drone operator. Once Demko explained the situation, he was all in.

Demko planned to leave Tina and Juliette. But Juliette reminded him that she was the one with the medical training. Tina agreed to scout from the air in the police helicopter, and to coordinate with their ground support, engaging the FBI after they'd spotted their target.

Tina and her pilot were in the air before they'd left the bay. They continued west, unsure whether to turn south in the direction of their travel or north to intercept. The possibility of missing them by guessing incorrectly kept them angling west.

"Tina?" Demko used the agreed-upon radio frequency, unsure if their phones would prove reliable.

"I'm here. We're looking north." There was a pause. "We got one, but the nets are out. Want us to keep going?"

"Get the name."

"Hang on."

He waited for the endless minutes.

"It's… *Reel Lady Jane*."

"Keep going. Call when you get something."

The radio silence was deafening as they continued.

"Clint! Clint! Over?" Tina sounded breathless.

"Here, Tina."

"I've got her. *Miss Faro*. I can see the boat."

"Stay back. Don't let them spot you."

"Roger."

"Any sign of Nadine?"

"No. Just the shrimp boat and… I can't see anyone on board. We've passed it and then came around. Want me to make another pass?"

"No. Give me your position and head away."

"Yes. Okay." Tina relayed what the pilot said. "He says we've got another hour fly time. We'll move out of sight and stand by."

Their captain gunned the motor and swung them to the north.

"Five nautical miles," he said.

"How long?"

"Twenty minutes."

After ten minutes, the copilot, a patrol officer with two years in, retrieved a large case.

"A drone?" asked Demko.

"Yup. New toy and I'm one of two trained to operate this baby."

"How far can it go?"

"Five miles."

"I don't want them to see it," said Demko.

"Or hear it," said Juliette.

"Can't hear it over their engines and I'll stay just below cloud cover."

He had the white drone set up in moments. It lifted into the air, heading north below low clouds.

Demko, Juliette and their captain watched the computer screen as the green water turned blue as it deepened.

"There it is!" said Juliette.

On the screen appeared a sky view of a shrimp trawler.

The operator worked the camera and the image enlarged.

"Don't get too close," said Demko.

"Zooming," said the drone operator.

"I only see one man in the wheelhouse."

Demko looked at the small image.

"That him?" asked the copilot.

He narrowed his eyes, squinting at his target. "Yes."

Juliette peered at the screen. "Where's Nadine?"

"Likely below decks," said the operator.

"When he spots us, we need to look like a charter fishing outfit."

"How will you get on board?" asked Juliette.

"We have to get close enough to jump."

"You'll land in the water."

The captain spoke up. "I can skim the side."

"Juliette, radio Tina. Tell her we made a positive ID on Lionel Decristofaro and to call in the coast guard and FBI."

"Are we waiting for them?"

"No. We're hitting him right now."

*

The sedative's effects still clung to her, making concentration difficult. When Lionel dragged in the fisherman, Nadine was seeing double and couldn't lift her head.

Now she pushed herself up on one elbow and closed an eye, making it easier to focus.

The man lying on the floor below her wore dirty coveralls, a tan canvas work shirt and one rubber boot. His other foot was bare. His full dark beard covered much of his cheeks and his wavy hair grew in a wild cap.

Nadine inched across the vinyl mat to get a better look. Her wrists were taped before her, as were her ankles. The pointed shape of the compartment and the up-and-down motion told her this was the front of the boat.

What was her best course?

During her FBI training, an instructor had advised to take an inventory of available resources.

She had only the flannel shirt. The compartment was empty, and the twin berths were padlocked shut. The only other obvious resource was the unconscious man. Nadine worked her legs off the compartment and eased to the floor. She spent the next few minutes searching him and recovered a red folding multitool from his front pocket.

Jackpot.

The awkward position of her bound hands increased the difficulty in both opening a blade and wielding the tool, but Nadine was determined. With a knife, she might escape this room and find a better weapon to confront Lionel.

She knew from the man's arrival that beyond the door were three short steps and then cloudy skies. The width of the compartment meant this was a small vessel, perhaps thirty-five feet.

She could barely recall coming on board. Everything in her mind was fuzzy.

Nadine sat with her back braced against the berth and the open blade of the multitool clutched between her bare feet as she sliced through the tape wrapping her wrists.

Every second she expected Lionel to return. If she could just get her hands and feet free, she could defend herself. And if she could reach a radio or cell phone, she could bring help.

At last the tape gave way. Nadine used her teeth to rip away the bonds. Then she turned to her feet, making quick work of the tethers.

Free at last, she turned to the unconscious man. This was his brother. Is that what he'd said? A second search yielded nothing to identify him or prove useful.

Then she studied the coveralls. In a few minutes she had dragged them off and slipped them on, grateful for the adjustable suspenders that allowed her to wear the overlarge gear.

What next? Force open the cabinets and see what might lie inside or work on the door. Likely there would be ropes and gear. Might she find a grabbling hook or club? Nets?

It was a crapshoot.

She turned to the door, trying the latch and finding it locked. The hinges seemed a better option. All she needed to do was remove the pins.

Using the plier tool, she wiggled the pin. Once she gained a half inch, she beat the closed multitool against the pin like a hammer in time to the crash of waves against the hull, hoping to disguise her work. When the last pin dropped to the deck, she paused to stretch her cramped hand and examine her blistered palms. The torn skin stung, and clear fluid dampened her hands.

Then she tugged at the door and eased a gap between the hinges and frame and slipped out. She paused at the bottom step and selected the largest blade, extending the four-inch steel.

Her mother had killed eight couples in total with a blade this size: a carpet knife, the handle flecked with blue paint.

Now Nadine stood at the start of a journey that included using this blade to attack or kill Lionel. She paused at the ice that crystalized along her spine. If she plunged this blade into his body, what irrevocable damage would she be doing to herself?

She pressed her back to the rail and shivered, paralyzed with indecision. Suddenly she was afraid for herself in a whole different way. She wasn't a killer. But was she prepared to kill if forced? Was she prepared to live with the scars to her soul that came with taking a human life?

If she were not prepared to defend herself, was she prepared to die?

A worse possibility dawned. What if there was no damage to her soul? What if she felt nothing at all after killing a man, or what if she enjoyed it?

She dropped the blade.

Nadine considered returning to the cabin. She did not want to kill Lionel. Nor did she want to die. What she wanted was to live to see Clint and tell him what she should have told him from the start, that she loved him and wanted to share her life with him.

She retrieved the blade.

Her bare foot slipped onto the next step, creeping toward this showdown with a slow deliberate tread of a gunfighter at high noon.

The boat lurched, throwing her violently back down the stairs. The crash and shudder told her that they'd struck something, or been struck.

Nadine fell, her shoulder slamming into the door, throwing it farther askew.

Out here, what could they hit? There was nothing but water… and other boats?

The shout from above brought her scrambling to her feet.

She gripped the knife and dashed up the stairs, pausing like a gopher to glance about from her burrow. Lionel leapt down from the wheelhouse, charging past her.

Nadine emerged to the deck to see Demko airborne as a sports fishing boat scraped along their side behind him, heading in the opposite direction. He landed hard as the vessels detached, sending their craft tilting. The rolling deck threw him against the winch.

Nadine stumbled and the knife skidded away back down the stairs.

Lionel regained his footing first, shouldering the shotgun. Nadine saw her future flash before her eyes as she rushed forward, lifting a metal rake and howling like a banshee.

Lionel turned, swinging the barrel away from Demko and spotting her too late. She brought the rake down on his arm. The long handle struck the weapon as the metal teeth of the rake-head sank into his shoulder.

He roared and used the barrel of the shotgun to knock away her rake, then seized the head in his opposite hand. He thrust and she toppled, striking the gunwales and sliding to the deck.

Lionel glanced back to Demko, lifting his shotgun.

She flinched at the rapid *pop, pop, pop* of Demko's weapon. Lionel staggered, the barrel floating upward as he fired.

Nadine screamed at the blast, scrambling forward in time to see Demko fall.

# CHAPTER THIRTY-TWO

Three bloodstains bloomed on Decristofaro's shirt. The shotgun clattered to the deck as he swayed. Demko saw his spread of bullets. Each one had struck the center of the man's chest. His opponent had minutes left before death.

The pain in his shoulder took a moment to register. Seeing blood on his shirt shocked him. The blast had been high. He was certain.

Where was Nadine?

There she was, pausing at Decristofaro as he reached for her, his hand grasping. She stepped back, clear of his grip. He said something, but the ringing in his ears from the shotgun blast made it impossible for him to hear.

Her lips moved, but there was no sound, and then she was past the bleeding man, running to him, falling beside him, her arms around him, clinging, sobbing.

He held her tight, closing his eyes to savor the feel of her, the smell of her and the familiar silk of her hair.

"Got you," he said.

"Clint, I'm so sorry."

"No need."

"I never should have dragged you along."

"You stopped him, Nadine. We stopped him."

There was a bump as the two boats scraped against each other again.

Demko lifted his gaze to the fishing craft and her captain, high above the deck, at the wheel as Juliette threw a rope over to them.

"Nadine!"

She lifted her head and then hurried to grab the line, tying it awkwardly to the winch, allowing the two boats to touch.

Juliette scrambled from the sleek fiberglass hull over the wooden gunwales of the shrimp boat. She rushed to Nadine and hugged her, and the second in command headed to the wheelhouse. A moment later, the engine cut. The two women rocked back and forth, reunited sisters as the waves lapped the side of the boat.

Demko smiled. When he sat up, the twinge of pain made him gasp. He tugged at the sleeve of his shirt and located the cause of the shooting agony ripping through his muscle. A shard of wood stuck through his skin like the plug in a cork.

He lifted his opposite hand.

"Don't do that!" shouted Juliette as he tugged the sliver free and blood poured from the wound.

*

Nadine sat up in the hospital bed, clear-eyed and rested from the night's sleep. She'd survived it. Somehow Jack had gotten her message to Demko and he had found her out there amid hundreds of commercial boats.

Demko had been here last night when she'd finally tumbled into sleep, holding his hand as he assured her that she was safe. Juliette had stanched his wound. A sliver of the winch system had been blown away by the shotgun blast and punctured his shoulder. His treatment had involved antibiotics and several stitches.

She'd thought she had been fine until Clint brought her aboard the second vessel and she began experiencing what she thought was a stress reaction. It turned out she also had a fever and was dehydrated.

Part of her felt lucky. Decristofaro was dead, sparing them the trauma of a trial. The victims' families would never have to witness the man who killed their daughter, sister, wife, girlfriend, sit remorseless at trial, or suffer the indignation of knowing he still walked and talked and breathed while their loved ones were gone forever.

His brother, Leonard, had been released without charges, as he had no knowledge of his brother's plans.

Nadine turned her head to look at Demko, sitting in the vinyl chair at her bedside. The dark stubble of beard growing on his face and red-rimmed eyes showed she had slept far better than he had. His arm rested in a sling so new, it still had the fold marks from packaging.

"Good morning," he said and took her hand, gently offering a kiss on the knuckles past the finger monitor.

"Hey there." She lifted her chin to accept a kiss on the mouth. He lingered and she slipped her tongue along his, igniting a fire between them. Her heart rate monitor beeped at a faster pace, making her laugh.

He drew back.

"You're feeling better." He cast her a wicked smile.

"So much better. Care to join me?" She lifted the blanket.

"Too tired to climb over the rail," he said and grinned. "Almost."

"You planning to head home and shower?" she asked.

"That a hint?"

She smiled. "You smell like the catch of the day."

He dropped his smile, suddenly looking serious.

"Clint?"

He grasped her hand. "Nadine, when I thought I'd lost you, I went crazy. I've never been so scared."

"I'm sorry."

"He took you right out from under our noses. He could have killed you."

"He didn't."

"Because you were right. He wanted you."

"To bear him an entire litter of psycho killers. He told me I had the perfect lineage. Just what he needed to build a dynasty." She looked away. The pain in her heart too raw to allow him to see.

"Nadine. I'm so sorry."

She shook her head, pressing her lips together as she struggled to rein in the tears that made her throat ache.

"He wasn't wrong, Clint." She risked a look at him and saw nothing but confusion. "About my lineage. My mother's side is a nightmare of murder and death. My brother, my grandfather and my mother are felons. And who even knows what horrors are lurking on my father's side."

"What are you saying, Nadine?"

"It's why I asked for time. I didn't know how to tell you this. How afraid I am." The tears came, but she wouldn't let them stop her from getting this out this time. "What if I marry you and… I know you want children."

"I never said that."

"But you do. You're the perfect dad. You should have kids. As many as you like. But not *my* kids. My kids might be… damaged. They might carry that same killer code that runs through me."

"That's ridiculous."

She took his hand and shook it. "It's not. Some families have breast cancer, fibroids, diabetes, heart disease. I have murder."

"I don't believe that, Nadine. It's how they are raised. There is no killer code."

He rejected the importance of the research, just like Juliette. She knew better. It wasn't some unfounded fear. She had it. So did Arlo.

"It's real, Clint."

"A combination of factors. That's what experts say."

He'd been doing research, she realized.

"A proclivity," she countered. "Innate."

"So what if it is? You're telling me that everyone born with that gene sequence or chemical thing grows up to be a killer?"

"No. Not all. But the percentages…"

"Percentages." He scoffed. "Nadine, you're not a killer. Because you choose not to be. It's a choice we all make. Follow the law and rules of society, or don't. You are not your parents. And as for children, we can have them or not. We can adopt. We can work all that out, but only if you'll give us a chance."

Nadine met his gaze and knew he was right. He was brave and strong and so good for her. She'd lived with guilt and shame and fear for so long. She'd balked because of her past and nearly been lost to him forever. Now she needed to be brave enough to stop living in the past in favor of a future with Clint Demko as her husband.

The knock at the door brought an end to their conversation. Gabriella Carter stepped in, carrying a vase of sunflowers, which she set on the side table.

"How are you, Dr. Finch?"

"Feeling better, Agent Carter. These are lovely."

"I spoke to your doctor. He tells me that he'll discharge you today, sometime after he makes rounds."

"That's good news."

"Yes. We're going to need you to make a statement. Would you be willing to come to the Ocala field office tomorrow?"

"I'm sure I can make it." She turned to Demko. "Where are we staying?"

"Safe house. No reason to leave now."

"You'll be returning to the Tampa office while we finish up here," said Carter. "That might be a few weeks yet. We'll need you to help. Paperwork. Interviews and so on."

"I'd like to request that Tina Ruz's position as my assistant be made permanent."

"I can work that out." Carter went to leave, then turned back. "Oh, one bit of news that Agent Wynns asked me to pass on. Decristofaro resided in Miami for over a year. That's why he didn't pop on the searches because he wasn't officially residing here. Paid under the table by the Kilpatrick family who gave him a trailer on their property as part of the arrangement. His mailing address is still Miami. But Wynns said, you were still right."

"Untraceable," said Demko.

"Seems so." Carter turned to Nadine. "I'm glad you're doing better. I'll see you tomorrow then."

She strode out like a woman on a mission. Was she on her way to see Skogen?

Demko left her shortly after Carter's departure.

Nadine used the call button and accepted help getting washed up. Unfortunately, she was not able to dress and the intravenous line remained in her hand. But she was eating and drinking on her own.

Upon return to her bed, she ate her breakfast and awaited her doctor, impatient to be discharged.

From the nurse, she discovered that Skogen was on her floor. Her nurse agreed to accompany her to his room, promising she wouldn't miss her physician making rounds, because she'd receive an alert.

Nadine walked slowly down the hall in her underwear and hospital gown, one hand gripping the stainless-steel stem to the rack holding her IV drip.

From the hallway of Skogen's room, she spotted several bright bouquets of flowers. Moving inside, she noted a Mylar balloon tied to his bedrail. Layah Coleman sat beside his bed, an eReader in her hand.

"Dr. Finch." She sounded surprised. "You're up."

"I'll be discharged today." Nadine beamed.

Coleman rose and met her beside the bed, first offering her a hug and then the seat.

She turned her attention to Jack. The swelling at his face distorted his features. But his color was better. His lips were cracked and his chest bare except for the bandage that wrapped around his ribs. Above and below, the reddish purple bruises blossomed.

Beside him sat the usual monitors, IV drip and a medical dispenser for on-demand morphine.

"He been awake?"

"Axel spoke to him last night. He's been out since I got here. He's still in a lot of pain."

"Demko told me he had surgery."

"They removed his spleen. His kidneys are bruised." She motioned to the bag of urine hanging at his bedrail. The blood turned the fluid pink.

"But he's out of the woods. That's what they say. Everything will heal with time."

Not everything, thought Nadine, looking at his bandaged hands, recalling the sight of the raw wounds where his nails had been.

"The doctor said the soft tissue damage will leave scars and they don't know yet if the nerve damage is permanent," said Layah.

Nadine silently took it all in. The man in the bed had nearly lost his life because of her. But had she saved him, too?

"Did they find an engagement ring on Jack's hand?"

"I don't know. I can find out."

"Thanks. And, Layah, could you please advocate for counseling? He'll need to speak to someone."

"He'll be required to do that."

Nadine exhaled a breath, feeling slightly better. Jack's mental wounds would be less obvious but just as serious.

"What about you?" asked Layah.

"I already have a therapist. I'm sure this will keep us busy for years." She tried and failed for a laugh.

"Dr. Finch, I have a question. Dr. Hartfield told us what happened on the boat. She said you knocked the barrel of his gun away, giving Detective Demko time to shoot."

Nadine nodded.

"She also said that afterward, he spoke to you and you said something to him before running to Detective Demko."

"Yes."

"I'm wondering, what did you say?"

Nadine thought back to that moment, Decristofaro reaching for her and calling her name.

"I told him that natural selection also leads to extinctions."

Coleman's brows shot up and then she smiled.

Nadine stepped up beside Jack's bed, moving in close to whisper into his ear.

"You did it, Jack. You saved me. Thank you for my life." She stroked the hair back from his forehead and dropped a kiss on his forehead, forgiving him for lying to her and everything else.

He'd been the leak that had brought the Huntsman after them. He'd have to live with that. But had his actions helped them find Decristofaro sooner? Had he saved unknown victims a terrible fate?

She didn't know. But she was happy to be free and safe and on the mend.

"I'll see you at the office," she said to Layah, and walked back to her room pushing her IV stand and accompanied by her nurse.

She was surprised at the visitor waiting there to see her.

"Dr. Crean?"

## THREE DAYS LATER

Juliette Hartfield popped her head into Nadine's bedroom office in the safe house. She and Tina had returned this morning to collect their belongings before heading back to Tampa and Nadine's new assignment with the FBI field office there. Clint would be returning to his position in the Sarasota Police, Homicide department, and Juliette would be resuming her post as a medical examiner for District 12.

"How's Skogen?" asked Juliette.

"Still on a morphine drip for the pain, but his body is healing."

Juliette had told them that, although internal injuries would heal and so would the broken bones, there was some doubt that his fingers would ever recover from the torture.

"What does that mean for his career?" asked Tina.

"Well, if the scarring on his fingers causes contractures and permanent nerve damage, he won't be able to continue in the field. It will be up to him to decide on reassignment or retire from the Bureau."

"That's terrible," said Nadine.

"Not so terrible. He's got a literary agent and ghostwriter lined up. Rumors of a major book deal."

"And Crean's book is out." Tina spoke of their old supervisor, Margery Crean, who had been shot and recently delivered a signed copy of her book to Nadine's bedside.

"Why don't you write a book?" asked Juliette. "Everyone else is cashing in."

Nadine smiled. She was no longer afraid of the publicity. No longer running from the limelight. But that didn't mean she cared to turn it on herself.

"Someday, maybe. After I've put a few more bad guys in prison."

"I'm keeping notes," said Tina.

Both women turned to her.

"You're what?" asked Nadine.

"Case notes, calendars and journal entries. To help you remember when you decide to write it all down."

Nadine had thought she might start doing that, but it seemed she did not need to.

"Thank you, Tina."

Her assistant beamed.

"Dr. Crean came to see me at the hospital," said Nadine.

The two women gaped.

"What?" asked Juliette at the same time Tina asked, "Why?"

"She wants me to write the foreword for her next book."

"No!" said Juliette. Though whether this was shock or her reply, Nadine didn't know.

"I said I would."

"That's a surprise," said Juliette. "I thought you were avoiding the limelight."

"Time to accept that I'm out there and get a grip on the narrative."

"Hurrah!" said Tina. "Our book will blow hers away."

Nadine laughed. "Not so fast. I think I'll start by accepting a few interviews from our Florida newspapers."

"I can set that up," said Tina.

"You'll have to. I've asked Carter to make your position with me permanent."

Tina rushed forward and threw herself against Nadine, sending them back a step. Nadine hugged her as Tina pressed her face into her neck for a moment before drawing back.

Then she clasped her hands and lifted her shoulders. "I'm so happy."

"Looks like me and Demko are the only ones heading back to Sarasota," said Juliette.

"It's only forty-five minutes to Tampa."

"Without traffic," they said in unison and then, also in unison, "There's always traffic!"

Nadine laughed.

"Juliette, are you interested in working for the Bureau? I'm certain you could if you liked."

"And leave Demko behind?"

Tina glanced over her shoulder and stepped aside. She looked positively gleeful as Clint Demko appeared in the doorway.

"Who's leaving me behind?"

Clint joined them looking fit and healthy. He'd got rid of the sling and so there was no outward evidence of the injury to his shoulder. He cast them all a winning smile.

"Tina is going to Tampa with Nadine," said Juliette.

Demko nodded at this and glanced to Nadine's luggage, all packed.

"You still lugging that brick around?"

"Well, you'll be the one lugging it, if you're putting those suitcases in the SUV."

"Can we see it?" asked Tina.

She lifted the smaller roller bag to the couch and unwound the Bubble Wrap, thinking it ridiculous to protect a brick. Then she held out the mark of achievement, with its brightly painted *Yellow Brick Road*, the year and her graduating class number in black.

"It's yellow!" said Tina, looking surprised as she came forward to admire the object marking Nadine's accomplishment.

"For the Yellow Brick Road," said Nadine.

"So badass!" Juliette touched the surface with reverence.

Clint took his turn to admire the unwieldy trophy and handed it back. "It's such an incredible accomplishment."

Nadine smiled, warm inside and out from the approval of her closest friends. Then she set the trophy in the bag.

Juliette wrapped an arm around Nadine and Tina, dragging them against her as they all admired the yellow brick. Her family, Nadine thought, and sighed, suddenly happier than she'd ever been in her life.

"We're proud of you," said Demko.

Nadine choked the words out past the tears. "I love you guys."

Demko cleared his throat. "Might be getting one myself, next year."

All three women turned to him. Nadine gaped. "What?"

"I got a nudge from Supervisory Special Agent Carter. She'd like to recommend me."

"That's wonderful!" said Juliette, offering Demko a quick hug.

"So cool!" said Tina.

"Another separation," said Nadine.

"Yeah, but maybe you can arrange additional training. We could share a bunk in the dormitory."

She laughed. "Yeah, that isn't a thing."

"What do you think?" he asked.

She stepped forward and into his arms. "I think it's marvelous."

Nadine kissed him, then leaned back, but he kept her locked in his arms.

She heard Tina say, "Dr. Hartfield? Could I speak to you outside?"

That was her signal. Nadine sucked in a breath and tightened up, the nerves engaging, making her muscles go rigid.

Clint released her. His expression showed confusion.

He watched the pair make a hasty exit. "We having a cake or something?"

While it was true they had no time to celebrate her graduation from the FBI National Academy, it was not cake waiting, but champagne, and it would remain in the refrigerator unless Nadine got the answer she sought.

Clint cocked his head, trying to work out what was happening. He turned to Nadine and found her opening her nightstand.

Her throat had gone dry as the Mojave and her hand shook as she withdrew the velvet box he had given her. It now held the ring, thanks to Agent Coleman wrangling it out of evidence.

Clint spotted the box. "Nadine?"

She stepped before him.

Now she understood his tortured, nervous expression when he'd proposed. Sweat trickled down her back.

"Clint, this last case clarified the precious gift of each moment we have together. It helped me realize what I want. Please forgive me for my delay."

He sank to the couch beside her open suitcase.

"I'm finally getting my answer. Aren't I?"

Did he think she meant to return his ring?

She needed to make clear what she really intended.

Nadine dropped to the carpet to kneel before him as words tumbled from her. "Yes. That's the answer. Yes, I want you. Yes, I love you. Yes, please make me your wife. I'm so sorry I let my fears keep us apart. I was wrong. Will you marry me?"

She opened the box and there was her ring.

"Is that…?" He glanced to her. "*Your* ring?"

She nodded, tipping the box so that the diamond flashed.

He peered at the familiar contents of this special box. "They confiscated the ring."

She smiled. "Yes. But Layah convinced them to expedite clearing it from evidence."

"Do you still want *that* ring?" he asked. They both knew this ring was inextricably tied to this case. But it was also the ring he had chosen for her, to mark their commitment to one another.

"I want it."

He nodded.

"Is that a yes?"

"Nadine, I haven't changed my mind."

She threw her arms around his neck, collapsing on top of him. He held her tight. The kiss they shared heated her inside and out. She wanted to shout and dance and strip him out of his traveling clothing. Instead she drew back. He reverently took the ring and slipped it on her finger.

All worry melted away. He still wanted her. He believed, as did she, in them, their relationship and the life they would share. The warm glow of joy filled her.

"Partners," she said, beaming up at him. He took her hand, turning it to admire the ring, now seated on her finger.

"It looks just right. Exactly how I imagined it."

Demko gave her another long kiss. The pressing of their mouths over each other and the warmth of his embrace assured her that she had finally found the home she longed for, here in his arms.

The moment was interrupted by a knock on the open door. Nadine turned, expecting to see Tina carrying champagne and Juliette holding long-stemmed glasses. Instead she spotted the Marion County sheriff standing in the adjoining room.

The smile dropped from Nadine's face. Both the sheriff's grim expression and Tina wringing her hands broadcast that this was unwelcome news.

Now her heart raced for different reasons.

The sheriff stepped forward. Tina followed looking apologetic.

"I'm sorry. He said it was urgent."

"Sheriff Douglas," said Demko, obviously recognizing the man on sight. "This is a surprise."

He stood, drawing Nadine up beside him.

She tried to convince herself that Sheriff Douglas was here about some detail that needed attention and could not quite manage it.

"Dr. Finch, I wanted to alert you of a private matter." He glanced to Tina and to Demko.

"It's all right. You can speak before them."

"I just received a call from the correctional facility in Lawtey. We have been contacted as the arresting law enforcement agency of record."

Nadine's heart began pounding, anticipating the subject of this private matter.

"As a courtesy, we wanted to inform you in person that your brother, Arlo Howler, has just been released from federal prison."

# A LETTER FROM JENNA

Dear Reader,

A great big thank-you for choosing to read *The Hunted Girls*. I appreciate you joining me on Nadine Finch's second exciting case! To be the first to know about all my latest releases, sign up at the following link. Your email address will never be shared and you can unsubscribe at any time.

*www.bookouture.com/jenna-kernan*

Going home again can be difficult. I was obsessed with the idea of sending the daughter of a serial killer back to her childhood home, which is also her mother's old killing ground.

I grew up in my father's hometown, which was his father's hometown, and his father's as well. My family has people tucked under sod on the ancestral land in Upstate New York with sturdy Vermont marble to mark the year, day and, on some, the exact hour of their deaths stretching back to the late 1700s. Nadine and I both share the sense of the strange superimposing the familiar, as past and present occupy the same geography.

In addition to bringing you along on Nadine's homecoming, I am so pleased to present to you a bit of Central Florida. This is one of the most beautiful parts of our state and also the wildest, least visited and most underappreciated. The natural springs throughout Florida have clear turquoise-blue water that averages a constant 75°F/23°C, making the springs cool in summer and warm in winter. In the heat of summer, these springs are cool, refreshing swimming spots for locals and visitors alike. The springs close from November to March to allow space for the manatee to raise their young. The Ocala National Forest is immense with hundreds of lakes. As part of my research, I rented a houseboat and traveled upriver on the St. Johns, from DeLand to Silver Glen Springs. I've never seen so many eagles. We camped on the boat, moored to a small island, and watched a flock of turkeys arrive to eat acorns. Guess what animal arrived next? If you picked alligators, you are correct. If you ever get an opportunity to visit one of the natural springs or travel down the St. Johns River, jump at the chance. But definitely don't jump in the river water. It really is full of gators. ;)

I hope you enjoyed *The Hunted Girls* and would be so kind as to leave a brief review on Amazon or the reader's site of your choosing. Your review helps new readers discover a story you enjoyed. Even a line or two can make an enormous difference in the success of this book.

I'd love to learn what you thought about Nadine's stormy return to her childhood home. Please get in touch on social media, Goodreads, in an Amazon review or on my website.

Be safe. Stay Well.

Happy Reading!
Jenna Kernan

authorjennakernan

@jennakernan

@jenna_kernan

@authors/jenna-kernan

@jennakernan

www.jennakernan.com

# ACKNOWLEDGMENTS

Working with a UK editor has been fab! I'm learning to use new expressions, like chuffed, keen and brilliant! In return, I've taught my Bookouture editor, Ellen Gleeson, how to make gator bites and what to expect in a mangrove tunnel. A true collaboration! And once again, Ellen has elevated this story through excellent editing and advice. She flagged issues and offered insightful suggestions to make this story shine. I'm so grateful for her hard work on this series!

Special thanks to my longtime friend and literary agent, Ann Leslie Tuttle, of Dystel, Goderich & Bourret. Without Ann Leslie's belief in this series, it never would have found a home. I appreciate her support and friendship over many years and many projects.

I'm grateful to all the wonderful folks at Bookouture. So many individuals helped with the creation, production, promotion and marketing of this series that I had to start a list. So, thank you to the editorial manager, audio production department, the art team, contracts, book production, publicists, and social media, advertising and marketing teams who all ensure this story reaches you. This crew is both brilliant and fab. I'm chuffed to bits to continue working with them.

In addition, I offer my thanks to the writing organizations providing education to mystery, suspense, thriller and police procedural writers. Thank you to Sisters in Crime, Mystery Writers of America, Mystery Writers of Florida, International Thriller Writers, Writers' Police Academy and Novelists, Inc.

Special thanks to my siblings, Amy, Nan and James for buying and reviewing my books, sharing and liking my posts and offering praise and support!

And to my husband, Jim, who bought a box of my first release at full cover price, and when I told him I could buy them at cost, replied, "I don't care."

I'm so lucky to have you in my corner (and to take appropriate action when I've once again left something burning in the kitchen!).

Finally, I am grateful to my readers. This story doesn't live until it is in your hands!

Printed in Great Britain
by Amazon